# BRACO

### A NOVEL

## LESLEYANNE RYAN

P.O. Box 2188, St. John's, NL, Canada, A1C 6E6
WWW.BREAKWATERBOOKS.COM

LIBRARY AND ARCHIVES CANADA CATALOGUING IN PUBLICATION
Ryan, Lesleyanne
Braco / Lesleyanne Ryan.
ISBN 978-1-55081-334-0
I. Title.
PS8635.Y357B73 2012      C813'.6      C2012-904975-1

We acknowledge the support of the Canada Council for the Arts which last year invested $24.3 million in writing and publishing throughout Canada. We acknowledge the Government of Canada through the Canada Book Fund and the Government of Newfoundland and Labrador through the Department of Tourism, Culture and Recreation for our publishing activities.

PRINTED AND BOUND IN CANADA.

 Canada Council     Conseil des Arts
for the Arts        du Canada     Canadä      Newfoundland Labrador

Breakwater Books is committed to choosing papers and materials for our books that help to protect our environment. To this end, this book is printed on a recycled paper that is certified by the Forest Stewardship Council®.

 MIX
Paper from responsible sources
FSC
www.fsc.org     FSC® C016245

DEC 0 5 2012

FOR JACQUES AND ATIF

# PREFACE

THE PEOPLE OF the former country of Yugoslavia are the original inhabitants of that region of the Balkans and are racially identical. For more than two thousand years, the great empires of Europe–including the Holy Roman Empire, the Byzantine Empire, and the Ottoman Empire–shaped the identity of the area that would become central Yugoslavia, dividing the people along religious lines: Roman Catholic Croats, Eastern Orthodox Serbs, and Muslim Bosniaks.

The three groups were united under the Kingdom of Yugoslavia in 1929, and it became the Federal People's Republic of Yugoslavia in 1946 when a communist government was established. Communism blurred the lines between the three groups for the next forty years. During this period, they intermarried and lived side by side in peace.

The Republics of Croatia and Serbia were dominated by Croat and Serb populations respectively, but Bosnia and Herzegovina mixed all three groups with approximately 44% of the population identifying themselves as Bosnian Muslim, 31% as Bosnian Serbs, and 17% as Bosnian Croat.

The death of Yugoslav President Josip Broz Tito, in 1980, led to a resurgence of Serbian nationalism under Slobodan Milosevic. As a result, the Serbs dominated the military and political structure of Yugoslavia into the 1990s. When Communism failed across Eastern Europe, Croatia and Slovenia declared their independence, leading to a short war between Croatia and the Serbian-dominated Yugoslav army in 1991. United Nations peacekeepers were deployed to Croatia to implement a tentative ceasefire, but not before the Serbians had claimed one third of the newly independent country.

In 1992, war erupted in Bosnia where an arms embargo hobbled the Bosnian Muslim army. They could do little against the Bosnian Serbs, who had easy access to the former Yugoslav army's equipment and ammunition. By 1995, the Bosnian Serbs had claimed more than half the country while an alliance between the Muslims and Croats struggled to hold on to what remained. Attempts at a peace deal collapsed largely over the issue of the Muslim safe areas of Srebrenica, Zepa, and Gorazde in Bosnian Serb territory. .

While peace negotiations continued into the summer of 1995, the Bosnian Serbs secretly made their own plans to deal with these issues. The ethnic cleansing of Muslim areas started with Srebrenica in July, 1995.

This story takes place over the five days following the fall of Srebrenica.

BRACO

# CHARACTERS

**BOSNIAN CIVILIANS**
Atif Stavic
Marija Stavic

**DUTCH PEACEKEEPER**
Jac Larue

**BOSNIAN SOLDIER**
Tarak Smajlovic

**SERB SOLDIER**
Niko Basaric

**CANADIAN PHOTO-JOURNALIST**
Michael Sakic

# PROLOGUE

*YOU LIE STILL and stare at the sky.*

*Curious.*

*The fog cleared hours ago, but the clouds remain low. The layers move, join, and tear apart. A speck of blue disappears. A wisp of black drifts into view. You draw in a long breath. Soot coats your throat.*

*Buzzing.*

*A bee? Mosquito?*

*You raise your arm and swat around your face. Your hand comes back red. You blink, trying to focus. You can't understand why it's red.*

*The buzzing grows louder.*

*A black cloud invades, moving from right to left. With effort, you move your head to follow the cloud from the heavens to the earth. White concrete homes line the street. One alley is familiar. An overturned car blocks the entrance and the black cloud billows up from behind.*

*The buzzing crackles. Voices join the chorus.*

*Someone touches your shoulder.*

*You ignore them and concentrate on the car, on the alley. The place seems important. Someone shakes you, but your eyes rest on the alley. You struggle to focus. Your vision clears.*

*A small arm hangs limp between the car and the wall.*

# TUESDAY: ATIF STAVIC

ATIF STAVIC WOKE to hands shaking his shoulder. His head rolled from side to side. He tensed and sucked in air like a newborn.

"Please," a woman's voice said. "You'll hurt her."

Atif rubbed his eyes. "What?"

The young woman held a scarf tight around her pale face and pointed. Atif raised his head. His feet had pinned a little girl against the rusted metal railing at the foot of the bed. She moaned, holding her hands to a blood soaked cloth wrapped around her head. Atif jerked his feet back and sat up, drawing his knees close to his chest.

"I'm sorry. I didn't mean it."

"I know," the woman replied. "You were dreaming."

*It was a dream?*

Atif looked around. A bright sun lit the room through a cracked window high on the aging concrete wall next to him. The light flickered as legs rushed by in both directions. Across the room, three children shared another bed. Injured and dying people carpeted the floor: groaning, crying, talking. The stench of urine and vomit mingled with antiseptic and infection. Atif's stomach churned. He leaned against the wall and closed his eyes.

*Was the dream real?*

His head pounded in rhythm with the beating of his heart and he fought the growing nausea. The memories formed in a haze.

They had played two on two using a wrecked Lada tipped on its side as a goal. Jovan and Ramo had paired up against Atif and Ramo's little brother, Dani. Excited that the older boys had invited him to play, Dani paced back and forth between the front to rear axle of the wreck with his arms held wide enough to hug an elephant. He had not been able to stop a single shot. Atif played near the goal to help him.

Jovan and Ramo advanced, passing the ball between them. Dani stayed close to the car.

"Come out," Atif had said. "You can't stop a ball if your back is up against the drive shaft."

The boy took a step forward, his arms still up. Atif looked back as Ramo made a clumsy attempt at a back pass to Jovan.

*He thinks he's Elvir Bolic.*

Jovan bounced the ball back to Ramo, who made a chip shot. The ball took flight and sailed high. Atif turned as Dani's short frame rose in the air, his fingertips scraping the bottom of the ball. It bounced on the car and disappeared from sight.

"Thirty-two to nothing," Ramo said.

"That wasn't in," Atif replied. "That was over the goal."

Jovan laughed.

"Fine. Thirty-one nothing."

"I'll get the ball," Dani said.

Atif spun around. "What? No. I'll get it."

He plucked the boy off the transmission, scaled the wreck, and ran after the ball as it skipped over rocks and garbage in the gutter across the street. He picked it up and stood still, scanning the hills for movement.

*The snipers can see the street.*

*But the hills are quiet.*

Atif faced the alley and held the grimy ball over his head, ready to throw it back.

His memory blurred.

*Why didn't I hear the shell?*

"Bad dreams?"

Atif looked to his right. A young soldier sat slumped in a chair next to the bed, his eyes fixed on the far wall. His name, Omar Pasic, was scribbled on a scrap of paper pinned to the heavy bandages wrapped around his gut. A cigarette hung between his fingers. The long ash threatened to drop.

"No." Atif turned away. "I wasn't dreaming."

"Don't worry about it. We all get them."

The door opened, striking a leg stretched out in its path. A female voice yelped. A nurse glanced inside and left, leaving the door open. People moved back and forth in the dim light of the corridor, pushing and shouting. The nurse returned, shoving a gurney into the room across the hall. The door to the room slammed shut, its faceplate swinging from a single nail. Atif tilted his head and read the word on the plate: morgue. A man backed into the morgue, cradling his injured arm. A woman followed a doctor down the corridor.

"Mama?"

"She's here, somewhere," the soldier said. Atif turned. "She's trying to find a doctor. Wants to make sure it's okay for you to leave."

"Leave? Why?"

The soldier lifted his arm and looked at the cigarette, then crushed it against the wall. The ash left a black scar on the peeling white paint.

"You don't know?"

"Know what?"

"Chetniks are coming. The tanks are just outside the town. They'll be here in a few hours."

Panic stabbed Atif's chest. He thought back, struggling to remember, but his memory stopped at the alley. Ramo and Jovan laughing. Dani's bright blue eyes staring out from behind the wrecked car. Then nothing.

"I don't remember. Where'd they come from?"

"They're coming up from Skelani," the soldier said. "I heard there were twenty thousand troops. We never stood a chance."

"But the UN, the Dutch."

"The bastards don't care about us. They promised us air strikes. They warned us last night to evacuate our front lines. They said there would be massive air strikes. A zone of death they called it." The soldier paused, pulling in a laboured breath. "And what did we get? Nothing! Not a single aircraft showed up and the Chetniks walked in and took our trenches."

Atif swallowed, his throat sticking. He tried to formulate a thought through the shellfire in his head. The Dutch had hundreds of peacekeepers in the area. The UN had sent them to protect the town, but Atif knew a few hundred Dutch could do little against the Serbs without air strikes.

Unless.

"Maybe the planes didn't come because the blue helmets are bringing in more troops," he said.

The soldier laughed and the laugh degenerated into a fit of coughing.

"There are no troops coming." He wiped blood trickling from his mouth. "They don't give a damn. To them, one Dutch life is worth more than fifty thousand Muslims."

"That's not true!"

"Believe what you want," the soldier said. His head settled back and his eyes focused on the far wall. "If you were smart, you'd follow the men."

"What are you talking about? Follow what men?"

As the soldier opened his mouth to respond, a familiar voice drew Atif's attention to the door. His mother stood in the hall, speaking to a doctor. She was wearing a white blouse and a long dark skirt and she had his sneakers in her hand. Atif glanced at her feet. She wore her walking shoes.

"Mama."

The doctor left and his mother stepped inside, bringing her hand to her nose for a moment. She slipped through the minefield of injured and dying and laid Atif's sneakers on the bed.

"You can leave," she said, handing him a bottle of water. "Drink some."

Atif drank while his mother pushed the sneakers on his feet and tied the laces. He capped the bottle.

"Where's Tihana?"

"She's waiting at the house with Ina and the twins. They should be packed by the time we get there."

Ina and her twin seventeen-year-old daughters had shared the same house in Srebrenica with Atif's family for three years. Ina worked as a nurse in the hospital.

*And she's not here now?*

"Why? Where are we going?"

"Potocari. We're going to the Dutch base."

"But he told me the Dutch weren't going to help us," Atif said, motioning over his shoulder with his thumb.

"Everyone is going there. They'll protect us."

Atif turned to the soldier.

"See, I told you."

The soldier's head slumped forward.

"Mama?"

She finished tying his laces.

"Should we call the doctor?"

"We have to go." She took his hand. "Now."

Atif slid off the bed and followed his mother to the door, glancing back. Two women had claimed his spot on the bed. Behind them, the soldier remained motionless.

Atif's mother pulled him into the corridor. A gauntlet of injured people lined the hallway on stretchers, beds, and the floor. An old woman stopped a nurse, blocking the hallway.

"My husband needs help."

Atif followed the woman's finger to a man curled up on the floor. Bandages hid his face.

"We're starting an evacuation," the nurse said. "You have to take him to the Dutch base in Potocari."

"Potocari. That's five kilometres. I can't carry him that far."

"I don't know what to tell you. You'll have to wait to see if the Dutch can transport him."

The nurse sidestepped the old woman and shouldered her way through a growing traffic jam. Atif followed his mother as she picked a way for them through the hall and up the stairs to the main entrance. They walked through the doorway and stepped into a brilliant sun. Atif winced, turning away from the bright light. Spots clouded his vision and sweat rolled through his eyes. He wiped his forehead, his fingers brushing something on his right temple. Gauze and medical tape. He counted eight bumps under the gauze.

*Stitches?*

His mother wrapped an arm around his shoulder and they walked down the driveway. Atif blinked his vision clear. Thousands of men, women, and children clogged the main road flowing east like a raging river that could not be stopped. No one could move west against the torrent. Men carried children on their shoulders and women carried bags. A donkey struggled to pull a cart filled with wounded. Two men pushed a wheelbarrow with a television in it. Soldiers walked in groups.

*Have they all given up?*

A pillar of dirt and debris rose up suddenly behind the houses across the street. The report punched the air an instant later.

Whomp!

The sound always reminded Atif of ice sliding off a roof onto a bed of fluffy snow. A sharp but muffled sound of air trying to escape. A sound that meant death.

Atif's knees failed him. He slid towards the pavement, dragging his mother down with him.

"We can't go down there."

"It's okay, Atif. They're not shelling the road. That's why we have to move now. We'll be safe in Potocari."

A second shell struck a parking lot, driving shards of concrete, rock, and mud into the air. Atif climbed to his feet, staring at the twin columns of dust drifting between the houses. He clamped his arms like tongs around his mother as they joined the river of refugees. People pushed, not caring who they knocked down in their panic to get away from the town and the encroaching Serbs. Sweat clouded Atif's vision again.

They approached the small Dutch compound called Bravo within minutes. White trucks sat parked in the motor pool. Blue helmets scurried between them, carrying equipment and stretchers. A truck roared to life and moved forward. Peacekeepers hefted stretchers into the back.

A cloud puffed up behind the trucks, the report following a moment later. Atif and his mother ducked with the rest of the crowd. He looked back. A second pillar of dirt sprouted behind the camp.

"They're shelling the blue helmets. What's going on, Mama?"

She pulled him forward. "We have to hurry, Atif. The soldiers are saying the tanks are in the town."

Atif watched the camp, hoping to glimpse a familiar face. The peacekeepers ran back and forth between the buildings and trucks carrying boxes, packs, and blankets. Sentries watched the crowd. A woman approached the wire fence and spoke to a peacekeeper on the other side. He stepped inside a bunker and returned, tossing a bottle of water over the fence.

A line of peacekeepers stretched across the main gate.

"Go to Potocari," one of the Dutch shouted in English. A truck idled behind him.

Atif turned away and spotted the top half of their house across the street. The white concrete face was pitted from shrapnel. The second-story balcony had no rail and was piled with split firewood. Thick clear plastic covered the windows and a hole in the roof had been repaired with scrap lumber.

Atif's mother fought against the current of refugees and they emerged on the shoulder of the road. The front lawn had been converted into a vegetable garden and now swarmed with people digging up the potatoes and carrots. Atif released his mother and ran into the yard.

"What are you doing?" he asked a man, tugging on his shirt. The man ignored him. "Those are our carrots. Get away."

"Leave him alone, Atif."

He looked up. Ina stood in the doorway dressed in jeans and a flowered blouse. She ran her hand through her short black hair and pointed inside.

"We have all that we can carry," she said. "Come get your pack."

"But it's ours."

His mother took him by the shoulders and directed him up the steps. "Go get your pack. We have to go."

Atif walked up the rotted wooden stairs, his feet pounding each step. He was careful to skip the second-last one. He expected the spongy tread to fail soon.

His mother followed him into the poorly lit kitchen. Firewood covered the windows and the only light came from the door. Empty cupboards lined a wall and dishes sat unwashed in the sink below them. Ina's twin daughters, Lejla and Adila, stood at a table sorting through a pile of carrots, potatoes, and clumps of soil. They wore head scarves, long sleeved blouses, and brightly coloured baggy trousers, despite the heat. Atif knew the twins preferred jeans and short-sleeved tops. He had never seen them wear head scarves or *dimijes*. They turned to Atif and smiled.

"We left your pack on your mattress," Lejla said. "We didn't know what you wanted to bring."

"Pack light, Atif," his mother said, helping the girls. "You don't need any clothes. Leave room for the food and water."

Tihana sat on a stack of split wood next to the stove, watching everything that moved. He stood above her and peered down into the reflection of his own green eyes.

"Hi," he said, crouching next to his seven-year-old sister. "Did you miss me?"

She nodded but said nothing, her eyes following Adila across the room. Atif stood and turned to his mother.

"What's wrong with her?"

"She hasn't said a word since," she whispered close to his ear. "She ran to the alley after the shell hit, but some men had taken you to the hospital before we got there. We didn't know for hours. She thought you were in the alley when the shell hit. And she saw Dani."

"Why didn't you tell me?"

"You had a concussion. I doubt you remember much from the last couple of days."

"She'll be okay," Ina said, touching his arm. "She just needs time. Now go get your pack. Hurry."

Atif stared at her then nodded. He trusted her judgment.

He turned away and took the stairs two at a time into the basement. Mattresses covered with clothes and blankets lined the damp foundation walls. A broken light bulb hung from a loose wire in the middle of the ceiling. A wool blanket with sewn up holes separated his space from the girl's section of the room. He brushed by the blanket and knelt on his mattress. His black knapsack sat in the middle and he picked it up, dumping the clothes out.

*What do I need?*

He picked up a red hardcover journal and skimmed through the pages of notes, numbers, and dates until he found his identification booklet and cards.

*All there.*

He wrapped the book in a plastic bag and stuffed it inside the pack then checked the outside pocket. Empty.

*Where are my cigarettes?*

He checked around the mattress but couldn't find them.

*Mama must have them.*

His eyes swept the mattress and spied his favorite neon-yellow A-Team t-shirt. He stripped off the blood and sweat-stained shirt he was wearing and pulled on the clean yellow shirt and then he surveyed the wood stacked on one side of the room. He picked up four die-cast toy soldiers sitting on a piece of split wood and dumped them into the single outside pocket.

He stood up and looked around the room that had kept them safe for three years.

*The farm. The cabin. Now this. I hate running away.*

"Did you take my cigarettes?" he shouted as he scaled the stairs.

"I have them," his mother said.

She tossed a small plastic container to Atif. He opened it and counted nine cigarettes.

"I had to buy some water containers."

Atif followed his mother's gaze to Ina, who pointed to a large green container the Dutch usually used to store gas. Two smaller clear plastic bottles were on the table. Lejla had carried in a bucket from the rain barrels in the backyard and was pouring it into the green container.

He had been saving the cigarettes to buy winter boots for Tihana for her birthday.

*But nine cigarettes can buy more valuable things now.*

His mother took his pack and dropped the two small bottles inside. Ina picked up a handful of potatoes and stuffed them in between the bottles. Adila handed her carrots and she laid them on top.

"Is this too heavy?"

"It's fine," Atif said, without picking it up.

People shouted outside.

"What's going on?" Lejla asked.

They went outside and leaned over the railing, looking south.

"I don't see any tanks," Ina said.

The people in the crowd looked skyward. Fingers pointed to the north. Atif ran into the yard and looked up, shielding his eyes from the high sun. He scanned the clear blue sky above the steep hills surrounding the town.

Thunder rolled and faded then rolled again.

*A helicopter? No.*

The noise didn't have the chopping echo of a helicopter.

*A plane?*

His thoughts skipped to the early days of the war when the Serbs used to bomb the town from slow-moving propeller-driven airplanes. They were easy to recognize. They sounded like mosquitoes.

But this wasn't a mosquito.

*Bigger. Louder.*

*Hornets?*

Two silver-grey blurs split the air like lightning.

Thunder clapped. The crowd screeched.

Atif slapped his hands against his ears and bent over as air rushed in to fill the vacuum left behind the fast moving aircraft. His ribs vibrated. He straightened up and swung around to look at the planes as they threaded the needle between the hills and disappeared towards the south. He made a fist and punched the air.

"Yes! Yes! They came. I knew they'd come. I knew they'd save us!"

The crowd slowed down; thousands of eyes settled on the southwestern horizon. The distant rumble changed pitch. An explosion echoed between the hills. People burst into cheers and applause.

"Yes, yes!" Atif screamed at the sky. "I knew you'd come. I knew it."

The planes rose, two dots above the horizon. As they turned, the sun glinted off their wings. Then they dove again.

"Come on. Come on." Atif eyed his mother. She was smiling, but it was a reserved smile. He glanced at Ina; her expression was like his mother's.

*They should be happy. We don't have to leave now.*

Thunder grew in the south. The planes rose into the sky a second time. He waited for more explosions.

Nothing.

The aircraft dove and disappeared from sight. Smoke drifted up behind the southern hills. The crowd scanned the sky, looking for their saviours. Fingers pointed in every direction and then the roar returned. A single jet came down the same path from the north, swooped low over the edge of town and then streaked straight up into the sky. A second bomb detonated.

"Go, go, go. We're going to be okay, Mama. We're going to be okay."

They waited for more, but the thunder faded and the glints vanished from the sky. The crowd resumed their walk to Potocari. More people entered the yard and dug for potatoes.

"Come on, Atif," his mother said, stepping inside. "We have to get ready."

"What? No," he said, climbing the steps and following her. "We don't have to go. They'll come back. The Chetniks won't come in now."

His mother took him by the shoulders.

"Listen to me, Atif. We both know that two bombs mean nothing. There are too many Chetniks and, until we know for sure, we're better off in Potocari."

Atif glared at her.

"Look at them." She motioned through the open door to the

refugees; a Dutch peacekeeper was walking among them. "We have to follow them. We're not going to turn back until they do."

"To Potocari," the peacekeeper shouted. "Chetniks come. To Potocari."

No one turned back.

Atif's elation evaporated. He looked at his mother. She returned his gaze, her lips tight. He drew in a sharp breath, remembering the last time he had seen the same expression.

Atif had woken to his father's touch that spring night three years earlier, back on the farm near Kravica.

"Get up," his father had said. "Get dressed. Quickly."

Atif had sat up in his bed and wiped the sleep from his eyes before looking up. His father's eyes darted away, his calloused fingers fidgeting with the buttons on his own shirt.

"What's wrong, Tata?"

"Chetniks are coming. We have to leave."

"Now?"

His father didn't answer. He'd reached under Atif's bed and pulled out a knapsack they had packed months earlier. The war in Croatia had convinced his father the fighting would spread to Bosnia and he had set to work building a place to hide in the woods behind their farm. He had stocked it with enough food and supplies to last them for months and traded Yugoslav currency for Deutsche Marks and American Dollars. He'd bought cartons of cigarettes even though he didn't smoke.

"Get dressed," his father had said. "Bring a sweater and the pack. Nothing else. Understand?"

"Yes, Tata."

"Come downstairs when you're ready," he'd said, pulling the door closed as he left.

Atif had dressed and wrapped a light sweater around his waist. He looked around his room.

*Nothing else?*

His eyes had scanned the room, seeing the wool blankets rumpled on his bed, the blind teddy bear sitting next to his soccer trophies on the dresser, and the poster of the 1990 Yugoslav World Cup team.

*I hate penalty shootouts.*

A line of die-cast metal soldiers the size of his hand sat next to the billowing curtain. He'd picked two infantry, one machine gunner, and a mortar man, stuffing them into the knapsack. Light flashed in the distance. Thunder rumbled.

*A storm? Now?*

He'd taken one last look at his room and left. When the Serb army swept through the town, his family hid in the cabin while their Muslim neighbours were murdered.

Atif tore his gaze away from his mother and looked down at his sister.

*I wish you were here now, Tata.*

"Okay," Atif said. "But if they turn around, we can come back, right?"

"I don't think anyone is going home this time," she said, holding up a length of white rope. "I want you to tie yourself to Tihana. That's all you have to worry about. If we get separated from you in the crowd, I want you to meet us at the bus depot in Potocari. Get as close to the fuel tanks as you can. I'll find you there."

Atif took the rope and stared at it. His vision blurred and his knee felt weak.

*Am I still dreaming?*

He rubbed his eyes and walked over to Tihana. She sat on the wood, holding her knees to her chest. She was shaking. Atif crouched down next to her.

"Come on, Tihana," he said, holding up the rope. "We have to go."

She shook her head. A shell struck high on the hill across the street, a dirty cloud of dirt erupting among the field of stumps that covered the hillside. Tihana sucked in air, staring at the window. Atif glanced back at his mother. She was helping the twins with their bags.

Atif retrieved his bag from the table and returned to Tihana. He took one of the toy soldiers from the pack and held it up. Her eyes widened.

"Remember him?" he said. "I told you the machine gunner is really good because he can shoot a lot of bullets, right?"

She nodded.

"Why don't you hold on to him? He'll take care of you. I have the rest so that no one will be able to hurt us. Okay?"

She took the toy soldier.

"Don't let go of him, okay?"

She wrapped her fingers tight around the soldier. Atif offered her his hand and she stood up. He wrapped the rope around her waist, tying a tight knot, and did the same to himself.

"Are you ready?"

She held the toy soldier close and then looked up, smiling.

"Not too much slack," his mother said. She loosened a knot and pulled them closer together, tying it back up securely. "There's going to be a lot of pushing and shoving. Keep her close to you and stay away from the trucks. Understand?"

"Yes, Mama. I'll take care of her."

"I know you will." She kissed him. "Don't forget. The fuel tanks."

"Yes, Mama."

He pulled on his pack. The weight unbalanced him and he grabbed a chair to steady himself. Everyone slung their bags and the twins picked up the green water container between them.

Atif led Tihana outside. His mother closed the door.

She didn't lock it.

Three shells plowed into the hill above the camp in quick succession. The crowd dipped like a rolling swell before moving on.

"I'll stay in front with the girls," Ina said, eyeing the hillside. "I think we should stay in the centre of the crowd. In case a shell falls short."

"Agreed," his mother said, leading Atif and Tihana down the steps and through their looted garden. They followed Ina and the twins into the chaotic crowd. The shelling intensified as the last few homes and factory buildings of Srebrenica faded behind them and gave way to countryside dotted with homes, farms, and forests. Two shells detonated among the trees on a hill far to the right and another fell in a cultivated field to the left. The crowd paused each time and then continued walking.

Atif understood. The Serbs weren't trying to shell the people. They were herding everyone towards the Dutch base.

He encouraged Tihana to quicken her pace.

The shelling persisted, close enough to drive the crowd like cattle but never close enough to hurt anyone on the road. Atif's group walked for more than an hour, stopping twice in the shade of trees to rest and drink water before rejoining the crowd. With each step, the scorching sun and blistering pavement sapped their strength, slowing their pace. They watched people too exhausted to continue collapse on the edge of the road or seek shelter in the houses.

A Dutch troop truck crept along, the crowd streaming around it like the wake from a ship. Atif kept glancing back as it got closer, astonished at the number of people clinging to the vehicle. They sat on top of the tarp, hung from the sides, and occupied every open space on the cab. They positioned and repositioned themselves like bees working a hive.

*How can the driver see the road?*

Two men carrying an unconscious woman on a door brushed by Atif and laid their burden in the middle of the road in front of the truck. The rusted hinges clinked against the asphalt and the doorknob propped the makeshift stretcher up on one side. The men slipped back into the crowd. Atif looked at the truck.

"He doesn't see her, Mama!"

His mother stepped in front of the woman and waved her hands above her head.

"Stop," she screamed. "Halt! Halt! You'll run her over."

Atif crouched next to Ina and wrapped his arms around Tihana. The truck lurched to a stop, the passengers falling forward. A boy slid off the hood and another one took his place. A blue helmet surfaced between a group of teenage girls holding on to the driver's door.

"I can't take any more," the peacekeeper shouted to Atif's mother in English. "Tell them to move her."

Atif studied the peacekeeper's shaded features.

*Is that Jac? No. Can't be.*

His peacekeeper friend was at the observation post near Jaglici, a village north of Potocari.

*But is he still there?*

Atif's mother darted into the crowd in search of the men. She returned alone and shook her head at the driver. Another blue helmet appeared from the passenger window and shouted directions. The wheels of the truck cut to the right until they squealed and it edged its way around the stretcher. People shuffled aside as the tires crushed gravel along the shoulder. The truck veered back onto the pavement and kept going. The woman remained on the door in the middle of the road.

"Keep moving, Atif," his mother said. "There's nothing we can do."

She placed her hands on his shoulders and steered him forward. He glanced back, watching the crowd swallow up the woman.

"Why isn't anyone helping her?"

His mother said nothing. Tihana pulled Atif forward. People ran after the truck and tried to climb on board. They were pushed back down. Someone loosened the straps on the vinyl tarp and part of it collapsed. People on top scrambled forward or clung to the side, fighting others for space. Some fell among those inside the truck. One was pushed off the truck. Women on the road begged the occupants to take their children. One woman threw her infant into the back of the truck and it was thrown back. An old man collapsed on the road. A peacekeeper pushed a woman in a wheelbarrow. A cow trotted free. Gunfire echoed in the hills.

*It's happening too fast. Too fast.*

Atif squeezed his eyes shut, hoping to wake up warm in his own bed back on the farm. Instead, Dani looked at him with wide blue eyes. Ramo waved. Jovan laughed. His father kissed him on the forehead and walked off into the fog. Atif shook the images from his mind.

*Don't think about it.*

He opened his eyes and looked at his sister. She licked her lips.

He had to take care of his family now. That's what his father would have wanted.

Atif tugged on his mother's arm.

"Maybe we should stop for a few minutes. I think Tihana wants some water."

Ina looked back at them and then pointed to the side of the road. They moved out of the sweltering throng and took refuge next to a vandalized VW that hadn't moved in three years.

Atif pulled one of the bottles from his pack and passed it around. He used his shirt to wipe his face and then surveyed the area. They were close to Potocari where roadside homes outnumbered farms. People ransacked the line of houses across the street, throwing mattresses and furniture from the second-story balconies. At the white house directly across from Atif, a man pushed a table over the edge of the balcony, flattening a row of tended yellow roses lining the front wall. Men entered the houses empty handed and left carrying sacks.

Atif looked to his left and spotted the turnoff to Susnjari and Jaglici, villages seven kilometres to the north. The road was jammed with people.

*Why are they walking away from the Dutch camp?*

Potocari and the Dutch camp lay less than a kilometer away on the main road to the east. Atif stood up and studied the scene. Men were hugging their wives and children and then turning north. Teenage boys were joining their fathers and brothers. No women followed.

"Where are they going, Mama?" he asked, pointing towards the road.

His mother turned to look.

"They're going through the woods," Ina said. Her eyes flicked towards his mother. "They're probably walking to Zepa or Tuzla."

*If you were smart, you'd follow the men.*

The soldier's warning flashed across Atif's mind.

"Should I be going with them?" he asked his mother.

"No. You're too young."

Atif clenched his teeth and looked away.

*I'm always too young.*

"We should get going," Ina said.

Atif stuffed the bottle into his pack, took Tihana's hand, and followed Ina into the crowd. They approached the turnoff and weaved around people stopped in the middle of the road. A man had his arms around his wife; both were crying. A woman passed a baby to her husband to hold. An old man was arguing with his wife. Bosnian soldiers made the turn without stopping. A teenage boy kissed his mother and then walked away with his father.

"Why are the boys going?" he asked.

"I don't know, Atif."

"But they don't look more than sixteen."

"Enough, Atif," his mother said. "You can't go with them. You'll be safe with us."

Atif ushered Tihana forward. He looked back, watching the men and boys walk away. His documents said he was only fourteen, but people always said he looked older. Tihana wrapped an arm around his thigh and squeezed.

"It'll be okay, Tihana," he said. "Those boys probably don't have any identification to prove they're too young to fight."

He only hoped that mattered.

The crowd closed in and Atif draped an arm over Tihana's shoulder, pulling her close. He felt his mother's hand on his arm. The pace slowed.

"What's going on?"

Ina glanced back. "The Dutch have two trucks on the road. They're funneling us between them."

Atif strained to look over Ina's shoulder. A peacekeeper stood on one of the vehicles, coaxing the crowd forward.

"Stay together," he shouted. "Follow directions to the base."

They passed through the funnel and found they had more room. People moved quickly towards the Dutch base. Atif hadn't seen Potocari by daylight in three years; he looked for familiar landmarks. The Energoinvest building came into view on his left, windows smashed but otherwise intact. People sat along the edge of the parking lot. The long narrow zinc factory was next with the bus depot on the opposite side of the road. Wrecked buses grew out of the tall grass in front of the building. Peacekeepers blocked the main road, directing everyone towards the depot.

"Can't we go to Bratunac?" a woman asked. The Serb town lay only a few kilometres up the road on the Serbian border.

"Too dangerous," the peacekeeper said. "Just stay together."

The crowd slowed as they moved past a factory that used to produce brake shoes before the war. Pockmarks marred the concrete facade. Part of the roof hung over the edge of the building, threatening to fall.

Ina looked back.

"Do you hear it?"

Women shouted. Children cried. Peacekeepers gave orders.

"What is it?" his mother asked.

"It sounds like they're going through the fence."

Atif turned an ear forward and concentrated until he heard the familiar rattle of a chain-link fence.

"So, we're going inside." The load on Atif's shoulders lightened. He squeezed Tihana with one arm. "We'll be safe in there."

She nodded, holding the toy soldier close to her chest.

The crowd turned right and skirted along the fence towards the opening. Atif looked inside. The Dutch base was on the site of an old battery factory. A four-story building shaped like a cube dominated the centre of the camp; there was a large guard bunker on top of it. A wooden sign hung from the side of the building with the word *Dutchbat* painted in blue.

As they moved closer to the opening, the pace slowed to a shuffle. With every step, people jockeyed for a position as far forward as they could manage.

"C'mon, c'mon," Atif whispered to himself.

The column narrowed and the space around Atif shrank. He kept Tihana in front. Gulping in the superheated air, he considered picking her up.

Then the crowd stopped. People in front shouted.

"What is it?" he asked Ina as she stood on her toes.

The fence rattled. Atif picked up Tihana and pressed against the metal links. The Dutch manipulated the chain link section they had cut, rolling it back and securing the hole they had opened, using wire to tie the ends together.

"Why have you stopped?" his mother shouted to one of the peacekeepers in English. "Why can't we get inside?"

Women collapsed on the ground crying. Children screamed. An old man shook his fist at the Dutch and spit. The peacekeeper turned, his eyes shadowed by his Kevlar helmet.

"We can't take any more inside." He crushed a half-smoked cigarette under his boot. "The building is full."

Atif searched the faces of the peacekeepers inside the fence, but he recognized none of them.

"We don't need to go into the building," his mother said.

Other women echoed her words in several languages.

"There's more than enough room inside the fence," she said. "We'll sit on the ground. Please. You have to let us inside."

"I can't," the peacekeeper said, raising his hands, palms out. "The Serbs said they'd shell the compound if we took refugees inside. If we left you all outside in the open, they will see you and one shell would be disastrous. Do you understand that?"

"We'll take the chance."

"I'm sorry. I have my orders."

"Then go get whoever gave you those orders. Let me speak to him."

The crowd shouted the same message. A rock sailed over Atif's head, rebounded against the fence, and struck the woman behind him. She grasped her head and staggered away.

A man appeared from one of the buildings and approached the fence. He stopped to talk with the peacekeepers. He wore a blue helmet, but there were civilian clothes underneath his flak vest. Atif tapped his mother on the shoulder and pointed.

"Translator. Maybe he can do something."

The translator turned towards the crowd. "We are opening up the factories down the street," he told them in Bosnian. "You can go there."

"We won't be safe there," someone said from behind.

"The base will be extended to include the factories," the translator said, stepping forward. "The Dutch will be there. They will try to find some food and water for you. They will provide medical attention. A clinic will be set up at the bus depot."

"Why so far?" a man asked. He pointed to the factory behind them. "Why can't we stay in that building?"

The translator spoke to one of the peacekeepers.

"The building is full of asbestos. It's piled everywhere inside. It will make you sick. Go to the other factories. The Dutch will secure the area."

"We should go," Atif whispered to his mother. "Now. Before the factories fill up."

"Go back the way you came," the translator said. "Don't go near the main gate. The Chetniks can see that side of the camp."

The refugees drifted away from the fence.

"He's right," Ina said.

She wrapped her arms around her daughters and turned. His mother's features softened and she nodded. Atif dropped Tihana on her feet and they followed Ina into the crowd. Tihana stopped and sat down on the ground. People bumped into them and tripped.

"She's tired," Ina told Atif.

"We need to get to the factory," he said. "Before it fills up."

"We'll worry about that when we get there," his mother said. She directed them to the brake factory wall and then bent down to untie the rope around Tihana's waist. "I'll carry her."

Atif untied his end of the rope first and let it drop.

"No, it's okay, Mama. I'll carry her."

"You're sure?"

"I don't mind. She can sit on my shoulders."

His mother hesitated then nodded.

"Okay."

Ina passed around a cup of water from the green container. After they drank, his mother picked up Tihana and swung her up and over Atif's head, positioning her half on his shoulders, half on his pack. Atif grunted from the extra weight and fought to keep his knees from giving out. Tihana wrapped her hands around Atif's head, her nails digging into his skull. The toy soldier dug the tip of its machine gun into his temple.

"Are you okay?" Ina asked.

"Yeah. Let's go."

They rejoined the crowd, trudging through the narrow gap between the brake factory and other buildings. Atif held his sister's hand to keep the toy soldier from impaling his eyes. Her fingernails found his stitches. Sweat dribbled into his eyes. He could see nothing, plodding behind Ina and the twins. A Dutch voice called out, shepherding the crowd towards the zinc factory. People dropped out of the line, sitting on the road or the grass.

"Almost there," Ina said.

They reached a door which kept opening and closing, making a high-pitched squeal. Next to it, a larger door hung open. They stepped through the open door and shuffled to the right. As his eyes adjusted, Atif made out a choppy sea of bobbing heads belonging to people who occupied the long, narrow factory floor. Some were moving upstairs into the offices. Dust filled the air; it was like standing in a hot oven.

*Could there be asbestos here too?*

"We might be better off outside," Atif said.

"By the buses," Ina replied. "It's shelter at least and won't be as crowded."

They turned around and fought against the tide. When they got back outside, Ina led them across the street to the side of a wrecked bus partially tipped on one side. They settled down against it, out of the sun. Atif laid Tihana in the tall grass. She went to sleep, the toy soldier nestled under her chin.

Atif leaned against the fender of the bus. People were claiming every open patch of ground, placing blankets, plastic, and cardboard on the grass or pavement.

"What do we do now?"

His mother rolled up a blanket and placed it under Tihana's head.

"We wait."

Atif didn't want to wait. He wanted answers.

*Why only two planes? Why did the men go into the woods? What are they going to do with us?*

He stared at his backpack, remembering the young journalist who had ridden into Srebrenica with the first convoy three years earlier.

"I want to show the world what's happening here," the Western journalist had said in flawless Bosnian. "They need to see that you don't have a lot of food. If they see that, they won't be happy about it and they'll send food."

Atif stared up at the young man, whose eyes were hidden behind sunglasses.

"How can I do anything about that?"

"You're pretty skinny. Let me take your picture. The rest of Europe will be angry to learn that you're not getting enough to eat."

"But I've always been skinny."

"That doesn't matter."

"I'll have to ask my father."

"That's fine. Perhaps I can take a picture of your family."

"My little sister, too?"

"Yeah. Sure."

Atif had stared at the journalist's backpack, chewing on his lip. The pack had a gold embroidered emblem with three words underneath.

"University of...."

"Manitoba." The journalist crouched down and let Atif take a closer look. "I went there for a few years."

"Where is Manitoba?"

"In Canada. Do you know where that is?"

"Yes."

"Manitoba is a province in the middle of Canada. I was born there, but I live in Toronto now."

"But how come you speak our language?"

"My grandparents emigrated from Croatia to Great Britain before the Second World War and then they went to Manitoba during the war. My grandmother never learned English, so I had to learn her language."

Atif smiled, staring at the pack again. He liked the gold embroidery.

"Do you want it?"

"What?"

"Consider it a gift, for letting me take your picture."

The journalist opened the pack and transferred most of the contents to his camera bag. Atif took the bag and looked inside.

"I left some treats in there," the journalist said. "You can share them with your sister."

"Any cigarettes?"

"Aren't you a little young to be smoking?"

"I don't smoke them. I trade them. For food and stuff."

"Oh. Right. Hold on a moment."

The journalist had gone to his truck and returned with a white plastic container the size of a cigarette pack. When he opened it, there were twelve cigarettes and a lighter inside.

Atif stuffed the container into the bag. "Thanks."

Later, he had traded the lighter for a pound of salt. The cigarettes had bought meat and a winter jacket for Tihana. His father agreed to the pictures, standing silently to one side as the journalist snapped shots of his son wearing only a pair of shorts.

The journalist asked him to suck in his stomach each time he took a photo. Atif didn't like doing that.

He stared at the road leading to the Dutch base and wondered if there were any journalists there now.

*Do they know what's happening? Do they care?*

# TUESDAY: MICHAEL SAKIC

MIKE GROANED AND rolled his head into the pillow trying to silence the thumping between his ears. He wondered if he had any Aspirin left but didn't have the energy to open his eyes to look.

"Never again."

The pounding came from outside now and his name came with it. He tilted his head.

"Mike!"

"Goddamnit."

He rolled his head back into the pillow and pulled up the sides, covering his ears. The thumping stopped and he slipped into sleep.

*Burning furniture. Table legs. Armchairs.*

Keys jingled.

A click followed.

Mike opened his eyes on a bright window. A moment later, a shadow eclipsed the light and a hand shook his shoulder. Mike's vision adjusted; Brendan's stocky frame stood in front of him.

"Get up, Mike."

"I am up."

Clothes landed on his head.

"You're awake. You're not up. For God's sake, you said you'd go."

Mike squinted, wondering what he had said. The last thing he remembered was a soldier leading him into a basement full of black-market alcohol.

"I wouldn't have wasted my time if I knew you were going to fall off the wagon."

"Wasn't my fault," Mike said, wiping drool from his chin.

Brendan shook his head. His short, flaming red hair mirrored his mood. "What? Does Bosnian beer have legs? Did it walk up to you and force its way down your throat?"

Mike chuckled into the pillow.

"Fine." He heard zippers. "Where are we going?"

"Srebrenica, you fool. I expected you in the lobby an hour ago. I thought you of all people would jump at this chance."

Mike rolled onto his back; the room spun. He swallowed bile and looked up. A blurred form stuffed a black bag.

Brendan worked for an American news affiliate, but neither he nor his cameraman spoke Bosnian. In the last month, the pair had lost their translator to the BBC and their driver to a sniper. Mike had offered to do both jobs; it supplemented his income enough to keep him in the country longer than he had anticipated. The agreement also landed him more photos.

"I didn't think we'd go," Mike said. "The UN said there would be air strikes today. The zone of death, remember? They won't let us anywhere near the town."

"Christ, Mike. Have you been asleep all day?"

Brendan sat down on the edge of the bed and handed him his glasses and a cup of coffee. Mike stuffed a pillow behind his back and sat up, taking a sip. He glanced at Brendan who glared back.

"What?" Mike asked.

"They dropped two bombs and went back to Italy. We're guessing the Serbs threatened to kill the Dutch they took from the observation posts. The Serbs are probably in the town by now. Last I heard the population was heading for Potocari."

"Goddamnit," Mike said. The coffee repeated and he swallowed the acidic sludge. "There's going to be a lot of body bags."

"And we need to leave now if we want a front row seat."

"Fine. Fine. I'll meet you downstairs."

Mike dug into his jeans pocket and pulled out his wallet, opening it.

"What the...."

"They drank you dry, didn't they?"

"Bastards."

The soldiers he'd met the previous night had told Mike they would take him to meet a man who helped people escape from Sarajevo through a tunnel in the hills. Mike rubbed his forehead and pushed his glasses up.

*I should have known better than to accept that first drink.*

Brendan dropped the packed bag at the foot of the bed.

"Look. Shit, shower, and shave and get down to the lobby in fifteen minutes. I'll take care of the bill. Consider it payment for your translating services this week. And next week."

"I'm still doing your soundman's work. How about we call it even?"

"Then you're out of luck. He's cutting through the red tape in Zagreb. I expect him here in a week or so." Brendan moved towards the door then hesitated. "On second thought, skip the shit and shower. Just piss and pack."

He stood at the door, staring at Mike.

"I'm up. I'm up."

Brendan shook his head and left. Mike swung his legs over the side of the bed, immediately regretting the motion. He dropped his head into his hands to steady the rotating room. The coffee repeated.

After a few deep breaths, he stumbled to the bathroom and turned on the hot water faucet. Cold water sputtered from the tap. He soaked a towel and held it to his face. Feeling half awake, he dressed and then checked his camera bag to make sure the soldiers hadn't made off with everything else.

Cameras, lenses, film, meter, filters, batteries. Everything present and accounted for.

A metallic noise suddenly shattered the silence of his room. Mike's knees gave out and he dropped to the floor behind his bed.

*Damned garbage containers.*

He stood up, walked to the window and looked out over a pile of sandbags. On the street below, teenagers were diving into dumpsters looking for the food they knew the Western journalists wasted without a second thought. Three dogs sniffed the rubble at the base of the containers, roving back and forth like caged wolves.

Then a cat scrambled to the top of a container, startling the teenagers; it took a long leap through a broken window. A dog tried to follow. It yelped as it hit the window sill and dropped.

Another lid crashed down.

Mike shivered.

As much as he hated the noise, he preferred it to the alternative. The hotel routinely assigned journalists to the rooms facing Putnik Street, a wide multi-lane Sarajevo roadway in front of the hotel. On his first trip into the battered capital he learned that the road was visible to Serb snipers.

He closed his eyes, remembering every detail.

The first time he had heard the popping sounds outside his window, he didn't flinch or duck. He thought a car had backfired. Then he'd looked outside.

Two women lay in the middle of Putnik Street, the contents of their bags strewn around them. One lay still in a puddle of blood. The other cowered behind her friend's body, shrieking. A French armoured personnel carrier rolled into the middle of the street to protect the women.

Mike had done the one thing he had come to Sarajevo to do: he grabbed his camera and rushed outside to take pictures. The next day, the same thing happened. A repeat on the third day had bewildered him and he'd buttonholed a British officer in the hotel lobby.

"Why are there no sea containers there to protect them? You've got them on the road behind the hotel. Why not here?"

"They won't let us," the officer had replied, glancing around.

"What do you mean they won't let you? Who?"

"The city government." The officer had turned and pointed to the crowd of reporters huddled near the hotel entrance. They looked like they expected Tom Hanks to walk by at any moment. "This is what the Bosnians want. A sniper victim falling dead in front of the media. This way, they make sure the world doesn't forget what is going on here."

Mike had turned away from the peacekeeper in disgust and walked over to the front desk to request a room change. When he sent out the photos he'd taken the day before, he included a commentary on the politics behind the killings. They'd published the picture but cut the "unsubstantiated" story.

"Ready?"

Mike opened his eyes. Brendan's new cameraman, Robert, stood in the doorway. He carried a video camera on his shoulder, which looked too big for his slight frame.

"Brendan said to tell you the escort leaves with or without us in ten minutes."

Mike tossed the towel on the dresser.

"I'm coming."

Robert didn't move. "He told me to help you."

"No, he told you to make sure I was up and moving." Mike picked up the black bag and tossed it at Robert's feet. "Go on. I'll be right down."

Robert picked up the bag and walked away. Mike turned to the dresser and shuffled through some papers. He picked up a laminated black and white clipping that showed an emaciated boy wearing only a pair of shorts.

The caption read, "Starvation in the heart of Europe. Twelve year old Atif Stavic weighs only 63 pounds. Food drops and convoys are doing little to alleviate the hunger. Should the UN intervene?"

Mike had never returned to Srebrenica to tell the boy his face was known worldwide; at least it had been for a few days. His photos and the footage from other journalists had sparked outrage over the Serb blockades. Within months, the UN designated Srebrenica and a fifty-square-kilometre area around the town as the first United Nations Safe Area. Only the Canadians responded to the UN request for troops, sending in one hundred and fifty peacekeepers when ten thousand were needed. Eight hundred Dutch replaced them a year later.

Mike liked to think the photo had made a difference. The truth usually did.

"Where are you now, *Braco*?"

He dropped the picture into his knapsack, checked the room over, and left.

# TUESDAY: ATIF STAVIC

ATIF STARED AT the blood-red disk setting through a pillar of smoke. The air had started to chill and he rubbed his arms, his gaze moving to the field of corn behind the factories in Potocari. People wandered through the stalks, stripping the plants bare. Others swarmed the houses sitting on the edge of the field, looting anything they could eat or sell. Artillery echoed in the hills, too distant to be a threat. The steep hills and deep valleys could make the sound carry a very long way.

Or conceal it altogether.

Atif turned away and took a step closer to the water spigot. The woman next in line didn't have a container. She cupped her hands under the water, gulped down mouthfuls, and then gave water to her little boy to drink. Afterwards, she dunked his head under the water and soaked a towel. Someone tapped on Atif's shoulder. He turned; a young woman held up a paper bag.

"I need a container," she said.

She opened the bag to reveal a large chunk of red meat. Atif stared at enough calories to feed his family for two days.

"I can't," he said, his mouth watering. "I'm getting water for six people."

The woman frowned and walked on without a word. She moved along the line until an old man gave up a small bottle for the beef.

*How would he cook it?*

A woman behind Atif grumbled. He turned back to find the spigot free. Sliding his container under the stream, he waited until it overflowed and then capped it. When he picked it up, he was surprised at his strength after so many days in hospital. He couldn't remember if he had eaten.

*Mama must have made me eat something.*

Getting food over the last few months had not been as difficult as he expected. The Bosnian army had rejected his application, telling Atif he was too young to join and that, without a weapon, he would be useless to them anyway. Instead, they hired him as a courier and Atif had spent the spring and summer carrying messages, food, and ammunition to the trenches closest to town. They paid him with cigarettes and Deutsche Marks and enough food to ensure he would have the strength to make the runs every day. Now he had the strength to take care of his family.

"You're a man now, Atif," his father had told him on a late summer day three years before. "While I'm gone, it's up to you to take care of them. Can you do that?"

Atif had stood tall before his father and accepted the responsibility. Three months into the war, they were still in the woods, their food supply dwindling. Any hope the war would be short had vanished. His father said they had to do something before the winter set in. He decided to chance a walk into town to get news and to see if he could find someone to smuggle them to Srebrenica or Tuzla.

Atif remained standing next to his mother as his father walked into the darkness. His father returned before dawn. Atif had hidden his shame; he had done nothing except sleep.

"They slept in peace, Atif. You did a good job."

Six days later, they were in the back of a VW heading for Srebrenica.

*So long ago.*

Atif dragged the water container through the ocean of refugees, their hands and feet lapping at him like waves against a boat. He stopped to rest and looked around. Dutch peacekeepers were handing out towels and bottles of water. People pleaded for food.

"Soon," the peacekeepers replied to every inquiry.

Atif studied every peacekeeper he saw but none were familiar. Some of the people in the line-up had told them the Dutch were evacuating their remote observation posts. One person said that some of the Dutch had been taken hostage. From the southern posts, another had added. Jac had been sent to a post called Romeo near Jaglici in the north. Atif wondered if he was still there or back in Potocari.

He dragged the container towards the bus depot where the peace-keepers had set up a medical tent. People lined up for help. Dutch medics spoke to them through translators. Atif pulled the container through the line of people and made his way to the side of the wrecked bus. His mother was tucking a blanket under Tihana's head as his sister slept in Lejla's lap. Ina came to his side and helped him the last few steps. They laid the container down next to Adila and his mother stood, giving him a quick hug and kiss.

"I was beginning to worry," she said, "but someone said the line was long. Did you have any problems?"

"No, Mama."

Atif stepped over his sleeping sister and sat next to his mother, surprised to find a pot sitting on top of a small camp stove next to Ina.

"We borrowed it." She pointed to the far end of the bus where an older man sat with his wife and daughter. "I promised them all the water left in the pot and half dozen boiled potatoes."

Atif helped his mother pour the water and light the stove. They dropped twelve potatoes into the pot and waited for them to boil. Hungry eyes in the crowd watched their every move.

"Maybe we should boil them all," Atif said.

His mother followed his gaze.

"We don't know how long we're going to be here," she whispered. "We don't know if the Dutch have any food to give out and we don't know how long before they can get the trucks here to get us out. We could be here for days."

"Don't worry about them, Atif," Ina said. "There's plenty of water. People can last a long time without food as long as they have water."

Atif ate the half-cooked potato with his back to the crowd.

His mother returned the pot to the family with six potatoes in the water. Lejla woke Tihana; she ate only after Lejla pretended to feed the toy soldier. Atif's mother peeled the skin from her own potato and gave it to Tihana. She pulled one of the water bottles from Atif's pack and then dug into her own pack, taking out a small plastic bag containing the last of their salt supply.

Salt had been a rare commodity in Srebrenica. The humanitarian convoys seldom brought salt into the town; the residents had to buy what they could off the black market. The peacekeepers told Atif the Serbs usually stripped the convoys of salt destined for the town. Atif didn't understand why until Ina told him the lack of natural iodine in the area meant an increase in the risk for diseases like goiter. Some people found clumps of road salt and boiled it to use in place of table salt, but Ina said they were wasting their time. Road salt contained no iodine.

As time went on, it became harder to find salt, even on the black market. Atif had lucked into the small bag one day when he'd brought up the army's supplies. He'd traded a soldier three cigarettes for the bag of salt and considered it a steal.

His mother took several pinches, mixed it with the water, and passed it around. When they finished, Atif offered to refill the containers.

"We should wait till morning," his mother said. "It'll be dark soon."

"That's okay," Atif replied. "I know the way. And there won't be as many people there this time."

His mother glanced at Ina.

"Perhaps he should," Ina said. "It's better than facing the crowds in the morning when it's hot."

"Okay," his mother said. "But don't go near any of the rivers. We don't know where the mines are around here."

Atif kissed her and then emptied the water from the large container into the smaller ones. He left the bus and made his way through the crowd. A woman tried to calm a screeching infant. Two women held each other, crying. Another woman held her young daughter's hand as the girl urinated next to their spot. An older woman vomited. Two peacekeepers carried a woman in labour to the medical tent. A blanket was held up, offered in exchange for food. Atif said no and kept walking.

He stopped and stared at a boy. The blond hair and pale blue shirt were familiar. Atif walked towards the boy and then hesitated. He closed his eyes tight and saw Dani's face, the little boy's eyes staring at him from behind the car.

A flash, brilliant white.

Darkness.

Atif opened his eyes.

"It can't be," he whispered to himself. He stepped forward and looked down.

"Dani?"

The boy turned and looked up.

"Who?"

Atif turned away. Ahead of him another blond boy sat with his back to him. He blinked, but the boy remained. Atif walked towards the boy and touched him on the shoulder. A stranger's eyes peered up.

"Sorry," Atif said

He turned away, took two steps, and then reached out to steady himself against a tree. His head spun as he lowered himself to the ground. He squeezed his eyes shut, rocking back and forth.

It's not happening, he told himself. Just tricks. The mind plays tricks. Remember? The soldiers used to say that.

Someone touched his shoulder. Atif flinched.

"Are you okay?" the woman sitting next to him asked. She was rocking a baby in her arms.

"Yes," Atif replied. He pointed to the bandage on his temple. "I just have a headache."

"Sorry. Are you going to get water?"

Atif nodded. The woman held up a baby bottle.

"Could you? Please. I have nothing to give you."

"That's okay." He took the bottle.

"Thank you."

Atif got to his feet and looked around. A sea of women, children, and old men surrounded him.

*Women, children, and old men?*

For the first time since he'd arrived in Potocari, Atif took a close look at the crowd. Almost every face was female. The few male faces were very old or very young. He could see no young men, no older boys. His heart vibrated in his chest as he walked towards the water line, searching for another young male face.

*Have they all gone? Am I the only one left? They couldn't have all been missing their documentation.*

His eye shifted from face to face until they fell on the features of a middle-aged man sitting with his wife and two young children. Then another young man. And a teenage boy. Atif drew in a long breath of relief and took his place in the water line. But the anxiety remained.

*What is going to happen to us?*

He knew the entire population would have to leave, most likely for Tuzla. He imagined the blue helmets trying to put together a convoy of trucks and buses. *But will the Chetniks let them in?*

The sun had sunk below the horizon and the moon had risen in the southeast before Atif had his turn at the water spigot. He filled the containers and returned the baby bottle to the woman. When he got back to the bus, the twins were asleep with Tihana between them. Ina was talking with the man who had lent them the pot.

"Any problems?" his mother asked.

Atif shook his head and sat down next to her.

"Have you heard anything? Do they know what's going to happen?"

"Nothing yet," she replied. "The Dutch must be working on something."

"Everyone is talking, passing information around," Atif said, pointing towards the water line. "Someone said the Chetniks have forty thousand troops coming this way."

"I don't believe that."

"What if it's true?"

"Even if it is true, they won't hurt us. They could have shelled us on the road this afternoon and they didn't. In fact, they went out of their way not to shell us. They know if they start hurting us, the planes will attack. They don't want to risk that."

"Then why did the men go into the woods?"

"I don't know, Atif. Maybe they didn't want to take the chance."

Atif wanted to ask more questions but resisted. She didn't know the answers any more than he did. He sat in silence for a long time, watching. A woman force fed a fussy child. An old man washed the stump of his amputated leg. A family prayed.

"Is Tata dead?"

"What?"

"I mean is there something you know that you're not telling me?"

"No. Absolutely not." She laid a hand on his shoulder. "You were there when the soldier came to the door. He said they found no bodies. He said he was sure the snowstorm took them by surprise and they just got stuck somewhere."

"That was three months ago. Why isn't he back?"

"They were probably forced to go elsewhere. They might be in Zepa or Tuzla. One soldier said they might have crossed the Drina into Serbia and simply can't get word back to us."

Atif stared straight ahead. His chest ached as he tried to haul in a full breath.

"If Tata were here, do you think he would have gone with the men?"

"Well, he knows the way. I'm sure they would have used him to lead a group."

"Would he have taken me?"

"I don't know." She smiled. "Do you remember the first time you went into the woods alone?"

Atif returned the smile as the memory surfaced. He had been six-years old and had stayed in the woods behind their farm until dusk. After a lecture from his mother, Atif went to sleep but woke an hour later to find his father sitting on the edge of his bed.

"You scared her," his father had said.

"I didn't mean to. I just lost track of time."

"You need to be more careful, Atif. There are things in the woods; things that can be dangerous."

"All I saw were rabbits."

"That's good, but there are other creatures there. Has anyone told you about the *blautsauger*?"

He pulled the blanket to his chest. "You mean the *lampir*?"

"No. Not quite the same thing. I've never seen a *blautsauger*, but those who have survived an encounter have told us about it." His father raised a hand above his head. "It is a tall creature without a skeleton. It has large eyes and its body is covered with hair and it can change shape. Sometimes into a rat and sometimes into a wolf."

Atif had pulled the blanket to his chin.

"At night, it comes out of its tomb and walks around. It picks up a handful of dirt and holds it behind its back and then it goes looking for a victim. When it finds one, it puts the dirt into their mouth and turns them into another *blautsauger*."

"How do you stop it, Tata?"

"Hawthorn flowers. If you put hawthorn flowers on the tomb of the *blautsauger* and the ground around it, it will have no choice but to pick them all up. If there are enough flowers, it will keep the *blautsauger* busy until the sun rises. Sun is its enemy; if sunlight touches it, it will be destroyed."

"I know where there are some hawthorn flowers. I can put them on its tomb."

"But we don't always know where its tomb is. We keep the flowers on the ones we know about, but we can never be sure. That's why you have to be careful and stay out of the woods when the sun starts to go down."

Atif had nodded his head with enthusiasm.

"Don't worry, Tata. I won't go back in."

His mother laughed.

"And you didn't go back in the woods for years after that."

*And never alone*, Atif added to himself.

Her arm draped itself across his back.

"We have to hope, Atif. Until we know for sure we have to believe he is out there somewhere trying to get into contact with us. We both know people who have been split up for a long time and somehow find their way back together. Until the war is over, we can't be sure."

"That could be years."

"Then we'll wait years. All that matters is that you and Tihana are safe. That's what he would have wanted."

"I guess."

"I miss him, too," she said, kissing him. "Now, why don't you try to get some sleep?"

"No." The word caught in his throat. He swallowed and faced his mother. "I slept most of the day. We should take turns keeping an eye on our stuff. You should sleep now. I can wake you in a few hours."

His mother studied his features for a few moments then smiled.

"In a few hours?"

"Promise."

She curled up next to Tihana and fell asleep in minutes. Atif wondered how long it had been since she had last slept.

He leaned against the rusted wheel rim and looked around. Children slept. Parents stayed awake next to them, watching everything that moved. Some cried while others prayed. Atif sought a glimpse of the peacekeepers, hoping to recognize Jac or one of his friends. He wasn't sure if Jac could get them inside the compound, but he might have some answers.

There was a distant rumble; Atif stood up and moved a few short steps away from his family. A Dutch armoured personnel carrier with smoke pouring from its engine was creeping along the road towards the compound. Peacekeepers walked with it, in the shadows. Atif guessed the vehicle had come from one of the observation posts.

Jac would be among them sooner or later.

Atif sat down against the tire rim and kept watch.

# TUESDAY: JAC LARUE

SOMEONE SHOOK JAC'S foot.

*Mom?*

His foot rose and fell, the heel catching on a metal edge. Jac sat up, smacking his head on kit strapped to the ceiling of the armoured personnel carrier. His book and pen flew across the cramped compartment. A thin sheet of stationary floated to the floor. He swung his legs to the side.

"Goddamnit."

Maarten Wendell stepped inside and sat down next to him. He slipped his helmet off his shaved head and leaned forward.

"Didn't mean to startle you."

"Sure you did," Jac said, rubbing his face. He took note of the growing stubble then peered at his watch.

*A full hour?*

He rubbed his face again, trying to wake up. An hour of sleep had done little to compensate him for the last three days without any. He leaned back and looked around at the gear piled up to the roof of the vehicle, which had been their home for two days. The armoured personnel carrier was a metal box on tracks meant to transport, not house them. The engine and driver occupied the front; the crew commander and gunner's hatch was behind them. Two benches ran the length of the passenger compartment in the rear with enough room to seat half a dozen troops. They could exit the vehicle down the back ramp or through a large hatch on top.

All the hatches were wide open, but two days of oppressive heat and six men who hadn't showered in more than a week meant that the interior smelled like a mixture of oil, lubricants, and sweat.

"I thought I said to give me fifteen minutes," Jac said.

"Oops." Maarten picked up the book. "*Lord Jim*. Where'd you get this?"

"Found it. I think one of the Canadians left it behind."

Maarten fingered through the first few pages and stopped, clearing his throat.

"He was an inch, perhaps two, under six feet, powerfully built, and he advanced straight at you with a slight stoop of the shoulders, head forward, and a fixed from-under stare which made you think of a charging bull." Maarten closed the book and tossed it to Jac. "Well, what do you know? It's about you. Except the part about being an inch or two under six feet. Four or five is more like it."

"Yeah? I'd like to see you brag about that the next time we have to dig a trench deep enough to hide your head."

"Oh, I don't mind, except when I have to find a box for you to stand on."

Jac raised a middle finger then flipped through the book. He stopped and looked around the cramped space.

"Where's the letter?"

Maarten moved his foot, which was pinning a light blue sheet of paper to the floor. He picked it up.

"Dear Mother." He laughed. "Are you serious?"

Jac tore the sheet from Maarten's hands and folded it inside the book.

"What am I supposed to say?"

"Hi, Mom. How are you doing after...." He hesitated, counting on his fingers like a first-grader. "Seven months? By the way, you were right, Mom. This place is screwed up and I should have gone to university like you wanted."

"Forget I asked." Jac poked the book into his thigh pocket. "What's going on?"

"We just bombed Srebrenica."

"Seriously?"

"Yeah. Two planes. Two bombs."

"And?"

"And what? They went back to Italy in time for dinner."

"After two bombs?"

"Budget cutbacks."

"What did Sergeant Janssen say?"

"Nothing. He's gone into Jaglici to speak to the Bosnian commander."

"Nezir?"

"Yeah," Maarten said, pointing. "That's Nezir's family over there."

Jac leaned forward. A woman sat near the carrier's rear ramp with three children around her. She held an infant in her arms.

"Does Janssen think he'll let us go?"

"Might," Maarten said. "A lot of men passing by are saying something about walking to Tuzla."

"Long walk," Jac replied. He hauled a bottle of warm water from a half empty case sitting on top of their gear, swallowed a mouthful then pulled a towel from around his neck and soaked it. He ran the wet towel over his face, hung it around his neck, and then poured the rest of the water through his hair and down his chest and back. He secured his flak vest.

"Some of the men said Zepa has fallen," Maarten said, glancing outside. "Believe that?"

"I don't know what to believe anymore."

Jac looked outside. Refugees had been gathering since the morning; mostly women and children left behind by their husbands and fathers. A hundred metres up the road, the remains of their observation post smouldered. The Serbs had shelled it two days earlier, only minutes after the Dutch evacuated the structure.

After the observation post had been destroyed, the peace-keepers had boarded the carrier, intending to return to Potocari. Nezir heard of the peacekeepers' impending departure and ordered his soldiers to stop them. He believed that if the Dutch left, there would be nothing to keep the Serbs from taking the northern towns. The Bosnian soldiers had set up a machine gun in a nearby house; one other soldier walked around carrying an anti-tank missile. Nezir ensured the Dutch he didn't want to harm them. He only wanted to keep them from leaving the area.

A rumble overhead drew Jac's attention outside. He slipped his helmet on and picked up his Uzi submachine gun. He slung it over his shoulder and let the weapon hang against his chest. Maarten followed. They stepped onto the ramp and stared into the sky. Two jets circled like hawks high above.

"Think they're the same planes that hit Srebrenica?" said a voice from above.

Jac glanced back. Erik Klein, their gunner, sat cross-legged on the top of the carrier.

"No idea," Jac replied. "Definitely good guys."

"Probably American," Maarten said. "They're flying high and fast."

"Yeah."

The Americans had lost a plane to Serb anti-aircraft fire the month before and since then they had been flying higher and faster in order to avoid the missiles.

"Bad guys!" Erik shouted.

Jac and Maarten wheeled around and looked up. Erik pointed; two missiles were punching through the air towards the high-flying jets. They missed by a wide margin and the planes disappeared into the west.

"Well," Maarten said. "We won't see them again."

*Good guys my ass*, Jac thought.

"We have to be neutral," the officer had said. "No good guys, no bad guys." That was the theory. In practice, each side played both roles. One day the Serbs would agree to a ceasefire then shell the town, killing civilians who had left their homes believing they were safe. Another day, Bosnian soldiers would crawl across the front lines so they could shoot at the Dutch observation posts. The Bosnian soldiers hoped they would be mistaken for Serbs who were firing on the UN and invite reprisals against the Serbs. Both armies hated the presence of the UN and manipulated the peacekeepers for their own ends.

Jac crossed his arms and rested them on his Uzi and then surveyed the growing crowd of civilians. They were the real losers, he thought.

For three years, the Serb army had Srebrenica under siege. The civilians had used every opportunity to get out of the enclave, but the Bosnian army had prevented as many as possible from leaving. They even shot civilians caught trying to walk through the woods. From the Bosnian army's perspective, the town would be lost if the civilians were allowed to leave and so they kept them there in squalor and with less food to eat than those who endured the

Siberian gulag. Now the army had abandoned the civilians, leaving them at the mercy of the enemy.

"Hey, Jac."

He turned to see Karel Meyer leaning against the carrier. Karel pushed his helmet back and lit a cigarette. The smoked swirled around his sunglasses.

"What do you call a Bosnian, a Serb, and a Croat woman standing together?"

"Give it up, Karel."

"A full set of teeth." Karel blew smoke through his nose.

Maarten looked back.

"Are you still telling that stupid joke?"

Karel held up a middle finger and tapped himself on the forehead. Maarten laughed.

"Only if you buy me dinner."

"Go to hell, *flikker*," Karel said.

"Oh, isn't that sweet, guys. He still thinks insults mean something to someone over the age of twelve."

"Will you two give it up," Erik said.

"*Kankerjood.*"

Jac turned and walked up to Karel.

"I'm not gay or Jewish, so what's your problem with me?"

"You like them," Karel replied and then laughed.

"Go stand somewhere else."

"Learn to take a joke, Jac." Karel sauntered away.

"Might be time for the sergeant to have a talk with him," Maarten said.

Jac nodded. The last thing Karel had wanted was a tour in Bosnia. He took his frustrations out on everyone, including the locals, but it had gotten worse in the past few days. One of their own had been killed three days earlier. Karel had known him and took the death hard. Now all he cared about was getting home.

"Jac."

He looked up at Erik.

"Some of the men are saying that the Serbs are killing civilians in Srebrenica."

"Sergeant Janssen didn't say anything about it the last time he spoke to Potocari. Don't worry about it, Erik. They'll be fine."

Jac stepped off the ramp. Their medic, Arie Smit, was examining a pregnant woman. Two other women held a blanket over them as a sun shield. A man stood nearby holding two cows by a tether.

"We're not going to be able to transport them all," Maarten whispered from behind.

Jac glanced back and up. Maarten was tall and lanky like most of the guys in their unit. Jac, on the other hand, had inherited his Dutch mother's blue eyes and black hair but none of her height. His French father had burdened him with shoulders so broad he had to get his uniforms custom made.

The pregnant woman squealed and Jac turned around. More women were crowded around Arie.

"You're right," Jac said. "We're not going to be able to transport them all. If they can walk, they'll have to walk."

"If they let us go."

"They'll let us go." He motioned towards a group of soldiers walking towards Susnjari. "They're all going that way sooner or later."

Arie stood up and called for help. Jac and Maarten carried the pregnant woman to the carrier; they stacked up their gear to make room for her on one of the benches. A shell whistled overhead and slammed into the forested hill beyond the observation post. The refugees shifted closer to the Dutch.

"Jac. Maarten. Karel."

Jac poked his head up through the passenger hatch. Sergeant Janssen was marching towards them. He stopped next to the carrier and took a bottle of water from Erik, drinking half before pouring the rest through the bristle on his head. He threw the bottle away and ran his fingers along his moustache.

"We're going," Janssen said.

"With the refugees?" Maarten asked.

"Yes. I want you to walk out front. I need Jac and Karel to stay back here and keep them calm. Nezir is telling the women they can follow us to Potocari. Lead them to the upper road. The Serbs won't be able to see you up there. I'll take the carrier around on the lower road and meet up with you on the other side. It'll be dark soon, so the rest of the way shouldn't be a problem. Just keep them calm. And for God's sake, keep them behind the carrier. Got that?"

"Got it, Sergeant," they replied in unison.

"Good. Now let's get the hell out of here before they change their minds."

The peacekeepers secured the vehicle, closing the hatches and tossing the remainder of their equipment inside. Arie rearranged the gear around the pregnant woman and closed the ramp. Janssen jumped on top and gestured to the crowd to stand up. Everyone stood and surged ahead. Jac held out his arms and shifted from side to side like a cowboy trying to corral a loose horse.

Janssen lowered himself into the driver's hatch until only his helmet and sunglasses were visible. Erik dropped into the gunner's hatch, everything above his waist still visible from the outside. The vehicle roared to life, spooking the refugees. They stepped back, falling over one other. The carrier lurched ahead and then slipped sideways, heading for a ditch. The saturated embankment gave way and the carrier slid farther. The tracks rotated, spitting dirt and mud as they dug twin ruts into the loose soil. Jac stepped back, avoiding the flying lumps of earth.

"He's going to have to take the pads off the treads," Karel said. "We'll be here all night."

Men shouted.

Jac looked back. A group of Bosnian soldiers emerged from the woods, weapons pointed at the peacekeepers. The soldier carrying the anti-tank weapon on his shoulder ran to the front of the carrier, shaking his head and waving his free arm. The carrier powered down. One of the soldiers walked up to the peacekeepers.

"No," he said. "You stay. You can't leave or Chetniks come."

Another soldier raised his rifle to Karel's chest.

"Stay," the soldier said. "You go, Chetniks come."

The sergeant pulled himself halfway out of the driver's hatch and twisted around.

"What's going on?"

"They're not letting us go," Karel said.

A third soldier pointed his rifle at Erik who raised his hands away from the machine gun mounted on the hatch.

"Goddamnit." The sergeant hauled himself up on top of the carrier then dropped to the ground and faced the first soldier. "Will you make up your goddamned minds? Do we go or don't we?"

Jac heard a commotion among the refugees and turned. Nezir had pushed his stocky frame through the crowd and was shouting in Bosnian at the first soldier. The soldier hollered back, motioning to the carrier and the refugees.

Nezir fell silent. He wiped the sweat from his brow and dropped his hand to his hip. His eyes shifted between Jac, Maarten, and the sergeant. Jac's gaze drifted down. Nezir's fingers had unbuttoned the clasp of his holster and his hand was grasping the butt of his pistol.

Jac looked up. Nezir's eyes had moved back to the first Bosnian soldier and, without a word, Nezir raised the pistol and shot the soldier in the head.

Jac sucked in a sharp breath and stumbled backwards, bumping into Maarten.

"Jesus!"

The second soldier swung his rifle around. Nezir shifted his aim and shot him in the face.

Blood splattered Janssen.

Nezir shouted at his men; muzzles lowered and the soldiers trudged away. Nezir turned to Janssen.

"Now Sergeant, you can go to Potocari," he said. "My soldiers will not stop you. So, please, take my family and go."

Nezir jammed his pistol back in the holster, patted the sergeant once on the shoulder, and walked over to his family. He kissed his wife and hugged his children then vanished into the crowd.

"My God," Jac said, staring at the two bodies.

Janssen wiped the blood from his cheek and turned away from the dead soldiers.

"Let's get the hell out of here."

Jac tore his eyes away from the bodies and followed Janssen towards the carrier.

"Keep them back, Jac," Janssen said, climbing to the top of the vehicle. "I need some space to get out of here."

"Yeah. Okay."

Jac stepped away and motioned to the wary crowd to stay back. The carrier came to life and the sergeant battled to pull the vehicle out of the ditch. The metal box pivoted to the left and then to the right, launching earth and rock like missiles. The crowd ducked. Some ran away.

Jac glimpsed movement in the corner of his eye; someone was running towards the carrier. He swung around. A cow trotted in front of the carrier just as the vehicle dug in and surged ahead. Erik shouted to the sergeant, but the animal was out of Janssen's line of sight. The carrier struck the cow. The animal cried out, but the sound was lost to a chorus of cracking bones and popping organs. The vehicle came to a halt and Janssen stood up in his hatch. He stared, wide-eyed, at Erik.

Erik raised his hands and pointed as he spoke to Janssen over the headset. The sergeant nodded and relaxed. Jac crossed in front of the carrier to inspect the damage. A layer of red covered the muddy white metal skin. Pieces of shattered bone poked out of the treads. Rivulets of blood flowed into the ditch.

"Is it dead?"

"Oh yeah. It's dead, Sergeant." Jac glanced at the crowd, convinced the incident would make his job easier. "Go ahead. We'll meet you down below."

The carrier moved away, but the crowd remained. Karel and Maarten joined Jac. They waved their arms, encouraging the anxious refugees forward.

"Come," Jac shouted. "To Potocari. Come."

They led the crowd along a road sheltered from the Serbs while the carrier rumbled down the lower road. After a short distance, Jac spotted Janssen standing on top of the carrier, motioning to the refugees to come forward. They approached the vehicle and stopped behind it.

"Rest," the sergeant said.

A few refugees sat down. The rest stayed on their feet, staring at the peacekeepers.

They think we're going to take off on them, Jac thought. He took Maarten's arm and pulled him to the edge of the crowd.

"Sit down with me. Show them we're not going to leave without them."

The peacekeepers sat down in the middle of the road and, one by one, the refugees followed suit. They drank water and adjusted their belongings. One woman emerged from the forest, leading a white horse with two children on its back. Gunfire popped in the south. Mortars flew overhead and slammed into the hills above the crowd. People flinched and ducked.

"Jesus, Jac, I know they're not trying to hit us, but if just one shell falls short."

"I know." He looked back. Janssen was on his feet, motioning to Jac. "I think he has the same idea."

"Get them going," Janssen said. He dropped into his hatch.

Jac stood. The crowd stood with him

"To Potocari," he said. "Come. To Potocari."

Maarten walked to the front of the carrier as it started up. Jac and Karel waved everyone forward. The carrier crept ahead at a pace slower than the slowest refugee. They walked with Jac, crowding him but staying behind the carrier.

Ahead, a road to the northwest led to another Dutch observation post. The post, Tango, was manned and, the last Jac had heard, it was under fire. He imagined the crew huddled inside their bunker waiting for the attacks to end. Jac trotted up to the carrier and waved to Erik.

"Any word from Tango?" Jac asked.

Erik shrugged and picked up his binoculars, scanning the road ahead.

"Oh my God!"

"What is it?"

Erik pointed towards the intersection while he spoke into his mic, reporting to Janssen. Jac peered ahead.

"I don't see anything."

"Refugees. Go, go."

Jac joined Maarten and they jogged ahead of the vehicle. Then they slowed down; thousands of people were cramming the road from Tango. People who had taken refuge there but were now rushing towards them.

"They must have heard the carrier," Maarten said.

Jac looked at the vehicle and then the crowd. The mob would swamp the main road before the vehicle could pass the intersection.

"What do we do?" Maarten asked.

Jac motioned to the carrier to speed up, but wave after wave of refugees poured onto the road ahead of the carrier. The vehicle stopped and they swarmed it like ants, crawling up the sides and fighting for space on top. The peacekeepers worked to pull down people who were capable of walking, but for every person they removed two more scrambled on top of the vehicle.

"This is useless," Maarten shouted to the sergeant.

The refugees sat two and three deep on the carrier when the sergeant gave up. He waved to Jac who propped himself up on a track next to the sergeant's hatch.

"Sergeant?"

He rubbed the sweat from his forehead. Speckles of blood remained. "Don't waste your time. We're going. Just keep them away from me, okay?"

"Yeah. No problem, Sergeant."

Jac dropped to the road and surveyed the scene. People trying to crawl on top of the carrier were pushed back or pulled down by others trying to scramble up the side of the vehicle. Others gave up and walked ahead. A woman shrieked.

He turned around just as two young men dumped an old woman out of a wheelbarrow. They shoved her husband to the ground and picked up stereo equipment and piled it in the wheelbarrow. Wires hung over the edge.

"Jesus," Jac said. He stepped in front of the men and dropped a heavy hand on the wheelbarrow. "What are you're doing?"

The young men stared at Jac. One shrugged.

"How the hell are we supposed to help you if you don't help yourselves?"

They tried to move forward, but Jac kept his grip on the wheelbarrow. And then he seized a speaker and threw it into the ditch. When he grabbed the other speaker, one of the men tried to take it away from him.

"Fuck you, Blue Helmet."

A pair of hands appeared and tore the speaker from both of them. Karel tossed the speaker into the ditch then laid his hand on his Uzi.

"Get lost."

The men backed away, crouched to pick up the rest of their equipment and melted into the crowd.

"Why do you bother, Jac?" Karel asked.

Jac ignored him and picked up the wheelbarrow, rolling it back to its owner. As he placed the woman inside, she kissed his hand and arm. The man tried to kiss him as well, but Jac stepped back and pointed.

"To Potocari."

"*Danke, danke.*" He wheeled his wife away.

"Christ, Jac," Karel said from behind. "If they want to kill each other, let them. It's not our problem."

Jac turned his back on Karel and walked away. The carrier roared to life and he shooed people away from the tracks.

They began their slow march to Potocari.

# WEDNESDAY: MICHAEL SAKIC

MIKE LEANED AGAINST a truck, listening to a Pakistani captain argue with a Serb soldier through a translator. Beyond them, Serb soldiers loitered around their checkpoint. The barrier was down and a row of anti-tank mines were strung across the road. A large guard shack sat on the edge of the forest. Beside it, a group of soldiers encircled a fire, drinking and singing.

*They look like boy scouts.* Mike glanced at his watch. *Almost midnight.*

After he had heard enough, he turned and walked the length of the convoy. He passed a Dutch armoured vehicle, a Pakistani tanker, a Norwegian ambulance, and three UN transports full of humanitarian aid. His truck, which hadn't moved in three hours, was second from last. With the obvious breakdown in negotiations, the convoy would likely spend the night on the mountainside. He climbed into the driver's seat.

"I was getting ready to send out a search-and-rescue mission," Brendan said. "What were you doing for the last two hours?"

"Your work, of course." Mike fished out two Aspirin from a bottle in the glove compartment and chased them down with a Coke. "I just found my newest, bestest friend."

"Who?"

Mike glanced at Robert. The cameraman had folded the back

seat down and made a bed out of the bags and equipment. He lay on his stomach with his head between the front seats and his hands propped under his chin like a first-grader waiting for story time.

"The Pakistani captain. I know the translator, a guy named Jure, and between the two of them, I got a few juicy details."

"Yeah?" Brendan raised an eyebrow. "Either one up for an interview?"

"Not if they want to keep their jobs."

"Then that information is pretty well useless to me."

"Well, it may be second and maybe even third-hand, but it's a starting point for a few questions in Tuzla, don't you think?"

Brendan's mouth opened and then closed shut.

"Thought so."

"So, what did your newest, bestest friend tell you?"

Mike chuckled and flipped back a few pages of his notepad.

"Well, according to them, all this started when the Serbs came up from Skelani on Thursday and attacked the Dutch OPs down there."

"OPs?" Robert asked.

Mike looked back at the cameraman.

"He's still a virgin when it comes to military terminology," Brendan said. "Among other things."

Robert slapped Brendan's shoulder. "Hey!"

"Did you know last night was the first time he saw *The A-Team*?"

"It was in Greek," Robert said.

"It could have been in English and it would have still been Greek to you." Brendan looked at Mike. "His parents were pacifist hippies. They didn't own a television."

Mike eyed Robert. "And you grew up to be a television cameraman?"

"Ironic, isn't it?" he replied. He had arrived in the country two days before, replacing Brendan's regular cameraman whose wife had gone into early labour. When he first saw him, Mike thought Robert was no more than eighteen, but his passport proved he was twenty-two.

"Well, an OP is an observation post," Mike said. "The Dutch have their main base in Potocari. There's a smaller camp in Srebrenica called Bravo. The OPs are basically bunkers manned by about a half dozen guys. There are a bunch of them stationed on the edge of the enclave to keep an eye on things."

"Oh. Okay."

"Anyway, after the Serbs attacked the OPs, the Dutch called for air strikes several times, but nothing happened. The guys on top had a variety of excuses: no evidence of the peacekeepers being directly targeted and so on and so forth. Probably the most important thing to happen over the weekend was that a group of Muslims stopped a Dutch crew who were retreating from one of the southern OPs. They demanded the Dutch go back to stop the Serbs, but the Dutch refused. So, one of the Muslims threw a grenade and killed one of the peacekeepers."

"I heard something about that," Robert said.

"Yeah." Mike took a swig of his Coke. "That made the news, but what's important is when the other crews were forced to leave their OPs, the Serbs gave them a choice between going back to Potocari or staying with them. Of course, those crews knew what happened when the first OP crew tried to go through the Muslim lines, so they opted to stay with the Serbs."

"Instant hostages," Brendan said through a whistle.

"Precisely," Mike replied, pointing his pen at Brendan. "So the Serbs kept advancing and the Muslims kept withdrawing until they got close to the town where the defenders were dug in pretty good." He flipped forward a page. "Okay. Again, the Dutch reported being attacked by the Serbs and demanded air strikes. So finally, last night, the UN agreed to send in the planes to bomb the crap out of the Serb tanks, but by the time they get their act together, it was too dark, so they decided to wait until this morning."

"The planes can't attack in the dark?" Robert asked.

"Planes can attack after dark," Mike said. "I think they were a little wary about striking near Srebrenica because the town is in a long valley surrounded by steep hills. They probably didn't want to risk flying into a hill.

"It's as good an excuse as any of the others," Brendan said.

"Oh, you haven't heard the best of it." Mike pushed his glasses up. "The Dutch in Srebrenica told the Muslims there were going to be massive air strikes in the morning, so the Muslims had little choice but to abandon their trenches. When the sun came up this morning, they were all waiting for the planes, but nothing showed up."

"And the Serbs happily took those unoccupied trenches, right?" Brendan asked.

"Who's telling the story here?"

"Sorry. It's just that this crap is becoming predictable."

"Yeah." Mike flipped to the next page. "So, where was I? Okay, no air strike and Potocari checked with Tuzla this morning to find out what happened to the planes. Now, listen to this. They were told the request was filed on the wrong bloody form."

"What?"

"Oh, that's still not all. Potocari resubmitted the form and it gets rejected because the targeting information wasn't right. Then the fax in Tuzla broke down."

"Holy shit," Brendan said. "Next thing you know, they'll be saying the dog ate the request. You can see what's happening here, right?"

"What?" Robert asked.

"The UN is dragging its feet," Brendan replied. "Srebrenica is in the way of a peace deal. The Bosnian Serbs don't want a Muslim community smack dab in the middle of their territory and they're not going to make peace until it's gone."

"The UN wants peace," Mike said. "The Serbs want Srebrenica. The Muslims get screwed."

"Okay," Robert said. "So, what happened with the planes?"

"Well, we know two Dutch planes made a run this afternoon. They dropped two bombs and, as we expected, the Serbs threatened the Dutch hostages. That was it for air strikes."

"So, what's going on now?" Brendan asked.

"Nothing they could tell me. The latest they've heard is that most of the Dutch are back on the base in Potocari and they estimate some twenty-five thousand civilians are either on the base or in the factories surrounding it."

"Twenty-five thousand?" Robert's eyebrows were almost at his hairline.

Mike flipped a page over and tapped his pen against the pad. "That's what he said."

Robert looked at Brendan. "Didn't you tell me there were almost fifty thousand people there?"

"Yeah. A conservative estimate really."

Robert turned to Mike. "So, where're the other twenty-five thousand?"

The two Americans stared at Mike.

There was a sharp tap on Mike's window. All three men jerked their heads around. A Serb soldier was standing on the other side of the glass, motioning to them to leave the vehicle. Mike opened his door and stepped out. The tail gate dropped.

"What's going on?" Robert asked.

"They're searching for weapons," Brendan replied, stepping outside.

Robert slid over the tailgate. The Serbs soldiers were pulling equipment and bags out of the truck and dropping them on the ground. They checked every compartment they could open. One soldier let the air out of the spare tire. Another used a mirror to check underneath the truck.

A soldier walked up to Mike and held out his hand. "Passport. Press cards. Travel papers."

Mike collected the documents and passed them to the Serb. The soldier took his time examining the paperwork. His flashlight moved from each document to the corresponding face and settled on Mike's. The Serb shone the light back down at the passport and then up into Mike's face again.

"You are Michael Sakic?" he asked in English.

"Mike Sakic. Yes."

"Come with me," the soldier said.

"What's the matter?" Brendan asked.

"It's fine," Mike said. "This isn't the first time."

"First time for what?"

"It's fine." Mike walked away with the soldier.

Brendan and Robert followed. The soldier led them to a corporal and handed over the documents. The corporal examined them and the two soldiers began speaking in their own language.

"I'm not Croat," Mike said to them in the same language.

The soldiers stared at him.

"I'm not Croat. I'm Canadian."

"Sakic," the corporal said, holding up Mike's passport. "You're Croat."

Mike shook his head and pointed to his passport.

"No. I am Canadian. Look. I was born in Winnipeg. It's in Canada."

"You speak the language very well for a Canadian."

"My grandparents taught me. They were Croat. I'm Canadian."

"What's going on?" Brendan asked, elbowing Mike.

Mike explained the situation to him.

"Does he speak English?"

"I do," the corporal replied.

Brendan took the Serb corporal aside and they spoke in whispers.

"What are they talking about?" Robert asked.

"No idea," Mike replied then sighed. "But I can guess."

The corporal laughed and patted Brendan on the shoulder. Brendan glanced at Mike and then passed something to the Serb. The soldier gave the documents to Brendan and he walked back to the truck. The soldiers returned to the checkpoint, leaving the luggage and equipment on the ground.

"So," Mike said, leaning on the driver's door and checking his documents. "How much of my fee did that cost me?"

Brendan poked his wallet away and smiled.

# TUESDAY: JAC LARUE

EXHAUSTION.

Jac rubbed his face hard with the towel and drew in a long breath. Nothing could give him his second wind.

Or was it his fifth wind? He had lost count.

The carrier trudged along beside him and the moon brightened as it rose. It lit the road so well, the carrier could move without headlights. Jac never imagined he would, as a soldier, be so grateful for a full moon. Headlights and flashlights usually attracted the wrong kind of attention.

Ahead, a boy latched onto the grate holding a fuel can. He slipped sideways, a foot bouncing against the rotating track. Jac sidestepped a woman and dove towards the boy, pulling him off the side of the carrier.

"No," Jac said. He slapped the side of the carrier. "Dangerous. You have to walk."

The boy ran, disappearing into the moonlit crowd. When Jac turned around, two young men were trying to untie the fuel can. Their eyes met and the men raised their palms and backed away.

"They're empty," he yelled after them.

A mortar whooshed overhead and struck the woods behind them.

*That was too damned close.*

Jac stopped. Screams erupted in the distance. A man broke through the crowd carrying a little girl, her face full of blood. Jac drew her hair back. A shard of metal protruded from the flesh above her ear.

"Ah, God." Jac looked at the carrier. People sat two and three deep on top. Even if there was room, she'd get pushed off. He turned back to the man. "I don't think the shrapnel is in too far. Can you carry her? To Potocari? See doctor in Potocari?"

A woman spoke to the man in Bosnian and he nodded.

"Tell him to stay close," Jac said to the woman. "And tell him not to pull it out."

"Yes, yes." The woman translated Jac's message and then she placed a rag against the little girl's head.

The boy returned and tried to scale the carrier again. Jac pulled him off just as the vehicle slowed and stopped. Sergeant Janssen climbed out of his hatch and waved to the crowd.

"To Potocari. To Potocari."

He wiped his brow, took a long swig on a bottle of water, and dropped back into the hatch. The vehicle lurched forward. Maarten waited until the vehicle moved ahead and then walked with Jac.

"Know where we are?"

Jac gazed forwards; he recognized the stretch of road. The shoulder dropped off steeply on the left and on the right a rock face skirted the edge of the road. The narrow passage forced the refugees to squeeze into the tight space. Some ran ahead of Jac and the carrier, others waited to fall in behind.

"Yeah," Jac replied. "We're almost home."

Maarten patted Jac on the back and walked ahead, moving in front of the carrier.

Jac checked his watch. Just one more hour, he thought. The refugees would be safe and he could finally lapse into a coma and dream of the bedroom he hadn't seen in seven months. The double bed with clean sheets and a thick quilt his mother had made for him.

Warm. Secure. Safe.

Another mortar struck above the rock face. Jac ducked then straightened up and glanced around. The carrier stopped and the sergeant climbed out of his hatch. Erik motioned to Jac.

"It's a boy," he shouted over the engine.

"What?

The moon lit up Erik's smile.

"The pregnant woman. She just had a boy."

Jac had just started to return the smile when the sky above Erik turned red. A tracer round split the air directly above the gunner and ricocheted against the rock wall. Another followed; five rounds struck the cliff for every tracer that lit up the sky. Bodies rolled from the carrier like logs falling off the side of a lumber truck. Flailing arms struck Jac in the face and he fell backwards. People fell on top of him. Some scrambled up and ran. Others remained still.

"Get inside!" Erik yelled. He disappeared inside his hatch.

Jac climbed to his feet and ducked around the back of the carrier. He slipped on something wet and fell hard, his helmet catching on a metal corner. The hatch swung open. A pair of arms slid in under Jac's and scooped him up. Maarten pushed him through the opening. Karel brought up the rear, slamming the hatch closed.

Metallic pings peppered the side of the vehicle.

A baby cried.

Jac crawled over the mass of arms and legs. Sweat blurred his vision. His arm slipped between two bodies. His head hit a torso. He struggled to pull an arm up, using someone's knee as leverage. He finally yanked it free and grabbed a strap hanging from the roof, pulling himself forward. He reached the front of the passenger compartment and rubbed his vision clear with his towel. A flashlight stabbed through the darkness and Jac caught a glimpse of the sergeant safely in his seat.

"They're shooting at us," Jac shouted to anyone who would listen.

"We have to move," someone else shouted from behind. "If they put mortars on us, they'll kill them all."

"Get out of here," another voice added to the noise.

Jac hauled his helmet off and wiped more sweat from his face. Erik listened to the sergeant over his headset. Then the gunner gave a thumbs up and climbed back into his hatch where he had some protection. Jac tugged on Erik's pants.

"What are you doing?"

"They're shooting at us," Erik shouted from above. "We have to move or the Serbs will cut the crowd to pieces."

Jac heard the vehicle's horn and light filtered in from Erik's hatch as the carrier's headlights flooded the road. The vehicle lurched forward and Jac lost his balance, falling against the engine wall. He held on as they picked up speed.

The metallic pings continued.

A woman screamed.

Men shouted.

Next to Jac, the engine was revving higher than it had all day. Then the right side of the vehicle suddenly rose and fell, then the left side. And the right.

*Are we off the road?*

Erik dropped down from his hatch, screaming into his headset. Jac could hear nothing over the engine, but he was sure Erik's lips were mouthing the word *stop*, over and over. Jac pulled himself over mounds of gear until he could see the sergeant. The headset hung around Janssen's neck; his head was jammed against the hull so he could watch the road through the periscope. Erik grabbed Jac and yanked him back.

"We're running them over," he shrieked next to Jac's ear. "For God's sake, tell him to stop!"

Jac turned, pushed aside their kit and reached towards Janssen. Three times he tried to poke the sergeant in the back, but he fell each time the vehicle shifted to the left or the right. Finally, he managed to grab the back of the sergeant's seat and steady himself. He pulled on Janssen's uniform.

No reaction.

The carrier swung right and Jac fell back. They jolted to a stop and the engine switched off. Jac looked up.

Janssen was gone.

Erik's legs slipped up through the gunner's hatch. Jac crawled up behind him and then dropped to the ground. Refugees were sprinting in all directions. Some were hiding behind the vehicle, others moved forward. The carrier had come to rest around a bend in the road.

*We're safe here.*

He turned around; Erik was arguing with the sergeant.

"We have to go back," Erik said. "We have to help them."

"They'll only shoot at us again. I've got a woman bleeding to death in there and I have to get her to a doctor. Now get back up in your hatch."

The sergeant walked away. Erik slammed his hand against the side of the vehicle.

"What's going on?" Jac asked.

"Goddamnit, Jac. We ran them over." He drew an arm across his face. "They were up against the rock wall and there wasn't enough room. Don't you see? They pushed people in front of us to make room. Women and children. They just pushed them in front of us. Bloody bastards."

Erik climbed the vehicle and dropped into his hatch, wiping his eyes. Jac looked down the road, but he couldn't see anything except desperate faces running by. The sergeant waved his arms at the refugees.

They don't need any urging, Jac wanted to say.

Arie was at work helping the refugees. Jac helped the wounded climb back on top of the carrier. He recognized some of the injured civilians.

"Are they all shrapnel wounds?" Jac asked, passing a little girl up to the medic.

"As far as I can tell."

"No crush injuries?"

"Crush injuries? No. Why would there be?" he asked then drew in a sharp breath. "Jesus. We didn't, did we?" A baby shrieked. "Can you take care of this?"

"Yeah, sure," Jac said. "Go on."

Arie disappeared inside the carrier.

"Keep them moving," the sergeant said.

Jac followed Janssen around the carrier.

"Shouldn't we go check, Sergeant?"

"Jac, even if I wanted to risk them firing on us again, I can't drive back through all those people."

The sergeant turned around and climbed onto the carrier. He dropped into his hatch.

"I can go with Maarten. We can bring the injured up here."

"We can't stay. These people need medical attention now." Janssen pointed to the side of the carrier. "Get him off."

Jac turned; a boy was trying to scale the side of the vehicle. By the time he pulled the boy down, Janssen had disappeared inside the carrier.

Jac looked back at the road. Refugees scurried by. A woman tripped on an abandoned bag. A man helped her up. A little girl walked alone, crying. Jac stepped forward; a woman scooped the child up. She looked at Jac.

"Safe here?"

"I think so."

She started to walk away.

"Wait," Jac said. He pointed down the road. "Are there people hurt down there? On the road. Anyone hurt?"

The woman followed his finger and then looked back, confused. "I not see anyone. Very crazy. Lots of people running."

"Thanks."

The woman left. Jac stared down the road and then looked back at the carrier. Karel pushed a man away from the rear hatch and pulled a girl down. Arie sealed the rear hatch as Jac turned away and walked deeper into the crowd. People bumped into him, knocking him from side to side. Tracer fire popped. He looked back. The crowd hid the carrier from sight. He kept walking, watching the crowd for injured refugees.

Then the crowd opened up before him, running around something on the road. Something metallic.

He leaned down and touched the cold metal handle of a wheelbarrow. The steel reflected the moonlight and had been twisted into an unnatural position. The short axle held onto the punctured tire.

Jac followed the trail of parts until he found the crushed metal bin. Next to it, the shattered remains of a stereo. Feet kicked wires and circuit boards in every direction. A speaker cone rolled from one foot and was crushed by another.

He looked up the road. *This can't be all there is.*

Mortar struck the side of the hill. Jac covered his eyes and ducked. Women screamed. Some stopped and covered their children.

The carrier started up.

Jac stood still. Another mortar struck the ditch.

He backed up.

The engine revved. Tracks rattled.

"Damn it."

He turned and walked with the crowd until he reached the carrier. For the next hour, he watched the dark road behind him, waiting for someone to bring the injured forward, but no one appeared.

The vehicle turned left onto the main road where Dutch carriers blocked their path. The sergeant got out to speak to the officer in charge. The refugees flowed around the blockade like a forked river.

Jac walked to the front of the carrier. Erik was in his hatch, leaning on the machine gun. He stared straight ahead. Jac left him alone. He walked in front with Maarten as their carrier crossed the blockade and crawled through the sea of refugees.

"Unbelievable."

"There must be thousands," Maarten said.

They woke people sleeping on the pavement and helped them move aside as the carrier crept by. They entered the camp at midnight and pulled up next to the hospital. A group of medics helped offload the wounded and then the carrier rumbled towards the vehicle bay. Erik remained on top, his eyes drilling a hole through a distant wall.

After Jac delivered the last wounded civilian to the clinic, he left Maarten with Arie and went looking for Erik. He walked through the main building to the vehicle bay expecting to find the carrier. Instead, he found thousands of refugees; men, women, and children occupied every scrap of open space on the floor of the vehicle park. Heads turned in his direction. Mouths formed questions in Bosnian.

"Jac."

He turned. Albert, a mechanic, waved to him. Jac backed out of the building.

"I'm looking for Janssen," the mechanic said, wiping his hands with a rag.

"Last I saw, he was talking to the major. Why?"

"You don't know?"

"Know what?"

"They're going to hose down your vehicle now." Albert motioned over his shoulder with a thumb. "Go take a look for yourself. I'm going to find Janssen."

The mechanic walked away.

*Erik?*

Jac sprinted towards the maintenance bay. He heard water splashing against the hull before he turned the corner. Two maintenance corporals held a hose, soaking the left side of the vehicle. Fresh dents and scars pitted the carrier's metal skin. Erik stood staring at the right side. Jac released the air in his lungs and walked up to him.

"What's going on?"

Streaks of clean skin trailed through the dirt on the gunner's face to his chin. He said nothing, his lips tight. Jac followed his gaze. Blood was mixed with mud on the side of the carrier. Tissue and bone stuck to the treads.

"No, no," Jac said, turning to Erik. "That's from the cow we ran over."

Erik shook his head and held up a piece of white cloth soaked with blood. Jac stared at the rag in Erik's hand and then turned to inspect the track. There was more bone and blood on the vehicle then he remembered.

Seven kilometres on the road would have removed most of the cow, Jac thought.

He crouched and reached into the track well; his hand came out holding another piece of white material. The remains of a cuff.

*Goddamnit. I should have gone back.*

# WEDNESDAY: ATIF STAVIC

ATIF MOVED A step closer to the water spigot, pushing the green container forward with his feet. The midday sun assaulted him from above and shade was still a dozen people away. He licked his cracked lips, wishing he'd left a little water in the container.

"I don't know," a voice said in English.

Atif turned. A peacekeeper walked along the line.

"Don't know what?" Atif asked him.

The peacekeeper slowed. "I don't know when they're going to send trucks or buses to get you all out of here."

"But they're going to send them, are they?"

"Like I said, I don't know." The peacekeeper kept walking.

"They know nothing," the old woman behind Atif said. He turned around to face her. "They won't be able to do anything."

"We should walk to Serbia," a younger woman said. "We could get there before sunset."

"That would mean you'd have to cross the lines," Atif said.

"Better that than waiting for the Dutch to do something."

"Atif. Atif."

*Ina?*

He looked around until he saw Ina weaving in and out of the line. He waved to her. She stopped, taking a moment to catch her breath.

"I didn't think you were so close. Your mother wants you to go back. I'll fill this up."

"It's okay. I can take care of this."

"No, Atif. You need to go back to her. Now."

Before he could protest, Ina pointed towards the road near the Dutch compound. Atif surveyed the area. There were three soldiers pacing along the edge of the crowd. They weren't wearing blue helmets.

*Chetniks!*

Two of them were bareheaded and dressed in green camouflage uniforms. The third sported a mismatched assortment of army green and had a red bandanna wrapped around his head.

*He thinks he's Rambo.*

"But they can't come in here," he told Ina. "The Dutch said this was part of their compound now."

"We don't know what they can and can't do, Atif. Best if you stayed with your mother."

Atif frowned and gave up his spot in the line to her.

"Go directly back, Atif."

He walked away, pausing to watch the soldiers. When he glanced back at Ina, she had her arm raised, pointing towards the bus. He took a shortcut through bushes and walked through the crowd watching every step, avoiding arms and legs hiding under blankets and sections of open ground used as a latrine.

Checking to make sure Ina was out of sight, he made a left turn and crossed the street near the soldiers. Some of the peacekeepers were stringing white and red tape between the soldiers and the civilians; others stood in a line behind the tape. Some of the Serbs were sitting on the grass and singing songs. Others were tossing treats to the children. A piece of wrapped candy dropped at Atif's feet. A little girl bounced over a bag and grabbed it.

"Don't eat that," he told her. "They could have poisoned it."

The girl ignored him, tearing off the wrapper and devouring the sweet. Two military trucks lumbered down the road and parked near the tape. Soldiers jumped from the back. A car pulled up behind them and a television crew stepped out.

*The Dutch will keep them out.* Atif watched the peacekeepers form a loose human chain. *They promised.*

Atif turned his back on the Serbs and made his way to the wrecked bus. His mother stood next to the three girls, scanning the crowd. The moment their eyes met, she stepped forward, waving to him to hurry. She wrapped her arm around his shoulders and sat him under the bus next to Tihana.

"You don't have to worry, Mama. They're not coming in. The Dutch put some tape up."

"Do you honestly think a bit of tape is going to keep them out?"

"No. The Dutch will. This is part of their camp. They won't let them in."

"Listen to me, Atif," she replied, taking him by the shoulders. "The Dutch can't stop them. They have no food, water, or transportation and we both know the Chetniks won't let any trucks through. They can do whatever they want."

Atif looked away. "What do you think they'll do?"

"I don't know," she replied. "But I know the Dutch are not going to be able to stop them. The sooner you start believing that, the better. We'll just have to wait and see."

Atif leaned against the rusted axle, rubbing his hands together. He hated waiting. For three years, he had waited in lines for water and food or in dusty basements for the shelling to stop.

Waited for his father to return.

"You should sleep."

"I'm fine, Mama." Atif picked up one of the bottles next to his pack and drained the last few drops.

"You haven't slept in almost twenty-four hours."

"I'm fine. Really."

He wiped his forehead with his shirt. He couldn't sleep with the Serbs so close.

He needed to watch.

Ina returned with the container full of water. They borrowed the stove to boil the remaining potatoes. When they were done, Atif's mother returned the stove and pot to the old man, the last of their potatoes in the water.

Atif ate his potato and Lejla fed Tihana's toy soldier. His sister watched and, when the soldier had had enough, she ate. Then Ina and his mother turned away and spoke in whispers. Atif stared at them, chewing on his lip and wishing he could hear.

He remembered the first time his father had spoken to his mother in whispers. They had probably done it before, but he hadn't noticed. This time, though, he felt left out, sitting at the empty table in their new home in Srebrenica. His father had given their farm to a Serb neighbour in exchange for the Serb's house in the town. The neighbour helped smuggle their family into Srebrenica. Though Atif didn't think *smuggle* was the right word. They sat in the back of a VW and drove down a gravel road to a checkpoint. The soldier on duty accepted the Serb driver's identification and the stack of Deutsch Marks inside without saying a word.

When he saw their new home, Atif thought the deal favoured their neighbour. The house had a basement as promised, but the entire structure needed work. And, it was already occupied. Ina and her daughters had moved in months earlier, believing it abandoned. Atif's father had insisted they stay. He knew Ina's nursing skills would be invaluable.

"What are you talking about?" Atif had finally said to his father.

His parents stared at him.

"Your father is going to follow the soldiers. When they attack a village, he'll go in and find as much food as he can carry."

"Then I should go with him. We could carry more."

"It's not safe for someone so young, Atif," his father had said. "Besides, like I told you before, I need you to look after your mother and sister for me. I want to know they will be safe."

*How can I respond to that?*

He knew he couldn't face his father if something happened to his sister and his mother while he was gone, but what could he do to protect them? His father had returned in the morning carrying a sack of potatoes on his back. He didn't tell Atif where he found the food or if anyone had been killed. He rarely spoke about the raids.

Atif looked away from his mother and Ina to watch Tihana play with the toy soldier. She walked it along and then mimed an explosion. The machine gunner lay dead in the crushed grass.

"What happened, Tihana? Did the soldier get hurt?"

Tihana smiled and repeated the scene.

"C'mon. You can tell your big brother. Does he need help?"

A single gunshot popped.

Atif flinched and turned around, looking at the zinc factory. The crowd shifted and settled.

"What's going on?"

"I don't know, Atif," Ina replied. She avoided his eyes. "I think the Serbs are celebrating."

Atif stared at her.

*Why do they think they can lie to me?*

The gunshots had started earlier in the day, but then they had been in the hills lying towards Srebrenica. This one was closer, much closer.

And they're not celebrating, he thought, still gazing at Ina. Celebrating soldiers didn't fire single shots. They switched their rifles to full auto and emptied the magazine into the air in a matter of seconds.

*Enough of this.*

He leaned close so that only Ina and his mother could hear his words.

"They're shooting people, aren't they?"

Ina's eyes darted to the ground.

"Why won't you tell me?"

"She's not sure," his mother whispered into his ear. "She said some of the Chetniks are inside the tape now. She saw one of the soldiers take an old man behind the factory. Then the soldier came back alone, carrying a bloody knife."

"An old man?"

Ina nodded.

"But the Dutch are watching."

"Hey, boy."

They looked up. A tall figure eclipsed the high sun. Atif raised his hand to shield his eyes. The Serb soldier wore a dark uniform, which had a tiger emblem on the sleeve. A rifle hung from his shoulder, lazily pointing in their direction.

"How old are you, boy?"

The women stood.

"He's fourteen," his mother replied.

"No, he's older," the Serb said. "He's a soldier. I've seen you, boy. On the front line."

"I'm not a soldier."

"Yes, you are. I've seen you. You've killed Serb women and children." He pointed to Atif's temple. "You're a soldier. You were injured."

"One of your shells did that while he was playing," Ina said. "This boy has been at home, helping us grow food and helping his mother teach the younger children. He's never held a rifle in his life."

"We can test his hands for residue. If he has fired a weapon, we'll know." The soldier moved towards Atif. "We need to question him."

Both women stepped in front of the soldier. The Serb moved

towards them, stopping inches from Atif's mother, scowling. His eyes dropped to her chest and he reached across to touch the crucifix around her neck. She pulled back.

"Why do you wear this?"

"Because I'm a Christian," his mother said.

"Your husband is Muslim."

"He was."

"He was a soldier."

"No. He was a father trying to feed his family."

"No. He was a soldier. He taught your son to fight."

"He taught him how to farm."

The soldier bared his teeth and returned his attention to the crucifix. "You're not Christian." He tore it from her neck. "You're a Turk whore."

Pushing her aside, the soldier snatched at Atif. He backed up under the bus as far as possible. The Serb crouched, reached his hand under the bus, snagged Atif's ankle, and pulled. The twins grabbed Tihana and turned away, crying. Atif yelled and kicked; the hand released him.

It didn't return.

*Where is it?*

Atif wrapped his arms around the driveshaft and waited for the claws to reappear. A second pair of combat boots appeared instead.

Dutch boots.

A familiar voice.

"What's going on here?"

# WEDNESDAY: JAC LARUE

JAC SUBMERGED HIS head into a sink filled with cold water and kept it there until he ran out of breath. He straightened up, letting the water roll down his neck and drench his shirt. He soaked his towel and slung it around his neck. He closed his eyes for a moment, savouring the only cold he was likely to feel for the rest of the day.

"Get any sleep?"

Jac looked behind him. Bram Vogel, a tank driver, was squeezing the last of his toothpaste onto a brush.

"Five hours."

"You're joking?"

"Sergeant kept me up until eight this morning but promised me five hours of uninterrupted sleep if I stayed on sentry."

"And he delivered?"

"Yeah." Jac pulled out a razor and began dry-shaving his face. "What about you?"

"I sat outside the fence with your friend Karel," Bram said, spitting into the sink.

"He's not my friend."

"Well, he was pretty pissed." Bram gathered up his shaving kit and moved towards the exit. "He went to bed after you guys got back last night, but Janssen woke him up around three."

Jac kept his smile inside. He dunked his head, rubbing the loose whiskers from his face. When he surfaced, Maarten's reflection was beside his in the mirror. He flinched.

"Jesus. Where did you come from?"

"My mother. So I'm told." Maarten grinned. "Ready?"

"Almost," Jac replied, shaving his neck. "What's going on anyway?"

"Serbs are here. Major said he doesn't want them beyond the barricade. Though I'm not sure I'd call a piece of tape a barricade."

"A piece of tape?"

"Yeah. Does anyone really think that's going to stop them?"

"No, but enough of us might."

"Seriously, Jac? Do you think we possess any semblance of authority over these bastards? I mean, after everything we've seen?"

"What do you suggest? That we hide in here and let them do what they want to the refugees?"

"That's not what I mean."

"I know." Jac nicked his neck. "Damn."

He cleaned it with the wet towel and then threw the dulled razor in the garbage. He sealed his flak vest around his chest, picked up his Uzi, and slung it over his shoulder.

"Let's go."

Outside, Jac drew in a lung full of super-heated air.

*I should have worn my shorts.*

He and Maarten walked through the main gate and turned left towards the refugees. Vehicles lined the road. Serb soldiers were massed near the tape. Some wore green camouflage, but many were Rambo types; they wore mismatched uniforms with bandannas on their heads and had bandoliers crisscrossing their chests. A Serb civilian was directing a camera crew shooting video of soldiers throwing candy to the children.

Jac spotted one of their local translators walking away from a group of Serb soldiers. The young man was taking quick strides and glancing over his shoulder. He bumped into Maarten and started to walk around him.

"Amir," Jac said.

The translator hesitated.

"What's wrong?"

"Nothing." The man rubbed his thumb over the UN identification card in his palm. "It's just...."

"It's okay, Amir," Jac said. "They can't hurt you. What's going on?"

Amir's eyes darted towards Jac. "Are you sure about that? Do you think anyone here or in the camp is really safe?"

"Of course they are," Jac said. "What did they say to you?"

Amir swallowed hard and he stepped close to Jac.

"I overheard a Chetnik officer speaking to one of his men," he whispered. "The officer grabbed the soldier by the belt and said that no man or boy taller than his belt could get on the buses."

"Buses?" Jac asked.

"Yes, buses," Amir said. "The Chetniks are going to transport everyone to our territory. The buses are coming now." He glanced back at the soldiers then. "Don't you see? They can do whatever they want with us on the road. If I get on one of those buses, they will kill me."

"No, Amir," Jac said. "You're safe with us. You work for us."

"Yeah? What about the rest of them? There are hundreds of men in the crowd. My two little brothers are in the camp with our mother. Do you think you can save them all?"

"They wouldn't dare try," Jac said. "They know we're watching."

"Somehow, I don't think that will be enough," Amir said. He looked back at the Serbs and then walked towards the camp entrance.

Jac moved to follow him, but Maarten held him back.

"Let him go. He's just scared and I can't say I blame him."

Jac and Maarten walked to the edge of the tape, passing a fire truck distributing water. From the back of another truck, two Serb civilians were throwing bread at the outstretched hands of hungry refugees. A Serb officer was giving an interview with the bread truck as a backdrop. Serb soldiers loitered among the refugees.

"Jac." Janssen laid a hand on his shoulder. "Get your five hours?"

"Yes, Sergeant. Thanks."

"Good. I need at least one corporal out here who has a clear head."

"Did you know the Serbs are inside the line?"

"Yes. Orders say we're not to cooperate with them, but we can't do anything to provoke them either."

"Don't cooperate with them, but don't provoke them. Seriously?"

"Don't shoot the piano player, Jac," Janssen replied, absently playing with the gold band on his finger.

"Do you think the refugees are safe?"

"I don't know. I really don't. All I know is that I have a few dozen exhausted guys and more than twenty thousand refugees to care for. I'm trying to get guys out here to keep an eye on the Serbs in the crowd, but we're spread too thin." He pulled out a handkerchief and wiped the sweat from his face. "Let's just focus on getting as many of the refugees out of here as we can. Alive."

"What do you want us to do?"

"Go into the crowd. Do what you can. There's a medical tent out by the bus depot if anyone needs medical attention. Some of the guys have been passing out wet towels, but I think we're pretty well out of them now. Other than that, they seem to be getting enough water from the houses and the rivers. I think they've pretty well looted every house in the area as well, but that's the least of our problems. Don't bother with looters. Maarten can stay with you. Karel and Erik are already out there. Arie is with the doctors."

"Erik's out there?"

"Yeah, why?"

"No reason, Sergeant. Just thought he might be better off in the camp on sentry duty."

"I know, Jac." The sergeant stifled a yawn. "But I need every warm body I can get. Check back with me at supper time."

"No problem, Sergeant."

Janssen walked away, his head and shoulders lower than usual.

"Did he get any sleep last night?" Maarten asked.

"I don't think he's going to sleep until he gets home," Jac replied.

"Did he say anything about the blood on the carrier?"

Jac hooked his thumbs inside the flak vest. "He wants to think it was from the cow. He just doesn't know."

Maarten grunted and then turned to face the road. "Something's coming."

Jac listened to an engine accelerate in the distance.

Diesel, he thought. Another fire truck?

Sun glinted off the windshield of a bus which pulled up and parked on the shoulder. Within minutes, a dozen buses lined the street like a row of boxcars. Refugees rushed the tape.

"Hold them back," Jac shouted.

He touched Maarten's arm and pointed; the other peacekeepers were forming a human chain. But before they could secure the refugees, one of the Serbs shouted at the crowd, motioning to the buses. Jac didn't understand the words, but the refugees did. They broke through the chain of peacekeepers and stampeded towards the buses. Two men bulldozed over Jac, knocking him to the ground. Maarten grabbed the shoulder of his flak vest and pulled him away from the rampaging mob.

The crowd stormed the buses. In minutes the vehicles were over-flowing with people. The stampede slowed and the peacekeepers worked to herd the remaining refugees behind the tape. Then Jac spied two Serb soldiers pulling an old man up into the back of the empty bread truck.

"Come on, Maarten."

The peacekeepers moved through the refugees until they stood next to the fire truck. Serb soldiers were hauling more men from the crowd and loading them into the bread truck. One soldier grabbed a boy, pulling him away from his mother. She shrieked and grabbed the boy's dragging feet. Jac walked up to the Serb and seized his hands, removing them from the boy.

"What are you doing? He's just a kid."

"Fuck off, Blue Helmet."

A Serb sergeant walked up to Jac.

"We are taking them to be questioned," the sergeant said.

"Questioned? For what?"

"To see if they are war criminals."

Jac pointed to the boy lying on the ground with his mother.

"He's not a war criminal, for God's sake. He can't be more than twelve."

The sergeant gestured to the soldier with a finger. The soldier stepped back and the boy left with his mother. Maarten tapped Jac on the shoulder and pointed to a pile of documents on the ground. Jac picked up two of them. They were identification documents the Bosnians used. He approached the Serb sergeant with the papers in his hand.

"How are you going to identify war criminals without their papers?"

"We know who they are." The Serb smiled. "We don't need their papers."

"What do you mean you don't need them?" Jac looked into the truck. Six elderly men pleaded with their eyes. "Where are you taking them?"

"None of your business. If they're war criminals, they'll be tried. If they are not, they will go to Tuzla."

*They can do whatever they want with us on the road.*

"I don't believe you."

"I don't care." The Serb jerked his thumb at a house. Jac's eyes followed the thumb. On the second-floor balcony of the house, a fifty-calibre machine gun had been set up and was pointed at the Dutch compound. The weapon could cut down hundreds of people in a matter of seconds.

"Jac," Maarten whispered, tugging on Jac's arm. "Janssen said not to provoke them."

Jac pulled away.

"Provoke them? For God's sake, Maarten, they're taking these men away. They're probably going to kill them."

"No kidding," Maarten replied in a quiet voice. "But just how do you suggest we stop them? Look, maybe we should report this and let the major take care of it."

A gunshot cracked.

Jac and Maarten twisted around, looking for the source. They waited for a second shot, but none came.

"Where was that?" Jac asked.

"I don't know."

Jac surveyed the refugees. There was a disturbance in the crowd near one of the factories. Some of the refugees were standing and pointing, some were moving away. Others cowered under blankets and sheets. He turned around, looking for the Serbs he had been speaking to.

They had vanished.

The bread truck pulled away.

"Damn it!"

"What do we do now?"

Jac looked at the crowd, rubbing his face with his towel.

"Whatever we can, I guess."

They passed through the human chain and stepped into the crowd. Jac covered his nose and mouth with his towel. The heat amplified the stench of urine, feces, and vomit mixed with smoke drifting in from burning homes and haystacks. Women cried and children screamed. One young man spit at Maarten. A little girl relieved herself in the grass where she sat. Women grabbed at Jac's hands and his uniform, asking questions in Bosnian and English.

"They've taken my husband," one woman said, pointing to a house across from the compound. "Please. Can you help him?"

"We haven't eaten in two days," another said, holding up her young daughter.

"What is going to happen to us? Are they going to kill us?"

To his left, Jac saw a man with half a dozen loaves of Serb bread. He dropped the towel from his face, leaned down, tore three loaves away, and passed them to the hungry women.

He and Maarten kept moving. There were more Serbs walking among the refugees. Some hurled insults at the women. Others greeted old friends and neighbours with hugs, kisses, and an exchange of cigarettes. One soldier gave a long and passionate kiss to a young woman.

"Good guys or bad guys today?" Maarten asked from behind.

Jac shook his head. They walked to the far side of the crowd where the carriers sat blocking the road to the southwest. When they reached the other side of the blockade, they stood and stared at the Jaglici road.

"The Serbs are transporting troops from Srebrenica now," the officer on duty told them, motioning at an approaching truck. "They drop them here and go back for more."

"Are they going north after the men?"

"Not that I've seen," the officer said, shaking his head. "To tell you the truth, I don't think they know where the men are gone. The soldiers are all going into the crowd."

Jac nodded, staring at the road.

"There are still refugees coming south." The officer leaned close to Jac. "I haven't seen any with crush injuries."

Jac nodded again. "Thanks."

The Serb truck stopped, dropped off eight soldiers and then turned around.

"Anything you need, Sir?" Jac asked.

"No. Just keep an eye on those guys as best you can."

Jac and Maarten followed the soldiers into the crowd but lost track of them when Maarten stopped to help a woman. She was lying alone on the pavement, her skin flushed, her breathing rapid. He felt her head.

"Heatstroke," he said. "We have to get her to the doctor."

He and Jac carried the woman to the medical tent, leaving her outside in the shade with a bottle of water.

A single gunshot rang out near the zinc factory. A peacekeeper close to the building drew their attention to a Serb in a dark uniform. Jac and Maarten shadowed the Serb, watching from a distance as the soldier harassed the refugees. Then the Serb stopped.

They slowed as the soldier spoke to someone next to a wrecked bus. Two women stood up, arguing with him.

"Oh my God," he said, waving Maarten over. "I know that woman."

Jac made his way towards the bus, watching where his feet landed. When he got there, the soldier had pushed the women aside and was leaning under the bus. A boy yelled. Jac approached the Serb from behind.

"What's going on here?"

The Serb dropped the boy's foot, straightened up, and turned around. He glared at Jac.

"None of your business, Blue Helmet."

Jac bent down to look. Atif remained under the bus, his arm wrapped around the rusted driveshaft and his face drained of blood.

"I know this boy," Jac said. "He's fourteen. He's not a war criminal or a soldier. He helped me translate sometimes. Nothing more."

The Serb stepped closer to Jac. His breath stank of cigarettes.

"Listen, Blue Helmet. This isn't your problem anymore. Never was. You come here then you go home. We live here. This is our problem."

"That boy isn't a problem."

"Perhaps not now," the Serb replied, "but in a year or two. We have to keep their numbers down. They breed like rabbits you know. They're here now. In a few years, they'll be in your country. Then you will see. We learned at Kosovo and now we have a solution to this problem."

"The boy isn't a problem."

The Serb glanced at Maarten and then smiled at Jac, exposing rotten teeth.

"Fine. He's your problem. One boy will not make a difference. We will still get our revenge for Kosovo." The Serb pulled an armour piercing rifle round from his pouch and held it up. He tapped Jac's flak jacket with it. "That will not protect you, Blue Helmet."

Jac stared at the Serb, his lips tight. The soldier slid the round into one of Jac's chest pockets.

"Keep it. As a souvenir."

He walked away, laughing. Jac resumed breathing.

"Christ, Jac," Maarten said. "What part of don't provoke them didn't you understand?" He scratched his head. "Or was it the part about not cooperating that confused you?"

Jac turned away, knelt down, and extended his arm under the bus. Atif grabbed his hand and he helped the boy climb out.

"Are you okay?"

"Yes, *Korporaal* Jac."

Atif's mother crouched next to Jac and hugged him.

He pointed at the bandage on Atif's temple. "What happened?"

"He was too close to a shell."

Jac glanced around, looking for Atif's little sister. Tihana was sitting between the twins.

"They're all okay?"

"Yeah, they are, but some of his friends were killed."

"What?" Jac felt queasy. "The boys?"

"Yes. Little Dani too."

Jac bit his lip hard. He turned to Atif. The boy's eyes were lowered.

"Sorry to hear that, little brother."

Atif shrugged. Jac pulled a half-melted chocolate bar from his pocket and gave it to him.

"I think this is the last scrap of chocolate on the whole base," he said. Atif gave Jac a brief smile. "Go ahead. Share it with them before it melts. I want to talk to your mother for a minute."

"About what, *Korporaal* Jac?"

"Nothing important. Just stay down so the soldiers can't see you."

Atif pushed himself back against the bus. Maarten crouched down to speak with Atif and the girls. Jac stood and led Atif's mother a few steps away.

"Marija," Jac began, not sure how to broach the subject. "I was just wondering." He took a quick breath. "Why is Atif still here?"

"What do you mean?"

"The men are walking through the woods. Why didn't he go with them?"

"I couldn't let him," she said. Her eyes darted between the pockets on his shirt. "He would be alone. Besides, he's only fourteen. I have documents to prove that."

Jac placed a hand on her shoulder.

"I don't pretend to understand half of what is going on around me right now. In fact, I'm having a hard time trying to swallow a lot of what I'm seeing with my own eyes, but do you honestly think they're going to stop to look at his papers?"

"I don't know anymore," she said; her eyes still hadn't met his.

"Okay," Jac said, pausing to haul in a deeper breath. "Let me put it to you from my point of view. The Serbs are taking men away. I've seen them put old men on a truck and throw all their identification away. Some of these men were far too old to be soldiers. One of my translators told me the Serbs have been ordered to keep any male that is taller than a man's belt from boarding the buses."

Marija's eyes glistened.

"I don't know for sure," Jac said, "but I'm willing to bet those gunshots behind the factory are executions. I can't get close enough right now to see and, frankly, I'm not sure what I can do about it even if they are shooting the men. I can't tell you what to do. All I can do is tell you what I've seen."

"But it's too late," she said, her voice shaking. "The men have left."

"No, no, no. It's not too late. When I left Jaglici late yesterday, the men were just starting to gather. Marija, there were thousands of them. Soldiers. Civilians. Boys. Even some women. They probably didn't leave until late last night and they would be moving very slow. Atif is strong. He can catch up to them easily, but not if he waits much longer."

A tear ran down her cheek.

"But if you help, we could get him on a bus."

Jac looked from left to right before he answered.

"That's possible. But we won't have much control once the buses leave here. Even if we can get one soldier on every bus that leaves, the Serbs could still stop and search them on the way. I doubt a single peacekeeper is going to have much say about what the Serbs do or don't do."

"You think I should send him after the men?"

"I don't know. I just know that his options are limited. You've seen what can happen if he stays. It may take two or three days for the buses to get you all out of here. Do you think you can keep the soldiers from taking him for that long?"

"No," she said, shaking her head. "Can you get him inside the compound? He would be safe in there with you."

Maarten appeared next to Marija.

"To tell you the truth," he said. "I don't think anyone on the base is any better off. Even the civilian employees are afraid and they all have UN identification."

Marija finally raised her eyes; they had a plea in them.

"I think Jac is right," Maarten said. "Given what I've seen."

"Atif is a smart boy," Jac said. "He'll be okay. He told me he used to hunt in those hills with his father."

Marija nodded.

"He knows the area. The men will have crossed the minefields and marked them. In fact, I'm guessing the minefields have slowed them down a lot. Some of them are probably still trying to cross just north of Susnjari. It's still early in the afternoon. I think Atif could be there in less than two hours."

"The road to Susnjari is clear right now," Maarten said. "The lieutenant on duty down there said the Serbs were coming up from Srebrenica, but none of them were turning onto the road going north. From what they've told us, I don't think the Serbs know where the men have gone. At least not yet."

"We can give him some food and Maarten's spare boots," Jac said. "It'll be enough for two or three days."

Marija's eyes moved between the peacekeepers. The fingers of one hand covered her mouth and she swiped a tear away with the other.

The hand dropped from her lips. "I don't have a choice, do I?"

Jac hesitated, the full impact of what he was doing suddenly hitting him.

*I'm telling a mother to let her son run off by himself into the forest that's going to be filled with Serbs trying to track him down along with the rest of the men.*

He looked at the waiting buses. Two Dutch carriers pulled up into view and parked on opposite sides of the road. The vehicles became a funnel for the refugees moving towards the buses. Jac realized the funnel would make it easier for the Serbs to pick the men out of the crowd.

*Atif's chances just got slimmer.*

Jac turned to Marija. "No. I don't think you do."

"Are you talking about me, *Korporaal* Jac?"

The three adults looked down.

"If you're talking about me, don't do it to my back. Please."

Marija rubbed a hand over her face. Jac passed her his towel and she dried her eyes.

"You're right, Atif," Jac said.

Marija laid a gentle hand on Jac's arm.

"Let me tell him."

Jac nodded. Marija sat with her son.

"Do me a favour," Jac said, turning to Maarten. "I'll stay here and keep an eye on him. I need you to go back to the carrier. Grab some rations and anything else you think he might need."

"Like my boots?"

"Put it on my tab."

"You think he's going?"

"I think so. We should be ready."

"Okay. I'll be quick."

"Oh, and grab one of my green shirts. The long sleeved one."

Maarten gave Jac a mock salute and disappeared into the crowd.

# WEDNESDAY: MARIJA STAVIC

"MAMA?"

Marija pulled her thoughts together before turning to face her son. She tried to draw in a full breath, but the pain growing in her chest made it difficult.

*Am I doing the right thing?*

She trusted Jac. He had been good to them. Atif had met Jac late last January, speaking to him one day in English when the peace-keeper was on guard duty. The next time they saw Jac on duty, Marija had made him a loaf of bread and Atif delivered it hot. They'd been friends ever since. Jac had given them extra food and cigarettes to help them through the winter. He refused to accept money in exchange for the cigarettes and had even turned down his vacation because he was afraid the Serbs wouldn't let him back into the safe area.

*Jac wouldn't lie to me. He cares about Atif, worries about him. And he's right.*

If she kept Atif with her, the Serbs would get him.

*He has to follow the men.*

A tear dropped.

*How do I let him go?*

She crouched next to Atif and brushed the dirt from her son's shoulder as she tried to find the right words.

*How do I convince him that he is better off in the woods?*

"What's going on, Mama?"

"We think…." she started and then stopped. "I think it's too dangerous for you to stay. I want you to follow the men to Tuzla."

"What? No, Mama. I have to stay with you."

"No!" Marija took a breath. "You can't, Atif, you can't. You've seen what the Chetniks will do. *Korporaal* Jac can't be around all the time. The next time, they might get you."

Atif gazed up at Jac.

"She's right," the peacekeeper said.

"But the men are gone," Atif replied. "The Chetniks are everywhere."

Jac crouched next to Atif and repeated to him everything he had told his mother. Atif looked dazed, but he seemed to soak up every word. He didn't cry.

*Has he cried since his friends were killed?* Marija thought back. *Has he cried since his father disappeared?*

"I can take you as far as the Jaglici road," Jac said. "You can go north from there. The Serbs haven't been seen on that road. It's possible they don't know where the men have gone yet."

"But I promised Tata I would take care of my mother and my sister," Atif said, shaking his head. "I can't leave them."

"They can get on the bus, Atif. I'll make sure they do and, if I can, I'll ride the bus with them."

"But you don't even know if they're letting the buses through."

"They are," said a breathless voice from behind. Maarten was back with a bag and a pair of boots. "I just spoke to our sergeant. He said the first bus arrived in Tisca. They're being allowed to cross over and should be in Tuzla in a few hours."

"You see," Marija said, raising her hand to Atif's face. "We'll be all right. We have to think about you now. You have to go."

"No. I can't go. Tata told me to take care of you."

"He's not here, Atif. I am. We can take care of ourselves now."

"No. You need me."

"We don't need you. We'll be fine. If you want to take care of us, you need to start by taking care of yourself."

"I can't do it by myself, Mama."

"You won't be alone. You know the way to Susnjari. You've been there with your father several times. You'll find the men there and they will take you to Tuzla."

"But what if...." he started. "What if...."

She took his hands.

Warm, sticky. Trembling.

"Please, Atif. Do this for me."

Atif's eyes wandered. His mouth tried to form words.

"Your father taught you how to take care of yourself. You're smart. You'll know what to do. You just have to try."

"But Tata always said we should think before we act. We need to think about this. We're acting too fast."

She rubbed his hands between hers.

"Some things don't require a lot of thought, Atif. There are times when we just need to act."

He looked away. Ina touched his shoulder. The twins watched, wide-eyed. Tihana sat in Lejla's lap, scratching off the faded blue paint from the toy soldier's helmet.

"We'll be okay, Atif," Adila said. "You should do this."

Atif looked his mother in the eyes. "Are you sure, Mama?"

*No, I'm not, my dear, dear child.*

"Yes," she said, holding his gaze. "I am."

"I don't know what to do, Mama."

His mother took him into her arms and held him tight.

"Yes, you do," she whispered into his ear. "You need to do this. Catch up to the men. They'll take care of you."

She kissed him on the forehead and pulled back. He looked at her, dropped his head, and drew a long breath. Then he turned to Jac.

"You'll keep an eye on them?"

"Yes, I will. I promise."

"Then what do I do now?"

Jac handed Marija the pair of boots.

"They're a bit big, but they're better than what he has on."

Atif stripped off the ragged sneakers. Marija untied the laces and handed the boots to her son. He found wool socks inside.

"Use them," Jac said. "They'll absorb the sweat."

Atif pulled on the socks and then the boots. Maarten knelt next to the twins and pointed to Atif's bag. They passed it to their mother who took the remaining carrots out, leaving the bottle of water. Maarten added several ration packs, a green shirt, and another two-litre bottle of water.

"You can refill the bottles in the rivers," Maarten told Atif.

"With all the rain we've gotten lately, you shouldn't have a problem finding enough water."

Marija stood up and moved a few feet away from the group while the two peacekeepers prepared her son. She crossed her arms, tucking her hands underneath and holding them tight against her body. Another gunshot echoed from behind the factories. A shudder rippled through her body.

*What if they had taken him? Could that shot have been for Atif?*

Jac passed the pack to Atif and he looked inside.

"There are some ration packs in there. They'll last a few days or more if you're careful. You can put on the green shirt once you're in the woods." Jac smiled and pointed to the neon yellow *A-Team* t-shirt Atif wore. "They'll see you in Belgrade with that on."

The peacekeepers stood up. Atif stared up at them.

This is it, Marija thought, biting her lip.

"Say good-bye to your sister," she said.

Atif turned; Tihana was playing with the toy soldier. He reached into his pack and pulled out another toy soldier.

"Tell you what. Since I'm not going to be around, I'll leave an infantryman here to help the machine gunner." He gave her the soldier. "Keep them with you. And when you get to Tuzla, put them on a window sill so they can watch over you. Okay?"

Tihana nodded and introduced the two soldiers to each other.

Atif leaned back. Adila rubbed his arm and Lejla kissed his cheek. His face flushed.

"We'll see you in Tuzla."

Ina laid an arm over his shoulder and squeezed.

"You're doing the right thing," she said.

"I know."

Marija's mind raced.

*Does he have enough? Is there anything else?*

She looked at her bag.

*The salt.*

Marija's hand reached into her bag and pulled out the small plastic bag of salt. Atif stood and she held it out to him.

"You should take this, too."

He pushed it away. "No, Mama. That's all you have left."

"We might be in Tuzla by tonight. You'll need it more than we will." She stuffed the bag into his front pocket. "Keep it in your pocket so you won't spill it. If you run out of food, you only need a little each day to keep your head clear. You know what to do with it."

"Yes, Mama," he said, choking on the words.

Marija wrapped her arms around him.

"You'll be okay. You're strong and smart. You'll get through this and we'll be waiting for you in Tuzla. You know where your uncle Vlatko lives, right?"

Atif nodded against her head.

"I spoke to him on the shortwave a few weeks ago. He hasn't moved. So I'll be at his house waiting for you. I won't leave until you walk out of the woods. I promise you. I won't leave, okay?"

"Yes, Mama."

Marija could feel his heart beating like a hammer. She pulled back and stared straight into his eyes.

*He's going to be tall. Like his father.*

"I love you," she said, willing the tears not to come. "Don't ever forget that."

Atif dropped his head on her shoulder.

"I love you too, Mama."

Marija fought the emotion in her chest that was threatening to crush it and willed her feet to step away from Atif. She put her hands on his shoulder and turned him towards Jac.

"Go. Go before it's too late."

*Go before I change my mind.*

Jac picked up the pack and laid a hand on Atif's shoulder. They walked away with Maarten a few steps behind them.

Atif looked back twice and waved. The trio melted into the crowd.

When she was certain Atif was well out of sight, Marija collapsed next to Ina and sobbed.

# WEDNESDAY: ATIF STAVIC

ATIF MOVED THROUGH the crowd in a fog.

Everything is going too fast, he thought. But it must be okay. Mama wouldn't let me go if she didn't think I would be safer in the woods.

Now he understood why so many boys had turned off the main road with their fathers and brothers the day before. They didn't trust the Dutch to protect them.

Walking between Jac and Maarten, Atif watched the Serbs move among the refugees. Few gave them a second glance. The carriers blocking the end of the road came into view. Jac, Maarten, and Atif passed between them and turned right onto a street parallel to the Jaglici road.

The street was lined with homes, their lawns covered with garbage. A man stepped from a house carrying a sack over his shoulder. He stopped and stared at the peacekeepers. Atif looked back over his shoulder. The man had moved on to the next house. When they got near the end of the street, Jac glanced behind him. Then he pointed at the last house on the left. Maarten posted himself in front of the house and Atif followed Jac into the trees behind it.

Atif's head began to spin and he slowed.

*This is a dream.* He touched a tree. The sap came back sticky.

"Can I sit down for a minute?"

Jac looked back at him and nodded.

"Yeah, this should be close enough."

Atif dropped to the ground. A bottle of water appeared in front of him.

"You're flushed. You okay?"

Atif drank some water and returned the bottle to Jac.

"I don't know if I can do this, *Korporaal* Jac."

The peacekeeper sat down next to him and pulled his field pad from his side pocket. He took out a pen and a folded map.

"Do you want to go back with your mother?"

Atif felt a sudden sharp jab in the pit of his stomach.

"Maybe."

But he couldn't go back. He was too tall and the bit of fuzz on his chin that he was so proud of only made him look older. When he'd tried to join the army, he made the mistake of telling them his age. If he had lied, they would have believed he was sixteen.

Now I might really have to fight, he thought, fidgeting with his sticky fingers.

"I wouldn't have suggested this to your mother if I didn't think you were capable," Jac said, opening up the map. "I know you are. As far as I'm concerned, you could out-soldier some of our own guys."

"Yeah?"

"No doubt in my mind. Look what you've put up with for the last three years. Constant shelling and sniping, starvation, your father." Jac paused. "You still function like any teenage boy I know." He tapped Atif on the head. "You're strong. Up there. That's what will get you to Tuzla."

Jac tore away a section of the map with Susnjari at the bottom and the outskirts of Tuzla at the top. He drew a few lines on it.

"You've been up in the hills with your father, so you know about some of the minefields."

Atif nodded, his mind flashing back a year.

"You can come," his father had said. He'd dropped a packed bag at Atif's feet. "I'll take you as far as the minefields and lead the others into Kravica. I'll bring the food to you and go back for more."

"Why now?" Atif had replied.

"You're bigger now. You can handle the walk and the load."

Then why didn't you take me with you last month, he'd thought.

What has changed?

His father had looked at Atif as though he were reading his mind.

"I think it's important that you get to know the woods."

*Know the woods.*

His father had foreseen the end of the safe area. Just as he had foreseen everything else.

*Mama is right. I have to leave.*

"The men will have made a path through the minefields."

Jac's words brought Atif back to the present.

"They shouldn't be hard to follow," the peacekeeper said. "Thousands of footsteps will have left you a clear path across."

Atif turned his attention to the map. Jac pointed out the road that ran north from Bratunac then west. It encircled the area Atif had to walk through like a horseshoe.

"This road is going to be the biggest hurdle," Jac said. "My guess is they'll start to patrol it very soon. You'll have to cross it at night. But I have no doubt you'll catch up with the men long before that. Once you're across the road, you need to keep going north by northwest and you'll eventually cross the front lines. You'll probably do most of your travelling at night."

"What if I don't catch up to them? How will I know which way to go at night?"

Jac licked his lips and stared straight ahead for a few moments.

"The moon," he said with a quick smile. "There's a full moon tonight. It's in the southern sky. It rises in the southeast and sets in the southwest. It should be visible for the next few nights. You just have to keep it at your back."

"That easy?"

"Yeah. I wish I had a compass or pocket knife to give you, but I lost it all at the observation post." He raised a finger. "Don't forget that a full moon can light up the countryside. It'll be easy to see movement."

Atif nodded. He had rations, clothes, water, directions, and now a hint of confidence.

Jac wrote something on the back of the map, folded it, and poked it in the outside pocket of Atif's pack.

"I wrote my address on the map. I'm not sure how much longer we'll be here or where they'll send us, so I may not be in Tuzla when you get there. I'd like it if you would send me a postcard."

"Yeah. I'll do that. I promise."

"Last night the men moved through Jaglici to Susnjari. They're going to wait there for a while before proceeding. Now, the Serbs can see part of the road, so you might want to hug the treeline and rivers between here and Susnjari. I'm guessing you know which parts are safe."

Atif nodded.

"You're going to come across others walking back. They'll try to convince you to turn around. But whatever you do, keep going. You know what's waiting for you here."

"I won't come back."

"Keep a steady pace. Watch where you put your feet. The last thing you need is a broken ankle."

"I'll be careful."

"I know you will."

Atif sensed that Jac didn't want to let him go. The peacekeeper's eyes moved back and forth as though he were looking for something else to say.

"I guess I should go then."

"Yeah." Jac stood up and helped Atif pull on the pack.

"You'll keep an eye on my mother and sister?"

"You know I will."

"Thank you, *Korporaal* Jac. For everything."

Jac looked at his feet. The toes of his boots kicked at the dirt.

"Just send me the postcard. That's all the thanks I need."

Jac offered Atif his hand. Atif ignored it. He wrapped his arms around the peacekeeper and hugged him. Jac returned the hug then released Atif and stepped back.

"Don't forget. A steady pace."

Atif smiled at Jac and then turned away. He started to move off into the trees.

"Atif?"

He looked back. Jac's eyes were fixed on a point somewhere past him.

"I just wanted to say...." The peacekeeper swallowed, then began again. "I just wanted to say I'm sorry."

"About what?"

"About all this. We were supposed to take care of you, protect you, and we let you down. I feel like we're abandoning you."

Atif shrugged. His father had said the peacekeeping mission would fail unless the Americans got involved. Until then, the Serbs would continue to do as they pleased against the lightly armed peace-keepers.

"You didn't let us down, *Korporaal* Jac. I know what you've had to deal with. The Chetniks didn't let your men back in after their vacations. They stopped a lot of your convoys. You don't have a lot of ammunition. No big guns. No tanks. And the Chetniks know how to lie and be believed. I think, *Korporaal* Jac, we were both abandoned."

"Yeah."

"Can you do one thing for me, *Korporaal* Jac?"

"Name it."

"Make sure they all know what happened here. Make sure the world knows. Make sure they know the truth."

"You have my word," Jac said.

"Good."

*That's all I needed.* Atif turned away and stared at the trees and the Jaglici road beyond them.

"Remember," Jac said. "Walk away from the moon."

Atif glanced back at the peacekeeper, wondering if he would ever see him again. He took the first steps. When he got to the edge of the treeline, he looked up and down the road. A woman with two young children was trudging towards Potocari. The rest of the road was deserted.

Atif looked back at the house.

Jac was gone.

# WEDNESDAY: MICHAEL SAKIC

MIKE HESITATED OUTSIDE Brendan's room and glanced at his watch.

*Two o'clock. Do I wake them?*

He raised his fist to the door then paused. Their convoy had arrived at six and it had taken another two hours to settle into the hotel. Mike had managed a few hours of sleep on the mountain, but Brendan had stayed awake. He hated sleeping in the truck.

Mike dropped his fist and walked away. He took a set of narrow stairs into a small dining room which served as a bar in the evenings. The hotel owner, Sabir, was sitting behind the bar smoking a pipe and reading a paper. His wife was wiping off the three empty tables.

"Would you like something to eat?" she asked in Bosnian.

"Sure. Whatever you have."

She nodded and limped behind the bar. Shrapnel wound from early in the war, Sabir had told Mike the first time he had stayed in the five-room hotel.

He sat down at the bar and watched Sabir's wife crack two eggs against the side of a frying pan. The yolk plopped inside the pan followed by the mucus-like whites.

*Eggs?* The thought made his stomach tighten.

"Scramble them, please," he said, making a circular motion with his finger. "Well done."

The woman gave him a sideways glance and kept cooking. The wall behind the bar was lined with empty shelves. They kept the plum brandy and vodka in the cupboards below and the food in the back room.

"Got any Coke, Sabir?"

The man laid down the paper and reached under the bar. He put a can of warm Coke and an empty glass in front of Mike. The woman placed the eggs next to it, scrambled and brown. Mike pulled out a pouch of ketchup he had stolen from McDonald's on his way out of Toronto and squeezed it over the eggs.

"You won't get into Srebrenica," Sabir said. "My cousin should have been here hours ago with the eggs. If he can't get through the checkpoints, they won't let you through."

"It's probably just temporary." Mike shovelled the eggs into his mouth and swallowed before they could leave a taste. "There might be more air strikes."

Sabir snorted. "The planes are not going back."

"They did for Sarajevo."

"Yes, for Sarajevo." Smoke poured from Sabir's nose. "They won't go back for Srebrenica."

Mike scooped up the last spoonful of eggs and chased them with a mouthful of Coke.

"Do you know anyone there?"

"I have many friends there." Sabir's eyes wandered. "Good friends. They're in the woods now."

"What do you mean in the woods?"

"The men can't stay with the women. Chetniks won't bother the women too much, but they will kill the men. So they are going to the woods and walking."

"Walking where?"

"To Zepa most likely. Or Serbia."

Mike straightened up. He knew getting into Zepa would be harder than getting into Srebrenica. *But Serbia?*

"Would they go to Serbia if they thought that Zepa had fallen?"

"But it hasn't," Sabir said, inhaling on his pipe.

"They may think it has if they're listening to Serb radio."

"Then I think most would come here rather than go to Serbia."

"You think the Serbs will let them through?"

Sabir leaned forward on the counter and pointed his pipe at Mike.

"My friend, Sakic," he said, smoke puffing from his mouth between the words. "You have a Croat name, but you still don't understand. Chetniks will not let a single man cross the lines. They will hunt them like deer and slit every throat."

"But most of them will be civilians."

"The Chetniks don't care what you wear. If your last name is Muslim, you are a threat to a Greater Serbia."

"There could be twenty thousand men in the woods. They can't possibly kill that many men and think they can get away with it. Look at what happened last year. They killed sixty-eight in that Sarajevo marketplace and NATO pushed them off the mountains."

"And a few months later, the Chetniks were right back on those mountains. The world has a short memory, my friend."

"They'd be insane to kill that many men."

"And war is sane?"

"Do I smell eggs?" Robert pulled up a stool. "Can I get a couple?"

"I think I had the last ones," Mike said. "He can make you a sandwich. Beef, I think."

"Sure. One for Brendan too."

Mike translated the order and Sabir moved off into the kitchen area.

"Nice place," Robert said, glancing around. "Sleep well?"

"I don't sleep."

"You slept till four yesterday."

"I wasn't asleep. I was passed out."

"Oh."

"Let me guess. You've never been drunk."

"Never felt the need to drink."

"Stay here a while. That'll change."

He reached for his Coke and grasped empty air and spun around on his stool. Brendan was holding the glass to his nose.

"Christ, man. I'm not drinking."

"Just screwing with you," Brendan said, handing the drink to Mike.

"Keep screwing with me and I'll stop doing your job."

"No shit. The briefing isn't until four. Where'd you go?"

"Nowhere."

Mike told them everything Sabir had said.

Brendan was shaking his head. "It wouldn't be insane. It'd be stupid. The American satellites are reading licence plates for God's sake.

No way can they expect to get away with killing twenty thousand men."

"So what are they going to do with them?" Robert looked at Brendan then Mike. "Put them in a prison?"

"They won't get away with concentration camps again," Mike replied.

"Maybe they'll funnel them into Serbia," Brendan said. "Make the Serbian government relocate them to other countries."

Sabir laid the sandwiches on the counter.

"They don't believe you either," Mike told Sabir. "A few hundred, maybe, but we can't see them killing thousands. Not in this day and age."

"Believe me, don't believe me." Sabir stuffed tobacco into his pipe. "In a few days, you will see. We have long memories."

# WEDNESDAY: ATIF STAVIC

ATIF JOGGED NORTH along the Jaglici road, staring at his feet.

*Keep a steady pace. Don't break an ankle.*

"You're going the wrong way."

Atif glanced at the woman as he passed her.

"The Chetniks are there," she shouted at his back.

Atif slid to a halt. He turned around and stared at the woman. She shifted a child in her arms.

"You saw them there?" he asked. "With your own eyes?"

"Well, no. But everyone is saying they're there."

"Keep going to Potocari," he told her. "There are buses there that will take you to Tuzla."

Atif faced north again before she could reply. He stuck his thumbs inside the straps of his pack and picked up his pace.

*Steady pace. Watch where I put my feet. Don't break an ankle.* He glanced at the waning sun. *Five, maybe six hours of light left.*

He passed an elderly couple trudging south. Another woman herded two cows along the road and an old man pushed his wife in a cart. Mortar echoed in the distance.

*Steady pace. Steady pace.*

He jogged along the edge of the road, ready to plunge into the ditch if necessary, but no one fired near the road. The closer he came to Susnjari, the fewer people he met. He turned a corner and found himself exposed to a hill in the near distance. People were standing in a clearing on the side of the hill, some hiding from the heat in the shadow of artillery and trees.

*Chetniks?*

Atif dropped into the rocky bottomed ditch and walked north.

*Steady pace. Don't break an ankle.*

He climbed out of the ditch when he was confident he was sheltered from the hill. When he reached the edge of Susnjari, he stopped in a clump of trees and listened for tanks, trucks, or men, but heard nothing.

Except birdsong.

Atif studied the road leading into the town. Automatic gunfire echoed in the distance

No engines. No footfalls. No voices.

*Is it deserted?*

He left the trees, crossed a street, and followed a trail of discarded luggage to the town's soccer field, stopping under bleachers to rest. Garbage, clothes, bags, and burnt wood covered the field. A fire pit contained the smouldering carcass of a cow. The smell of roasted meat lingered in the air.

*They can't be that far ahead.*

He drank the last quarter litre of water in one bottle and wiped his face with the edge of his shirt. His head pounded from the heat, but he didn't want to open the second bottle until he was sure he could refill it.

He stashed the empty bottle in his pack and looked around. Nothing moved. He stepped out from under the bleachers and jogged around the edge of the soccer field. The trail of garbage led into the woods.

Atif knew the area from the trips he had made with his father, but they had made those journeys in the dark and he had relied on his father's directions. He only hoped he remembered where the mine-fields were. Jac's map was not that precise.

The pavement became a dirt road and then a wide path. Thousands of footsteps had flattened the brush on either side of the trail. Atif trotted along until the path opened wide into a pasture. He stopped and studied the land before him.

*Is this the minefield?*

He looked down at the crushed grass then moved forward, scanning the ground. Disturbed vegetation meant there were no landmines. He glanced at the map.

*Is it here or on the next plateau?*

He gazed across the field for a long moment. The crushed grass and discarded luggage indicated the men had cut a wide swath through the meadow.

*Is it safe?*

"Hey, boy."

Atif spun around.

Three men sat in the shade of some bushes near the treeline. One man lumbered to his feet like a small elephant.

Atif tensed. The only people who had remained fat in Srebrenica were those who controlled the black market and the shipments of aid from the UN. As the man approached, Atif took a step backwards.

"What are you doing here?" the man asked.

"I'm following the men to Tuzla."

The other two men climbed to their feet, shouldered bags, and joined their friend. The trio stood in front of Atif.

"Not a good idea, boy. They won't make it to Tuzla. The Chetniks will stop them at the road."

"Well," Atif said, his eyes shifting between the three men, "where am I supposed to go?"

"Zepa," the fat man said. "It's closer."

Atif understood why that appealed to him.

"Someone in Potocari said that Zepa had fallen."

"Propaganda," the man replied. He motioned to Atif's pack. "What are you carrying?"

Atif stepped back again. *Am I stepping into a minefield?*

"Nothing. Just some water and clothes."

The man motioned Atif closer.

"Let me see."

"It's just water and clothes."

An arm darted towards Atif's pack. He jumped, evading it, but tripped over his own feet and fell hard. A water bottle dug into his back.

"Take it off," the man shouted.

"Leave him alone!"

Atif thought the voice belonged to one of the other men, but when he propped himself up on his elbows he saw a soldier standing behind them, his legs planted apart and a rifle held tight against his shoulder.

The soldier aimed the rifle at the fat man.

# TUESDAY: TARAK SMAJLOVIC

"TARAK!"

Tarak blinked, the dirt scrapping the inside of his eyelids. Someone screamed. He sat up, rubbed the grime from his eyes, and searched for the voice. Smoke and debris clouded his view. Splintered trees lay on the ground or threatened to topple.

"Tarak!"

He turned around; the trees rotated with the motion. His throat stung.

*Fadil?*

He rubbed his face and tried to focus.

*Where am I? What happened? A tank shell. Chetniks. Invasion. And we're losing.*

Tarak spit dirt and bile. When he glanced up, he saw Salko leaning over a pair of kicking legs.

"Get with it, Tarak. I need a dressing."

He looked around. His pack and rifle were leaning against the tree that had stood between him and the tank shell. He crawled over and pulled a dressing from an outside pocket, tossing it to Salko.

"Are you okay?"

"Yeah. Yeah,". Tarak mumbled, using the tree to help him stand. His head pounded and his ears rang. He looked at the kicking legs again.

"Who is that?"

"Omar."

"Oh, no." Tarak fell to his knees and crawled to the side of the young soldier. Omar lay still, his chest rising and falling rapidly. Dirt and blood covered his face. Salko was tearing away clothing around Omar's stomach. Dark liquid leaked from three holes.

"You're going to be fine, Omar," Tarak whispered, unsure if the man could hear his words.

Salko wrapped the dressing around Omar's gut and tied it tight. "We have to get him to the hospital."

"How?"

"We'll have to carry him. Or take a truck from the blue helmets if we have to."

"Put him on my back," Tarak said, getting up and grabbing his pack and rifle.

"You can barely stand."

"I can do it. Get him up."

Salko frowned and wrapped an arm around Omar. The half-conscious soldier grunted as Salko pulled him to his feet. Tarak crouched down and took Omar's full weight on his shoulders. He straightened up and Salko led them down the hillside. When they hit the pavement, Tarak looked back. A Serb tank was coming towards them. Soldiers walked behind it.

Tarak and Salko jogged away from the invaders. Two Dutch armoured vehicles came into view, blocking the road. Tarak knew the UN vehicles were no match for a tank and he expected them to run the moment the tanks came into view.

Tarak followed Salko through the UN blockade and found a Dutch Mercedes jeep preparing to leave on the other side. Salko jumped in front of it and raised his rifle.

"We need a ride."

The driver opened his door, leapt out, and raised his Uzi.

"Get out of the way!" he shouted in English.

"You have to take him," Salko said, motioning to Omar. "To the hospital."

"I don't have the time."

Tarak opened the rear hatch, slid Omar gently off his back, and laid him inside. The peacekeeper slammed the driver's door shut and walked to the back of the vehicle. Tarak raised his rifle and then jammed it into the peacekeeper's chest.

"Cowards. You're supposed to stop them. Now you are running away like frightened hens. Where are the air strikes?"

"I don't know where they are," the peacekeeper replied. "They told us the planes would come this morning. I don't know what to tell you."

"You're lying."

"No," the peacekeeper said, his features softening. "But I think someone is lying to us." He glanced at the carriers. "Look, I'm going to Bravo. I can drop you on the road by the hospital."

"Fine," Tarak said, lowering his weapon. He climbed into the back of the vehicle and returned his attention to Omar. Salko and the peacekeeper jumped in the jeep and it screeched away, navigating among the people fleeing the town. The number of refugees grew the farther they drove. The jeep slowed to a crawl short of the hospital.

"Let us out here," Tarak told the driver

The vehicle came to a halt. While they were taking Omar out, fleeing civilians took their place in the jeep. The peacekeeper didn't try to stop them. By the time Tarak had Omar across his shoulders again, the vehicle was swarming with refugees, inside and out.

Tarak struggled up the steep driveway; Omar was unconscious, a dead weight on his back. He and Salko pushed their way into the crowded hospital and walked from room to room, looking for help. A nurse stopped them and then led them to a gurney in the main hallway. When Tarak placed him on the gurney, Omar groaned and his eyes flickered.

"You're at the hospital," Tarak whispered close to Omar's ear. "They're going to take care of you, Omar. You're going to be all right."

Omar's eyes shifted up. He grunted a word Tarak couldn't understand. The nurse inspected Omar's wounds and then she wrote his name on a tag and pinned it to his shirt.

"I need to take him in now. You can wait if you want."

Omar grabbed Tarak's arm and moved his head from side to side.

"Okay," Tarak said, taking Omar's hand. "But we'll be back to see you in a few hours, okay?"

Omar managed a smile and raised two fingers to his mouth. Tarak fished a half pack of cigarettes out of a pocket and stuffed them into Omar's shirt pocket, patting it as the nurse pushed the gurney into the examination room. The door slammed shut.

"Shit," Tarak said, shaking his head.

"I know, friend."

A doctor halted in front of the soldiers.

"Good, they sent someone. The stretchers are outside. We need you to take them over to the Dutch. They're taking them to Potocari."

"No one sent...."

Salko slapped Tarak's arm. The doctor moved off.

"Nothing we can do on the line. We might as well help here."

Tarak slung his pack onto his back and followed Salko outside. A dozen occupied stretchers lined the sidewalk. Tarak looked at the steep hill leading to the road and at the mass of people moving towards the Dutch camp a short distance away.

"I think I'd rather go fight."

"The Dutch aren't going to be able to stick around on that road and, once they pull back, the town is gone. We need to get as many people as possible to Potocari."

Tarak turned back to the stretchers. A soldier lay on the closest one. He was unconscious and his thigh was tightly bandaged. A nurse indicated to Tarak and Salko with her hand that he should be taken first.

They fought for more than an hour to carry the stretchers through the panicked crowd, struggling to keep the stretchers level. At first, the Dutch had been hesitant to accept the wounded men, but then an officer appeared and opened the gate. He had directed them towards a troop truck on which other stretchers waited for transportation. As they returned to the hospital for the seventh time, they passed a number of men and several peacekeepers carrying stretchers.

"Last one," Salko said as they deposited the seventh stretcher. "We need to see what's going on."

They left the camp and turned towards the post office. The small red brick structure functioned as their headquarters. Tarak expected to see soldiers hanging around the door, but the entrance was vacant. He took the steps two at a time, lunged though the door, and ran from room to room.

Empty. Even the short wave radio was gone.

He walked back outside. Salko was speaking to a familiar face in the thinning crowd.

"Rasim," Tarak shouted. He walked over to greet his friend.

"*Zdravo*, Tarak," Rasim said, lighting a cigarette. No one smiled. A soldier standing off to the side was crying.

"Where is everyone? What's going on?"

"They've given up," Salko told him. "They're gathering at Susnjari. They want to go through the woods."

"So they're not even going to try?"

"What's the sense?" Rasim pointed to a man with a radio. "Alija made a broadcast demanding that the blue helmets intervene. He said forty thousand Chetniks were waiting to take the town. Not much we can do against that with six thousand men and no weapons or ammunition."

Tarak shook his head. Alija Izetbegovic was the president of Bosnia and Herzegovina. Tarak knew he would have access to Western intelligence. If the president said forty-thousand Serbs waited to take the town, Tarak wouldn't question it.

Or, he wondered, is Izetbegovic inflating the numbers to make the blue helmets act?

"Fuck the blue helmets," one of the men said. "They've sold us out."

"Fuck France. Fuck Britain and America," another said. "They've made a deal with the Chetniks. Srebrenica for Sarajevo. They've signed our death warrants."

Tarak looked at Rasim.

"Who knows?" Rasim said with a shrug. "Look, you and Salko should gather up all the food you can carry and get up to Susnjari."

"What about my grandfather?"

Rasim took a long draw on his cigarette and blew the smoke from his nose.

"I don't know what to tell you, Tarak. If you can get him to the Dutch, they'll probably take care of him."

Tarak felt sick. His grandfather was eighty-six and stubborn enough to refuse to go with the Dutch. He didn't trust the blue helmets any more than Tarak did.

"I have to get him," Tarak said, leaning down to pick up his pack. "I'll check on Omar and I'll see you in Susnjari."

No one responded. When Tarak looked up, the others were staring into the sky as two fighter jets split the air above them heading towards the Serb lines.

Tarak stopped and leaned against a street sign to catch his breath. He was carrying his grandfather in his arms and a full pack on his back. His grandfather had managed to walk only the first kilometre. Tarak's attempts to convince him to go to Potocari had failed.

"They're puppets," his grandfather had mumbled as Tarak grabbed the few cans of food sitting in the cupboards. "They do what the West thinks is best. They will abandon us. You saw. They dropped two bombs and didn't come back. Srebrenica is in the way of peace. That is what the West wants. They don't care about us."

"There are thousands of people there now, Dada. The Dutch will watch over them. They'll get trucks and send them all to Tuzla. You'll see. You will be okay."

"No. I'll go with you. I'd rather die on my feet, where and when I choose."

Tarak locked eyes with his grandfather.

*I'm not going to win this one.*

When they got to Susnjari, men were gathering at the soccer field. Thousands were sitting in small groups on and off the field. Some cooked meals, others prayed. There were a few women and soldiers, but the rest were civilian men and teenage boys. Tarak found an open spot next to the bleachers and left his grandfather alone with a bottle of water and some crackers before going to search for someone in charge. He recognized a group of men arguing on the edge of the field. Salko was crouched next to them, jamming supplies into a pack.

"*Zdravo*, Salko."

"Where's your grandfather?" Salko asked, securing the flap on his pack.

"He's here," Tarak replied, cocking a thumb towards the bleachers. "What are they arguing about?"

Salko rolled his eyes as he straightened up. "What don't they argue about?"

Tarak smiled.

"They're a bureaucracy," Salko said. "They have to argue. Some want to go to Tuzla. Some want to go to Zepa. Some want to stand and fight."

"What is wrong with Zepa? It's closer than Tuzla and the Chetniks would have a hard time advancing in that terrain. They have more food there and we could join up with their forces. We could keep Zepa safe. Maybe keep the Chetniks occupied long enough to save Gorazde."

Salko nodded as Tarak spoke. "That's what I've been telling them, but someone said Zepa has fallen. They don't want to take the chance."

"Fallen? Are you sure?" Tarak bit his lip. He had hoped to join a group going to Zepa. He didn't think his grandfather would make it anywhere else.

"No one is sure about anything," Salko said, glancing at the arguing men. "That's the problem. All I know is the longer we sit here scratching our asses, the closer the Chetniks will come."

"They should let groups leave now. If Zepa is gone, we should all head north in small groups; some towards Zvornik, some towards Tisca, some towards Nova Kasaba."

"Listen!" a boy shouted. He stood and ran towards the arguing men. "Listen!"

The men became quiet. The boy held up a radio; Tarak strained to hear the words, but he couldn't make them out through the static. Suddenly, the men cheered. Some kissed one another. Some didn't react at all.

Salko spoke to one of the men and then turned back to Tarak.

"He said the Chetniks are going to open up a corridor to let anyone through who is not a war criminal."

"What good is that?"

"Can't you see what they're saying," Salko shouted at the men. They stopped to listen. "As far as the Chetniks are concerned, we're all war criminals. Every last one of us. It doesn't matter how old, young, or infirmed we are, they will kill us all. Don't be taken in by this."

Tarak stepped up next to Salko.

"Enough with the arguing. We need to go now."

The men turned away and started arguing again.

"Let me know when they're done. I have to see to my grandfather."

Salko nodded and then joined the heated discussion. Tarak picked up his pack and walked back to the bleachers. His grandfather held up the water and two crackers.

"No," Tarak said, pushing them away. "I have plenty. Go ahead, finish them."

The old man hesitated and then ate the crackers. Tarak sat down and sorted through the supplies he had dumped into his pack. He had enough food for both of them for only three days, but he wasn't concerned. Early in the war, the Americans had dropped thousands of ration packs over the enclave in an attempt to bypass Serb blockades. Tarak had found dozens of packs in the woods and buried them in several locations for just this type of emergency. If they decided on Tuzla, there was enough food buried along the route to last them both at least two weeks. The only question was how to get his grandfather that far north.

The arguing stopped and the men dispersed. Salko walked to where Tarak was sitting and threw his pack on the ground.

"Idiots," he said. "We're going as one group. To Tuzla via Zvornik."

"Seriously?"

"They think because it's been fairly quiet over the last few months the Chetniks will just conveniently not notice thousands of men going for a walk through the woods. Don't those fools remember anything?"

Tarak sighed hard and looked at his grandfather. The fifty kilometre walk involved steep hills, swamps, thick forests, and minefields. He had no doubt they would be under fire for part of the journey.

"Are they leaving now?"

"As soon as they can get the units ready. We're bringing up the rear. Some guys are going on ahead now to make a path through the minefields. All the politicians and most of the soldiers are going to the front. They're hoping they'll be able to open a passage across the road so that everyone can get to the other side."

"You don't think it'll work?"

"You were at Cerska. You know what it's like. By daybreak, the Chetniks will have a clear view of us in the hills and fields. We'll be sitting ducks."

Salko crouched down and said hello to Tarak's grandfather and then he pulled Tarak aside.

"What are you going to do?"

"I don't know," Tarak said. "He doesn't want to go to Potocari. I guess I'll have to carry him."

Salko leaned closer.

"We both know you can't carry him that far. With all the rain we had, the rivers will be swollen and the swamps will be barely passable. The mud on those hills will make them slicker than a ski slope."

"I know, I know," Tarak said. "But he's my grandfather."

Salko reached into a pouch on his web belt.

"He's an old man, Tarak. He has lived a good life. If you truly love him, you'll find a nice spot on the side of a hill, somewhere he can see the sunrise, and give him this."

Salko dropped a grenade into Tarak's hands and walked away.

# WEDNESDAY: TARAK SMAJLOVIC

TARAK PICKED A long blade of grass and chewed on it while his grandfather slept. The climb had taken most of the morning and left his grandfather exhausted. They were out of sight of the Serb guns and had a good view of the rolling hills that extended to the western horizon.

After spending the night at the soccer field, Tarak had bid farewell to Salko and walked into the fog with his grandfather. Most of the men had left by then. Watching from the hillside, he saw only a few hundred lingering in the area after the fog had cleared and by noon the trail was deserted. Tarak glanced up at the late afternoon sun. He knew he had to leave soon if he were to catch up to the men by sunset.

"You should go."

Tarak helped his grandfather sit up against the tree.

"I have a few more minutes, Dada."

"No, you don't. You should have left hours ago."

His grandfather ate crackers and washed them down with water. Tarak cleared his throat.

"I can still take you to Potocari."

"If you take me to Potocari," his grandfather said, pointing a half-eaten cracker in his grandson's direction, "the Chetniks will get me and they may get you, too. You're all that's left of our family. I will not put you in harm's way."

"I'll be fine."

"That's what your father said."

Tarak opened his mouth to respond, but then he shut it. Tarak had been serving in the Yugoslav army when the war in Croatia broke out. The Croat soldiers had already deserted and more and more Bosnians were following their lead as the Serbs took full control of the army. Tarak waited until Vukovar to leave. By then, he knew the war would spread. He knew the Zvornik region would be a primary target because of the industry, roads, and rail lines in the area. Tarak warned his father and their neighbours, but few believed him.

His grandfather believed. He had seen it sixty years earlier.

When it happened, Tarak was visiting friends in Srebrenica with his grandfather. Unable to return to Zvornik, they took over an abandoned house near Jaglici. The army gave him enough food to keep his grandfather fed and healthy.

Tarak didn't want to admit to himself that three years of struggling with his grandfather against shells and starvation had all been for nothing.

His grandfather laid a hand on his arm.

"You need to forgive yourself, Tarak."

"Dada...."

"No. Please, Tarak. You've been a good boy. You took care of me. Now, I have to take care of you." He paused to draw in a long breath. "You must go. They need you out there. I will be okay. I have food and water and a nice view." He fingered the grenade in his lap. "I won't be cold."

Tarak looked away.

"You're all I have left," his grandfather said, squeezing his arm. "You have to survive. For me. For your parents. For Fadil."

Tarak's head dropped as he fought the emotion rising from his gut.

"You don't have to say anything. Just pick up your stuff and go. You must go. You must survive."

Tarak drew his arm across his face and nodded. He leaned sideways and kissed his grandfather on the cheek.

"I love you, Dada."

"Take care of yourself, Tarak."

Tarak grabbed his pack and rifle and walked away from his grandfather. He picked his way down the side of the hill, his feet growing heavier with each step. When the ground levelled out, he paused and looked back at the hill. His grandfather was well out of sight, alone near the top.

"I can carry you, Dada."

Branches swayed but did not respond. Tarak dropped his rifle and threw his pack to the ground. Tears blurred his vision. He stood motionless, glaring at his equipment as memories flashed through his mind.

His father trying to teach him how to drive his new Yugo and breaking down before they had turned off their street. His grandfather teaching him how to hunt. His mother pruning her favorite roses.

Holding Fadil for the first time.

Tarak's teeth clenched so hard his head hurt. His breath came rapidly. He turned around and started to walk back up the hill. He stopped.

*You must go. They need you out there.*

"What difference is one rifle going to make, Dada?" he whispered to empty air. "I can carry you. Why won't you let me try?"

He swore under his breath and trudged back to his gear, collapsing to the ground. He wiped the tears from his cheeks.

"I can't do this anymore, Dada. I'm tired."

There was no future except war. Nothing but more killing and suffering. He picked up his rifle and laid it across his lap, staring at it for a long time.

A twig snapped.

Tarak raised his head and then returned his attention to the rifle. He'd taken the weapon from a wounded Serb two years before. He'd shot the soldier in the head afterwards. He didn't regret it. The Serb would have done the same to him. Tarak drew his hand across the weapon, feeling the worn wooden stock, the cold steel of the barrel. A Yugoslav made AK-47 semi-automatic rifle. Exceptional quality. He was lucky to have it.

His heart slammed against his ribs.

*You're all I have left.*

He felt his grandfather's hand squeeze his arm.

*You have to survive.*

He propped the rifle up until the steel barrel lay against his cheek.

*For me. For your parents. For Fadil.*

Tarak's finger played with the safety switch, flicking it on and off. Then on again.

*You must go. You must survive.*

He flicked the safety off again.

*You need to forgive yourself.*

Another twig snapped.

Tarak dropped to the ground, bringing the rifle up to bear on the trees in front of him. He held his breath and listened. Muffled footfalls slowed their pace a few metres away.

*Am I that close to the trail?*

He let the air seep out of his lungs and then reached for his pack, pulling it on. The footfalls continued away from him. Tarak climbed to his feet and shadowed the sound, stepping carefully until the sound ceased. Whispering voices drew Tarak's attention to his left. He moved closer to the sound and caught a glimpse of three heads in the brush. An overweight man stood up with some effort and then called out to someone else. He walked away and the other two followed.

Tarak made his way to the edge of the treeline, crouching behind bushes. The three men were walking towards a teenage boy. Tarak slipped the pack from his shoulders, lowered it to the ground, and then moved in to get a better view of the boy. The overweight man told the boy they were going to Zepa.

"What are you carrying?" the man said.

The boy backed up, giving Tarak a clear view of him.

*Fadil?*

"Nothing," the boy said. "Just some water and clothes."

"Let me see."

"It's just water and clothes."

The man made a grab for the boy who ducked the oversized hand but fell backwards onto the ground. Raising his rifle, Tarak stepped from the treeline.

"Take it off," the man was shouting, hovering over the terrified boy.

Tarak brought the rifle tight to his shoulder and drew a bead on the fat man.

"Leave him alone."

# WEDNESDAY: ATIF STAVIC

ATIF STARED AT the young soldier holding the automatic rifle levelled at the three men. He wore a mixture of uniforms: Canadian boots, Dutch pants, and a Yugoslav army shirt. The harness and pouches of his webbing were not the same colour green. His long hair was tied back in a ponytail and there was a white band around his left arm.

"Who do you think you are?" the fat man said. "Do you know who I am?"

"I know who you are," the soldier replied. He shifted his feet, taking a step forward. "And don't imagine for a moment that I'd think twice about putting a round through your well-fed skull."

"I don't believe you." The man moved closer to the soldier. "In fact, I'm guessing they left you behind because you don't have any rounds for that piece of junk."

One of the soldier's eyebrows arched and then his hand came up and cocked the weapon. A single brass round tumbled through the air.

"There are twenty-nine more."

The large man's chest rose and fell. He expelled air in a huff and then raised a pudgy finger. "You're making a mistake."

"It's mine to make." The soldier pointed west with the barrel of his weapon. "If you fools want to go to Zepa then leave. Now."

The man turned to his friends. "Let's get out of here," he said, retrieving his bag. His friends paused, looking between Atif and the soldier. "I said, let's go."

The men said nothing. They picked up their bags and followed the fat man westward. Atif remained on the ground. The soldier kept his rifle high, waiting until the trio disappeared from sight. Then he lowered the barrel, bent down, and retrieved the errant round and returned it to the magazine.

"Are you all right?" he asked.

"Yeah."

The soldier offered a hand. Atif stood up on his own and took a step back.

"Don't worry. I have no interest in your pack," the soldier said. He walked to the treeline and picked up a rucksack. "You see, I have my own." He returned and stood before Atif, cradling the rifle in his arms like a baby. "What's your name?"

Atif looked around.

"I'm alone," the soldier said.

"Why aren't you with the men?"

"I was...," he started, his eyes darting away for a moment. "I was delayed. What about you?"

"It wasn't safe in Potocari." Atif told the soldier about the Serb in Potocari and how his mother and Jac made him leave.

"How old are you?"

"I'll be fifteen in October."

"Really? You look older. Your mother and the Dutchman were right to make you leave. At least out here you have a fighting chance."

"I'm not so sure my mother thinks she was right."

"Of course not. She's your mother."

"It's just...." Atif said, glancing south. "I don't know if I'm doing the right thing."

"You're more worried about your mother than yourself. Right?"

Atif looked down at his feet.

"You said they're taking the men away in Potocari. If you go back, they will have you. You may make it to a bus, but then you have a long drive to Tisca. The Chetniks will board and search the buses."

Atif kicked at the dirt.

"If you want to live, you need to walk to Tuzla."

Atif lifted his gaze.

"And since we seem to be walking in the same direction, I wouldn't mind a little company."

"Really?"

"Tell you what. Promise you'll listen to me. If I say run, you run. If I say get down, you get down. If I say shut up, you shut up. Do that and I'll get you to Tuzla in one piece. I'll get you back to your family. How's that sound?"

"How do I know you won't leave me if I get in the way?"

"I don't think you will."

Atif glanced at the trail leading to Potocari.

"I had a little brother like you once," the soldier said. "I would like to think that you would have done the same for him."

Atif met the soldier's gaze. Tired eyes. Like his father.

"Okay."

The soldier smiled.

"So, what's your name?"

"Atif."

"I'm Tarak." The soldier untied his white armband and tore it in half. "First thing you'll need is a white armband."

"Is this to tell us apart from the Chetniks?"

"Yes, exactly," Tarak replied, tying the piece of material around Atif's left arm. Then he held up his rifle, flicking the safety on. "Do you know anything about weapons?"

Atif took the rifle and held it, his left hand under the barrel and his right on the grip. He laid his finger straight along the trigger guard and pointed the weapon down and away from Tarak. He studied the weapon. The metal gleamed and gave off a strong scent of gun oil. The wooden stock was worn but cared for, the magazine rusted along the seams.

"A Yugoslav-made Kalashnikov automatic rifle or AK-47," Atif said. "Selective fire, 7.62 mm gas operated assault rifle with a thirty round magazine. Mikhail Kalashnikov created it in 1947. It's the most reliable automatic weapon out there and is used more than any other assault rifle in the world."

Tarak stared at him.

"Mr. Kalashnikov is still alive, too," Atif said, with a shrug.

Tarak took the weapon back.

"Forget I asked," he said. "Reciting the textbook answer is one thing. Do you know how to use it?"

"I fired one once to test it. My father taught me how to repair them."

"Well, you could come in handy," Tarak said, slinging the rifle over his shoulder. "Now, we need to move quickly if we want to catch up with the rest of the men before dark. You have water?"

"Two bottles."

"Good. Drink as much as you want as we walk. There are some rivers ahead. Okay?"

"Yes," Atif said. "Thanks."

"Don't thank me, *Braco*." The soldier's eyes shifted to the hillside. "We're both getting something out of this."

Atif cocked his head. The soldier looked at the hill for a long moment. Then he turned away, motioning with his head for Atif to follow. Atif glanced back.

*Does he think the Chetniks are following?*

He eyed the hill. A swaying tree caught his attention, but then the motion moved along with the rest of the trees on the hill like a wave on a lake.

*It's only the wind.*

As his eyes made a final sweep of the area, a pillar of dust rose up between the trees. A sharp pop followed. Atif flinched and looked at Tarak. The soldier stopped but didn't turn around. Then he continued walking.

"Are the Chetniks that close?" Atif asked, catching up to the soldier.

"No. Don't worry about it. It's nothing."

Tarak kept a brisk pace and said little as he led Atif through an abandoned Serb trench. They climbed the first of three steep ridges. Trampled vegetation, garbage, and bodies marked the trail in the dense brush. They came across the first body during the climb from the base of the second ravine. An old man with a ragged suit jacket draped over his head lay next to the trail, his feet bare. There were two more bodies near the top of the ridge. The white bones of skeletons gleamed on the other side of the trail.

A steep slope led into the third ravine. Atif navigated through the brush and then pressed the tip of his boot into the exposed roots of a tree. He grabbed onto its branches but missed the next foothold, slipping onto his back and sliding more than a metre before Tarak snagged the straps of his backpack.

Atif looked up and nodded.

He felt like a puppet as Tarak held on to the straps while they descended the final few metres into the base of the third ravine. Tarak released him at the bottom and then Atif took a step forward. He stepped on something soft. He jerked his foot back and looked down. An arm lay motionless on the ground, reaching out from the bushes.

"Another body," he said to Tarak in a hushed voice. Tarak leaned forward and pushed the branches aside with the barrel of his rifle. Behind the bushes, three bodies lay side by side. A jacket covered their faces; their shoes were gone. Unlike the others, their chests and legs were sliced open from shrapnel or gunfire.

Tarak crouched and Atif followed suit. The soldier pulled out a pair of compact binoculars and scanned the area. Atif looked west where the setting sun cast long shadows.

"They must have been fired on from those hills. I don't see anything there now. Not that it means anything. Come on."

They kept low as they shuffled across the shallow river. On the other side, they sat down in the shadow of the next hill. Atif shed his pack and pulled out the water bottles. A few mouthfuls swished in the bottom of one.

"I'll refill them," Tarak said. "If you want to eat something, do it now. We'll rest here for a few minutes."

Atif passed the bottles to Tarak. The soldier crawled to the edge of the river, dipped the bottles into the fast-moving water, and then dunked his head. Atif examined the half-dozen ration packs Jac had put in his bag. The meals were like the American, Canadian, German, and British rations he had tried in the past. He preferred any one of them to the American meals although nothing compared to the German rations. They all had a big chocolate bar. The rations usually contained a main meal, drink crystals, candy, and a variety of crackers or bread as well as plastic cutlery, matches, and packets of salt, pepper, and sugar. Atif opened one and checked the English NATO label on the main meal pouch.

Pork and beans.

Atif stared at it. He had never eaten pork, but not because his father adhered to Islamic law. They simply didn't eat pork the same way his mother refused to eat meat on some Fridays.

Tradition.

He only had a few rations and it could take up to a week to walk to Tuzla.

*Do I throw it away?*

Tarak crawled back and returned Atif's bottles. He looked at the meal pack in Atif's hands.

"What is it?"

"Pork and beans."

Tarak laughed, spitting the water he had been about to swallow. He reached over and took the meal pack, feeling the contents inside the soft pouch.

"Reminds me of when the Americans started dropping the packs. I didn't know which was funnier: dropping rations older than me or dropping rations with pork to a community full of hungry Muslims."

Atif suddenly understood why his father had taken some of the American meal packs to trade.

"Do you practice?" Tarak asked, handing the meal back to Atif.

"My father promised to take me to mosque," Atif replied, shrugging. "Promised me for years, but he didn't. I don't think he believed anymore."

"Your mother?"

"She's Croat," he replied, still surprised he would describe her that way. Until the war started, he had no idea she was Croatian or that it mattered. "I think I know more about her religion than I do my own."

"There's not much pork in it anyway, but leave it to last if you're not comfortable. When you get hungry enough, you'll eat it."

Atif didn't argue. He knew what the empty, gnawing ache in his stomach felt like. He stuffed the pouch inside his bag and pulled out another.

Beef stew. Atif opened it and chugged half the pouch.

Tarak took a Canadian and German ration from his own pack, looked at both, and then tossed the German one back into his pack. He tore it open and scooped out the contents with a plastic spoon.

"What about your father. Is he out here?"

*Somewhere.*

"No. He used to guide soldiers and others through the woods. They say he got caught in that big snowstorm in April."

"I remember that. There were about a dozen of them?"

"Yes. They were going north."

"Well, if I remember correctly, they never found any bodies. He could still be alive."

Atif kept his eyes low.

"I lost my family when the Chetniks took Zvornik," Tarak said after a few quiet moments. "My grandfather survived. Stayed in Srebrenica with me. What about your grandparents?"

"They're all gone. My father's parents died in a car accident before I was born. My mother's parents died in Vukovar."

"Really?"

Atif eyed the soldier. "Why?"

"I was at Vukovar."

"How could you have been there?"

"I was in the Yugoslav army finishing up my year of service when everything started to crumble. Of course, that early on, I never thought the war would spread. As far as I was concerned, I was Yugoslav and wanted to keep my country together. I thought we were just going to quell some dissent in Croatia. I stayed with them until Vukovar, but after the hospital massacre, I decided I had had enough. So, I deserted like all the others. By that time, most of the army was Chetnik anyway."

"Did you actually fight in Vukovar?"

"No. I was Muslim. All I was good for was digging trenches and latrines."

"Oh," Atif mumbled, not sure what else to say. He finished the beef stew and pulled out a packet of drink crystals, pouring it into a bottle of water.

"So, what happened to you?" Tarak asked, motioning to the bandage on Atif's head.

"Shrapnel."

"The shell that hit the alley?"

Atif glanced up and nodded.

"They were your friends?"

"Yeah."

"I'm sorry," Tarak said. "I really am. This bloody war has been hard on everyone."

"It's stupid."

"That too." Tarak chewed through a row of crackers, his eyes fixed on the southern face of the ravine.

"How come you were so far behind the others?" Atif asked.

Tarak washed the crackers down with water.

"I had to leave my grandfather behind."

"Oh. Sorry."

"We seem to be digging up a lot of hard stuff, *Braco*." He forced a quick smile and shrugged. "He was old, stubborn. He had a good life."

Tarak finished his meal and tossed the empty pouch away. Artillery fell in the distance and he straightened up to listen. Gunfire echoed through the hills. He took a swig of his water and then stuffed it into his pack, gesturing to Atif to do the same.

"We're making good time. If we keep up the pace, we should catch up with them before the sun sets."

Atif hauled his pack on and stared at the steep hill ahead. He didn't remember climbing so much when he helped his father bring back food from Kravica.

"How many more hills like this?"

"This is it," Tarak said.

Atif jammed his toe into the craggy roots at the base of the hill.

"What's after this?"

"A plateau," Tarak whispered from behind. "It's a minefield."

# WEDNESDAY: MICHAEL SAKIC

MIKE TAPPED HIS fingers on the steering wheel; he was waiting for the Pakistani peacekeeper to finish filling out their passes. He looked into the distance where a city of white modular tents had grown up from the tarmac of the Tuzla air base.

"They don't use the airport?" Robert asked.

"It's not safe," Brendan replied. "The Serbs have guns in the hills and part of the airport is mined."

The peacekeeper passed the documents through Mike's window.

"You know where to go?"

Mike nodded and then motioned towards the tents.

"You're expecting refugees?"

"They're coming by bus," the peacekeeper replied. He glanced at his watch. "The first ones should be here soon. They'll tell you everything at the briefing."

"Thanks."

The peacekeeper threw a mock salute and Mike drove onto the base. He pulled up to the administration area and parked and the three men stepped out of the truck.

"Coming?" Brendan asked.

"You go on," Mike said. "I'm going to wait for the buses."

Robert hoisted the camera onto his shoulder and picked up a bag. Brendan took another bag and they walked towards the door.

"Take notes," Mike shouted after the pair.

"That'll cost you." Brendan opened the door and looked back, a smile plastered across his face. They disappeared inside.

Mike took his camera from the back seat and walked towards the tents. He stood on the edge of the tarmac, snapping pictures. Peacekeepers were assembling long metal pipes into triangular skeletons and dragging heavy white canvas over them. They slipped under the canvas and pushed up the poles on one side and then the other. They emerged from under the tent and carried on to the next one. A white truck backed up to one of the tents. Peacekeepers offloaded tables, chairs, and cases of water.

Shouting near the base entrance caught Mike's attention. Two peacekeepers jogged towards the gate and a third pointed down the road.

Rumbling.

Mike moved closer. A white bus approached, its brakes squealing as it slowed. The peacekeepers raised the barrier and the bus tipped from side to side as it made the turn. Mike jogged alongside until it came to a halt near the tent city.

The door cracked open.

Mike raised his camera.

An old woman stepped gingerly to the ground. A little girl followed, grasping the woman's hand. They took a few steps and then stopped and looked around.

Lost.

Within minutes, the area was filled with men, women, and children. Two Dutch peacekeepers moved among them. Mike snapped pictures of the exhausted and bewildered faces and then stopped.

There are men here, he thought, remembering what Sabir had told him. Was he wrong? Maybe the Serbs are letting the men leave with the women.

More blue helmets and berets appeared among the refugees. A Pakistani peacekeeper crouched next to a sobbing girl. He wiped her tears and gave her a white teddy bear. Then he picked her up and motioned to the crowd to follow. Mike took pictures as the peacekeeper walked away, the teddy bear swinging across his back.

He spotted a man walking alone.

"What was it like there?" Mike asked in Bosnian.

"Chaos," the man replied. "The Dutch had nothing for us. All they could do was stand there while the Chetniks gave us bread and water and transportation."

"The Serbs provided the buses?"

"Yes, yes. They dropped us off near Tisca. More are coming."

The sound of a woman crying captured Mike's attention. He followed the noise and found an older woman struggling to stand. She screamed at one of the Dutch.

"My husband," she wailed in Bosnian, falling back to her knees. "They've taken my husband. Why are you doing nothing?"

The Dutch soldier shrugged and walked away. Mike snapped a photo and then crouched next to the woman.

"Who took your husband?"

The woman raised her arms to the sky. "Chetniks. Chetniks took him," she screamed, falling forward and slapping the pavement with her palms. "They took him. Dragged him away."

Two women helped her to her feet.

"But there are men on the buses," Mike said to one of them.

"They are the lucky ones," she said. "The Dutch did nothing while the Chetniks killed our men."

"What? They're killing men in Potocari?"

"I saw them kill a child," a hoarse voice said behind him.

Mike turned around and looked down. An elderly woman pulled a scarf tight around her head and stepped closer to Mike.

"Chetniks," she whispered. "They killed a little boy sitting next to us in Potocari."

Mike pulled a notebook from his camera bag.

"How little?"

"Eleven or twelve. All he did was cry. One of the Chetniks came over and told him to shut up. His mother said she could do nothing. She said he was hungry." The woman paused, her lips tight, her eyes wet. "Then the Chetnik took out his knife and slashed the boy's throat."

A teenage girl wrapped an arm around the woman's shoulder. She looked at Mike.

"The Chetnik laughed and said the boy would not be hungry again."

Mike stared at the women.

"It is true," the girl said.

"No. Sorry. I believe you. Do you know the boy's name?"

"No. We didn't know them. We were sitting next to them." She turned around so that Mike could see the back of her blouse. "We sat too close."

Mike examined the blouse. Blood spots formed a straight line pattern across the back.

"What about his body?"

"The Dutch took it," she said. "I'm not sure where. Someone said they buried the bodies on the base."

"Bodies?"

"Mostly older people, I heard. Heat exhaustion."

Mike raised his camera.

"Can I get your names and take your picture?"

The old woman looked up. She was wiping away tears.

"Do you have some water?" the girl asked.

Mike nodded and pulled a bottle from his camera bag. The girl gave the bottle to the woman and then helped her sit down on the curb. She took Mike aside a few paces.

"My father is still in the woods," she said. "I don't want to risk his life. If the Chetniks find him and find out what we just said."

"It's true then? The men are in the woods?"

"Yes. They left last night."

Mike pointed his pen at a young man walking away from the bus.

"Where did they come from?"

"There are a few hundred left in Potocari. We were the first to board the buses. It was madness. My mother was knocked down twice. Some of the men made it on to the buses. Some were taken out of the line before they could get to the bus. Some they shot behind the factories."

"In front of the Dutch?"

The girl sighed, watching her mother.

"What can they do? The Chetniks are too strong. They needed the planes to come. Not one or two. They needed dozens. They needed them to drop a hundred bombs. Not two."

Mike nodded, jotting notes.

"How many men do you think are in the woods?"

"Thousands. And the Chetniks are waiting for them. We saw soldiers patrolling along the road." She hesitated, choking back her worry. "Most of them are civilians, not soldiers. They have no weapons. Or food. They left so quickly."

"I don't need your names," Mike said, placing a gentle hand on her shoulder, "but can I take a picture of you and your blouse?"

The girl stared at her mother for few moments and then nodded.

"My name is Fatima."

Mike took the picture.

"Do you know what is going to happen to us?" she asked.

"The Pakistanis here will take care of you. They have food and water and they'll have enough tents for everyone. There are doctors too. Was your mother hurt?"

"She's fine. She's just tired. Like all of us."

Fatima returned to where her mother sat and Mike followed. She leaned down and took one of her mother's arms and he took the other. The woman grunted and pushed herself to her feet.

"You're a Western journalist, right?" Fatima looked at him with her head inclined.

"Yes."

"American?"

"No. Canadian. But my stuff can be published anywhere."

"Good. Good." She smiled, picked up her bag, and walked away with her mother. They joined the line of refugees waiting to be processed.

Mike looked down at his notes. The Serbs had murdered a twelve year old boy in front of witnesses. They had pulled men from the lines and shot them in front of the peacekeepers.

*What are they going to do to the thousands of men behind their own borders?*

Mike flipped the notepad closed and walked back to the base.

*Goddamnit. I have to get into Srebrenica.*

# WEDNESDAY: MARIJA STAVIC

JAC CROUCHED NEXT to Marija and laughed.

"You have the process down to a science," he said, pointing at the girls.

Adila was holding Tihana while Lejla pretended to feed the toy soldiers. She dropped a morsel of food next to a soldier, catching it without letting Tihana see. Tihana chewed her own food as Leila fed the soldiers the same piece over and over. When they finished eating, Maarten poured a few drops of water over the soldiers and Tihana drank her fill from the bottle.

"Thank you for the meal," Marija said, touching his arm. "I haven't been able to get her to eat that much all week."

"Are you sure you don't want to try to get on a bus now?"

"I think it's better if we waited until tomorrow. We don't want to risk being on the road after dark with the girls."

Jac's eyes flicked back to the girls.

"Probably best," he said, standing. "We'll do another circuit and drop by again."

"Thank you."

Maarten joined Jac and they walked away.

"Did you hear?" a woman sitting beside Marija asked.

"Hear what?"

The woman pulled a shawl over her shoulder.

"Someone listening to the radio heard that the Chetniks are opening up a corridor so that the men can cross."

"That's wonderful," Marija said, smiling. The smile faded. "But it doesn't make sense. Why would they go after the men here but leave them alone in the woods?"

"There are a lot of soldiers with them. Maybe they don't want to fight them."

Marija relaxed against the drive shaft.

*Perhaps I did the right thing after all.*

She turned back to the twins.

"Have you finished?"

"Yes. I think she's tired," Adila said.

Marija took Tihana and placed her against the bus. A family next to them had left on the buses earlier in the afternoon, leaving flattened cardboard boxes on the ground. Marija had taken the cardboard and spread it under the girls. She covered Tihana with a blanket and kissed her.

"Mama's coming back," Adila said.

Lejla's brow furrowed. "Why is she running?"

Marija looked up. Ina was running, weaving her way through the crowd. When she reached the bus, she dropped the empty water container next to Marija and wrapped her arms around her daughters.

"Under the bus," Ina said, picking up a blanket.

"Mama," Adila said. "It's still early."

"We're not tired."

"Get under there, now."

The girls obeyed, sliding in next to Tihana. Marija helped Ina cover the twins, pulling the blanket up to their necks.

"Don't get out unless I tell you," Ina said. She turned and sat with her back to the girls, eyes darting left and right.

"What is it?" Marija asked.

Ina took a moment to catch her breath then leaned in close.

"Chetniks," she whispered, her voice trembling. "They just pulled a girl out of the factory and dragged her into the bushes."

Marija covered her mouth with her hand, her eyes scanning the crowd for soldiers.

"What do I do?" Ina asked. "I can't send them into the woods. And what happens when we get on the bus. Jac said they were stopping the buses along the road. What if they take them?"

Marija turned back to her friend and draped an arm around

her. They'd been hoping the Serbs wouldn't notice the twins. There were a lot of refugees, after all. But the number of soldiers had increased during the day and many were drinking now.

*That's all we need. A drunken Chetnik noticing a pair of pretty twins*—Marija's thought stopped mid-sentence.

"That's it! We have to dirty them up."

"What?"

"If they're not attractive, the Chetniks won't be interested. We can dirty their clothes and faces. One of them can carry Tihana to the bus. They won't be interested if they think she's not a virgin. And we can make them look sick. Anything so that they don't attract attention."

"Sick," Ina whispered to herself. "They're allergic to latex. Both of them."

"I don't understand."

"Don't you see? Certain types of latex make them break out into hives. It might take a few hours, but with enough contact they get pretty bad. A red rash can also be a symptom of hepatitis or scabies. A doctor could easily tell the difference, but I doubt a soldier would know."

"But wouldn't that be dangerous to them?"

"No, no," Ina replied. "They have a different type that just gives them a bad rash."

"So where can we find latex here?"

Ina pointed at the Dutch medical tent.

"Can you go? I'd like to stay with them."

Marija clasped Ina's hands.

"I'll be right back."

She threaded her way through the thinning crowd towards the green tent. People were clustered outside the entrance, exhausted from the heat. A Serb soldier rode a white horse through the sick and injured, forcing them to move aside. Marija looked around for a doctor, but there were only refugees. She poked her head inside the tent.

*I don't need a new pair of gloves. A few discarded pairs would do.*

She walked up to the first garbage container she saw.

"Excusez-moi, Madame," a woman said.

Marija turned. A young woman waved her hands and then touched the garbage container. She was wearing a shirt with Médecins Sans Frontières embroidered on the front.

"I speak French," Marija said.

"Oh, okay. I just wanted to tell you not to go through the garbage. There could be needles in there."

Marija jerked her arm back from the edge of the bin.

"What were you looking for?"

"Some gloves. Latex gloves. They don't have to be new. I just need a couple of pairs."

The doctor cocked her head. "May I ask why?"

Marija glanced around. "My friend has twin teenage daughters. They are...." she hesitated, trying to formulate the words without coming right out with an explanation. "They are very pretty girls."

"Okay," the doctor replied, drawing out the word. "So, why the gloves?"

"They're allergic to latex. If she can cause a rash, she says she can pass it off as hepatitis or scabies or something."

"I understand. Most people wouldn't know the difference. But I'm afraid all our gloves are latex-free."

Marija drew a sharp breath. The doctor patted her on the arm.

"Just a moment," she said. "Wait outside for me. I may have something that will help."

"Thank you."

Outside in the waning sunlight, Marija looked north, her heart aching.

*Where are you now, Atif? Are you safe? Have you caught up to them?*

She said a short prayer, hoping he would not have to walk the forest alone after dark.

"Madame?"

The doctor waved to Marija from the other opening in the tent. She was holding a paper bag.

"For the two pretty girls," the doctor said, handing the bag to Marija.

She looked; it was full of condoms. She grinned.

"It was all I could find. But they have latex in them. Do you think our friend will mind?"

"No."

A man holding an infant approached the two women. A Serb soldier walked behind him. Marija tensed, crushing the bag closed in her fist. The man began to speak, but the doctor raised her hand. She looked at Marija.

"My translator is inside the compound getting supplies. Can you translate?"

Marija nodded and turned to the man.

"I'm alone," he said. "Chetniks want to take me in for questioning, but I have no one to take care of my son. The soldier told me to give him to the doctor."

Marija took a moment to sort her thoughts before translating.

The doctor listened, drawing a hand through her short black hair. "I need their names. And the mother's name."

The man gave them the information and the doctor wrote it on the back of a prescription pad. Then he placed the baby carefully in the doctor's arms, kissed him on the forehead, and left, the soldier at his heels.

"This is the second one today," the doctor said, tickling the baby's chin. "Will you be okay with the condoms?"

"Yes, yes. Thank you."

The doctor went inside the tent with the baby and Marija made her way back to Ina. All around her, people prepared for the night, bargaining for blankets and scraps of cardboard to sleep on. Women huddled close together; they covered their daughters and kept watch. Shots rang out from the hillside.

Marija rounded the end of the bus and stopped. Three Serb soldiers stood a few metres away, arguing among themselves. She ducked under the rusted rim. Ina had covered the three girls completely and was sitting in front of them like a sentry. Marija joined her. The soldiers were standing above the old man, who was trying to attach his prosthetic leg.

"What were they arguing about?" Marija whispered to Ina.

"The two soldiers spoke to the man and then they left him alone. But the sergeant made them come back. He's ordered them to take the man to the little white house for questioning. They think he's a war criminal."

"But he can barely walk."

Ina raised an eyebrow and nodded slowly.

Marija looked at the two soldiers. The youngest didn't look much older than Atif. He wore a clean green camouflage uniform that seemed to be a size too large. The other soldier wore the same uniform and a helmet. Marija leaned forward, trying to get a better view. The soldier in the helmet turned, catching her gaze.

*My God, he's familiar.* But she couldn't put her finger on it. *A former student?*

The soldier held her eyes.

*And he knows who I am.*

The younger soldier interrupted the staring match. "Niko. Lets go."

*Niko Basaric!*

He'd been one of her pupils the year she filled in for a sick teacher at the school in Srebrenica. He had an amazing ability for math and languages. She'd met him again when he helped coach Atif's soccer team the year before the war. He had just gotten married and was thinking about becoming an engineer. The war had obviously interrupted those plans.

Niko turned away and helped his comrade pull the crippled man to his feet.

Marija opened her mouth to call out to him and then shut it again. No sense in attracting any attention.

The soldiers walked away, the old man limping between them.

Niko didn't look back.

# TUESDAY: NIKO BASARIC

NIKO BASARIC'S HEAD bobbed forward then back, striking the tree and driving his helmet down over his eyes. He woke up, pushed the helmet back, and hauled out his canteen.

*God, I hate the heat.*

He hadn't slept in two days and he'd been walking since early morning. His section had met little resistance on the road that led into Srebrenica, but that wasn't unexpected. The fighting would take place in the town, house to house. They were about twenty minutes from the town, but the advance had stopped an hour before.

He glanced at the sky.

*Probably planes in the area.*

He drank half the canteen and took off his helmet, pouring the rest of the water through the stubble on his head. He stuffed the canteen into his pack and stared at the laminated picture of his wife, Natalija, and his two-year-old daughter, Mira, jammed inside the helmet. Niko swallowed. He had been taken off the checkpoint so quickly there'd been no chance to return home to say goodbye. He'd sent word with one of the drivers. Had Natalija received it? Would he ever see them again?

Niko hated the army. He'd resisted the pressure from his Serb father to go to Croatia to fight and when the war spread to Bosnia, he thought he could sit it out in Srebrenica. The people in the town didn't care that he was half Serb. They were grateful to have some-one who could repair rifles. But the war dragged on, getting uglier as winter approached. A Muslim soldier, distraught over the death of his wife during an artillery attack, tried to kill Natalija because she was Serb. The soldier had shot Niko in the shoulder before neighbours could wrestle the attacker to the ground. With his shoulder still bleed-ing, Niko packed what he could and moved to Bratunac, a Serb town a few kilometres east of Srebrenica near the border with Serbia.

Once there, Niko had no choice but to join the Bosnian Serb army in order to get a place to live. But he was a Serb of mixed heritage and he found the soldiers constantly tested his loyalty. He told them he was Christian, that his father was a Serb, but they didn't care. His mother was Muslim and that somehow made him less human.

He rubbed his aching shoulder. *Damn it, I just want to go home.*

His parents had fled to Austria soon after the fighting broke out and they'd left the house in Srebrenica to him. He doubted Natalija would want to return, even for a house. Recently, she'd started hinting about joining his parents in Austria before the winter set in. He knew Mira would be safer there and, if he survived this day, he would give it serious consideration. He just wanted to have a look at the house in Srebrenica first.

"Niko."

Petar Kadija was approaching along the ditch in a low crouch. The young, skinny recruit carried two bottles of water. He handed one to Niko.

"Thanks," he said, stuffing the bottle into his pack.

Petar dropped to the ground and swallowed a mouthful of water, then stowed the other bottle in his own pack.

"How much longer do we have to wait?"

"No idea," Niko said. "There must be planes nearby. They're probably watching them on radar. When the planes run low on fuel, they'll go back to Italy and we'll move on."

"They're not worried about the planes attacking?"

"We've gotten this far. My guess is they're still trying to cut their way through the red tape in New York."

Petar laughed. Niko eyed the recruit. The boy was eighteen, fresh out of basic training, and excited about the prospect of going into combat so quickly.

Too quickly, Niko thought. And too excited.

Two weeks earlier, the training captain had assigned the rest of Petar's class to combat units. He hadn't known what to do with Petar; the boy had barely scraped through basic training. Niko had volunteered to shape the eager recruit into a soldier. That was the official story, the one Petar's father was told. In reality, Petar's mother had pleaded with Niko to keep her naïve son away from the front lines.

"I could use the manpower," Niko had told the training captain. There had been a list of assignments for recruits on his desk. Petar's name was listed under a combat unit but circled in red. Niko laid a bag on the desk and took three bottles of plum brandy and a carton of Marlboros out of it. "I can whip him into shape. Maybe in a few months he'll be useful to you."

The captain dropped the brandy and the cigarettes into a desk drawer.

"Keep him, Niko. You'll be doing all of us a favour."

Niko could still feel the kiss Petar's mother had planted on his cheek when she learned that her son would be assigned to his checkpoint. Niko had stopped short of promising her that Petar would be safe. As he watched the young recruit fiddle with his helmet, he was thankful he'd had the foresight not to make such a promise.

"Shouldn't we keep up with the tanks?" Petar asked.

"We're fine here. They'll let us know when it's time to move."

"I just wish...."

"Quiet!" Niko said, turning his head.

Rumbling.

*That's not the tanks.*

The noise grew from the east, rolling in like thunder.

*On a clear day?*

"Get down!"

Niko grabbed Petar and pulled him to the bottom of the ditch. The two jets screeched above them. A moment later, the ground quaked. Petar grabbed his ears and screamed and tried to wiggle out from under Niko.

"Stay still, you fool."

"They're bombing, they're bombing. We have to get out of here!"

Niko shifted his weight, pinning the recruit.

"If you run out into the open, the shrapnel will tear you to pieces. Don't move. Do you hear me?"

"But if we stay here, the bombs will fall on us."

"You're better off here. Now shut up."

The planes climbed into the sky and the thunder faded. Niko couldn't turn around to watch without letting Petar go. He listened instead. The roar returned from the east.

"They're coming back, Petar. Don't move."

Images of Natalija and Mira filled Niko's thoughts as the ground shook and dirt rained.

"Don't move," he yelled next to Petar's ear.

"I'm not moving," the recruit screamed back.

"Okay. Okay."

Niko returned his attention to the planes. The roar faded. Seconds. Minutes.

"Do you hear the planes?" Niko finally asked.

"No. No. I don't hear anything."

Niko sat up, releasing Petar.

"Anything now?"

"Nothing," Petar said, swallowing twice. "What do we do?"

"Wait until everyone else starts to move. They'll know if the planes have gone back to Italy or not."

"Okay. Yeah. We'll wait."

Niko smiled. *Was I ever that nervous?*

He settled back against the tree and hauled a Dutch ration pack he'd found in one of the abandoned observation posts out of his pack. He tossed the meal pouch to Petar.

*Nothing like food to take his mind off the aircraft.*

He crawled to the edge of the road. Soldiers were climbing out of the ditches. Some loitered in the area. Others walked towards the town. Black smoke obscured the road ahead. A tank, two armoured personnel carriers, and three trucks filled with infantry drove by and disappeared into the smoke. Niko listened, expecting to hear the echoes of a firefight in the houses below. He heard nothing except their own mortar and artillery.

"Basaric!"

Niko glanced back. Ivan Radic was gesturing to him to come forward. A hardened veteran, Ivan was the only other corporal in the section besides Niko. The tall soldier was a physical fitness fanatic and it showed in his chest and shoulders.

"We'll meet you farther down," Ivan said. "Get moving."

"We're coming." Niko climbed out from under the shade of the tree. Petar tossed away the empty meal packet and followed Niko as they moved towards the wall of smoke. The smell of burning diesel and flesh assaulted his senses. Niko pulled out a bandanna and covered his mouth and nose. Petar did the same and they jogged through the acrid air.

A burning tank lay on the edge of a crater, thick black smoke pouring from the open hatches. A jeep sat nearby, its windows smashed. Soldiers were draping canvas over three bodies on the side of the road.

"Oh my God!"

Petar was staring at the front of the tank. The blackened remains of an arm hung over the driver's hatch.

"C'mon," Niko said, pulling the recruit's shirt.

Petar resisted and then gave in. He kept glancing back as they walked.

"I don't understand. Why didn't they get out? They must have seen the planes."

"Like we did?"

Petar looked back again. "I mean, have you ever seen anything like that?"

"Will you shut up," Niko said, grabbing Petar by the arm and pushing him forward. "And stop staring at it."

"Will you stop treating me like a child?"

"Fine. You want to stare at it, go ahead." Niko pulled Petar back towards the tank. "Go ahead. Memorize every last detail. The flesh burned from the bone. The wedding ring on his finger. The smell you can't wash out of your clothes or your memory."

He wiped away the sweat dripping into his eyes and pushed Petar closer to the tank.

"You'll dream about it at first. You'll wake up drenched to the skin, shaking so bad you can't stop. If you get back to sleep, you'll only dream about it again except this time you'll dream that *you're* on fire. You'll wake up screaming. You'll wake up trying to beat the flames out on your chest. Is that what you want?"

"No, but...."

"If we survive this day, you're going to see things you don't want to remember." Niko pulled him away from the tank and led him to the opposite side of the road. He pointed through the trees at the houses below. "When we get down there, we're going to be looking at snipers in every window and booby traps in every house. It may take weeks to clear the town. This is real. This is life and death and if I have to worry about you getting distracted by something as mundane as another burned body then you're no good to me. Understand?"

Petar's eyes focused on the town.

"Hey, Turk!"

Niko turned. Sergeant Drach stood on their side of the road, drawing a towel over his shaved head.

*Damn it. The bombs missed him.*

The sergeant was an ultranationalist who didn't mind advertising his hatred for anything and anyone who wasn't pure Serb. Niko had been detached to Drach's section on several occasions, but this was the first time the sergeant was going to let him fight. The other times, Niko had been told to dig trenches or run errands.

The sergeant motioned to an approaching carrier, the black smoke swirling in its wake.

"We have a ride," Drach shouted, shouldering his rifle. "Grab your pet and move it."

The carrier slowed and the trio mounted the vehicle, joining the other four men in their section. They'd started out with more than twenty, but the rest of Drach's men were filling the ranks of the front line sections. Ivan was thirty and like Drach had been fighting from the beginning of the war. Vladen, Pavle, and Anton were new additions to Drach's section. They were all younger than Niko, but they'd seen their share of combat.

*If their stories are to be believed.*

"They're not meeting any resistance," Drach told them, shouting over the roar of the engines. "There's no one down there."

Niko glanced towards the town.

*No resistance at all? Where had they gone?*

"We're going to spend the day clearing houses," Drach replied to a question Niko had not heard.

The others mouthed words of disgust Niko had no trouble reading.

"Are you disappointed, Turk?" Pavle, the youngest soldier, asked. "You finally get a chance to prove you're not a coward and your people run off with their women."

"They're not my people," Niko muttered.

"He can still prove he is not a coward," Drach said. "We will let him kick in the doors."

Niko looked away, holding on as the carrier slowed for a sharp hairpin turn.

"Is there a problem, Turk?" Drach asked. "Would you rather be digging? I can arrange that."

"That's okay, Sergeant."

The carrier sped along the last stretch of road into the town. Niko sat up straight. He had no idea what to expect, despite what he had heard. He'd spoken to other soldiers in Bratunac who'd said conditions bordered on the medieval. They boasted about sneaking into the town to watch videos at the makeshift cinema, but Niko dismissed their claims.

*Who would risk their life to see* Rambo *or* Die Hard?

The carrier moved along the deserted main street, passing soldiers who were searching houses. Niko's heart sank to the bottom of his boots. This was the town he had once called home.

Medieval was a generous description. Shells had damaged every building and rubble covered the sidewalks. Some houses had burned to the ground. Others stood without roofs and shrapnel had left the walls pockmarked. Soot covered everything. All the windows had been smashed and replaced with ragged pieces of plastic. Split firewood was stacked against the first floor windows. There were mountains of rancid garbage between the homes and in open spaces. The smell of raw sewage overpowered the smell of the garbage. Niko raised the bandanna to his mouth.

"How could they live in this?" Petar asked.

Niko didn't have an answer. How had his friends endured three years in this hell? And what about Nina, the old woman who lived next door to them? When he was young, she used to bring him treats whenever she visited her daughter in Tuzla.

*Had she gotten out? Could she have survived all this time on handouts?*

The carrier slowed and Niko's eyes fell on the set of steps where he used to hang around with his friends and smoke.

*Lutvo, Alen, and Mersid. Are they still alive?*

The carrier stopped in the middle of the road and they dismounted.

"We've been given authority to inspect every home," Drach said as the carrier rumbled away. "If we find anyone, they will be taken to the soccer field. Nobody is to be harmed. Understand?"

The group grunted a collective affirmative as they followed him to the first house. They stopped at the front door.

"You first, Turk," Drach said, his smile exposing stained teeth and a chipped front tooth. "Watch out now. Your friends like to leave grenades on top of the door frames."

"Or wire them to the doorknob," Ivan said. He elbowed Pavle, chuckling.

Niko rolled his eyes as he brushed by Ivan. He thought it unlikely that they'd had time to set up booby traps. Word of the air strikes probably had given them false hope, keeping them in their homes. The failure of the planes to stop the advance meant a lot of people had fled the area in a short period of time.

Niko hesitated and eyed the door.

*Yes. They left too fast.*

He reached for the door handle and turned it.

The handle clicked.

Niko's heart skipped.

The door slid open, scrapping the floor.

No wires. No grenades.

He pushed the door against the wall and stepped inside. Piles of wood sat next to the window. Garbage covered the floor. A wooden table sat alone in the middle of the room.

"Good job," Ivan said, patting Niko on the back as he walked in.

The others followed, moving from room to room. Niko sat on the edge of the table and looked around. A well-used fireplace dominated the exterior wall, its mantelpiece covered in candle wax. He glanced at the ceiling: there were only wires and soot where the light fixture had been. Drach, Vladen, and Anton thundered up the stairs. Ivan and Pavle wandered about the main floor. Dishes smashed in the kitchen. Cupboard doors slammed. The ceiling above creaked. Dust settled in the room. Petar waited next to the door, his eyes darting to the ceiling. Something crashed to the floor upstairs.

A voice screamed in delight and boots scuffed the floor. Anton pounded down the stairs and dumped a box of jewelry onto the table.

"Jackpot," he said, sorting through the rings and chains.

"Why would they leave that behind?" Petar asked.

"Cause we scared the crap out of them and they ran like rabbits," Ivan said, removing the cork from a wine bottle. It popped like a gunshot and Ivan inhaled over the opening. "Damned Turks drink crap, too."

"We're out of it," Tarak said.

A high-pitched cracking sound echoed through the hills. Tarak turned around and grabbed Atif.

"Get down!"

They dropped together and Tarak draped an arm over the boy, listening as the shell whooshed overhead and exploded on the far side of the plateau. Tarak turned his head to look back at the growing column of dust.

*Was someone else there?*

Atif's body trembled.

"It's okay," Tarak whispered. "I don't think they're aiming at us. Don't move. We'll wait it out."

A second round split the air above them and then a third. Gunfire reverberated from another hillside. Silent minutes ticked by. Tarak risked sitting up. Dust and smoke lingered among the ridges and ravines they had crossed earlier. He pulled out his binoculars and scanned the impact area. Nothing moved.

*What were they shooting at?*

"Can you run?" he asked Atif, replacing the binoculars.

"Yeah. But won't they see us?"

"We'll be fine. Even if they do see us, it'll take too long for them to adjust their fire."

"Oh. Okay."

Tarak took a last look at the hills. Then he and Atif stood up and sprinted into the forest.

# WEDNESDAY: JAC LARUE

*DAMN, I HATE the heat.*

Jac leaned against the carrier watching the intersection of the Jaglici road. Refugees straggled in from the north. He resisted the urge to ask them if they had seen bodies on the road.

Or a boy.

He rubbed his head in the dry towel and turned to the crowd. Maarten was walking towards him, holding his hand under his flak vest.

"Thanks," Jac said, accepting the bottle of water Maarten produced from under his vest. He drank half and soaked the towel, then poured the rest over his head and down his chest.

"Two more women just died at the clinic," Maarten said. "Heat exhaustion."

Jac glanced at the setting red disk.

"It'll be dark in a couple hours."

"I'm not sure if that's a good thing or a bad thing."

A woman and a man holding a baby against his chest were approaching the carriers. Jac walked up to him.

"They're taking away the men," he told the young father. "I really don't think you're safe here. Do you understand me?"

"Yes, yes," the man said. "But I was never a soldier. I was a mechanic. I have my papers."

"It won't matter," Maarten said.

"I can't leave my family."

"They'll be safe here," Jac said. "There are buses taking the women and children to Tuzla, but they're not letting the men aboard."

"Listen to him, Danko," his wife said. "I said you should go with the men." She took the baby from her husband. After a short conversation, he gathered up what he had and bade farewell to his family. Jac walked him along the same road he had used for Atif.

When he got back, Maarten was arguing with a Serb soldier.

"For the last time," Maarten said, "they're not for sale."

The Serb raised a fistful of Deutsche Marks to Jac's face.

"I want to buy your Uzi. And your flak vest."

Jac laughed.

"Not a chance in hell."

"This too," the Serb said, raising his own rifle. "For your Uzi and flak vest."

"No."

"Cigarettes, too. I have Camels."

Both peacekeepers shook their heads.

"Why not? You don't need weapons. You don't fight."

"And we don't smoke," Maarten said. "Get lost."

The Serb frowned and walked away, stuffing the money into a pocket.

"I really need to eat something," Jac said, moving towards the front steps of the closest house. He dropped his helmet on the bottom step and expelled a long breath.

"You can say that again."

Maarten planted himself on the doorstep and pulled out two ration packs, tossing one to Jac.

"Your favorite. Macaroni and cheese."

Jac didn't bother with a fork. He opened the pouch and lifted it to his mouth.

Children giggled.

Jac glanced up. Two young girls, no more than five or six, smiled in his direction, but they were not smiling at him. They were staring at the food. He waved them over. The girls glanced at their mother for permission and then shuffled to the steps.

"Bonbon?" one asked.

Maarten dug into his pack and tossed another pouch to them.

The girls smiled, at them this time.

"*Hvala*," they said in unison and scurried back to their mother. She nodded at the peacekeepers and then divided the food between the girls. The woman's long dark hair curled around her shoulders, the ends split and ragged. Dirt coated her hands and fingernails. Her clothes were stained and worn.

Jac looked at the children again. His mother had been a child refugee during the Second World War. Her family had escaped the bombings in Rotterdam and then spent weeks moving from town to town until a complete stranger took them in.

*Would they have survived if he hadn't taken them in? I could owe my existence to the kindness of one man.*

Maarten elbowed Jac back into the present.

"Who's that?" Maarten asked, his mouth full. He was stabbing air with his fork to the left.

Jac looked across the ocean of refugees.

*Who is he pointing at?*

"The soldier," Maarten said.

Jac shifted his gaze back to a man he had thought was another peacekeeper walking alone among the refugees. The soldier was wearing a blue helmet, Dutch flak vest, and he was carrying an Uzi, but the camouflage of his uniform was different.

"I don't know who that is."

Jac slipped his helmet on and stood up with Maarten, shielding his eyes from the sun. He watched the soldier join one of the Serb soldiers who dressed like Rambo.

"Jesus, Jac. It's a Serb. Who'd sell him an Uzi? That's insane."

Jac nodded, surveying the rest of the crowd. He'd seen the odd Serb soldier wearing a blue helmet, but no one with all the gear.

"We should let the sergeant know."

Maarten tossed his empty meal pouch away and then they moved into the crowd. As they walked, the women assaulted them with questions in Bosnian. Jac understood the occasional word.

Please. Help. Husband.

*Da li govorite engleski?*

Do you speak English?

Jac felt a tug at his sleeve and glanced down. A little girl pointed and kept tugging.

"Okay. We're coming."

The girl led Jac by his sleeve until they stood over a woman with a belly the size of a basketball. Maarten dropped to her side and gave her his canteen.

"Labour," a woman nearby told them. She said something else Jac couldn't translate and then something he could: "doctor."

"I'll carry her," Maarten said, putting his Uzi on his back.

Through an array of hand signals and single words they understood, Maarten managed to pick the woman off the ground. Jac scooped up the little girl.

"Go to doctor now, okay?"

"Doctor. Okay," she said, kissing Jac on the cheek.

Jac smiled. He walked in front of Maarten, heading towards the medical tent. The same Serb, the one with the Uzi, was walking alone near the zinc factory. Jac slowed down and watched him. The Serb leaned down and pulled an old man to his feet and then pushed him forward. The man leaned on a cane as he shuffled towards the back of the factory ahead of the soldier.

"What's going on?" Maarten asked, adjusting his hold on the woman.

Before Jac could answer, a single shot rang out from behind the factory. The pair of peacekeepers stared at the building. The Serb reappeared, spinning the cane in his hands. He tossed it into the bushes in front of the factory.

"Jesus, Jac," Maarten said. "They really are killing them."

Jac tried to swallow, but his throat stuck. "Let's just get these two to the doctor. We'll talk to the sergeant. Find out what we can do."

They left the woman and her daughter with a physician from Doctors Without Borders.

"I have to go take a look," he told Maarten.

"Shouldn't we tell the sergeant first?"

"Tell him what? We've been hearing shots all afternoon. I want to show him a body to go with them."

"Show Janssen a body? The same Janssen who told us not to provoke these guys?"

Jac could feel the redness flood his face; his heart sounded like a trip hammer inside his head. "We're supposed to protect these people, Maarten."

"And just how do you propose we stop these guys?"

Jac looked at the factory.

"Listen, Jac. I'm with you. I'll go get that body with you, but don't try to convince me anything is going to change. Not when the alternative is artillery falling on twenty-five thousand helpless refugees and the UN too chicken to do anything about it. You told me when we got here to slap you on the head if I thought you were doing something stupid. All I'm saying is consider yourself slapped."

Jac smiled briefly then resumed walking. They picked their way through a dense section of refugees then reached the bushes where they found the cane.

"Hey, Blue Helmet."

The peacekeepers turned around. Three Serbs stood behind them wearing mismatched uniforms. They carried rifles on their shoulders and grenades hung from their webbing. The corporal who had spoken held a pistol in his right hand, pointing it at the ground.

"Your refugees are not back there."

"We have orders to patrol these areas," Jac said.

"No." The Serb shook his head. "Your safe area ends here. The rest belongs to us."

Jac looked at the bushes, gnawing at the inside of his cheek.

"Fine." He turned to leave, but the Serb blocked him. "What now?"

"I like your helmet."

"I like it, too."

Jac started to move away, but this time he was stopped by the Serb's pistol poking into his flak jacket.

"I like the flak vest, too."

Two rifles rose, pointed in their direction.

"In fact, we like your Uzis even more."

Maarten leaned close to Jac.

"So, do we provoke them or co-operate with them? Oh wait...."

Jac held up his hand and waved Maarten quiet.

"Fine," he said, and dropped his helmet on the ground. "Let's see how long you last in combat wearing a blue helmet."

The peacekeepers stripped off their flak jackets, pulled the magazines from the Uzis, and dropped them on the ground. The Serbs picked up everything.

"Thank you. You may go."

They walked past the soldiers and into the crowd.

"We have to pay for all that, Jac."

"I know. I know. Just be thankful."

"For what?"

"That they didn't ask for our uniforms."

Maarten laughed and slapped Jac on the shoulder.

"Can it get any more screwed up?"

"Yeah," Jac replied. "The moment the sergeant notices the missing Uzis, we're screwed."

They headed towards the carriers, which were funneling the refugees towards the buses. They fought their way through the mass of people and exited next to a chain of peacekeepers holding back a wall of refugees. Serbs sat on the road, some on couches and chairs pulled from nearby homes. Four soldiers were playing cards on a dining-room table. Buses were coming into view down the road.

"They get you, too."

Jac turned around. Hans Mesick was standing in front of him without his gear. He suddenly realized that none of the peacekeepers who formed the chain were armed or wearing their vests or helmets.

"Yeah," Jac said. "How's it going here?"

"We had to bring up the carriers to keep them from trampling one another. The Serbs tell us how many they need for each bus and we count them out."

"But doesn't that make it easy for them to separate the men?"

"Well, either kids get trampled to death or the men get taken for questioning. I prefer the choice that keeps people alive."

Jac stared up into Hans's eyes. "You're smarter than that."

Hans looked away. "What would you have me do, Jac? I can't control what happens to them once they're gone, but I can keep them from trampling each other right here, right now."

Maarten brushed up against Jac. "Erik's here," he whispered.

"Erik? Where?"

Maarten gestured towards the sidewalk with a thumb. Jac looked: the gunner was sitting down a few yards away, his arms wrapped around his knees.

"He's been there about an hour," Hans said.

"What's he doing?"

"Not much. Crying mostly."

"And you haven't sent him inside?"

"He won't listen."

"Hey, Blue Helmet," a Serb officer shouted. "Send us fifty."

"Go talk to Erik, if you want," Hans said. He turned away and started counting refugees.

Jac walked towards Erik. The gunner pulled his cap low, swiping his hand across his face. Jac sat down next to him.

"How are you doing, Erik?"

"Fine."

"Hans doesn't think so."

"I don't give a damn what Hans thinks."

"Why don't you come inside with me? See the doctor."

"I'm fine, Jac." Erik's voice was barely audible. "Just leave me alone."

A woman screamed. Jac's head jerked around. He scanned the fast moving crowd: a Serb was pulling an old man away from his wife. She was hanging onto his jacket and wailing like a banshee.

Erik filled Jac's field of vision.

"Leave him alone," the gunner yelled at the Serb.

Jac chased after Erik and grabbed his sleeve. "Leave it."

Erik tore his arm away and put his hand on the old man's shoulder.

"What's the matter with you all?" Erik shouted. "He's an old man. He's not some war criminal."

The soldier glared at Erik as if he were crazy then turned around and shrugged at the other soldiers. A Serb corporal came up behind him.

"What's going on here?"

Erik planted himself between the corporal and the old couple.

"He's an old man. He's no threat to you. You're no better than the Nazis. No, you're worse than the Nazis. Most of them didn't know better. You do."

"Don't call me a Nazi!" The corporal's nostrils flared. "My family fought the Nazis."

"And how is this any different? You Nazis are killing innocent people. You're tearing a husband away from his wife, for God's sake. He's old. He's no threat to you." Erik cocked his head and glared at the Serb. "Or is he?"

Jac grabbed Erik, but the gunner wrestled free and faced the Serb.

"Go back home, Blue Helmet. You don't belong here."

"Why are you so afraid of old men? Tell me. Is your army that bad that you have to murder old men who can barely walk?"

Maarten appeared and he and Jac took Erik by the arms and hauled him back.

"Get away from him, Erik."

"Why aren't you stopping him, Jac? You know they're killing the men, don't you? They're going to kill them all."

"Shut up," Jac said, shaking Erik. He nodded towards the crowd. "They can hear you."

"Maybe they should listen."

"Go back inside," Jac said, his outstretched finger pointing towards the camp. "And stay there before you get yourself or someone else killed."

"What about the old man?" Erik screamed, walking backwards in Maarten's grip. Tears rolled down his cheeks. "Why can't we help them, Jac?"

"I'll take care of it." Jac said. "Get inside."

Erik turned around and punched the air.

"I want him to apologize," the Serb told Jac. "Or they go nowhere."

"Look. He's just an old man."

"Why do you care? They're Muslims. If they're permitted to stay and fight then they will force Islam on all of us the way they did when the Turks were here. You see, you get to go home and forget about us. We live here. They are our problem. Not yours. This is our turn for revenge. For Kosovo. Now go get your friend. You make him apologize or the buses don't move."

"Look. I'm sorry about what he said. You have to understand that he is not handling this well. He's Jewish. His father lost his entire family to the Germans."

"That was fifty years ago. Why does he care?"

Jac leaned closer to the corporal. "Kosovo was seven hundred years ago. Why do you care?"

The Serb stared at Jac then stepped back and laughed.

"I like you, Blue Helmet," he said, pointing to Jac's head. "You're smart."

Jac smiled briefly and then eyed the old man.

The Serb followed his gaze. He waved at the old man, who stood up, brushed the dust from his pants, and joined his wife. They shuffled off towards the buses.

"Now, do me a favour, Blue Helmet. Go away and mind your own business."

Jac turned his back on the Serb and walked away.

*If only we could all do that.*

# WEDNESDAY: NIKO BASARIC

NIKO LEANED AGAINST a tree, playing with a cigarette. He stopped and stared at it. The last time he smoked a cigarette was the day Natalija told him she was pregnant. He looked up the road towards Bratunac.

*She must be going out of her mind.*

There'd been rumours about a celebration at the Hotel Fontana in Bratunac.

*Maybe I'll get a chance to see them tonight.*

He crushed the cigarette in his fist, tossed it away, and turned back to the small group of men he had been tasked to guard. Four men, all of them in their sixties or older, sat huddled together. Petar was pacing in front of them.

Buses arrived and a corporal shouted for fifty refugees. Niko pulled his helmet low as soldiers dragged men away from their wives and mothers and added them to his group. An argument broke out on the other side of the street. Niko straightened up, straining to hear the words being exchanged between the corporal and the peacekeepers.

"What are they saying?" he asked Petar.

The recruit shrugged and went to investigate. Niko listened to the sound of arguing and then saw a peacekeeper escorting a comrade inside the compound. Petar came back.

"So?"

"The peacekeeper called the corporal a Nazi. Can you believe it?" Petar glanced back and then stepped next to Niko. "The peacekeeper said we were killing all the men. Is that true?"

Niko's eyes dropped to the men sitting in front of them. They looked at him, wide-eyed. Jaws trembled.

"I don't know what to believe, Petar. The officer said they were being taken to Bratunac to be questioned. Why would he lie?"

"Would you be so calm if he said you were being taken to be killed?"

"I don't know what's going on, Petar. I really don't."

"You said they were trying people for war crimes. Isn't killing civilians a war crime?"

"Yes."

"Then they could go after us for this, couldn't they?"

Niko stepped away from the men, pulling Petar along with him.

"We don't know what they're doing," he said, keeping his voice low. "Even if they are, what can we do? Refuse? Drop our rifles and run? They'd shoot us."

"But you said following orders wasn't an excuse."

"I don't know that I'm following an illegal order. I really don't. Until that happens, I can't do anything about it. So stop worrying about it. Besides, there are thousands of men. They can't be stupid enough to think they can kill them all and get away with it. Just keep your safety on and if one of them runs, let him go. Let someone else shoot them and take the blame."

"Basaric?" the corporal called out. "Is that your name? Basaric?"

"That's me."

The corporal pointed to the men on the ground and then at the white house directly behind the group.

"Take those men into the house."

Niko turned away from the corporal and, with a slight motion of his rifle, told the men to stand and follow Petar. Niko brought up the rear. They moved through the front yard. Piles of discarded bags and clothes smothered rows of half-picked carrots. A white rosebush next to the steps was in bloom, the breeze carrying the fragrance to his nose. Niko paused to pull in a deep breath.

Inside, two soldiers took the men aside and searched them. They took money from one man and a ring from another then tossed everything else, including their identification documents, into a pile on the floor.

"Don't you need them?" Niko asked, indicating the discarded identification. "Aren't you supposed to compare their names to a list, to see if they're war criminals?"

The soldier ignored Niko. He pocketed the money.

"Take them upstairs."

Niko left Petar with the soldiers and climbed the stairs, the old men following him. The planks creaked under their weight. Niko stopped next to the first room and looked inside. Elderly men sat against the far wall. They stared at Niko.

"I'm sorry," he whispered to one of the old men he had led up the stairs. "It's this goddamned war. I wish it was over."

The man raised his eyes and placed a hand on Niko's shoulder. He left it there for a moment and then stepped inside the room. The others followed.

Niko walked back down to the main floor, his boots giving each step a sharp blow.

*Goddamn it. These people were my neighbours.*

He and Petar returned to their post near the Dutch vehicles.

*This fucking war.*

Some of the soldiers were taunting the refugees. He looked away, staring instead at the crushed cigarette on the ground, thankful he had bummed only one. Leaning against a tree, he watched the peacekeepers count out the next fifty refugees. Niko glimpsed a tall man about to pass through the Dutch line. He took a step forward, concentrating on the man's face.

*I know him.* He stepped up on the curb to get a better view. *Yes!*

He picked up a discarded blanket and waded into the crowd.

"Where are you going?"

"Stay there."

As he got close to the Dutch line, Niko spotted the man again. He had one arm around a woman and the other around a teenage girl. Niko walked up to the man and pushed his helmet back.

"Mr. Munic?"

They looked at him with the same expression he had seen in the house only minutes before.

"Do I know you?"

"You were a teacher here. Mathematics."

"Yes," the man replied, his eyes darting left and right.

"I was one of your students about eight years ago. My name is Niko. Niko Basaric."

The man was smiling before Niko had finished. "Yes, yes. You were a good student. I had hoped you would become an engineer."

"I thought about it. I still do." Niko looked at the Dutch line and the thinning crowd. He raised the blanket and put it over Munic's head. "Keep this on. Get on the bus and don't take it off."

Munic hesitated for an instant and then pulled the blanket around his face, obscuring as much of it as he could.

"Stay in the middle of the crowd. Go. Quickly."

Tears welled up in Munic's eyes and his wife reached up to kiss Niko.

"No, please. Go. There are only a few people behind you. Stay in the crowd."

Munic pulled his wife and daughter closer and stooped over.

As he walked away, the former teacher looked like an old woman. Niko followed them at a distance. The family passed through the gauntlet unmolested and boarded the last bus. He stepped back as the buses turned, trying to catch a glimpse of the family, but they were buried deep in the back of the overloaded vehicle. At the last moment, a woman near the front of the bus caught Niko's eye. She stood and waved at him. Niko stepped close to the reversing vehicle.

*Nina!*

She stopped waving and put up both thumbs. He smiled broadly and raised his hand to wave.

"What are you doing, Basaric?"

Niko dropped his hand and turned around. Drach, with Petar and the others, walked up behind him.

"Nothing, Sergeant."

"That's what it looks like." Drach pointed to a truck on the side of the road. "Get in. We have another job to do."

# WEDNESDAY: TARAK SMAJLOVIC

TARAK TOOK A long swig of water and then surveyed the area. Compared to the blinding sunlight in the open field, the forest was pitch black except for the lengthening slats of sunlight among the trees.

"Drink up. There's a river ahead."

Atif, breathing hard, nodded and spit out the water he had swished in his mouth.

"Do you think they're much farther ahead?"

"I'm surprised we didn't meet up with them at the minefield." Tarak stood up and jerked a thumb northwards. "I'm guessing they're probably at Kamenica by now."

"Is that good?"

"Encouraging. They're making good time. If the rear of the column is in Kamenica then the front should be close to the road. That means they can open up a corridor for the rest of us and we can all cross before dawn."

Tarak resisted adding a caveat. If the front of the column was unable to gain control of the road, the rest of them would be trapped between two roads from which the Serb army could flank them.

"Caught your breath?"

Atif drank the last of his water and stood up.

"I'm ready."

"Okay. Stick close to me. It's only going to get darker."

Atif's eyes shifted left then right.

"What?"

Atif grinned. "When I was little, I stayed in the woods behind our farm until it got dark one day, so my father told me about the *blautsauger*."

Tarak laughed. "Do you still believe the stories?"

Atif shrugged, his eyes fixed on the woods. Tarak shook his head and turned north.

*The blautsauger is going to be the least of our problems.*

"You mentioned a farm. You're not originally from Srebrenica?"

"No. We had a farm not far from here. Closer to the Drina. My father farmed in the summer. Mostly corn, but he grew enough potatoes, carrots, and onions for us. In the winter, he would set up his workshop in the barn and build furniture. He was beginning to get orders from all over Yugoslavia when the war broke out."

"What kind of furniture?"

"Anything, really. Mostly tables, chairs, and beds. He was planning to build an extension onto the barn for a permanent workshop when the war broke out. He hated having to pack it all up for the summer."

"What about your mother?"

"She's a teacher. She learned English, French, and German growing up, so she teaches languages. Mostly in the higher grades."

"Do you speak those languages?"

"Yes. And some Dutch now."

"Is that what you want to do? Teach languages like your mother?"

"No. I'm going to be a soldier."

Tarak stopped and stared at the boy.

"Why? With those language skills, you could emigrate anywhere in the world. Germany, France, England, Canada. Any one of them would take your family in a heartbeat."

"I don't want to go. I want to fight."

"Another soldier isn't going to make a difference."

Atif evaded his gaze.

*What's going through your mind, Braco?*

They resumed walking, following the trampled path through dense woods and over even terrain until they came to a creek. They stopped and refilled their bottles.

"Do you hear that?" Atif asked, facing north.

Tarak stepped away from the gurgling creek and listened.

"My hearing is shot," he said. "What do you think you heard?"

"I'm not sure." Atif took a few steps. "Voices. I think."

Tarak could hear nothing. "I guess they can't be far away."

"I hear them again."

Tarak waved Atif down and raised a finger to his lips. Atif nodded. Tree branches swayed. Insects chirped. Gunshots echoed far away. In between these noises, there was a low grumbling that changed pitch.

Two voices. In the trees.

Tarak held out his hand, gesturing to Atif to stay. Then he raised his rifle and moved forward a few yards, planting each foot so that it didn't disturb the vegetation. The voices became clearer. There were men to his left behind some bushes. Tarak used the rifle to push bushes aside. Two men were kneeling on the ground, their backs to Tarak. He leaned forward.

*Are they picking mushrooms?*

"*Zdravo*, gentlemen."

The pair jumped up and turned around. One man held his hand to his chest.

"Young man," he said. "You should think twice before scaring the wits out of your elders."

"My apologies," Tarak said, unable to stop smiling. "We're late. Are the rest far ahead?"

"Not far," the man said. "They've stopped to rest on the meadow near Kamenica."

Tarak's smile faded.

"On the meadow?"

"Yes. They want to wait until it gets dark before moving on. They haven't stopped all day. We saw these mushrooms earlier and decided to come back."

"Do you know where the officers are?"

"Not sure." The man glanced at his friend, who shrugged. "I saw some soldiers together on the far side of the meadow. Why? Is there a problem?"

The glint on the hill.

"Is everyone sitting in the open?"

The men nodded.

"They're exposed," Tarak said. "You two should stay here until after dark."

The men protested, but Tarak didn't have time to argue. He waved Atif forward.

"We have to hurry." Tarak broke into a trot and the boy followed suit.

"I don't understand. What's the problem?"

"The glint I saw on the hill. It might have been artillery or an anti-aircraft gun. The men are resting in a meadow directly across from it."

"But wouldn't they see it?"

Tarak slowed down and then stopped. He faced Atif.

"Not necessarily. I may have had a better angle back there. Okay, now listen. If they shell the meadow and we get separated, I need you to get to the bottom of the hill on the far side as fast as you can. Stop for no one. There's a river there. Cross it and wait for me. If I don't find you within thirty minutes, keep moving north."

"You're not leaving...."

"No, *Braco*. Please, stay close."

He took Atif's hand and they jogged towards the meadow.

*What are they thinking? Sitting exposed knowing the enemy is so close. Insane!*

With the majority of soldiers at the front of the column, the civilians at the rear likely overruled the few soldiers with them and stopped to rest. But if they didn't listen, they risked being left behind. The column was at least three kilometres long. The Serbs need only cut the column in half to separate the soldiers from the bulk of the defenceless civilians.

A crack echoed in the distance.

*Damn it! I'm too late.*

A second crack followed. Tarak stopped, yanking Atif backwards.

"We need to find cover."

He picked the boy up and carried him behind a clump of trees. They dove as the artillery plowed into the meadow ahead of them. Tarak pinned Atif to the ground and then pulled off his pack and covered the boy's head with it. Machine gun fire followed artillery shells.

The ground thundered. The air vibrated. Men screamed. Machine gun rounds split the air above them, cracking tree limbs. Branches fell. Tarak felt Atif stir beneath him.

"Don't move, *Braco*. We have to wait until dark. They won't stop until then."

Atif relaxed, but his muscles tensed every time a shell exploded. "It's okay," he said. "We're safe here."

*For now.*

Tarak imagined the scene ahead. Hundreds of men spread out on the hillside like sheep. With so many targets, he knew it wasn't a matter of aiming but a matter of how fast the Serbs could reload their guns. Dozens had likely died in the first few seconds. Dozens, if not hundreds, would be wounded and would have to be carried.

And they would be cut off from the front half of the column.

Tarak laid his head on his arm and watched the light fade.

# WEDNESDAY: ATIF STAVIC

FOR MORE THAN an hour the ground shook and the air screeched. Atif breathed in dust and cordite. He covered his ears. His teeth chattered and his heart pounded.

"Please stop," he whispered to himself over and over. He felt as though he was suffocating.

"Count them," his father had said.

Atif looked up into his father's eyes. They were huddled together in the corner of a church, sheltered from the worst barrage they had experienced since arriving in Srebrenica. The pews and the altar were gone, burned for heat. As a round threw shrapnel against the side of the church, Atif buried his head into his father's chest, trembling.

"Count them, Atif. And write it down when you get home."

"What? Why?"

"Someone needs to keep records. The information may be important someday. When the shelling is over, we'll find out if anyone was hurt and keep an account of that, too. Okay?"

Atif nodded eagerly and waited for the next rumble.

"One."

"What do you mean one?" Tarak said next to his ear. "You were somewhere around fifty-four."

Atif blinked and flipped the dirt from his eyes with a free finger.

"Was I?"

Another round slammed into the earth.

"Fifty-six."

As darkness encroached, the attack slowed; one-sided machine gun fire punctuated the night more often than shells. Tarak shifted his weight and sat up, keeping low. Atif rolled to his side and came up against a fallen tree trunk. He took the long-sleeved green shirt from his pack and pulled it on. Tarak picked up his rifle, dusted off the barrel, and set to work taking it apart. He placed the parts on his legs after wiping them with a rag.

"Salko would have my head if he saw this go muzzle first into the ground."

"How many rounds do you have?"

Tarak tapped the magazine on his lap. "That's it. Since I wasn't going up front, they took everything I had." He pulled a piece of cloth through the barrel several times. "So, why were you counting the impacts?"

"My father told me to."

Atif reached into his pack and poked around until he felt the hard cover of the journal wrapped in plastic. He pulled it out.

"I wrote it all down. The date of each attack, the number of impacts from the artillery and from the airplanes that used to fly over. Then after the attacks I would ask around to find out who was hurt and record their names."

Atif passed the book to Tarak. He examined a page in the moonlight.

"This is really detailed. Good way to keep occupied."

"I think that's why Tata got me started, but after I spoke to some journalists I decided it was important. One guy who was taking pictures said that nobody believed we were being attacked; nobody believed we were starving. He said the Chetniks told everyone they only attacked soldiers. He said he could tell them the truth."

"Not easy to do if no one is listening."

"I guess so."

Atif wrapped the book and stuffed it under the bottles. Machine gun fire strafed the meadow. Atif peered over the dead tree.

"So, what do we do now?"

"I'd like to wait, but the front of the column will be crossing the road soon. They won't be able to hold it open for long."

"Do we have to go through the meadow?"

"Yes," Tarak said, reassembling the rifle. "Like I said, it's a steep hill with a river down below. Once we get there, we should be fine for a while. The woods are pretty thick there."

"What if they start shelling again?"

"Then drop and don't move."

Voices echoed in the distance; some talking, some shouting. Others shrieked in pain.

"It seems to have died down. Are you ready?"

Atif nodded, but his legs refused to budge.

"Can we wait? Just a couple of minutes?"

"Yeah, sure, *Braco*. Are you okay?"

"My legs are asleep. And. And I just...."

"It'll be all right. I've been through much worse. All you have to do is follow my instructions. The stuff I've told you really works."

"I believe you," Atif said, massaging his calves. "What's it like?"

"What's what like?"

"Living in peace."

"What do you mean?"

"I don't know." He slapped his legs. "I was eleven when the war started. I can't remember what it was like before. I get flashes of stuff like going to the hospital when my little sister was born. I remember walking through the parking lot, in the open. I remember not being afraid. And then it all changed: every time I stepped out into the street, I wondered if a sniper was waiting for me. There could have been crosshairs on my head and I would never know."

"Well, just wait until you get to Tuzla. Imagine going to the market and finding tables piled high with fruit, vegetables, videos, CDs, and clothes. Imagine buying whatever you want. Then taking it home and sitting down to a big meal in the backyard on a hot summer afternoon."

"You know what you said, about going away?"

"Yeah."

"My mother said if we got out of Srebrenica, we would go far away and never come back."

"But you want to stay so you can fight when you're old enough."

*I'm not sure what I want anymore.*

"I'm ready to go," Atif said, wincing from the wave of pins and needles in his shins.

Tarak helped Atif to his feet.

"Follow my lead and stay quiet. Voices can travel in these hills."

"Okay."

With the rising moon directly behind them, they walked to the treeline. The moon lit the meadow brightly enough that they could see figures moving between the shadows. They crouched, watching. Voices in pain drifted over the meadow. Ghostly figures moved among the bushes and trees. Some were single men, others were pairs carrying bodies between them. All headed down the hill. There was no response from the Serbs.

"Chetniks may have packed it in for the night," Tarak whispered, moving forward.

Atif followed. They quickened their pace and crossed the meadow, picking up speed as they descended. Atif heard voices, groans, and screaming to his left and right. He caught glimpses of bodies in the grass. Some still, others moving. When he turned his head to look at one, he tripped over another, slamming into the dirt face first.

A hand grabbed his foot.

Atif rolled to his back.

A face looked at him through the grass.

"Tata?"

Atif blinked.

The face, young now, screamed, "Help me!"

Atif tried to jerk his ankle free from the iron-clad grip. "I'm just a boy," he said, kicking at the hand with his free leg. "Just a boy."

Tarak appeared and wrenched the man's hand away from Atif's ankle. He grabbed a strap on Atif's pack, pulled him to his feet, and pushed him forward.

"Don't go!" the man screamed. "Please. I beg you."

They sprinted away, hurdling over several bodies. Atif heard his feet strike water and tripped again, submerging himself up to the neck. Tarak dragged him out. The moment his feet struck dry ground, Atif started to run. Machine gun fire strafed the hillside behind them.

"We're almost there," Tarak said, panting hard. "Almost there."

The machine gun rounds punched the air above them but didn't move down the slope.

"They can't see us down here, can they?" Atif asked.

"Just keep going."

They scrambled farther into the forest. Tarak changed direction and guided Atif to a rock. They collapsed behind it.

"You did well," Tarak said, breathing in short gasps.

Atif gulped the air and shivered in his wet clothes. "There're wounded men up there. Shouldn't someone be trying to help them?"

"Nothing we can do for them. We have to get to the road tonight and we can't do it dragging them along."

Figures moved through the woods. Men rested nearby, others kept walking. Some carried makeshift stretchers between them. Atif remembered his father speaking to his mother after a group he had led to Kravica was ambushed.

"Out there," his father had said, "it's the law of the jungle. When the Chetniks attacked, it was every man for himself."

"Every man for himself."

"Yeah," Tarak replied. "Something like that. And if I get that badly hurt, you'll do the same for me."

"What? No."

"If you get hurt, I can carry you. You can't carry me and no one is going to help you. And I won't let you try."

He reached inside his shirt. Atif heard Velcro separating and Tarak pulled out a laminated identification card.

"This is my old Yugoslav Army ID. They can identify me with this. If anything happens, I want you to take this and tell the army where I am when you get to Tuzla."

"I don't know." Atif struggled with the notion that Tarak might get hurt. "Promise me, *Braco*. I have no family left. I need the army to know."

Tarak replaced the card.

"Promise?"

Atif stared at him, biting his lip. Tarak gave him an encouraging smile.

"Okay. I promise. But you're not going to get hurt."

Tarak patted Atif on the shoulder and shifted the rifle. He rose to one knee and looked around before standing.

"We have a long way to go to catch up with the rest of the men. They're not going to be able to keep the road open for long."

Atif stood, still sucking in air.

"Okay. Let's go."

# WEDNESDAY: NIKO BASARIC

NIKO SAT ON the edge of a stolen Dutch armoured personnel carrier watching flashes of white and red illuminate the southern sky. He glanced at his watch. Artillery and mortar had been falling for more than an hour. Heavy machine gun fire erupted between the shells. He dropped from the carrier and walked along the edge of the road. Petar sat on a guardrail, facing south.

"How can anyone survive that?" the recruit asked.

"You'd be amazed."

*It will barely make a dent in the thousands walking this way.*

After their section left Potocari, Drach had dropped them in Bratunac to eat. Afterwards, an officer told them they were needed to patrol the road to prevent the men from crossing. The officer suggested up to thirty thousand men were in the woods. The figure surprised Niko; he wondered if the officer had exaggerated the number to get more men and weapons.

"Did you get a chance to call your wife?"

"Phone wasn't working."

Niko never got a chance to try a second phone call before they were loaded into the carrier and driven to this dark stretch of road. The driver told them they were not far from Konjevic Polje.

They were sitting on the edge of the road near the lone carrier, waiting to face what might be thousands of Bosnian soldiers.

Niko shivered in the warm evening air.

"Are they sure they're coming this way?" Petar asked. "I mean, Zepa is so much closer."

"You should be happy they're not going that way. I'd rather fight them here than in those hills."

"I heard someone say Zepa had fallen. Said it was on the radio."

"But it hasn't fallen."

"I guess they don't know that."

Niko heard a sound to his right. He spun around, scanning the pitch black road. A shadow floated across the road.

And another.

"There's someone here," he whispered to Petar. "Stand up. Quietly."

"What is it?"

Niko walked backwards, pulling Petar with him.

A voice erupted from the woods. "Hey, Chetniks!"

In one swift motion, Niko and Petar dropped to the ground and raised their rifles.

"Who is that?" Petar shouted.

Niko slapped the recruit on the shoulder and raised a finger to his mouth.

The voice spoke again. "The entire army of Bosnia and Herzegovina. That's who. Ten thousand armed men are going to cross that road. I suggest you leave."

Behind them, the carrier roared to life.

"Go. Go." Niko grabbed Petar by the collar and pulled him towards the armoured vehicle, expecting to feel a rifle round penetrate his back any second. They turned the corner and dove inside the carrier. Niko pulled the hatch closed.

"We're in. Go. Go. Go!"

Moments after the carrier left the area, thousands of men poured across the road and melted into the forest on the other side.

No one stayed behind.

# WEDNESDAY: MICHAEL SAKIC

MIKE LOITERED NEAR the edge of the tent city. Peacekeepers were stringing wires between the tents and others were passing out lanterns to the refugees. A truck pulled up and off-loaded poles and canvas next to a group of women waiting for shelter. Local Bosnian soldiers had shown up a few hours earlier and they were moving among the tents, carrying food and stretchers. Men stood around in small groups, chatting and smoking. The hills in the distance were dark and silent.

"Michael?"

He turned to see Jure walking towards him. Mike pulled out a pack of Player's and tossed them to the lanky translator. Jure's face broke into a broad smile.

"Oh, you are a god."

Mike motioned to the tents. "What's on the go?"

"Buses are done for the night." Jure opened the pack of cigarettes and tucked one between his lips. "There are still people trickling in from Tisca, but the Chetniks have stopped dropping them off. We expect just as many will be transported tomorrow. They should have plenty to tell you."

"I don't think I need to hear the same story any more. Anything new from upstairs?"

Jure lit the cigarette and inhaled.

"Serb radio announced their glorious liberation of Srebrenica."

He rolled his eyes. "Said the population was free to stay or go and that they would all be treated in accordance with the Geneva Convention."

"I hear the Geneva Convention fits on a toilet roll very well around here."

The translator coughed, sending a mouthful of smoke out into the air. "And it comes in triple-ply."

Mike smiled. "What about the men?"

"They haven't heard anything certain." Jure took another long draw, deep into his lungs this time, savouring the smoke before blowing it through his nose. "The Americans are saying nothing. The Dutch are not saying much. The French are pushing for a rapid reaction force to retake the enclave. The rest, I don't know. These guys aren't privy to what's going on behind closed doors right now, but frankly, if they haven't done anything by now, I don't expect anything. It's simply too late."

"And Zepa?"

"The Chetniks are calling on them to surrender."

"So it hasn't fallen?"

"Not yet."

"Just a matter of time."

"I imagine the men there are already heading for the hills."

Mike grunted an affirmative.

"That's what I wanted to ask you about."

"Shoot."

"I need to get into the enclave."

Jure choked again, spitting more smoke. "And I want a Ferrari for my birthday." He held the pack of cigarettes up. "I do have a birthday coming up."

"Seriously, Jure."

"Who said I wasn't being serious? The enclave is cut off. Oric is pleading with the army to bring up troops to distract the Chetniks so the men can have a chance to break through. It's a bloody war zone. And I mean bloody. As in the red stuff you can't live without."

Mike chewed on his lower lip. Naser Oric was the commander of the Bosnian forces in Srebrenica. He had left the enclave in April and hadn't been able to risk a return by air after one of their helicopters was shot down.

"You don't know anyone who could get me close?"

"What do you expect to see?"

"Jure, they're going to kill those men and quietly bury them somewhere. Unless there's proof, the Serbs will say the men were killed in combat or that they just left the country. Most of them are civilians, for God's sake."

"You honestly think you can get close enough to see that?"

"Won't know if I don't try."

"You're a stubborn son of a bitch."

"Does that mean you can help me?"

"I don't know. Maybe I can get you close to Kladanj. The blue helmets are picking up the refugees there. Doubt you'll see much from there, though."

"Nothing better?"

Jure blew out the last of the smoke from the cigarette and squashed it under his sneaker.

"I know someone but he's away right now. I expect him back before the end of the month."

"Three weeks?"

"I doubt the corpses will rot by then. Besides, the Chetniks might want you to come visit their newly liberated town in a few days. It'll be an escorted tour but better than nothing."

Mike sighed and pulled out another pack of Player's.

"See what you can do about something a little less escorted."

He tossed the cigarettes to Jure.

"Ah, I foresee a happy birthday already."

Mike slapped Jure on the shoulder. The translator walked towards the gate, showing off the cigarettes to the peacekeepers as he went.

# THURSDAY: JAC LARUE

JAC CROUCHED NEXT to Marija, waiting for Maarten to return from the compound. He glanced under the bus where the three girls were sleeping. Marija and Ina sat in front of them. The moon lit their features.

"How are they doing?"

"Good," Ina replied. "Lejla's rash is already breaking out."

"I was talking to one of our guys a couple of hours ago. He said all the buses made it through to Tisca. But the Serbs searched the buses and took some men off."

Marija's hand went to her mouth.

"We're not sure yet, but there's word some nurses are missing too."

Ina laid a hand on Jac's arm. "What about the girls? Will they be okay?"

"I won't lie to you," Jac said. "God knows you've heard enough lies already. I think what you're doing is good. My sergeant said we're going to escort one of the convoys in the morning. If you can, find a spot close to the carriers when the buses arrive and we'll try to hook up for the same convoy."

"Thank you," Ina said.

Jac turned to Marija.

"You did the right thing."

"I know," she replied, motioning to the other end of the bus. "They've taken all the men from here. Some to the houses, others to the abattoir."

Jac's eyes followed Marija's outstretched arm. He'd heard screams earlier in the evening but couldn't pinpoint their location.

"Do you have a knife?" Ina asked.

"A knife. For what?"

"We want to cut the girl's hair in the morning."

Jac patted his pocket without thinking. "I don't have mine anymore."

A pocket knife appeared next to him.

"They can have mine," Maarten said.

Ina took the knife and thanked them.

"We'll check back." Jac stood up and glanced around. "If any of the Serbs give you a hard time, just shout out my name as loudly as you can. We shouldn't be far away."

"You know," Marija said, "it's getting hard to tell you apart from the Chetniks. Some of them are wearing exactly what you are."

"Well, none of us out here are carrying weapons anymore," Maarten said.

"We'll be back," Jac said.

As they left the wrecked buses, Maarten handed Jac a thermos.

"Just something to keep you warm," he said. "But I warn you, it's a little strong."

Jac poured himself a cup of coffee, wondering if he was ever going to get his second wind. He took a mouthful and choked.

"Jesus, Maarten. Did you put any water in with the coffee?"

"You'll thank me in about an hour."

"I'll probably be flying to the moon in about an hour."

Gunshots echoed from the hills. The pair stopped and looked north. Single shots and bursts of machine gun fire, which were not returned. Dogs barked.

The Serbs know the men are in the woods, Jac thought, glancing at his watch. Surely, Atif's with the men by now.

He finished the coffee and dropped the thermos into his pack, then checked his flashlight.

"This is going to be a long night."

*Where to start?* Jac's eyes rested on the zinc factory. *There.*

When he started for the factory, Maarten tugged on his arm.

"Where do you think we're going?"

"I have to look," Jac said.

"You're kidding, right? Losing the Uzi and our gear was not enough for you? Jesus, Jac, they really are stealing uniforms now. I don't exactly want to walk back into the compound in my underwear."

Jac shook off Maarten's hand and kept walking. As dusk approached, the number of soldiers had declined. Many had returned to Bratunac to celebrate. Others were celebrating in nearby houses.

When they got to the perimeter, Jac talked with the two peacekeepers posted there and then moved around the factory, Maarten at his heels.

"Wait here. I'll just take a quick look."

Maarten stopped and Jac made his way around the back of the factory by moonlight. Then he switched on his flashlight and scanned the ground.

Nothing.

*Had they taken the body so quickly?*

Earlier, Maarten had pointed out a van to him, which had been making trips to the area. Blacked out windows made it impossible to tell what the van carried. One of the refugees told them she had seen a line of men walking through the field towards some trucks. Jac wasn't sure if she was telling the truth. He'd asked around and none of the other peacekeepers could corroborate her story.

*As if that means anything. We're watching the refugees, not the fields around us.*

Jac returned to Maarten.

"Nothing there."

"Maybe they dragged the body farther away, knowing we like to risk our lives, not to mention life-long embarrassment from walking around in our underwear."

Jac turned around, facing the field stretching out behind the factory. Maarten moved closer to him.

"Keep looking out there and I will slap you."

"I'm not quite that stupid," Jac said. They turned around and headed back to the refugees and returned to patrolling the perimeter. They checked on the two-man teams stationed at intervals too far apart to keep the Serbs out. A man shrieked in the distance. Jac stopped. Marija was right. The sounds were coming from the abattoir.

The man shrieked again, the scream forming a word this time.

"What is he saying?" Jac asked.

"Sounds like 'Sanja.' I think that's a woman's name."

Jac stared into the darkness as the man's voice repeated the name over and over. He willed himself to move closer, but his second step brought him up against the tape.

"Damn it."

"C'mon Jac. We should check on the other teams."

Jac turned away, following Maarten. They walked the perimeter, returning to the zinc factory. There, they were bombarded by questions from the women in Bosnian, English, Dutch, German, and French.

"Where is my husband?"

"What are they doing to the men?"

"When can I see my son?"

"Have you seen my brother?"

"Where did the buses go?"

"Are they going to kill us?"

They answered what they could understand.

The next pair of sentries was on duty at the far end of the factory. Karel sat against the building, asleep, while Bram sat a few feet away from him. Jac tapped Karel with his foot.

"Get up!"

Karel stirred; Maarten leaned down, grabbed him by the collar, and pulled him to his feet.

"He said to get up."

"Get your hands off me," Karel said, pushing Maarten. "Sergeant said we could take a break as long as one of us stayed awake."

Jac turned to Bram.

"How long has he been on break?"

"About twenty minutes," the tank driver said. He was on his feet now, kicking pebbles.

Jac turned to Karel.

"Break is over."

Someone tugged on Jac's sleeve and he wheeled around.

"What?" he shouted, but the air in front of him was empty. He looked down: a young woman was sitting at his feet with a sleeping baby in her lap. She stared up at him. Jac raised his hands and produced a smile. "It's all right. It's all right. Did you want something?"

The woman pointed at the factory.

"What is it?"

The woman whispered in her language.

"I don't understand."

She glanced at the factory and then wrapped her scarf around her neck like a noose. She pointed at the building.

"Damn it," Jac said under his breath. "Come on, Maarten."

They stepped over people and walked through a doorway, the metal door wrenched off its hinges and lying on the floor. The stench assaulted them as soon as they were inside. Urine, feces, and vomit had been simmering in the heat all day. Jac pulled his towel up over his mouth and took a few steps. He played his flashlight over the interior. People scattered or turned their heads away. Women covered their daughters.

"They think we're Serbs," Maarten said.

Jac let the towel drop from his face and tried not to retch.

"It's okay," he said, mustering the strongest Dutch accent possible.

A woman pointed towards the staircase. Maarten led the way, stepping carefully. He started to climb the stairs and then stopped.

"Jesus, Jac. Under the stairs. There's something tied here"

Jac froze and stared. Maarten tugged on a piece of fabric tied to an open tread.

"Jac?" Maarten tapped his shoulder. "Go back down."

Jac took a long breath and then nodded. He went back down the stairs and climbed over a family huddled at the base. His flashlight illuminated a wooden door that accessed the area under the stairs.

Maarten's voice came from behind him.

"I'll get it." He grabbed the door with both hands and pulled it aside, scraping the floor. One hinge fell off.

Jac stepped forward and raised the flashlight. A boy, no more than fifteen, hung from one of the steps. Eyes as blue as his face stared straight ahead. Smurfs decorated the sheet around his neck.

"Goddamn it." Jac reached for his pocketknife. "I don't have a knife to cut him down."

"I'll hold him up," Maarten said. "You can untie him from above."

"Okay."

A woman's scream stabbed through the darkness, sending goose bumps down Jac's back.

"Where's it coming from?" he said, stepping in front of Maarten.

The next scream echoed inside the metal frame of the factory.

"Jesus, Jac. What's happening here?"

Jac raised his flashlight, scanning the crowd until it settled on the back corner.

"There's an office there."

People leaned away as the peacekeepers threaded their way through the crowd.

Another shriek.

*I can't go any faster, damn it!*

The office door was closed, but the large window frame next to it was empty, except for some jagged shards of glass. There was movement inside. Jac shone the light on the door. Maarten touched his shoulder and then Jac drove his foot against the doorknob.

The door swung open, struck the wall, and bounced back at Jac's face. He raised his hand in time to catch it and flung it back. A man wearing a Dutch flak vest passed through the doorway, knocking him back.

"Hey," Maarten's voice said.

Jac ignored the man and stepped inside. There were two men there, both wearing camouflage uniforms. One man's pants were around his ankles. Before Jac could react, the man grabbed his pants, pulled them up, and shoved past Jac. The second followed his friend.

"Forget them," Jac said to Maarten. He raised his flashlight; a young girl was struggling to pull her skirt down. The flashlight lit up the girl's nakedness. Her long curly hair partly obscuring her breasts. Her blouse lay in shreds beside her on the floor

*My God, she's beautiful.*

"Damn it," Jac muttered, swinging the flashlight away. "I need a blanket."

"You got it." Maarten disappeared into the crowd.

He turned back to the girl, pointing his flashlight at the floor.

"It's okay, it's okay."

The girl looked at him and screamed again. Spittle clung to her lip. She grabbed at her torn shirt, trying to cover herself. Maarten handed Jac a blanket.

"Find someone who speaks some English. Quick."

Maarten vanished. The girl kicked out wildly as Jac tried to wrap the blanket around her.

"I'm not a Serb. Not Chetnik. UN." He reached inside his shirt, pulled out his identification card, and pointed the flashlight at it. He placed the card next to his face. "Look! Blue helmet. Look."

A plump woman pushed her way past Jac and grabbed the blanket. She covered the girl, speaking to her in soothing tones.

"Tell her we're Dutch," Jac said, showing her the ID. "We can take her to see a doctor."

"Her ankle is hurt," the woman said. "Can you carry her?"

"Is she okay with that? She knows we're not Serbs?"

"With an accent like that? I will go with you."

Maarten volunteered to carry the girl. She held on to him tightly, sobbing into his shoulder. Jac led them through the factory.

Outside, he sent Maarten ahead with the women and turned to Karel.

"Did three men just leave here?"

"Might have," Karel said. He drew on a cigarette. "I don't know."

Jac glanced at Bram. He shrugged.

"Bastards." Jac stepped close to Karel. "If you're not going to do your job then go back to the base and trade off with someone who will."

"Last time I checked, Jac, my job description said nothing about chasing three guys across a dark field that might be mined."

"There's a boy's body hanging from the stairs inside. Go cut him down. I'll be back for him."

Karel blew smoke from his nose and tossed the butt into the crowd. A little girl crawled towards the smouldering butt and retrieved it. Karel drew a blade from a scabbard on his belt and held it up in the cloud of smoke pouring from his mouth.

"One less to deal with."

A fist formed at Jac's side, but he didn't give in to the urge to pummel Karel. Putting him in the hospital only meant the sergeant would have to find another peacekeeper to fill his shoes. Going to jail himself wouldn't help either.

He released his fingers. Karel wrapped a bandanna around his face and led Bram inside the factory.

Jac turned away, took a few steps, and stopped. There were gunshots in the hills. Children moaned. The man in the abattoir was still calling out to Sanja. Jac changed direction and walked the length of the factory wall. The man's voice stopped and then started again. It was full of agony. Jac clenched and released his fingers several times before he could force himself to stop. He started to leave, but another sound caught his attention. He froze. The noise was out of place.

A moan punctuated by sobs.

He moved towards the corner of the factory. The sound changed. Now it was a rhythmic grunting. He sprinted ahead and turned the corner, raising his flashlight. An old man was sitting in the tall grass, smashing his head with a rock.

"Jesus, Jesus, Jesus," Jac cried out, dropping down next to the man. He tore the rock from the man's hands and tossed it away. Then he put his flashlight on the face again. It was full of blood. The right side was bloated and bruised, the eye swollen shut.

"Doctor," Jac said, pulling the man to his feet. The old man trembled and Jac wrapped an arm around him. "This way."

The man shuffled along, mumbling. Behind them, the voice called for Sanja. The man stopped, turned towards the darkness, and shouted something in Bosnian. Jac caught a woman's name but nothing else.

"Come on. I have to get you to a doctor."

Maarten was waiting for Jac outside the green tent and helped him place the old man in a chair. Jac took a dressing off a table and pressed it against the man's forehead.

"Where's the doctor?"

"Ici," a woman said. She pushed her way in between the two peacekeepers and inspected the man's head. "Did he do this to himself?"

"With a rock," Jac replied in French.

The doctor finished inspecting the wound and then looked at Jac. "He'll be fine."

"Do you think you can get him out with the wounded?"

"No guarantees. But he's old. We'll try to get him out in the morning."

Jac patted the man on the shoulder.

"You'll be okay," he told him in English.

The man rocked back and forth, staring straight ahead. Jac rubbed his eyes hard.

"And how are you doing, *Korporaal*?"

He dropped his hand from his face.

"Just waiting for my second wind."

"You speak French very well."

"My father was French. I spent a lot of time in France with him." She smiled. "Well, *Korporaal*, there should be some coffee left in the back. It's strong enough to keep you awake for a week. Help yourself and let me know if you need anything else." She helped the old man to his feet and led him away.

Maarten leaned close to Jac. "What was all that about?"

"Nothing."

"A lot of talk for nothing."

"Did you tell them about the boy?"

"Yeah. She said to take him into the compound to be buried with the rest."

"Let's do that."

The two men left the tent. Jac paused, letting his eyes readjust to the darkness. Something wasn't right.

*What is it?*

No voice called for Sanja.

# THURSDAY: TARAK SMAJLOVIC

TARAK BLINKED THE sleep out of his eyes.

*When did I sleep last? Sunday?*

He took a mouthful of water and turned around, counting eight heads, including Atif's. The civilians had latched onto Tarak the moment they realized he was a soldier.

"Four more," a ninth man called from the trees.

Four men came straggling into the group.

"Are you injured?" Tarak asked.

"They attacked us near the road," a bearded man replied, wiping his face with his sleeve. "There were six of us. We lost two in the smoke." He wiped his face again. "I feel a little sick. Do you have any water?"

Someone offered the man a canteen.

Tarak cleared his throat. "Okay, listen to me. We have to move fast. The front of the column must be across by now and if they're holding the road open, they won't be there much longer."

"We're ready," the bearded man said.

Tarak looked at Atif. "Are you okay?"

"Just a little tired."

"We'll sleep on the other side of the road." Tarak checked his compass and pointed. "This way."

The men stood up and followed him. Tarak looked back. They

seemed able to keep up the pace, but their ability to remain silent was another matter.

"How much farther?"

"Are you sure you're going the right way?"

"I'm feeling sick. Can we stop for a moment?"

Tarak turned to face them.

"Will you please shut up." His whisper was as stern as he could make it. "We are walking parallel to the road. Kravica is nearby and if you keep talking, they'll hear you."

Twelve heads nodded.

"We'll take five minutes and then I don't care how sick you feel, we have to move."

"I'm finding it a little hard to breath," the bearded man said, wiping his face again. A hand holding a bottle of water was stretched out to him.

"Ration that until we get across the road," Tarak said. "We can refill it at the Jadar."

The man took a mouthful and handed it back.

"Okay. Okay. I'm better. We can go. Go. Yes. We can go."

Tarak looked at the man's companions. "Keep an eye on him," he said, and then turned to Atif.

"Much farther?" the boy asked.

"An hour at least, but we should be okay." Tarak took a mouthful of water and then stashed the bottle in his pack. "We have at least five hours until...."

"Chetniks!"

Tarak pushed Atif to the ground and raised his rifle. The bearded man was pointing up at the trees.

"Shoot him. Quick!" the man screamed, tugging at another man's rifle.

"Shut him up," Tarak said.

Two of the others wrestled the bearded man to the ground.

"They're going to kill us," the man shouted. "Shoot them. They're coming."

"Damn it. Gag him."

One of the man's companions pulled the white armband from his arm and made it into a gag, tying it across his mouth. The man kept struggling and pointing up at the trees.

"What's wrong with him?" Atif asked.

"I think it's getting to him," one of the men said. "Only so much the mind can take."

"We have to move," Tarak told them. "You two are responsible for him. If he gets too much for you, leave him behind."

The men nodded. Tarak returned to the head of his short column and held his compass out until the moon lit it up. He wanted to move away from the road. If those men were telling the truth about the earlier attack, the Serbs were patrolling the road below and might be in the woods as well. He decided to lead them deeper into the forest, away from the Kravica road. Crossing near Kravica was never a consideration. That would trap them in a narrow, heavily populated strip of Serb land between the road and the Drina River.

*We need to get closer to Nova Kasaba.*

They moved to the top of the ridge and descended the other side, walking northwest, keeping the ridge between them and the road. Someone at the back called out, asking Tarak to stop.

"That man is really sick. He's trying to vomit. Do I take off the gag?"

As Tarak opened his mouth to reply, a young man from the same group of four began laughing hysterically.

"What's happening?" Atif asked.

"I don't know, *Braco*. Just do me a favour. Stay here and stay down."

Atif nodded and slid to the ground behind a tree. Tarak went to the back of the column to help the laughing man's comrades subdue him. Fists flew. The man was bound and gagged.

Voices filled the trees.

"What's going on?"

"Could it be gas?"

"I saw smoke earlier."

"Smoke?" Tarak looked at them, his brow wrinkling. "Where?"

"Not far from where you found us. We had to walk through it."

"What did it smell like?"

"Like smoke. I thought it was a smoke grenade."

The bearded man began to convulse on the ground.

"Remove the gag," Tarak said.

"Don't do it!"

Tarak looked up. The third member of the bearded man's group was standing on the slope above them and aiming an Uzi in their direction.

"He's a Chetnik. Don't let him go."

"Put that down," Tarak said.

The man pointed the Uzi at Tarak and laughed. "Who do you think you are? Comrade Tito? You know we're all going to die out here, don't you? They have us surrounded."

The man suddenly spun around and pointed the Uzi up the slope. Two of the others dove for his legs and missed.

"Chetniks! You're all Chetniks!"

He fired.

The machine gun rounds sounded like firecrackers. Tarak hit the ground and rolled. His arm was burning. He stopped rolling, swung around a tree, and looked back. Atif was curled up next to another tree, his arms covering his head. Three men lay unmoving near the crazy man with the Uzi. He could hear the others plowing through the forest, breaking branches in their frenzy to get away. The man stopped to reload and then fired high into the trees.

"Paratroopers! Get down. They're coming."

The Uzi emptied in seconds. The man dropped the weapon and looked up, laughing and screaming at the sky.

"Come get me, you bastards. I don't owe you any money and I don't need your shoes."

He pulled out a grenade, removed the pin, and then placed it under his chin. There was a metal click; the handle popped free.

"Get down," Tarak shouted.

Seconds later, the grenade exploded.

*Enough of this.*

Tarak bolted from behind the tree and pulled Atif to his feet. They vanished between the trees.

# THURSDAY: ATIF STAVIC

ATIF STRUGGLED TO get his footing. Tarak was half-dragging and half-carrying him through the woods. Branches dug into his arm and snapped. Strong arms pushed him forward and upward.

*Is he afraid of the gas?*

Atif's mother had told him stories about gas attacks in the First World War. She said soldiers caught in craters or trenches during an attack without their gear had one terrible choice—to suffocate or seek higher ground where they exposed themselves to enemy fire.

The high moon lit their way as they crested the ridge and moved down on the opposite side towards the road. Then Tarak stopped, backtracked a few metres, and pointed at a fallen beech tree.

"Get down behind that," he said.

Atif obeyed; a few moments later, Tarak collapsed next to him. They sat in silence until each could breathe regularly again.

"Hear anything?"

"I don't think they could keep up to us," Atif replied, pulling a twig out from under a strap.

Tarak hauled off his pack, grunting.

"Are you okay?"

"Yeah," Tarak said. "Do you have any water left?"

Atif dug out a bottle and handed it to him. Tarak pulled back on his right sleeve and poured water over his forearm.

"Are you hit?"

Tarak held his arm up until Atif could distinguish it properly from the other shapes and shadows in the moonlight. Blood seeped from two holes on either side of his forearm.

Atif's mind flashed back to the alley. The arm hanging from the side of the car. The blood dripping to the ground. His stomach rebelled. The smell of vomit competed with the scent of pine needles.

Tarak held the bottle in front of him. "Drink some."

Atif took it, swallowed a mouthful, and threw it back up.

"Sorry," Tarak whispered. "I was going to ask you to help me wrap it up, but maybe not."

"No," Atif said. His throat was stinging. "I can do it. I just need a second."

"You sure?"

"Yeah." Atif pulled in long, measured breaths until his stomach settled. "Do you have anything to wrap it up with?"

Tarak handed him a roll of bandage and medical tape.

"That's perfect. We should wipe it down, make sure it's clean."

Atif tore off a piece of bandage while Tarak dribbled more water over his injured arm. A trickle of blood seeped from the wound every time he touched it. He took Tarak's hand and pulled it towards his chest and then unrolled the rest of the bandage, wrapping it below the wound and then over and above it. Tarak grunted.

"If I don't make it snug," Atif said, "it'll start to bleed again." He checked his work, pressing the arm on both sides of the wound. "Does it feel like it hit the bones?"

"No."

Atif tore off a piece of medical tape and placed it around the edge of the bandage.

"Lucky thing. There's not much room between the radius and ulna."

Tarak inspected his arm. "Where'd you learn so much about bandages and bones?"

"My mother's friend, Ina, is a nurse. She taught us all how to take care of an injury if we got hurt. You know, like how to make a tourniquet. She worked at the hospital, too. She even let me watch some operations."

"Do you want to be a doctor?"

"I did when I was younger. I don't know anymore."

Not after that day, he thought. He'd been waiting at the hospital for Ina when they brought in a little girl injured in a mortar attack. The hospital was out of anesthetic and they'd had to remove the shrapnel without it. He could hear her screams from the far end of the corridor.

*How could they do it?*

"You should think about it."

"Ina thinks I should...."

Something snapped in the forest. Atif's head jerked to the left. He peered over the tree.

"What is it?" Tarak asked.

Branches swayed.

"Nothing," Atif said after a few moments.

A twig cracked.

Tarak laid the barrel of his rifle on the tree trunk and pointed it into the darkness. The full moon made it easy to pick out individual trees, but a slight breeze had turned the shadows into a macabre ballet of dancing spectres. Atif squinted, trying to figure out if he was looking at a branch, a man's head, or the *blautsauger*.

Another twig snapped.

Atif held his breath.

A tap on the shoulder then Tarak's finger pointed. A spectre took human form. It was moving among the trees, pushing at branches, and holding them back for a second form and then a third.

"This way," the man in front said. "Yes. I'm sure of it."

Tarak's rifle shifted aim. The men were walking directly towards them.

"The culvert is just down here," the man said. He spoke too loudly for Atif's comfort. "Big enough to cross."

The man paused, waiting for the others to catch up. The moon lit up their forms but obscured their features. Atif tapped on Tarak's shoulder and pointed to the third man and then to the white bandanna wrapped around his own arm.

"Stay here," Tarak whispered in Atif's ear.

He slid over the tree and stood waiting for the men to approach.

"Who is that?" one of the men shouted. Atif watched them raise rifles to their shoulders. His stomach tightened.

Tarak said something unheard as he walked towards the men. Moments later, the barrels were lowered and Tarak was wrapping his arms around one of the apparitions. Atif let out a long sigh.

"Come out, Atif. It's okay."

He crawled out from behind the tree and sat on top of it.

"This is Juso," Tarak said, slapping the young soldier on the back. "We went through basic training together."

Atif didn't move. He counted six men. One of them was leaning on another. The shadows hid their faces.

"Where are you going?" Tarak asked.

Juso indicated the man in the lead. He was young, no more than nineteen, and wore a white shirt, jeans, and sneakers. He carried no weapons.

"This is Emin. We met up with him a while ago. He says he knows where we can crawl under the road through a culvert."

"A culvert?" Tarak asked, turning to Emin. "Along this stretch of road?"

"Yes, yes," Emin replied. "I grew up near here. We used it several times to raid the farms in Kravica."

Atif watched Tarak's head move up and down as he gave the man the once-over.

"You grew up in Kravica?"

"Yes. Just outside the town. My father was an accountant."

"You went to school there?"

"Of course."

Shadows crossed Tarak's face as he turned to Atif.

"Didn't your mother teach at the school in Kravica?"

Atif didn't like the way he sounded. "Yeah."

"What's her name?"

"Stavic. Marija Stavic."

Tarak turned back to Emin. "She taught mathematics."

Atif started to raise his hand and then dropped it again.

"Yes. I remember her, but she never taught in my class."

Tarak glanced at Atif.

*Why is Tarak asking him that? Did he think they had been affected by the gas?*

Atif wasn't sure he wanted to hear the answer. He slid to the opposite side of the log.

"We can catch up on old times later, Tarak," Juso said. "We should go."

"We're not going anywhere, Juso."

"What are you talking about?" The second man took his rifle down from his shoulder and stepped behind Emin. He was wearing jeans and a plaid shirt.

*A farmer?* The rifle looked like the one Atif's father used for hunting.

"If we don't go now," Emin said, "it may be too late."

"I've been through this area more times than I can count," Tarak said, stepping closer to him. "I don't remember any culverts big enough for a grown man to squeeze through."

"There is," the young man said. "Look. If you want to follow me, fine. If not, you can stay here and take your chances crossing on top. I don't care. I'm going now."

Tarak jabbed the muzzle of his rifle into Emin's chest.

"You're not going anywhere."

"Tarak?" The soldier called Juso sounded bewildered.

"Look at him, Juso. Look at his clothes. His shirt, his jeans. They're like he just put them on." Tarak pointed to Emin's feet. "And those sneakers look like they just came off a store shelf."

Atif looked down.

The sneakers were white, pristine. Atif glanced at his own boots caked in mud.

*But if Emin hadn't come from Srebrenica, where did he come from?*

"The clothes I was wearing were soaked," Emin said, his voice shaking. "I found some packs full of clothes and changed earlier this evening."

Tarak raised his hand and touched Emin's hair and then smelled his fingers.

"Shampoo. Smells like apples."

"I bought it off the black market."

The farmer raised the barrel of his rifle. Juso followed suit.

"What's going on?" Atif asked.

"He's a Chetnik, *Braco*. He was going to lead us into an ambush."

Atif stared at Emin. It had been so long since he'd seen a Serb out of uniform he had forgotten it was impossible to tell one apart from a Muslim or a Croat.

"What?" Emin said. "No. That's not true."

"He says he's from your area," Tarak said, glancing at Atif. "Do you recognize him?"

Atif looked up at the man and shook his head, but he wasn't sure. He no longer remembered the faces or names of his former neighbours.

"I am Muslim," Emin said. "Like you."

"Yeah?" said the man holding up his friend. "How many times a day do we pray?"

"Five," Emin replied.

"When? What are the names of the prayers? Can you recite them?"

Atif knew he couldn't answer those questions with complete certainty.

"My parents were Communists," Emin told them. "We didn't practice."

"We can't let him go," Juso said to Tarak. "He will tell them where we are."

Tarak rubbed his forehead hard and glanced at the other men.

"What do we do with him?"

"Kill him," said the man with the rifle.

"What? No. I'm telling you, I'm Muslim."

The young man's legs suddenly buckled and he was on the ground. Tarak reached down and grabbed Emin by the collar. Atif stood up.

"Do you honestly think we're that stupid?"

Emin said nothing. Blood dripped from his nose.

"*Braco*, throw me the tape."

The roll was sitting on Tarak's pack. Atif tossed it to him and then climbed on top of the log. Tarak handed the tape to the farmer.

"What's your name?"

"Murat."

"Tie his wrists and gag him."

Tarak held onto Emin while Murat bound him. Then he turned to Juso.

"Do you have any rope?"

"Some. Why?"

"We'll tie him to a tree and break his ankle. His own guys will find him soon enough."

"No," Murat said. "We should kill him. If he gets loose or screams, we'll all die."

"I'm not going to shoot an unarmed man."

"I don't have a problem with that," one of the other men said. He stepped forward, pulling out a pistol. "He's a Chetnik. They don't think twice about raping and killing our women and children."

"That doesn't make it right."

Atif gazed at Emin. The young man was struggling against the binds and shaking his head.

He's a Chetnik, Atif thought. A soldier. Was he the soldier who loaded the shell that killed Dani? The soldier responsible for Tata's disappearance? Atif's jaw hurt. His hands were shaking.

"Fine," Murat replied. "Let's vote on it."

"I say we break both ankles and leave him," Juso said.

The man leaning against his friend waved a hand. "I'm just a carpenter. I don't want anything to do with murdering an unarmed man. Allah has said that when angered, we should forgive."

Atif held his breath and looked at the other two men.

"Allah has also said to slay the aggressor wherever we find him. I say we slay this aggressor."

"You are wrong," Juso said, pointing at the shape in the shadows. "You take the words out of context. The Mujahidin mercenaries have corrupted you. They have corrupted our faith and twisted the words to suit their ends. This is not who we are."

"The fact remains that he had no problem leading us to our deaths," the other man said. "Revenge is mine, sayeth the Lord. Sound familiar, Emin? Well, now it's mine. I say kill the bastard."

"We have no proof. Killing him would be unjust and we all know what the Qur'an says about that."

"Doesn't matter," Tarak said. "It's a tie. We leave him."

Murat motioned to Atif.

"We haven't heard from the boy."

Atif stared at him.

"No," Tarak said. "He's only fourteen."

"He's old enough to be out here. He gets a vote. What do you say, boy?"

Atif's thoughts swam through mud. The years of starvation and shelling. The taste of cordite. The dead soldier in the hospital. Dani's smile from behind the car. His father's last wave as he walked into the fog.

"Boy?"

Atif blinked and glared at Emin.

"He killed my friends. He probably killed my father."

A pair of hands gripped Atif's shoulders.

"You don't know what this man did," Tarak said. "He could be a recruit, drafted out of school. He follows orders like I do, like Juso does. He didn't kill your friends or your father."

"You don't know that."

"Neither do you. *Braco*, please. If you do this, you'll regret it. It will haunt you until the day you die."

"I'm already haunted," Atif replied. "Because of him. Because of all of them."

"Let it go," Tarak whispered. "Let it go."

"I can't...."

A single gunshot exploded behind them. Tarak dropped to the ground, dragging Atif with him.

When they looked up, Emin was on the ground. Murat stood behind the body. He cocked his rifle and the spent casing flew away.

"What did you do that for?" Tarak's voice was rough with anger.

"Enough negotiating. I don't need a moral dictator to tell me about self-preservation. Let's...."

Murat's words became a gurgle. The farmer looked down at his chest as machine gun rounds sliced through him. When he collapsed, a red mist floated among the shadows.

The others scattered like deer. Tarak grabbed Atif and flipped him over the log.

"Stay down," he shouted, slinging his pack over his shoulder.

Atif hauled his own pack on as more rounds bit into the air above them. Branches snapped and fell. Trees splintered. Red tracers lit the sky. Someone cried out.

"Crawl, *Braco*, crawl."

Atif hesitated. He glanced under the rotted log. Emin's white shirt shone in the moonlight.

Tarak grabbed Atif's shoulder strap. He pulled him away from the log and deeper into the forest.

# THURSDAY: NIKO BASARIC

*I CAN'T BREATHE!*

A dozen soldiers and their equipment jammed the back of the carrier. Niko sat with his hands covering his ears, sucking in super-heated air, unable to move in the suffocating space. The carrier shifted right, then left, and powered down.

*About time.*

The ramp dropped. Niko followed the section outside, hauling in a lung full of cool night air. Another carrier pulled up next to a truck. Three mortar teams dropped from the back of the truck and went to search for an area in which to set up their weapons.

Niko found Petar; they crossed the road together, taking up station against a guard rail.

"Isn't this where we were when they came out of the woods?"

"I don't know," Niko replied, looking back. A second truck, carrying an anti-aircraft gun, pulled into the field behind them. Engines shut down. Lights faded.

Silence.

Niko could hear every voice, footstep, and snapping twig around him. Petar was looking over the guardrail at the forest.

"I think I can hear voices in there."

Niko waved him quiet. He had no idea if their presence would attract or scare off the men in the woods. Many of them would be armed and they wouldn't think twice about shooting their way across.

"What if they come up to us?" Petar asked.

"We'll tell them to surrender. Then the trucks will come pick them up."

"What if they start shooting?"

"Then keep your head down and let the mortars take care of them."

The moonlight highlighted every motion of Petar's head as it responded to the slightest sound in the woods.

"Basaric! Kadija!"

Niko and Petar stood up. Drach was coming towards them with Ivan, Anton, and Pavle in tow. The group stopped at the end of the guard rail and Drach pointed into the ditch.

"We can hear them in the woods," he said.

Petar turned to Niko, a smug smile plastered across his face. Anton pulled a cigarette from his pocket and stuck it in his mouth. Ivan snagged the cigarette and threw it away.

"Do you want your head shot off?"

"Listen to me," Drach said. "The lieutenant wants a patrol to flush them out on to the road. Ivan will lead." Drach pointed at Niko and Petar. "Let's see if he can teach you how to be real soldiers. You can prove you have a backbone after all."

"Yes, Sergeant," Niko replied.

"Move it." Drach turned away and melted into the darkness.

Ivan cocked his rifle and the others followed suit.

"Whatever you do," Ivan said, grimacing at Niko and Petar, "try not to shoot each other in the back."

For an instant, Niko wished Drach was going with them.

Ivan stepped off the pavement and slid into the ditch. Loose gravel followed him down. Niko cringed at the noise, dropping to a knee next to the guardrail. Pavle and Anton slid down next, pursued by an avalanche of rocks and dust. Niko motioned to Petar to go next. The recruit smiled like a schoolboy on a field trip and dropped into the ditch.

Niko followed, unable to descend without kicking the gravel loose. But once they were in the woods, the group moved like panthers. Every step was dropped with care, every branch carefully returned to its original position. Petar performed better than Niko expected.

*Then again, Petar's heart is probably ready to burst through his chest.* Niko pressed his hand to his own chest, surprised to feel a jackhammer at work.

The patrol moved away from the road. Voices drifted through the trees to their left. Shadows flickered in the waning moonlight. Ivan turned around and pointed south, opening his hand three times. *Fifteen men? Where?*

Ivan signaled to them to spread out and move south in an extended line. Niko backed up a few steps and turned left. He kept his eye on Petar to make sure the recruit didn't advance ahead of him or the others.

As they slithered through the brush, voices emerged. They carried easily in the heavy pre-dawn air. Niko waved to Petar twice to slow down, but Anton was even farther ahead. Niko couldn't see Ivan or Pavle at all.

A twig snapped on Niko's right and the voices ceased. He looked at Petar, who shrugged. When he looked back, an orange glow was floating among the trees, moving towards him.

*A cigarette?*

He waved Petar down and waited until the cigarette hovered within a few steps of him. Then he stood up and raised his rifle.

"Stop where you are. You're surrounded."

The cigarette fell to the ground.

"We want to sur...."

Automatic fire cut off the man's words. Niko dropped to the ground, unsure of who was shooting. He switched off his safety and pulled the trigger, spitting out thirty rounds in seconds. Men screamed and thrashed in the bushes.

No one fired back.

"Cease fire, you idiots," Ivan shouted from behind. "Who fired first?"

They looked at one another and then all eyes shifted to Petar.

"I did," the recruit said, standing to face Ivan. "It was an accident. I got such a fright when he spoke, I pulled the trigger."

"You were walking behind me with your safety off?"

Petar swallowed and nodded. Ivan switched his rifle from his right to his left hand and then drove his fist across Petar's chin. The recruit staggered back and collapsed. When Niko moved to help him, Ivan stuck his rifle in the way.

"Forget him. Check the Turks. See if they're alive."

Niko stepped over Petar and then over two bodies. Dozens of

rounds had sliced their chests open. In a small clearing a few metres away, four more bodies lay in a pile.

He checked the woods but found no one. When he returned to the others, they were crouched next to the bodies, rummaging through pockets.

"They're all dead," Niko said.

"Go get the recruit," Ivan replied, stuffing a pack of cigarettes into his pocket. "Take him back up to the road and keep him there."

Happily, Niko thought. He stepped over the bodies and then stopped. Another body lay off the trail. It wore a unique and familiar red and white track suit. Niko knelt next to the body and turned it over, brushing dirt and leaves away from the face.

"Goddamn it," Niko muttered to himself.

*Zahir.*

He had attended Zahir's wedding years ago; the mechanic had a wife and three young children. Niko swallowed hard.

*Did I kill you, my friend?*

He checked Zahir's pockets, surprised to find a wallet.

"I'll make sure they know where you are," he said to the unseeing face. "I promise."

# THURSDAY: TARAK SMAJLOVIC

TARAK SLID DOWN the side of a ravine and stepped into a small, slow moving river. He stared at the wall of trees before him; he didn't have the energy to scale another hill. Above him, the Milky Way painted the sky a dull white. He listened, but heard nothing.

"Are we lost?" Atif asked, submerging his bottle into the river.

Tarak looked at the boy. They were the first words he had uttered since the attack. "Not really," Tarak replied. "I have a good idea what area we're in, but I'm not sure how close we are to the road or to what part of the road."

Atif drank some water and dunked the bottle into the river again.

"I'm thinking we won't make it across tonight," Tarak said.

Atif looked up at him.

"The rest of the men are undoubtedly across by now and the Chetniks are on the road. I don't think we should attempt to cross until we know how many there are and exactly where they are. And I have no idea if they've laid mines or traps. We'll lay low for the day and try again after dark."

They crossed the river and Tarak surveyed the other side. He could see little beyond the thick brush.

"We'll be safe here until it gets light. We should try to get some sleep."

Atif settled down next to a tree. Tarak pulled off his pack and sat next to him.

"Are you cold?"

"No."

"Your clothes are still wet." Tarak hauled out his ranger blanket and untied the compact roll. "Put this around you. It's a lot warmer than it looks."

Atif took the blanket without a word.

"Hungry?"

"No."

Tarak heaved a sigh, unsure of what to say. He didn't know if Atif was upset because of his friends, his father, or the man they had just killed. Or a combination of the three.

"It's not your fault," Tarak said.

"Are you sure he was a Chetnik?"

"Right now, *Braco*, I'm not sure of a lot of things, but that guy just didn't seem right."

"They killed him because of me."

"You didn't pull the trigger. Murat was going to kill him one way or another."

"Maybe that was a good thing."

"Murdering someone who has no chance of defending themselves is not a good thing. I don't care how angry you are at them."

"I'm not angry."

"But you hate them, don't you? Because of your friends? Your father?"

"Yes."

"You want to kill them for all that, don't you?"

"Yes."

"Then if you're not angry, I don't know what to call you."

"Why does it matter? Why can't I be angry at them?"

Tarak leaned against the tree, his mind flashing back: burned-out houses, smoke mingling with screams from the bridge, women wailing. A little boy shrieking.

"Because it does no good," Tarak said. "All this anger and hate will burn you up inside. It'll change you into someone you don't want to be."

"How do you know that's not what I want?"

"Do you want to know why I stayed with the Chetniks for so long?"

"What?"

"I told you I was one of the last to desert. I stayed because I wanted to fight the Croats until there wasn't a single breathing bastard left alive." Tarak turned away for a moment. "We went into a Chetnik village in Croatia early in the war. The Croats had already expelled everyone, but some didn't make it out. We found the remains of one family in a basement. Sixteen people including four children. The Croats had barred them in there and lit the house on fire. They burned them alive."

Atif was staring at him.

"So for as long as they would let me fight, I killed Croats. Men, women. Even children. I was convinced if we didn't kill them, they'd come back and murder our families like they did with the Nazis." He hesitated, swallowing hard. "Until Vukovar. But even that didn't stop me because the Chetniks became my enemy."

Fadil's scream echoed in his mind.

"That's what hate gets you, *Braco*. It took me that long to wake up to what my anger was doing. It consumes you. Every day, you think about it. Every night, you dream about it. I killed innocent people who had never done anything to me and I will have to live with that the rest of my life. And I will answer for it later."

"So, when you get to Tuzla and your mother finds a way to get you to France or Canada or wherever, you go. You go as far from here as you can. Forget about being a soldier. Forget about all this. You go away and leave it behind. And when this war is over and you grow up, get married and have children, then you come back. You show your family where you grew up. Show them who you are. And you do it with some pride because you survived this insanity as a whole person."

Atif opened his mouth to speak, but Tarak raised his hand.

"Don't say anything. Just think about it for a while. Right now, we need to sleep."

"Okay," Atif whispered. He wrapped the blanket over his head and lay down, turning his back to Tarak.

Better this way, Tarak thought, leaning back against the tree.

He closed his eyes and willed the images from his mind. He didn't need that. Not now. He needed sleep. He had to think clearly if he was going to get them both across the road.

*Focus on that.*

In his mind, tanks and artillery lined the road like the Great Wall.

*But do they have enough troops to cover the whole thing?*

That had been the problem with the Serb army from the start of the war. They never had enough troops to do what they wanted. There would be gaps in the road. The army would concentrate on the areas where they expected the men to cross the road, primarily between Konjevic Polje and Nova Kasaba.

*We'll go west. We'll skirt south of Nova Kasaba and check the road. Somewhere on that stretch of road there will be a break in the coverage. In the darkness, we only need a few clear metres to get across.*

Tarak glanced at the boy.

*We'll get across, Braco. We'll get across.*

# THURSDAY: JAC LARUE

"WAKE UP, SOLDIER!"

Jac sat up, smacking his head against the roof of the carrier. Maarten was standing outside with a cup in each hand and he was wearing the widest smile Jac'd seen in days.

"If you keep doing that, you're going to give me a concussion sooner or later."

Maarten stepped inside the vehicle, sat down next to Jac, and handed him one of the cups of coffee.

"Small price to pay for fifteen minutes sleep. I think I'm closing in on thirty hours without a wink."

Jac took a mouthful of coffee and spit it back. "Keep drinking this and you won't sleep until the next century."

"Enjoy it," Maarten said. "It's the last of my stash."

"What's going on?"

"Quiet. Not a Serb in sight. They're probably all sleeping off the beer at that hotel."

Jac moaned. A hotel. Clean sheets, hot water, flushing toilets. And real coffee.

He took a bottle of water from the half-empty case next to him.

"It's going to be another hot one," Maarten said, as Jac soaked his towel with the water and wrapped it around his neck.

"Any sign of the sergeant?

"Just for a second. Said he has some guys out and needs us to help with the buses. He wants us easy to find when the convoy is ready to go."

Jac's shoulders dropped. He hated working the buses. His stomach churned at the thought of watching more men being separated from their families, of being spit on by some women and kissed by other women.

A rumbling sound echoed through the metal skin of the carrier.

"They're he-ere," Maarten said in a high-pitched squeak.

"Get out, Carol Ann."

Maarten laughed.

"I'm running towards the light, Mama," he said, ducking outside.

"You know," Jac shouted after him, "nothing pleases me more than the thought of that movie being shredded into a million pieces when the Serbs shelled our OP."

Maarten peeked back inside. "I'm sure it had another thirty or forty plays left in it."

Jac laughed, dropping the half-empty bottle into his pack. He stepped outside. The crowd was on its feet and waiting. Jac led Maarten between the two carriers, to where several other peacekeepers stood waiting. He looked around. The buses sat idling on the road with no Serbs in sight. He walked up to Hans.

"Where are they?"

"God knows. What do we do? Load them up?"

Another peacekeeper joined them.

"They're not here. Let's get the men on the buses and get them out before they show up."

"What about the Serbs on the road?" Hans asked. "They'll stop the buses."

"I think they're willing to take the chance," Jac said.

"Jesus," Hans said. "We better do it fast."

Jac and Maarten waded into the crowd.

"*Nema* Chetniks," Jac said to the people waiting between the armoured vehicles. "Men. Get men on the buses. Quick."

The crowd scrambled towards the buses. Jac fought against the tide until he came to groups of people sitting on the ground. He grabbed the first man he saw.

"*Nema* Chetniks. Go. Now."

The man understood. He and his wife rushed away. Jac looked around at the ocean of women and children.

*Where are the men?*

"*Nema* Chetniks," he said over and over. Only four other men appeared and Jac rushed them to the front before the buses were filled to capacity.

"Did you find any?"

Jac stepped away from the last bus and motioned the driver to leave.

"A few. I think they're all too afraid to show their faces."

"Or they're not there anymore," Maarten said.

"What about the men inside the compound?" Jac asked.

"I thought you said they were safe?"

"I don't know." He stared at the camp. "Are they?"

"They better be. There are hundreds in there."

Jac felt a tug on his sleeve. He looked down to see a little boy.

"Hello."

The boy looked away and then back at Jac. He raised a finger and pulled it across his throat and then pointed at one of the houses.

"I'm not sure I understand."

The boy repeated the actions and then ran off into the crowd.

"What was that all about?" Maarten asked.

Jac looked at the house and then at the empty road.

"Another suicide, maybe. We better go look."

"That's outside our area, Jac."

Jac walked towards the house and then looked back. "The Serbs are not here, Maarten. If we don't look now, we won't get another chance."

"You're not going to be satisfied until I get shot, are you?"

Jac threw Maarten a brief smile.

"Fine, fine. Let's hurry."

They trotted through the thinning crowd. There was no one in sight outside the house, although the refugees usually filled their water containers at the spigot attached to it. He glanced over at the other house: women were lined up there for water.

*But why not here?*

Jac entered the house and walked from room to room, finding only smashed furniture, broken windows, and garbage. He left through the back door. Behind the house, the land sloped towards a creek. Maarten was coming around the corner, having completed his circuit of the house.

"Nothing."

Jac stared at the creek. "C'mon."

"There could be mines down there, Jac."

"It's clear," he said, pointing to the ground. "Fresh footprints."

"Yeah," Maarten said, following. "Footprints of the guys who laid the mines. Did you consider that?"

Jac surveyed the area, slowing as he approached the creek. Deserted.

He crouched next to the creek and took a moment to soak his towel in the cool water. He flipped it around his neck and listened. Birds chirped in the trees. Tall grass swayed in the breeze.

"Oh shit!"

Jac turned. Maarten was standing a few metres upstream, behind a clump of bushes. And then he bent over and vomited.

"What's up?" Jac asked.

"Besides my caffeine breakfast?"

Maarten pointed just as Jac caught sight of a blackened hand sticking out between the bushes.

"I really didn't need to see this, Jac."

Maarten stepped aside. Behind him, the bodies of five men and one young woman lay in a row, their throats slashed and their skin darkening in the heat. Jac looked away before his stomach reacted.

"Got a camera on you?"

"A camera? Are you shitting me? Jesus, when is this crap going to end?"

Jac looked around. The tall foliage could hide anything lying on the ground. If the Serbs were able to remove the old man's body the day before, they'd be back for the rest today. Jac turned around and walked towards the compound.

"We need to tell the sergeant."

They re-entered the crowd of refugees without spotting a single Serb. The sergeant was outside the camp entrance; they told him what they had found.

"I'll take care of it," Janssen said, stifling a yawn. "But stick around. You'll likely be slated to escort the third or fourth convoy. I'm trying to siphon enough fuel from the other vehicles to last you to Tisca."

As Janssen walked back into the compound, another group of buses arrived.

Behind them were trucks carrying Serb soldiers.

# THURSDAY: MARIJA STAVIC

MARIJA WIPED HER cheeks dry as she watched the sun rise. She ate a carrot, but the ache in her stomach remained.

The girls stirred. Lejla mumbled in her sleep. People woke and stretched. Children cried. A parade of water containers moved towards the water spigot. A peacekeeper wandered among the refugees.

Peacekeeper? Yes, she thought. He was alone and unarmed.

Ina appeared next to him, carrying a full container. Water spilled through the loose cap with every step. She laid it next to Marija and sat down, breathing heavily.

"Glad I went when I did," she whispered. "I saw no Chetniks."

"They're drunk and asleep."

Ina took out a few carrots, scrubbed off the dirt, and then she poured the water into the bottles. The girls woke up and ate.

"I'm going to have to cut off your hair," Ina said to her daughters when they'd finished. She was holding up the pocket knife.

"Cut our hair?" Lejla said. "No, Mama. Please."

"It'll grow back," Ina said, opening the knife.

Lejla sat back, holding onto her long black hair. "No, Mama."

"Listen to me. You didn't see what went on here last night. You didn't hear what Jac told us."

"Lejla," Marija said. "You've been lucky to keep it this long. If you had gotten lice, we would have had to shave it to the skin."

"But you're not even sure it will help."

"It's not going to hurt," Ina said, holding out her hand.

Lejla cried as Ina sliced through her hair. The dull blade left a ragged edge.

Adila turned to Marija. "But if she makes it too obvious," she whispered, "they'll know she's trying to hide something."

Marija placed her hand on Adila's arm.

"She knows what she's doing. Please. Trust her. This isn't over until we are in Tuzla."

Adila leaned closer.

"I'm scared, Mrs. Stavic."

"You should be," Marija replied. "We're doing all that we can, Lejla. Just do as your mother tells you and we'll get through this. Okay?"

Adila said nothing when her turn came. Tihana picked up some of the discarded hair and wrapped it around the necks of the toy soldiers. She was still holding the carrot Ina had given to her when she awoke.

Marija wondered if she was saving it for Atif.

"What do you think?" Ina asked, cutting off the last of Adila's strands. "Should we go?"

Marija stood up and looked at the crowd forming around the Dutch carriers. No one was pushing or shoving the way they had the day before. Everyone knew the buses would come and they knew that the passengers had been dropped off near Tisca. She sat down and gestured to the twins.

"How are the rashes?"

Ina pulled back on Lejla's sleeve. The rash had become blister-sized blotches. Adila's rash covered her arms and neck. Lejla scratched at her arms.

"Don't scratch," Marija said.

"Maybe they should," Ina said. "Just a little. But don't use your nails." She passed Lejla a small towel. "We don't want them to scar."

The twin's heads popped up in unison.

"Scar?"

"Don't worry about it," Ina said. "Just don't drive your nails into them. Rub them with the towel."

Marija stood up and looked around. She spotted soldiers walking among the refugees.

*Or are they peacekeepers?*

She turned and surveyed the crowd near the carriers. Nothing had changed. She picked up her bag and slung it over her shoulder.

"We should get closer."

Adila stood, picked up Tihana, and offered her to Marija.

"I think it's best if you hold on to her and stay close to me," Marija said, glancing at the cardboard on the ground. She dropped to her knees and tore off four pieces. "It's going to be hot on the bus. We can use these to fan ourselves."

Ina stuffed the cardboard into her bag. Marija took one last look around the wrecked bus that had kept them safe for two days. Certain they had left nothing behind, she took Adila's hand and led her towards the armoured vehicles.

# THURSDAY: ATIF STAVIC

ATIF WOKE AND wiped dew from his face. He looked up at a narrow slice of blue sky wedged between the steep hills. A bird flew from one side to the other and then sat on an outstretched branch and chirped. Another bird flew by. The first left its perch and followed.

"Thirsty?"

Tarak sat next to him eating. He pointed to a full bottle of water sitting on his pack.

"Filled it up for you. Take your time."

Atif sat up, feeling every muscle in his body ache.

"Did I sleep?"

"You snored."

"I don't snore."

"Then there's a bear in the woods."

Atif smiled and opened his pack. He pulled out another Dutch ration.

Macaroni and cheese.

He ate and drank his fill and then topped up the bottles in the creek. The sun was still hidden behind the ravine wall when Tarak checked his compass and pointed north.

They walked through the thick brush for more than an hour, stopping every few steps to listen. The temperature climbed with the sun. By late morning, sweat soaked Atif's shirt.

A voice stopped Tarak mid-stride. He lowered himself to the

ground and looked at Atif with an index finger against his lips. They listened. The voice took form.

*Names?*

With Tarak in the lead, they walked to the side of a ridge, where trees gave way to tall grass and bushes. Then they crawled towards the bright morning sun on their bellies. Bushes rustled. Twigs cracked. Tarak brushed them aside, encouraging Atif forward until they had crawled to the edge of a rock face. Below them, a stretch of road swarmed with dozens of people.

"Take a look," Tarak said, passing Atif the binoculars.

He pressed them against his face and played with the knobs until everything came into focus. The first thing he noticed was a pair of soldiers wearing blue helmets standing next to a white armoured personnel carrier.

"Hey, it's the Dutch."

Atif began to push himself to his feet, but Tarak hauled him down.

"But it's okay," Atif said. "Don't you see? They must have forced the Chetniks to leave."

Tarak looked at Atif then raised a finger and pointed at the binoculars. "Look again, *Braco*. Look closely."

Atif stared at Tarak.

"Okay," he whispered, picking up the binoculars.

He refocused on the people below. They wore blue helmets and Dutch flak jackets, but the similarity ended there. The uniforms were mismatched like the ones he had seen in Potocari. Atif shifted his view. Other soldiers were walking behind the vehicles. Some wore bits and pieces of the Dutch uniform, but one had on purple and black camouflage.

"There's so many of them," he said, moving the binoculars over the area. He caught movement in the field on the far side of the road. Soldiers were guarding a group of men sitting in tall grass. A civilian walked among them with a television camera on his shoulder. He was following a soldier who had dragged a man to his feet and was hauling him forward.

"Slaven!" the captive shouted through cupped hands.

The cameraman focused on him.

"Mirzet. Come down. Come down out of the forest. There is food here. Water. They are going to drive us to Tuzla. Come down. Slaven! Mirzet!"

"Is he telling the truth?"

"What do you think?"

"I don't know." Atif raised the binoculars again. There were more men in the field.

*What are the Chetniks going to do with them if they were lying about taking them to Tuzla? Bring them to a camp?*

"The blue helmets are overseeing the evacuation," the captive said. "Please. Come down. They have food and water."

Two men crawled out of the woods. Serb soldiers searched them and then put them with the other captives. A few minutes later, another man stumbled out of the forest and the process was repeated.

"Slaven! Mirzet! Come down. Please."

"Who is he calling to?"

"I don't know," Tarak said. "Men he was travelling with. Maybe his brothers. Or his sons."

*Would a father lure his sons out of the woods if he thought they would be in danger?* Atif struggled with the contradictions. *Safe or not?*

They shared the binoculars, watching until the camera crew packed up its gear, boarded one of the trucks, and left. The man stopped shouting names and was led back to the group in the field. No one else left the forest. Atif passed the binoculars to Tarak. He took one more look.

"What are we going to do?"

"We'll keep looking for somewhere to cross."

Tarak suddenly gripped the binoculars with both hands and steadied them.

"What is it?"

Tarak didn't reply, but his jaw tightened. Automatic gunfire rattled below. Atif covered his head.

"They're not shooting at us."

He relaxed and looked at Tarak. He was still gripping the binoculars, knuckles white.

"What were they shooting at?"

Tarak pulled the binoculars from his face, swearing under his breath. "They're shooting the men down there."

"What?" Atif put his hand out for the binoculars.

Tarak held them out of his reach.

"I want to see for myself. I need to see it."

Tarak gave him the binoculars. Below, the scene didn't appear different. Men still sat in the field and soldiers loitered around them and on the road.

*They must have shot into the air. They're just trying to scare the men.*

A group of soldiers wandered over to the detainees. They selected six men and made them stand up. Then they herded them deeper into the field and lined them up.

One captive trudged away from the soldiers.

*Where is he going?*

The man took several stiff steps and the soldiers shouted. Then one of the soldiers left the group and raised his rifle.

Pop. Pop. Pop.

The man fell.

Atif blinked, searching the ground. The man didn't stand up again. Atif shifted his gaze to the soldiers. They were slapping the soldier who had killed the man on the back and laughing. They approached the next captive. Atif grasped the binoculars tightly. The man had on a blue shirt.

*Tata was wearing a blue shirt the day he left.*

A soldier poked the man in the back. He didn't move. The soldier jabbed him a second time. The man took a few steps.

Pop. Pop.

The man toppled into the tall grass and the soldiers moved on to the next one. Atif scanned the ground, trying to get a look at the man in the blue shirt, but could only see swaying grass. The soldiers shot the last four men and then sauntered back to the road.

When Atif passed the binoculars to Tarak, he realized he was holding his breath. He forced it out and tried to draw in fresh air, but his lungs didn't want to work. He felt a hand on his shoulder.

"Short breaths, *Braco*," Tarak said. "Through your nose."

"They're killing them," Atif said, swallowing. "My God, my God, they shot them in the back." He turned to Tarak. "Can't we do anything?"

"Do what? I have one magazine and there are at least two dozen soldiers down there."

Atif stared at the road, forcing air through his nose. "What do we do?"

"We get out of here and find a place to cross."

Tarak began to back up on his knees, but Atif remained still.

"What's the matter?"

"We're not going to make it, are we?"

Tarak crawled back to Atif.

"I don't know, but we have an advantage over a lot of them. We have food and water and we know the area. The people down there are mechanics or bakers or store clerks. One night in the woods is all they could handle. How many of them did you see wearing a uniform? I didn't see a single one."

"Because they all got across last night."

"Not all. We both know that."

At least two of the men they met the night before had been soldiers.

*But are they still alive? Or had they taken off their uniforms before giving up so that the Chetniks would think they were civilians?*

Atif dropped his head into his hands.

"Come on," Tarak said, touching his shoulder. "We have a long walk ahead of us."

Atif raised his head and nodded. His eyes rested for a moment on the tall, swaying grass where the dead men lay and then he turned away and followed Tarak off the ridge.

# THURSDAY: MICHAEL SAKIC

MIKE TOSSED HIS camera bag in the back seat of his truck and looked around. The sun hovered above the bustling tent city. Bosnian army trucks sat next to the tarmac; groups of soldiers were speaking with civilian men who had arrived on the buses the day before.

"Where are you going?"

Mike shut the door. Brendan leaned against the truck, combing his gelled hair.

"Jure came through with a way to get me to Kladanj. I'm his driver."

"In my truck?"

"Come with us."

Brendan opened his mouth to reply and stopped. He turned around to look at Robert, who sat on a step with his camera next to him.

"Tell you what. I'll stick around for the next briefing and you take him with you. He can get some footage and you can tell me what's going on down there."

"I'll try not to lose him."

"And keep him away from the land mines."

Mike smiled and pushed his bag aside to make room for another passenger. Jure appeared and got in the front seat.

"Let's get going. We're burning sunlight."

"Daylight, you moron."

Jure laughed and lit a cigarette. He rolled down the window and blew the smoke outside. Brendan was speaking to Robert. The young man's face brightened and he jumped up, hefted the camera to his shoulder, and walked towards the truck. He stashed his gear in the back seat and poked his hand in through the open front window.

"Hi," Robert said, shaking Jure's hand. "I guess you're the Muslim translator."

"Yes. I am. And I'm guessing that makes you the Christian cameraman."

"Umm..., actually, I'm American."

Jure pulled Robert's hand closer.

"I don't translate the religion, my friend. I translate the language."

Mike laughed and got in the driver's seat.

"Get in, Robert. Before he bites you."

"Is everyone in the West like him?" Jure asked in Bosnian.

"Pretty much," Mike replied. "Now you know why my job is so hard."

"That's okay. Until I met you, I thought all Canadians were nice people."

Mike started the truck and then he looked at Jure. "You want to walk?"

"Drive, Jeebes," Jure said in English.

"That's Jeeves, moron."

"You see what a blessing this man is," Jure said, turning to face Robert with his cigarette held high in one hand. "He brings me the finest tobacco known to man and gives me language lessons at the same time."

Mike looked at Jure and pushed his glasses back with his middle finger. He put the truck in gear and drove towards the gate. They passed through and turned south.

"Anything new this morning?"

"I didn't catch much," Jure replied. "No question everyone knows about the men. There's even word that they're calling on the Chetniks to let the men through to Tuzla."

"And what are the Serbs saying?"

"No idea, but I can guess."

"Okay, guess."

Jure cleared his throat.

"Yes, Mr. President, Mr. Secretary General, I assure you we are doing everything possible to ensure an orderly evacuation. Those that give themselves up will be treated according to the Geneva Convention and those that are not war criminals will be allowed to go home."

"What's wrong with that?" Robert asked, leaning forward between the seats.

"Well, you see, my young Christian American cameraman, we are all war criminals. If your last name is Omanovic, like mine, then you are a war criminal. If it's Karadzic or Mladic then you're not."

"That's pretty stupid."

Jure choked on the smoke he'd just inhaled.

"Ah, my friend, you are learning. Stick with me, Christian cameraman, and I will teach you so that you can go home and teach them."

"Yeah. Sure. Okay." Robert looked at Mike. "You sure he doesn't bite?"

They reached the checkpoint outside Kladanj. Jure raised his ID and they were waved through the barrier. Mike parked on the shoulder across from a line of buses. The men gathered their gear and walked towards the tents set up to dispense food, water, and medical assistance. Refugees trudging on the road were met by Pakistani peacekeepers and Norwegian medical staff. Some walked directly to the buses. Jure stepped inside a tent. Mike fished his camera out and strolled towards the approaching refugees, taking pictures. Robert followed, his camera rolling.

"Where are they coming from?" Mike asked Jure when he returned. "I don't see any buses."

Jure pointed down the road towards a short tunnel.

"Six kilometres away," he said. "They make them walk. The doctor said they've been trickling in all night. You should see them in there." His shoulders shuddered and he rubbed his arm. "I think I'm getting chicken skin."

"Goose bumps, you moron."

Mike already had goose bumps on top of goose bumps.

The road was full of refugees. Women carried their children, walking a few metres and stopping to rest then walking a few more. One old woman caught Mike's attention. She was pulling her husband, a double amputee, along the ground on a blanket and stopping to rest after every step. Two peacekeepers approached the woman and lifted the man and his blanket. His wife followed without a word.

Mike backed up, pulling Robert with him as he took pictures of the peacekeepers carrying the man. They disappeared inside the tent and Robert followed. A doctor pulled Jure aside to translate for him. Mike stood alone, staring down the road.

*Six kilometres.*

He'd hoped to get some pictures of the Serbs. He didn't expect they would be so far away.

*Not that a short walk has to stop me.*

"Jure," he said, tapping the translator on the shoulder. "I'm going for a walk. Okay?"

Jure spun around.

"Where?"

Mike walked away.

"Just as far as the buses."

"What?" Jure said, running after Mike. "You can't go down there."

"What are they going to do? Shoot me?"

"There are mines everywhere."

"I'm not going into the woods. I'll stay on the pavement and only go as far as they let me. If the first Serb I meet tells me to leave then I'll leave. Don't worry. I won't be long. And keep an eye on the kid. Don't bite him."

"Mike!"

"You know what they say, Jure. If your pictures aren't good enough, you're not close enough."

"Yeah?" Jure shouted after him. "Well. What about the one where if you're still breathing, you're not dead enough."

Mike glanced back, smiling. Jure threw up his hands and turned away.

He walked quickly through the tunnel. Women plodded along the road or sat on the shoulder, out of the sun. One woman was using a piece of cardboard to fan her infant. Another woman was trying to fill a bottle in a creek running alongside the road. Mike counted eight men in one group, but other than that, there were few men or teenage boys. Bags and clothes littered the road. Mike took pictures as he walked. The refugees asked him questions in Bosnian and English.

"What is going to happen to us?"

"Where are the blue helmets?"

"Do you know what they have done with our husbands?"

"How much farther?"

Mike pointed toward Kladanj.

"Not much farther," he told them. "Food and water."

Some who were on the verge of giving up took heart from his words and kept moving. Others remained on the ground, staring up at him as he took their picture.

Farther down, he came across a large tree lying across the road. Walking off the asphalt was a risk, so he pushed his camera bag underneath the tree and climbed over it. He stopped to take a picture of an old woman sitting against the tree on the other side.

"Where are you going?"

Mike turned, looking for the source of the question. A Serb soldier in a clean camouflage uniform was sitting on a guardrail. A rifle hung against his chest. He tossed a cigarette into the ditch and beckoned to Mike.

"What are you doing here?" He pointed at the camera around Mike's neck.

"They sent me here to take some pictures," Mike replied in Bosnian.

"Who sent you?"

Mike dug into his back pocket and pulled out a business card he had borrowed from a photojournalist who worked for a small paper in Novi Sad, Serbia.

"They want some pictures of the great victory over the Turks in Srebrenica."

The soldier inspected the card. Mike had used it once before to bluff his way across a Serb checkpoint. Luckily, he had learned the language without developing a strong accent. The Serb passed the card back.

"Novi Sad. I have two cousins there. Never been, though."

"You should visit and see our bridges."

The soldier fished out a pack of cigarettes, inspected the contents, and frowned. He crushed the empty package in his fist and tossed it over the edge. Mike dropped his camera bag to the ground, digging into a side pocket. He pulled out a pack of Player's. The Serb's mouth dropped open.

"I don't smoke," Mike said, tossing the pack to the soldier, "but I try to bring a pack or two with me to share with our brave soldiers." He raised his camera. "Can I take your picture? For your cousins to see."

The soldier smiled and poked the cigarettes into a pocket. He stood up straight, threw out his chest, and held the rifle high. Mike took a picture. The soldier pointed to the refugees.

"Another one. With the Turks in the background."

Mike took another shot. "Are the buses far away?"

"No," the soldier replied. "Not too far."

"Can I go?"

The soldier retrieved the pack of Player's from his pocket and sat back down on the guardrail. "Sure. Tell them I said you're okay."

"Keep up the good work," Mike said. He walked away, tasting the toast and marmalade from breakfast.

The last refugees had passed him on the road by the time Mike caught sight of the first bus, empty and turning around. A dozen soldiers loitered around the checkpoint. There were three men on the side of the road. Two lay on stretchers and the third was kneeling with his hands clasped behind his head. Mike started to repeat the bluff with the soldiers, but the moment he raised his camera, they stopped asking questions and smiled.

*Nothing like the prospect of being famous to make you forget about security.*

"More buses are coming very soon," the senior sergeant told him. The sergeant was two inches shorter than Mike, but his shoulders were twice as broad. His camouflaged shirt was unbuttoned, the sleeves too small to roll up over biceps as thick as Mike's thighs.

"The buses bring the women and children, but the men ran away. We have them trapped. We have soldiers on the road all the way to Bratunac. They can't escape. When we are done, Srebrenica will be Serbian once again."

"How many have been captured?"

"Thousands," he said. "They hide in the forest like deer, but we flush them out. They have no food or water. They'll all give up. They're cowards, as you know."

Mike nodded, his eyes drifting towards the stretchers. The man on the right was unconscious and had bloody bandages on his head. The other man's stomach and thigh were wrapped in bandages and he was coughing up blood. Neither wore a uniform. Mike raised his camera and focused on their faces.

"Take this man, for example," the sergeant said, kicking the thigh of the conscious man. "He is a soldier who stabbed himself in the leg hoping we would not detain him. But he is a war criminal. He killed Serb women and children. He raped them and burned them alive in their homes."

*Charred furniture. Crackling flames. Roasting flesh.*

Mike swallowed and refocused on the Serb. The sergeant turned to the kneeling man, pulled him to his feet, and dragged him to the edge of the road. The man's eyes were fixed on the ground and his whole body shook. Unlike the others, he wore camouflage pants and a green shirt. All three men were barefoot. The Serb pulled out his pistol and cocked it, pointing it up at the man's head.

"Come over here and take a picture. I will show you what we do to war criminals."

Mike lowered his camera and glanced down the road.

*Where are those goddamned buses?*

"Shoot," the sergeant said.

Mike's heart jumped. "Huh?"

The sergeant motioned to Mike with the pistol.

"Shoot your pictures. I have friends in Novi Sad. I want them to see that I have captured Turks. Come on. It's just a picture."

Mike used his shirt to wipe the sweat from his forehead. He raised the camera and centred the frame on the pistol pointing at the man's head.

"Let me know when you are ready," the sergeant said.

The prisoner's eyes flicked up.

Mike's finger hovered over the shutter release. He waited a moment for the lens to focus.

"I'm ready."

The pistol fired.

Mike's hand jumped. The camera clicked.

One picture.

Two.

Three.

The man collapsed to the ground.

Mike took a step back, struggling to hold onto the camera. His hands were shaking.

"Scared you, didn't I?"

Mike stared at the body. It stared back, sightless, blood seeping from the corner of its lips.

*Oh, shit, shit! Don't throw up.*

He looked up at the sergeant and flashed a brief smile.

"That picture will make you famous," the sergeant said. "Like the one from Vietnam."

Mike nodded, keeping his lips sealed tight. His throat stung. He pretended to play with the camera. The sergeant turned back to the body and kicked at it until it rolled into the ditch.

"Come look."

Mike willed his feet to remain still, but they moved anyway. And then he was standing on the edge of the road, looking down. Bodies littered the ravine.

"Go ahead. Take your pictures."

Mike pulled the camera up to his face. It was heavier than he remembered. He took pictures until the advance lever stopped.

"I'm out of film. I have to put in more."

The sergeant slapped him on the back.

"Do you like vodka? We have some good Russian vodka over here."

*That sounds good. Too good.*

"I'll be right there," Mike said, returning to his camera bag.

He crouched down, taking his time. His hands were still shaking. Every time he tried to insert the film into the reel, it popped out. He glanced at the soldiers. Most of them were pacing the road, smoking and chatting. One was taking a nap inside a truck. Another was leaning against a highway sign, staring at Mike.

Mike put his eyes back on the camera. After another fruitless attempt at inserting the film into the reel, he gave up. He closed the cover and slipped the film into his pocket. He stood up: the sergeant was coming towards him with a bottle. He opened it and held it in front of Mike.

He stared at the bottle and then his hand reached out and grabbed it by the neck. He took a swig. The burning liquid descended, warming his chest and stomach.

There was a growing rumble from the southeast.

*Oh, thank God.*

Mike handed the bottle back.

"Have some more."

"No. No. I'm fine. I need a steady hand."

"I think you need more to steady those hands."

Mike stuffed a trembling hand into his pocket. The Serb sergeant walked away to greet the bus. Mike followed, pretending to snap pictures of the refugees as they stepped off.

"Go. Your Turk brothers are waiting for you," the sergeant shouted, pointing towards Kladanj. "This is what Alija has done to you. Don't blame us. Your leaders could have gotten you all out years ago, but they let you suffer."

The soldiers posed with the refugees. A teenage girl squealed as a soldier draped an arm over her shoulder. A woman pulled the girl away and they shuffled off down the road. When the first bus was empty, Mike strolled up to the sergeant.

"I must return. My transportation will not wait for me."

The sergeant dropped a heavy hand on Mike's shoulder and walked him over to a truck. Mike held his breath. The soldier reached inside and pulled out a full bottle of vodka.

"For you, my friend."

Mike forced a smile and accepted the bottle, poking it inside his bag.

"I'll see to it your picture is on the front page."

"You should come back soon," the sergeant said, slapping Mike on the chest. "Come to Srebrenica. Your pictures of the liberated town will be in every paper in Serbia."

They shook hands and then Mike walked away and joined a group of women, asking questions as they melted into the crowd.

"What did you say your name was?" came a voice from behind.

Mike looked back. The soldier who had been staring at him was at his heels, his rifle slung over his shoulder. Mike gave him the name on the card.

"I lived in Novi Sad for a few years. I worked on my school newspaper. I knew some of the journalists. You're not familiar."

Mike shrugged and kept walking. The Serb kept up with him.

"I haven't been there long," Mike said.

The Serb grunted, unconvinced.

"Who do you really work for?"

Mike paused and stared at the young man.

"I told you."

"You're from the West, aren't you?"

"Does it matter?"

The soldier glanced at the checkpoint and then jerked his head forward.

"I'll walk with you awhile. Make sure no one bothers you."

Mike looked back; the sergeant waved to him, smiling.

"Yeah. Sure. Smoke?"

Mike hauled another pack of Player's from his bag and tossed them over. The soldier stuffed them into a pocket. They walked in silence, the soldier glancing back from time to time.

"My name is Nermin. I'm not sure how to say this, but what you saw back there, well, we're not all like that."

"I know."

"It's just...you took our pictures and I don't want to get in trouble for what the sergeant did."

"What did you say your name was?"

"Nermin. Nermin Jankovic."

Mike stopped and took out his notebook, writing the name under the sergeant's.

"You don't have to worry," he said, putting the notebook away and opening the back cover of the empty camera. "I don't have you on the other roll."

Nermin smiled.

"You know I have heard about the war crimes trials," the young soldier said. "I hope you can tell people we're not all like them. I wanted to be a journalist, like you, but when the war broke out, my father moved to Pale and I had to join up. All I want is for the war to end."

"You're not the only one."

Nermin looked at him, shaking his head.

"What happened back there, it had nothing to do with you. You know that, don't you?"

Mike said nothing. They approached the felled tree and Nermin slowed his pace.

"He was going to shoot them anyway. He hates the Muslims. Me? I had Muslim friends. Croat friends." He sighed. "I hope they're still my friends. I hope they're still alive."

"I understand."

The young soldier straightened up.

"Thank you. Whoever you are. I think I should go back."

Mike offered Nermin his hand and they shook.

"Take care, my friend."

Nermin jogged away, through the refugees. When he disappeared from sight, Mike turned and leaned against the tree. He stared straight ahead, his thoughts racing.

*"It had nothing to do with you. He was going to shoot them anyway."*

He heard a rustling sound near his feet. He looked down: the old woman whose picture he'd taken on the way in was sitting in the same position against the tree.

"Why are you still here?"

The woman touched the tree. Mike leaned down and took her hands.

"It's a long walk, Mother. Do you want a hand?"

She accepted his offer. Mike helped her over the tree.

As they walked away from it, hand in hand, two gunshots echoed behind them.

# THURSDAY: MARIJA STAVIC

MARIJA FORCED HER way through the sweltering crowd, hugging the side of the carrier until she broke free against the linked arms of the peacekeepers. She gulped in fresh air, leaning forward between two Dutch soldiers. The human chain stretched between the armoured vehicles, holding the surging throng of refugees. No buses were in sight. Marija looked around for Jac.

"Keep back," the peacekeeper said in English, pushing her.

"I'm looking for *Korporaal* Larue."

"I'm sorry. I don't know where he is. I think he's supposed to be escorting a convoy."

"I know. I...."

"Marija! Up here."

She looked up. Maarten was crouching on the edge of the carrier.

"I was ready to give up on you. Are the others close by?"

"Yes, yes. It took us a while, but they're just back there."

"Good. Jac's getting the jeep now. We're escorting the next convoy."

"Okay, I'll go get them. We should be able to get on."

"We probably won't see you on the road, but you'll be okay. The convoys are still getting through to Tisca."

"Thank you. And please, thank Jac for me again."

"I'll do that. Take care of yourselves."

Maarten stood up, walked to the edge of the carrier and dropped from sight. Marija took a long breath then turned back into the crowd and fought against the current. Behind her, buses rumbled to a halt. The crowd jostled their way forward.

She found Ina and the girls where she had left them. "We go now," she said, picking up her bag.

Adila offered Tihana to her, but Marija refused, wrapping her arm around the pair. "I'll stay close, but you hold on to her."

"We should try to stay near the centre of the crowd," Ina said.

They huddled together, moving with the flow, inching their way towards the centre. The pressure increased. Elbows and torsos pressed against them, threatening to drive the girls to the ground. Marija pushed back. A moment later, they were free. They shuffled through the line of Dutch peacekeepers with the rest of the crowd. On the other side, Serb soldiers closed in on them like wolves on a wounded deer. Marija adjusted Adila's scarf, covering the girl's head as much as possible.

"Where are your soldiers now?" one of the Serbs said. "They're drinking beer with your husbands."

"Turk whores," another said.

"Alija has abandoned you. The world doesn't care about you."

Marija ignored the taunts, holding Adila and Tihana close and fighting to stay in the middle of the crowd. Marija had lost sight of Ina in the quickly moving horde. She glanced back; Ina was waving her forward. Marija reached the last bus and climbed its steps. She found an empty seat half way down the aisle and placed Adila and Tihana next to the window.

"We did it," Adila said.

"Not yet," Marija whispered. "Just keep your head down."

Tihana cuddled into Adila's chest, clutching the toy soldiers hidden inside her shirt.

Ina and Lejla appeared a few moments later. "We'll sit apart," she said, and kept moving. Marija watched them find a seat on the rear bench with three others.

The bus driver stood up and rubbed the grey stubble on his cheek. He was balding and carried extra weight around his belly. Despite the heat, he wore a long-sleeved white shirt and a blue tie. He sealed the door and then walked the length of the bus, pulling candy out of his pocket and giving it to the children. He smiled at them and chatted with their mothers.

"Where are you taking us?" a woman asked.

"Don't worry," he said. "We are going to Tisca. The blue helmets are waiting for you up the road with food and water. Everything will be okay. Tonight, you will sleep peacefully in Tuzla. I promise you."

The women's eyes darted nervously. They looked at one another. Some shrugged. Others sighed. The driver took his seat and started the engine. The smell of diesel drifted in through the open windows. Marija looked out and spotted Maarten climbing into a Mercedes jeep. The jeep sped by and their bus made a three point turn and took its place at the end of the convoy.

Marija glanced back towards the town. It's almost over, she thought. She never expected to see Srebrenica again.

The buses crossed over the Yellow Bridge, passing the first checkpoint without stopping.

"Maybe we are going to be okay?" Adila said. "Maybe they won't stop us."

"We'll see."

The bus driver sang a few lines from an old Communist-era song. *"U ime svih nas iz pedeset i neke. Za zakletvu Titu ja spevao sam stih."*

Then he looked at the children in the first rows. He made a circular motion with his hands.

"I do not recall the past and the distant battle," he sang, "because I was born after them."

Soon the bus was filled with the surreal sound of children singing and laughing. Marija tickled Tihana's chin.

"'Count On Us.' You know the song."

Tihana smiled.

Suddenly, something struck their window and the sound of shattering glass broke into the song. Marija draped herself over Adila and Tihana. Children were squealing instead of singing. The bus kept moving.

Marija straightened up. A window four rows ahead was gone, the woman next to it pushing out the shards with her scarf wrapped around her hand. Marija's window had cracked, but it hadn't broken. The shattered core had grown multiple legs, making a web in the glass. She looked through a clear section between the cracks. People lined the side of the road. Men, women, and children were throwing rocks at the buses and screaming insults. Marija wrapped her arm around Adila.

"Are you okay?"

"Yes. Yes. It just startled me." Tihana was wrapped around Adila, trembling. Marija reached out and stroked her hair.

"Don't mind them," the driver shouted. "Now, what happened to my choir? *Računajte na nas!*"

As they put Bratunac behind them, the singing resumed. Marija noted landmarks she had not seen in three years. The bus stop where Yassir used to pick her up when she taught in Srebrenica. The gas station where they'd changed the flat tire. Cultivated fields covered the hillsides. When they got closer to Kravica, she felt a pang of homesickness. "You used to live near here, didn't you?" Adila asked.

"Yes. The farm is on this side of Kravica. It's beautiful this time of year with so much ready to harvest. We used to have fresh vegetables for dinner every night."

"How did you meet Yassir?"

"We went to school together. I was studying to become a teacher and he was taking agriculture. He had to drop out after his parents died. His brother, Vlatko, had no interest in the farm, but we made it work."

A hiss from the brakes and the bus rolled to a stop. Marija felt Adila tense. She looked past her, between the cracks in the window. Soldiers.

"Don't worry," Marija said. "They're just going to check for men."

The soldiers were standing around a donkey cart piled with manure, smoking with the old man holding the animal's tether. A soldier walked up to the white donkey and fed it an apple.

Marija licked her lips.

An impatient rap on the door: the driver lumbered down the steps and opened it. A soldier, wearing a blue helmet, stepped into the bus.

Jac? No, she thought. He wasn't wearing a helmet anymore.

The soldier turned to face the women. He had on a Dutch flak vest, but the rest of his uniform was mismatched camouflage.

"No men this time," the driver said to him. The soldier raised a hand and covered his nose as he scanned the interior of the bus. "Just ugly Turk women who need a bath."

The soldier glanced at the driver and smiled. Then he walked down the aisle. He stopped at the back and stared at the teenage girl with long blonde hair sitting next to Lejla. The soldier touched her cheek. The blonde girl turned away.

"What's your name?"

"Please, leave her alone," her mother said, adjusting the scarf on the girl's hair.

"I just wanted to know her name."

"Her name is Samira. Now please. You're scaring her."

The soldier grunted, turned around, and walked back to the driver.

"You're right. They're ugly."

The driver slapped the soldier on the shoulder and gave an exaggerated belly laugh. He had a pack of cigarettes in his hand and followed the soldier down the steps. They stood below her window, smoking. Minutes later, another soldier approached them. The driver gave him a cigarette and he poked it away behind his ear. The soldiers left and the driver flicked away his half-smoked butt. He boarded the bus and shut the door. Hesitating at the top of the steps, he looked at the women and winked.

When they pulled away from the checkpoint the bus filled with words of relief. Marija looked out the window: ahead of them Jac's jeep was sitting on the shoulder of the road. She stood up as they passed. Jac was arguing with one of the Serb soldiers. Maarten was standing off to the side, his face covered in blood.

"Are they beating them?" Adila asked.

Marija turned around and looked out the rear window. Jac's vehicle didn't move.

"I don't know."

She watched for several more kilometres, but there was no sign of Jac.

"We're on our own."

# THURSDAY: JAC LARUE

JAC POURED THE last jerry can full of fuel into his jeep and capped the tank. He laid the can aside and grabbed two backpacks.

"Jac."

He turned. Sergeant Janssen was lowering two jerry cans to the ground.

"Take one," he said, pointing, and then he lashed the other can to the jeep next to Jac's. "I'm taking the convoy after you."

Jac took the can and secured it to his own jeep.

"I'm ready to go. Anything else I should know?"

"Yeah. They stole some of the jeeps yesterday and we don't know where all the crews are."

"Maybe they put them on the buses. They could be in Tuzla."

"Let's hope so," he said, and started to turn away. He paused. "One other thing, Jac. Word has it that two buses went missing yesterday."

"Buses full of women? Missing?"

"That's what they're saying. In both cases, the convoy went straight, but the last bus just turned off onto some road, I don't know where."

"You're sure we can't take any weapons?"

"They'll only steal them." Janssen held out his hand. They shook. "Good luck, Jac."

"You too, Sergeant."

Janssen walked away. Jac began to open the jeep door and then stopped to stare in the direction of the morning sun.

*How do people handle this heat?*

He wiped his forehead with the towel and got inside, flipping on the air conditioning after he started the vehicle. Nothing happened and then he remembered. Albert had disabled the air conditioning in order to save gas.

"We're going to have a talk when I get back, Albert."

He drove to the entrance and gave his information to the sentry on duty and then drove out. Refugees streamed towards the buses. Jac pulled up facing the first bus and looked around for Maarten. The passenger door opened.

"I was getting worried," Maarten said, pulling one of the packs forward and inspecting its contents.

"I had to siphon fuel."

"Ah. And here I thought you were trying out a new cologne."

"Did you see Marija?"

Maarten tossed the pack into the back.

"Yes, actually. She was expecting to get on this convoy. I think I saw them get on the last bus."

"The last bus?"

"Yeah. Why?"

Jac tapped a finger against his chin. "Nothing."

"She said to thank you."

Jac looked at Maarten. He shrugged. They heard the first bus start.

"Told the driver we'd lead them out," Maarten said.

"Okay." Jac drove to the front of the six-bus convoy. He waited as the buses made their turns. Then the first bus honked.

"Here goes nothing."

Maarten was playing with the buttons on the dash.

"Where's the air conditioning?"

Jac laughed. "Right next to you," he said, pointing to the window. Maarten rolled it down.

"We can be comfortable or out of gas on the side of the road in the middle of a war. Your choice."

Maarten grumbled and then pointed forward. "Bad guys."

The first checkpoint was on the far side of the Yellow Bridge. The sentry had already pulled the barrier aside and waved them through.

"My mistake," Maarten said, waving back at the sentry. "Good guys."

"Somehow I don't think it's going to keep being this easy."

When the convoy approached Bratunac, Jac slowed to make the turn onto the road that would take them north to Konjevic Polje.

"Now, what do we have here?"

Jac geared the jeep down. Men, women, and children lined both sides of the road. Some were on the road, facing the approaching vehicles.

"Cheerleaders?"

Jac looked in the rearview mirror: the front grill of the bus behind him filled it.

"I think he wants us to speed up."

Jac honked and waved at the people.

"Get the hell off the road!" Maarten yelled out the window.

Some of them moved, but then a teenager stepped from the crowd. He was carrying a rock.

"Shit!"

The boy threw the rock at the jeep, shattering a headlight. Jac flattened the accelerator and swerved around the boy. Another rock bounced off the jeep's hood. Then Jac heard a dull thud.

"Jesus!"

Jac glanced at Maarten who was leaning forward and rolling up his window. "What's wrong?"

Maarten held up his hand. Blood was running down his arm.

"Just go, Jac. Go."

The back window cracked. A rock struck Jac's door. He looked in the rearview mirror: the first bus was latched onto their tail like a water skier, swerving with the jeep. Rocks pounded the side of the bus. Glass shattered.

Seconds later, the rocks stopped. The number of onlookers dwindled. Jac looked over at Maarten again: he had managed to get his pack out of the back and was digging a field dressing out of it.

"How bad is it?"

"Keep driving. I'm fine. It's just a cut."

"A cut my ass," Jac said. "Your face is covered in blood."

"It's not as bad as it looks. Just don't stop."

"There's water on the floor behind you."

Maarten grabbed a bottle and poured it over his head. He cleaned off the blood and tied the dressing tight around his head.

"Checkpoint," Jac said.

"Good guys?"

The sentry pulled aside the barrier, but then another soldier stood in the middle of the road and motioned them onto the shoulder. A group of soldiers was standing next to a donkey harnessed to a cart piled with manure. An old man held the reins. Jac followed the sentry's directions.

"What's going on?"

The soldiers surrounded the jeep, opening doors and pulling out anything that wasn't secured to the vehicle. They told Jac and Maarten to get out and herded them to the front of the jeep. A corporal was waiting for them.

"We have to search your vehicle to make sure you're not carrying any weapons."

"Damn it. Then hurry up."

The corporal picked the first-aid kit off the road and offered it to Jac.

"You should take care of your friend."

Jac took the kit from the soldier and opened it on the hood. Maarten untied the dressing and poured more water over his head.

"Jesus," Jac said, inspecting Maarten's wound. The gash had split his head below the right temple; blood was seeping from it. "You're going to need a few stitches."

"I'm not going back," Maarten said.

Jac cleaned the wound and then took some Steri-Strips out of the first-aid kit. He pulled the laceration closed and wrapped Maarten's head with a bandage.

"That's fine," Maarten said after Jac had wrapped his head three or four times. "Seriously. I don't need to be mummified."

Jac wrapped twice more and taped the bandage.

The first bus pulled out from behind them and headed north.

Jac turned to the corporal. "What's going on? You can't let them go without us."

The Serb ignored him. The buses disappeared from sight. The soldiers emptied the jeep, taking anything not screwed down. Their packs were all that was left.

"Can we go?" he asked the soldiers.

The corporal shrugged at Jac and then jerked his thumb at a young officer who was standing next to the donkey, scratching its ears.

"Well," Maarten said. "He doesn't look old enough to tie his shoelaces."

"Enough of this." Jac strode over to the officer. "I'm leaving now. I have my orders and I'm going to carry them out. You know about orders, don't you?"

The officer nodded and returned his attention to the donkey. Jac went back to the jeep.

"Get in," he said to Maarten, tossing the first-aid kit into the back. "We're leaving."

The jeep's tires spun in the gravel as they moved onto the pavement. There were hundreds of troops on the road now, patrolling the shoulder and ditches or sitting on the edge of the road looking south.

"Jac, look."

Jac glanced at Maarten, expecting to find his head bleeding again. But instead, Maarten was pointing at the window.

"I'm driving. What is it?"

"There are a hundred men in the field back there." Maarten shifted in his seat and looked out the back window. "No. More like two hundred. They're all kneeling down with their hands on their heads."

"Seriously?" Jac said.

"Do we stop?"

"No, we focus on the buses."

"Damn it. I wish I had a camera."

His camera had been destroyed in the observation post with his knife and compass.

"Jesus!"

"What?"

"Bodies," Maarten replied, rolling down his window.

Jac didn't need to look back. There were two more bodies on the shoulder of the road ahead. Serb soldiers loitered around them. When they saw the white jeep, the soldiers stepped in front of the bodies.

"Too late you bastards," Maarten shouted through the window. "We see them."

"Shut up, Maarten."

"There are more men up that road back there. No shirts on. They were marching in line with their hands on their heads."

"Okay, okay."

*What do I do? What do I do?* He had been tasked to escort the buses, not monitor prisoners. *But someone needs to know about it.*

"Got a notepad?"

"Yeah."

"Okay. Write it down," Jac said. "What you see and where it is. We'll let the sergeant know when we get back."

They drove past Konjevic Polje. Soldiers sat on the edge of the road two metres apart, watching the woods. Mortar, anti-aircraft guns, and armoured vehicles were parked at intervals. Dozens of empty trucks lined the road. Some Serbs were driving white Dutch carriers and jeeps.

"How are the men supposed to get through that?"

Jac shook his head, a lump caught in his throat. Atif would be trapped if he hadn't gotten across the road already.

"Buses," Maarten said, pointing forward.

Jac's foot pressed down on the accelerator just as a Serb soldier stepped out into the road and raised his hand.

"Goddamn it."

He slammed on the brakes, screeching to a stop less than a metre from the soldier. Then he turned the ignition off, threw the door open, and jumped out of the jeep, slamming the door behind him. He heard Maarten's door close.

"Are you trying to get yourself killed?" he shouted at the soldier.

A Serb captain approached him.

"We need your vehicle," he said in perfect English.

Maarten looked at Jac. "So, don't cooperate or don't provoke?"

"Sorry," Jac said to the Serb captain. "The jeep belongs to the Dutch government. It's not mine to give to you."

The captain smiled. A dozen rifles were suddenly levelled in their direction.

"As I was saying, I need your vehicle. If you have any personal gear, I suggest you remove it."

Jac cursed under his breath and then he turned and walked back to the jeep.

"Get your gear," he said to Maarten.

Jac reached in and pulled out his pack. The captain walked around the jeep and opened the driver's door. The other soldier got in the passenger side. The captain said something to a soldier standing beside the jeep and then he climbed in and drove off, leaving the two peacekeepers on the side of the road.

"Well," Maarten said, sitting down on his pack. "What do we do now?"

# THURSDAY: ATIF STAVIC

ATIF TORE THE spindly branches from a pair of trees and squeezed between their trunks. His foot slipped on roots growing like tarantula legs from the base of the tree. He caught himself and stepped forward, but his foot caught in the roots and he tripped and fell. He remained on the ground, willing his body to get up. Every muscle ached and his hands and face were scratched from the trek through the thick brush.

"Okay?"

Atif nodded. He stood up and weaved his foot out from the snaking roots. Tarak offered him a bottle of water and Atif drank it dry.

"The trees thin out from here. We'll rest ahead."

Tarak turned, took a step, and stopped.

"What is it?"

"I hear someone talking," Tarak whispered.

Atif stayed still. Voices drifted among the trees.

"Chetniks?"

"Stay here. I'll be right back."

Atif sat down and leaned back against a tree, pulling his legs up against his chest. He watched Tarak creep through the woods and disappear. The voices grew louder.

*An argument?*

For the first time since he'd fled into the woods, Atif didn't care who they belonged to. If the voices were Chetniks, it would be over.

*What would it be like? Were the men in that field happy it was over? What were they thinking? They must have known they were going to die. Were they scared? Did they hear the rifles fire? Did they live long enough to feel the pain?*

The questions prowled through Atif's mind, chewing at his sanity.

*Did they regret the decisions that led them here? Or did they accept it and die thinking of their families? Was it like that for Tata? Did they shoot him in the back and leave him in a field somewhere? Did Tata think of us?*

He felt tears rising.

"*I won't leave until you walk out of the woods.*"

"But what if I don't come out of the forest, Mama?" he said to himself.

*How would you know what happened to me? Would they just leave me in a field somewhere? No. They were killing too many men to leave them in the open. They would bury them all. They would bury me and Mama will never know.*

He remembered the notebook and dug it out of his pack. He flipped through dozens of pages containing dates, numbers, and names until he came to a blank sheet.

*Mama*, he wrote.

*You made the right choice, Mama. I found a soldier and he is helping me but I don't know if we can make it across the road. There are so many Chetniks and I know what they're doing. Please don't be mad at yourself. This was my only chance and I'm glad I tried. It is better this way. Right now, I'm just south of the road somewhere near Nova Kasaba. We're going to try to cross tonight. Tarak (he's the soldier) said we have a good chance of making it all the way if we can get across. I believe him and he really knows what he is doing. But I'm scared, Mama. I hate not knowing. I wish we had never gone to Srebrenica. I wish we had gone to Tuzla. Then we could have left for good. We'd be a family in some other country. I don't care where. I just want to be with you. I love you, Mama. Give Tihana kisses from me and tell her the soldiers will look after her from now on.*

Atif stared at the page. He wanted to erase the last part, but the eraser was a useless black stump. He didn't want his mother to cry. He considered tearing the page up. But it was the only way she'd know, if they found him. If they found the pack.

That's all that mattered.

Nothing he wrote would keep her from crying. And he wanted to say so much more.

*How would I tell her I don't think I can do it anymore? I don't want to die like them, Mama.*

He made sure his documents were inside the book and then he wrapped it up tight in the plastic bag and stuffed it in the bottom of the pack. There was a high pitched whistle: his head jerked up. Tarak was back, waving at him to come.

"It's five men," Tarak said as they walked along. "One of them is injured and can't go on. He wants to be left near the road where the Chetniks can find him. I'm going to help them bring him to the road and then we can move on."

"Do they know what will happen to him?"

"I told them. They understand."

*They're not afraid?*

Tarak led Atif into a small clearing. Five grey-haired men sat on the ground, looking warily in their direction. A man carrying a shabby suit jacket stood up and greeted Atif.

"My name is Kemal." He introduced the others. One man's leg was bandaged, but the bandage was soaked with fresh blood.

"If you're ready," Tarak said. "We should go."

"I've decided to go with him," the man named Sead said then gestured towards his brother, Izet. "We've spoken. My heart is weak and I can't walk much farther. The Chetniks will either treat me or shoot me, but it's better than dying under this cursed sun."

"I can't talk him out of it," Izet said.

"Okay." Tarak turned to Kemal. "Could you stay with the boy while we're gone?"

"Certainly," the man replied.

Atif gazed at the men, his head spinning.

*"The Chetniks will either treat me or shoot me."*

"No," Atif said to Tarak. "I want to go."

"It's better if you stayed here, *Braco*. Rest, eat something."

"No. I want to go to the road with them."

"What? No," Tarak said, stepping closer. "They'll kill you."

"So what? It's better than this. We won't get across."

"We haven't even tried. Why do you want to give up so easily?"

"I'm tired," he said, trying to catch his breath. "I can't take it anymore. The guns. The shelling. Snipers. I've had enough."

"You can't give up after three years. Only a couple of more days and you'll be safe in Tuzla."

"Until the Chetniks decide to invade there too. Then where do I go? Sarajevo? Don't you see? It's not going to end."

"What about your mother?"

Atif started to walk north. Tarak stood in the way.

"Leave her out of this."

"I can't," Tarak replied. "Your mother loves you. She's going to be waiting for you in Tuzla. What am I supposed to tell her when I walk out of the woods without you? That you gave up without even trying?"

"She'll understand."

"She won't understand. She's your mother. She wants you to grow up, get married, start a family. She wants you to be happy. She wants you to live."

"I can't live like this."

"She's not asking you to. She'll take you away from here. You said it yourself. You'll go west. You'll be safe there."

Atif looked away.

*"We have to hope, Atif."*

"What about your little sister? Are you going to make her grow up alone, *Braco*?"

"Stop calling me that!" he yelled. "I'm not your little brother. I'm not supposed to be out here. I'm only fourteen. I'm supposed to be in school or playing with my friends. I was supposed to be with my friends."

Atif backed away, his eyes sweeping the ground, unfocused. He couldn't erase the memory. The overturned car. Dani's smile. The smoke. The arm. His father waving goodbye.

"You're not thinking clearly, Atif. Do you think this is what your friends would have wanted?"

"Shut up." Atif pushed Tarak away and tried to walk past him. Tarak stepped back, blocking his way.

"I'm not going to let you commit suicide."

"That's my choice."

"Like your choice to go after the ball?"

*"I'll get it."*

"If Dani had gone after that ball and you had died in that alley, would you want him to give up? Wouldn't your last thought be that you were thankful he survived, that he could go on and do everything you wanted to do? Wouldn't you want him to live?"

"Yes," Atif whispered. Tears welled up in his eyes; he rubbed them away.

"But you lived. If you throw away your life then his death is meaningless."

"No, it's not."

"It is. He died and you lived. I can't understand why these things happen, but they do. All we can do is find some meaning in all this insanity. We can live. For them. Because if you don't then he will be forgotten."

"But it was my fault."

"It wasn't your fault. You didn't fire the shell."

"You don't understand. I went after that ball because I wanted to die. I stood there…." He paused, fighting for a full breath. "I stood there with the ball over my head wishing a sniper would see me."

"But they didn't see you, did they?" Tarak said, his voice softening. "How long have you been thinking like this?"

A tear welled up and threatened to spill over. Atif ignored it, swallowing hard.

"I don't know." The tear dropped. "I just miss him so much."

"Who? Your father?"

The tears came hard and fast and Atif sank to the ground under their onslaught. He hid his face in his hands. Tarak crouched next to him.

"Is that why you wanted to be a soldier?"

Atif nodded and looked up. His vision was still blurred.

"It would have been so easy. And mama wouldn't have known. I didn't want her to know. I just wanted to be with Tata."

"Do you think this is what your father would have wanted?"

Atif looked away, trying to catch his breath.

*"All that matters is that you and Tihana are safe. That's what he would have wanted."*

"Is it?" Tarak said.

"No! But I'm not strong enough to do what he wanted. I can't take care of them."

"But you did take care of them. You got them to Potocari. The blue helmet said the buses were making it through, that the women were safe. They're alive because of you. That's what your father wanted. And now he wants you to take care of yourself."

"I can't. I can't. I don't want to…."

"Don't want to what?"

Atif squeezed his eyes shut. The man in the blue shirt walked forward a few steps and then sank down in the tall grass.

"I don't want to die like them."

Tarak sat down next to Atif. A hand squeezed his shoulder.

"You're not going to die like them. I promise you."

Atif fell into Tarak's arms, tears flooding his face.

"I will get you to Tuzla. I promise."

# THURSDAY: NIKO BASARIC

NIKO PACED BACK and forth along the road; it had been a long day and he was sick of spending hours staring at the same clump of trees. Petar was sitting on the edge of the pavement, not saying a word. Niko found that odd. He had been certain the recruit wouldn't be able to shut up about his first few moments in combat.

*Although I can't really call it combat.*

Earlier, Drach had set up a checkpoint on the road for the buses. They hadn't found any men on the buses, but they'd confiscated money and jewelry from the women. More than two hundred men had walked out of the woods and surrendered. Trucks had taken them to the soccer field in Nova Kasaba.

*Another couple of days then it'll be over. I'll be rid of Drach and back on some quiet checkpoint somewhere, figuring out how to get to Austria.*

He glanced at Petar.

"See anything?"

Petar shook his head.

"You okay?"

"It's not what I expected."

"It usually isn't."

"I can't believe I shot them. I mean, they weren't even armed."

"You didn't know that."

"I know, I know. When I saw that first man, I thought I was

going to piss myself."

"You wouldn't be the first."

"What do you mean?"

"Drach did the first time."

"Seriously? How do you know?"

"The sergeant who led the patrol told me. It happened in Croatia. They had to send him back to get changed. They couldn't stand the stink."

Petar smiled for the first time in hours.

"You're just playing with me."

"No, I'm dead serious. I'll introduce you to his old sergeant when we go back."

The sound of engines broke into the conversation.

"Buses coming," Petar said.

Niko turned around. Sunlight glinted off a windshield. He crossed the road.

"Hey, Turk!" Drach shouted from the front yard of an abandoned yellow house. He was sitting in a chair next to a small table covered with bottles of wine and plum brandy.

*Damn it. The bastards are already getting drunk.*

"It's almost time to eat, Turk. Why don't you find us a pretty girl to share our meal?"

Niko ignored him.

Ivan appeared beside Drach and took a swig from one of the bottles.

"Don't leave it to him. You've seen what passes for pretty in Srebrenica. That's why he married a Serb."

"Could he be smarter than he looks?" Drach said. They laughed, reminding Niko of chimps in nature documentaries.

The last of the six buses hissed to a stop in front of him. The door opened and he climbed inside, bringing a hand to his nose.

"*Zdravo*, my friend," the bus driver said, rubbing the white stubble on his face. "There are no men aboard. I assure you. Just ugly Turk women who need a bath."

"Is there any other kind of Turk woman?" Ivan was standing just outside the door, lighting a cigarette.

Niko pulled his helmet low over his eyes. He walked along the aisle giving each woman a cursory glance.

"And what's your name?"

Niko stopped and looked back over his shoulder. Ivan, leaning over a woman, was removing the scarf from the girl sitting next to her.

"Is this your daughter? No, she can't be. You look too young to be a mother."

Satisfied the bus contained no men, Niko turned to leave. Ivan put out his hand.

"You haven't picked one."

The driver was standing behind Ivan, staring at Niko with eyes that held a plea.

"I thought you volunteered," Niko said.

Ivan pushed Niko aside and pointed.

"That one."

Niko turned around. Ivan's choice was a young blonde girl wrapped in her mother's arms.

"No," the girl's mother shrieked.

"Bring her," Ivan said to Niko.

"Please, sir, I am...." The driver shut his mouth on whatever he was going to say when Ivan shoved him aside.

"Bring her now, Turk. Or we go on another hunt. And this time, you will walk in front of me." Ivan stood by the door, his arms crossed.

Niko swallowed hard. He turned and went towards the girl. Her mother stood up, blocking Niko's path.

"You are not taking her."

"I'm sorry," Niko whispered. "I don't have a choice."

Another woman stood up. She gestured at her own dark-haired daughter.

"She is sick," the woman said. "It might be hepatitis and we've been sharing water."

"She is right," the driver said. "She has shared her water. They're probably all contagious."

"What's taking you so long, Turk?" Ivan's voice was mocking, impatient.

Niko stepped closer to the woman and her daughter. The dark-haired girl removed the scarf from her neck, revealing red blotches, and then pulled up her sleeve. Niko examined the sores on the girl's arm.

"I don't think that's hepatitis," he said to her mother. His uncle had died from the disease. He was sure the sores his uncle had were different.

The driver came up behind him.

"It's hepatitis," he whispered. Niko turned and they locked eyes. The driver gave him a slight nod. "Do you want to take the chance?"

"Turk!"

"Stay here," Niko told the blonde girl. He turned around. Ivan was drumming one hand against the driver's seat. "You don't want that one. She's been exposed to hepatitis."

"What?"

"She has," the driver agreed.

Ivan swore and turned, pounding his feet on the steps of the bus as he left. Niko felt a hand on his shoulder.

"Thank you, friend," the driver whispered. "What is your name?"

Niko faced the driver.

"I will remember this," the driver said. "We both know there are a lot of things happening. It would be wrong for some of us, people like you and me, to be blamed."

Niko took a last look at the women. His glance was arrested by a familiar face.

*The teacher?*

She met his gaze and nodded.

Next to her, a little girl was curled up on the lap of a teenager. The child stared wide-eyed at Niko with brilliant green eyes.

*The same eyes as her brother. She must be the baby the teacher used to bring to the soccer games.*

He wanted to step back and ask the woman where her son was, but the quicker he got off the bus, the better for everyone on it. He turned to the driver.

"Niko Basaric," he said and extended his hand. The two men shook.

"My name is Kovac. Alexandar Kovac."

Kovac offered Niko a cigarette, but he declined.

"Take care of yourself, Niko Basaric."

He gave the driver a quick smile and then glanced back: the blonde girl was sobbing in her mother's arms. The teacher was watching him.

He turned away and stepped off the bus. As the door shut behind him, he heard a girl squeal. He looked around. Ivan stepped from the second last bus in the convoy and walked towards the house, a girl slung over his shoulder. She wore shorts and a pink blouse, her face lost in long, tangled blonde hair.

Drach abandoned his chair, picked up a bottle of plum brandy, and followed Ivan into the yellow house.

# THURSDAY: ATIF STAVIC

ATIF SAT WITH his back to Kemal, his knees tight against his chest. He rubbed his eyes hard and then he licked his lips, tasting salt. He pulled a sleeve over his hand and wiped his face. The taste of salt remained.

Tarak is right, he thought. I have to try. I don't want Mama to spend her life watching the woods and waiting.

He looked up, searching for movement in the trees. Tarak and the other man had been gone an hour. They planned to carry the injured as close to the road as possible, leaving them where they could call out to the Serbs after Tarak and the others were at a safe distance away.

"Do you wish to join me?"

Atif looked around. Behind him, Kemal was unrolling his prayer mat.

"I don't know how to pray," Atif said.

"Well," Kemal said, considering Atif's words for a moment. "It's not my place to tell you how."

"I don't think my father believed anymore."

Kemal's eyes wandered. "Tito had a way of making us all forget our old ways and all our old hatreds. Brotherhood and unity was his way. Perhaps if he were alive today...." His words faded as he adjusted the mat, glancing up at the sun. "If you wish, I will keep you in my prayers."

Atif shrugged; Kemal knelt.

"Don't worry. Everything is as Allah wills it. If we are meant to survive, we will make it through. If not, then it is Allah's will."

Atif dug crackers out of his pack; Kemal prayed.

Bushes rustled.

Atif's head jerked around. Branches waved. A bird dropped from a tree, flying in a series of right angles until it disappeared in the foliage. Kemal got up from his mat and lay down on the ground next to Atif.

"Is it them?"

"I don't know," Atif whispered.

Twigs snapped. Movement.

*Chetnik patrol?*

A white armband appeared among the greenery.

"Yes, they're back."

Kemal patted Atif on the shoulder. "You see, my friend. Allah is watching over us."

Atif stared at the old man then looked away. "Tarak?"

Tarak emerged from the trees, looking at Atif as if he had half expected to find him gone. Izet walked behind him, wiping tears from his eyes. Vahid brought up the rear.

"Are you okay?" Tarak asked.

Atif nodded. "Sorry. I didn't mean for that to happen."

Tarak shook his shoulder. "Don't apologize. You seem to be holding a lot of emotion inside. Can't say I blame you, but it's good to get some of it out."

"I guess so."

Tarak looked at the men. "We should keep going."

Kemal rolled up his mat.

"What are we going to do?" Vahid asked.

"I wanted to go as far to the northwest as I can by nightfall and hope they don't have as many troops there. They seem to be concentrated in this area and they only have so many soldiers. Are you up to it?"

"We will try."

"Is that you, Tarak?" a voice asked from the woods.

The five men flinched like dogs avoiding an angry palm. Tarak straightened up and stepped forward.

"Who is that?"

Atif scanned the woods for movement but saw none until two

soldiers rose from the bushes a few metres away.

*So close?*

"Salko?"

The soldiers wore mismatched camouflage like Tarak. One carried a rifle and had three grenades hanging from his webbing; the other held a pistol loosely by his side. The first soldier, a burly man with a shaved head, walked up to Tarak and hugged him.

"I heard the boy shout and then I was sure I heard your voice. I was wondering what became of you."

"And you. I thought you would have crossed by now."

"I was across last night. I came back to help with the wounded and got trapped. Then we ran into a Chetnik patrol and had to leave the wounded anyway."

"Is it just the two of you?"

"Yes," he said, motioning to his young, lanky companion. "This is Ratib."

"Got any ideas on how to get across?"

"I have a secret way," Salko said. "I can get us all across."

"How?"

"We go under the road."

"They'll have all the bridges and culverts covered."

"Not this one." Salko raised his hands to animate their destiny. "It's like a bridge, but it's not. More like a square, concrete culvert. It's barely a metre across. It's so small you could be standing on the road and never know it existed. There used to be a creek running through there, but it's so steep, they built this small bridge instead of a culvert. The creek is dried up except when it rains a lot. The ditch on this side is heavily forested and steep. It would be impossible to see from the road.

"It's not far. Maybe an hour or two. I've used it a dozen times to cross over since the war started."

Tarak looked at Atif.

"How do you feel about that?"

We might really get out of this, Atif thought, working to stifle his excitement.

"Are you kidding?"

# THURSDAY: JAC LARUE

GRAVEL CRACKLED UNDER Jac's boot. He looked down, weeded out the larger pebbles with his boots and flipped them over the bank. Some bounced to the bottom. Others dragged along a miniature avalanche of stones, gravel, and dust. Maarten was sitting on the edge of the road, tossing pebbles into the dust cloud.

"So," Maarten said, wiping his hands against his pants. "Who do you think is going to shoot us first? The Serbs or Janssen?"

Jac eyed the Serbs on the opposite side of the road. Soldiers were stationed every few metres, their attention directed across a large farm to the south.

"Janssen said this might happen. He said they took some jeeps yesterday."

"And what happened to the guys in the jeeps?"

"No idea."

Maarten tossed another stone.

"Always wondered what the inside of a Belgrade prison looks like."

"You might enjoy that."

Maarten flipped a stone in Jac's direction.

The rumble of a truck engine caught Jac's attention. He turned: a troop truck was rounding a corner in the distance.

"Men or soldiers?" Maarten asked without looking up.

"It's going west. Men."

Maarten looked up as the truck passed with its cargo of civilian men stuffed into the back.

"I'd like to know how they can breathe in there," he said, taking notes.

Jac glanced up at the midday sun, wiping the sweat from his forehead. He stuck his thumbs against his chest, twice, expecting to hook them inside his flak jacket. After the second attempt, he mentally slapped himself. He slid his hands into his pockets, still feeling the urge to hang his thumbs in his phantom flak vest.

Another engine echoed from the road.

"Buses," Maarten said, standing. "The sergeant's convoy?"

A string of unescorted buses sped by the peacekeepers. They watched the empty road.

"Guess he's hitchhiking, too," Jac said.

"Hey, Blue Helmets!"

They turned around. A Serb waved to them from across the street.

"Wonder what he wants?"

"Our uniforms, probably," Maarten replied.

The Serb crossed the street with a half dozen heavily armed soldiers in tow. He held up his automatic rifle to Jac.

"We need help," he said.

Jac didn't touch the rifle. "Doing what?"

"Hunting Turks."

Maarten choked. "Say that in English."

The soldier pointed at the farm. "Come. We can hunt them."

Maarten pointed at the open fields. "Hunt where? I can see Greece from here."

Jac laid a hand on Maarten's arm and then the Serb tried to press the rifle into Jac's chest, but he raised his hands and stepped back.

"We're not going anywhere with you."

"So, you are cowards."

Maarten stepped up to the Serb. "Listen to me, you bastard...."

Jac pulled on his sleeve. "Leave it."

"Jesus, Jac. I'm sick of not cooperating. Maybe it's time we provoked...."

A green troop truck geared down next to them and stopped a few metres ahead of the group. Sergeant Janssen waved to them to climb aboard.

"Oh, thank God," Jac muttered as he pushed his way through the soldiers.

The pair scaled the back of the truck and it lurched forward.

"You're just in time," Maarten said. "They were ready to take us hunting."

"Hunting for what?" Janssen asked then shook his head. "Never mind."

"Where're we going?"

"To join the crews from the other convoys. Serbs stole every jeep that went out this morning." He pointed to Maarten. "What happened to you?"

"Open window. Flying rock. It's fine."

Janssen glanced at Jac, unconvinced. Jac shrugged.

As they approached the town, Maarten tapped Jac on the shoulder and then pointed towards a soccer field. Dozens of men sat in the middle of it. They were shirtless with their hands on their heads. Jac leaned out over the tailgate, looking for a young skinny boy among the men, but they were travelling too fast.

"Don't worry about him," Maarten said. "They all look like older men. He's a smart kid. He'll get through."

Jac motioned to the wall of soldiers lining the road. "You really think anyone can get through that?"

"Listen Jac, the men in that field were old men. Walking through the woods has to be hell on earth for them. They can't move fast and they don't know the woods like Atif does. I'm willing to bet he got here before most of these soldiers did and slipped across last night."

"You're full of it, you know that, right?"

"Not this time, Jac," Maarten replied, taking more notes. "I think the kid is okay."

They passed a line of men walking along the road, their hands on their heads. Jac examined their weathered faces. None wore army green.

"You see. They're all older men."

The truck slowed and turned onto a gravel road. They passed four Dutch jeeps sitting on the side of the road and stopped. Peace-keepers relaxed in the grass nearby. The tailgate dropped and a Serb corporal threw a thumb in their direction.

"Go on. Join your friends."

Janssen walked over to speak with a lieutenant sitting in the first jeep.

"Well, Potocari knows where we are," he told them a few minutes later, "so all we can do is wait. You might as well sit down and have something to eat."

Jac and Maarten slid down the short embankment and walked across the grass, joining the others under the shade of a large pine tree. Three bare-chested peacekeepers were lying on their shirts in the sun. Two wore sunglasses, the third's blue UN baseball cap covered his face.

"Well, what do you know? It's Jac and Jill," Karel said, tossing them each a ration pack.

Jac sat down next to Bram. "What's going on?"

"Well, now that the Serbs have stolen all our CD players and Game Boys, nothing much." He rolled his eyes at Karel. "He's keeping us entertained with his jokes. Again."

"Yeah, Jac, you missed the best ones," Karel said. "What would the people in Sarajevo ask Jesus if he showed up carrying his cross?"

"They'd ask him where he got the wood," Maarten replied. "Don't quit your day job, Karel."

"Okay. How about the one where the kid asked his friend why he was in the park swinging on the swings."

"He was doing it to screw up the snipers," one of the sunbathing peacekeepers answered.

"So, Karel, what would you do if you stepped on a land mine?" Maarten asked. Karel shrugged. "Jump two hundred feet into the air and scatter yourself over a wide area. Please."

Karel held up his fist, the middle finger popping up. Maarten laughed and raised the ration pack Karel had given him.

"Yeah, you bought me dinner, but be patient. We need more privacy, don't you think?"

The sunbathers laughed.

Maarten elbowed Jac and pointed to the road. Janssen was walking away from the jeeps with the lieutenant. They met with a Serb officer and an animated conversation ensued.

"What do you think they're up to?"

"No idea," Jac replied.

The conversation turned into smiles and an exchange of cigarettes. The lieutenant shook the Serb's hand and then went straight to the radio in the first jeep. Janssen approached the group.

"They're going to let most of you go back to the camp. Two of us will stay here and wait for the ride Potocari has already sent out."

The sergeant looked at Jac and smiled.

"That's us, right?" Jac said.

Janssen nodded.

"Make sure he gets his head checked," Jac said, motioning to Maarten. "And get them to check that ugly gash too."

Maarten slapped Jac on the back of his head and then followed the others to the jeeps. Jac went with them and Maarten tossed him a bottle of water out of the window as the vehicles turned around in a cloud of dust. They took a left at the end of the road.

The sergeant pulled out his field pad and strolled through the dust towards the intersection.

Jac walked behind him, opening the bottle. The water warmed his throat.

*Ice. What I'd give for a single cube of ice.*

He slowed and soaked his towel, wiping the sticky sweat from his face. A grenade exploded in the forest, a column of dust rising up between the trees. Serb soldiers jumped the guardrail and vanished into the forest. Others searched men who had come out of the woods to surrender and loaded them into the back of a troop truck. Serb soldiers returned from the forest with several more men. Another grenade popped. The sergeant wrote on his notepad.

"Don't worry, Blue Helmet," a voice said from behind Jac. A soldier walking with a group of comrades detached himself and came abreast of Jac. "The Turks are killing themselves with grenades. They're war criminals, you see. They would rather kill themselves than face justice."

The soldier laughed and rejoined his friends. Jac watched as they selected a number of men and searched them. The soldiers emptied pockets and bags, throwing away papers and pocketing other items. A soldier appeared from the forest on the far side of the road with two boys in tow. Jac stopped a few metres from the intersection, staring at the boys. One wore shorts and no shirt. The other wore jeans and a white shirt and both their heads were shaved. Jac moved closer. A soldier suddenly obscured his view of the two boys.

"What are you looking at, Blue Helmet?"

"Nothing."

"Then you should go do nothing with your friend over there."

A second soldier appeared beside the first. Their arms rested on the rifles slung across their chests.

Jac turned away. The Serbs followed him for a few steps and then left him alone. He slowed, looking for the boys.

*Have they been loaded onto a truck already?*

When he got to Janssen, he caught sight of the boys standing apart from the men. A soldier was standing in the middle of the road; he raised his arm to stop an approaching vehicle.

*Another truck?*

Brakes hissed.

Then a bus halted in front of the soldier and the door flew open. The soldier stepped aboard and spoke to the driver. The driver nodded his head and the soldier waved to the boys. They climbed into the bus full of women and children.

"Is that him?"

Jac turned. Sergeant Janssen made a last note and then took out his water and drank a mouthful. He pointed towards the bus with the bottle.

"Maarten told me what you did for the boy."

"I don't think that's him," Jac said. The bus crept through the crowded road. "He was taller."

"If your friend didn't get across, they probably did the same for him."

"Maybe."

A Serb officer walked up to them.

"Can I borrow your pen?"

Janssen passed his pen to the Serb.

"Can I borrow your notepad?"

Janssen flipped to a clean page and handed the pad to him. The Serb closed the notepad, stuffed it inside a pocket, and then walked away.

"Great," Janssen said, folding his arms. "That was my last pen."

The Serb officer stopped next to a group of men and pointed at the Dutch. Within minutes, five tall Serbs stood in front of the peacekeepers. Janssen walked away from the intersection and Jac followed.

"So, Sergeant, did you bring any cards with you?"

"What? And have them stolen too?"

Jac slowed down and turned his head. "That sounds like a jeep."

A white jeep turned the corner and stopped next to them. Four peacekeepers, including Maarten, piled out. A Serb truck pulled up alongside the jeep and deposited the other Dutch peacekeepers in the middle of the road. Maarten threw his gear on the ground.

"Bastards on the road stole the other three jeeps," he said. "And don't expect help from Potocari either. They stole that jeep too."

# THURSDAY: MARIJA STAVIC

ADILA SQUEEZED MARIJA'S arm as the bus slowed. The brakes hissed and the door clanked open. Tihana stirred in Adila's arms.

Another checkpoint.

"It's okay," Marija whispered, tucking Adila's scarf under her chin.

A green helmet appeared and the driver dug out a cigarette. The soldier lit up and then scanned the seats. Smoke poured from his nose.

"I could use some fresh air," the driver said.

The soldier nodded. The driver stood up and handed him another cigarette. They stepped off the bus. Adila's grip relaxed. Marija turned to look at Ina. She sat with her arm wrapped around Lejla, holding a blanket tight around the girl's head.

She must be sweltering under that, Marija thought. She turned away and checked their water supply. Two litres left.

Outside, the driver was talking to a small group of soldiers, passing out a cigarette every time one was smothered under a boot. Marija's eyes wandered to a farmhouse set back from the road. White with red trim.

*Like home.*

There were remnants of a child's attempt at a tree house under a large willow tree that was missing many of its lower branches; it reminded her of the fort Atif had built behind their house. Marija smiled to herself. Atif had borrowed his father's saw and hammer for the project, but Yassir had thought the tools had been stolen. He'd gone to Kravica to buy new ones, only to find the tools hanging in the proper spot when he got home. Atif got his own tool box after that.

*Is his fort still standing?* She stared at the rotted wood under the tree. *Where are you, my child?*

The driver boarded the bus and closed the door. The soldiers stepped back. The bus swayed as it pulled onto the road.

"How much farther?" Adila asked. "I don't know this part of the road at all."

"Well, we've passed Vlasenica, so it's not much farther." She leaned against the girl, trying to see ahead. They passed familiar buildings. "Yes. That's it. We're getting close. Shouldn't be long now."

"There's going to be soldiers there, right?" Adila's voice trembled.

"I don't know. But there will be so many of us. We'll try to stay in the middle of the crowd until we get to the other side."

Marija looked behind at Ina: she was tying a scarf around the blonde girl's head.

Gravel crackled underneath as the bus rolled along the shoulder of the road. The driver braked to a stop and then turned to face them.

"You have a long walk ahead of you, ladies. Don't worry. The blue helmets wait for you in Kladanj. In a few hours, you'll be in Tuzla. You'll have food and water and a place to sleep. Don't worry. The soldiers here won't bother you."

"There's a TV camera here," Adila said. "Are they journalists?"

Marija stood up and tried to find the camera. "I don't know, but it's a good thing."

"Why?"

"I'm guessing the soldiers won't do anything bad if it's going to be on film."

"What if it's the Chetniks who are filming?"

"I don't know. I'd still rather have them here."

The driver stepped off the bus and waited just outside the door. The women and children followed.

"Don't rush," he warned them, helping an elderly woman down the steps. "Take your time."

Marija waited until Ina and Lejla passed her before joining the line. As she stepped down, Ina was reaching up to kiss the driver on the cheek. He blushed and told her to keep going.

"Thank you, Mr. Kovac," Marija said, touching his arm.

"It's Alex to my friends." He smiled. "Alex Kovac."

Marija put her arm around Adila and walked behind Ina. They joined the refugees from the other buses, keeping their heads down. The Serbs were smiling at the camera as they helped the women step off the buses.

"Six kilometres," Ina said. "I heard one of the soldiers say the blue helmets were six kilometres ahead."

"Dear God," Marija said, looking around at some of the older women in the group. "In this heat?"

"Stay on the pavement," one soldier shouted. "There are mines in the woods. Don't go off the pavement for any reason. The blue helmets are in Kladanj. Six kilometres. They have food and water. Keep moving. Keep moving."

Tihana woke up and pulled the toy soldiers out from under her shirt.

"Do you think she can walk?" Adila asked. "She's getting heavy."

Marija glanced back, looking for helmets or short haircuts in the crowd. When she turned back, she walked into a wall of green. Two arms reached out and took her by the shoulders. She cried out.

"Sorry," a male voice said. "I didn't mean to scare you."

Marija looked up. The soldier stepped back, slinging his rifle behind him. He was looking at Adila.

"It's just that she looked like she needed help," he said in a voice that had yet to crack. "She doesn't look well."

Marija ushered Adila forward. "We're okay."

The soldier followed them. "Are you sure?"

"Yes. Please. Leave us alone."

"Okay. But my officer told me to walk with your group for a while. Some kids were throwing rocks, so he wants me to go along. Can you believe it? Throwing rocks at women and children."

"Yes, I can," Marija said, looking at him.

He held up a chocolate bar. "If it's all right, can you give this to the little girl? It's only going to melt."

The soldier was looking down at Tihana with a smile that reminded her of Atif. Marija looked away and then reached for Tihana. Adila laid her against Marija's shoulder.

"Do you want a little chocolate?"

Tihana's eyes bulged when she caught sight of the foil-wrapped bar. The soldier laughed and reached out with both hands.

"Seriously. Let me take her. It's hot and you must be exhausted."

Marija caught sight of Ina waiting on the side of the road.

Six kilometres at midday, Marija thought, sweat rolling between her eyes. And only two litres of water left.

"I'm not going to run off with her."

"Is it okay with you?" she asked Tihana.

Tihana nodded, her eyes on the chocolate bar. The soldier shifted his rifle and swung Tihana up and sat her on his shoulders.

"Here you go," he said, passing the chocolate bar up. "Try not to get it all over my cap."

Marija smiled. The soldier held on to Tihana just as Atif had the day before. Marija swallowed the ache rising in her throat and took Adila's hand.

"Let's go before we get left behind. Are you ready up there?" the soldier asked, peering at Tihana. She licked the chocolate from her fingers and nodded.

Marija stayed close to them; Ina and Lejla slipped in behind.

"Do you need any water?" the soldier asked after a few steps.

"We have some, thank you."

"I didn't mean to scare you," he said. "To tell you the truth, I recognized you."

"From where?"

"We have a farm just outside Bratunac. My father bought some furniture from your husband a couple months before the war started. I remember you took me into your kitchen and gave me cookies."

"I'm sorry, I don't remember."

"That's okay. Can I ask how your husband is doing?"

"I don't know where he is. I think he's been stranded somewhere since April."

"Then maybe you'll see him soon."

"What's your name?"

"Boris Racic."

"Racic? Yes. I remember your father. How has he been?"

"Good. I got a letter from him a couple of weeks ago. The farm is doing well. He was hoping for some rain, so I imagine he was happy last week. He is growing corn now. For the army."

"And your mother?"

"She's doing well," he said, shifting course towards the side of the road. He looked back briefly and then pulled a bottle of water from a side pocket and dropped it into the lap of an old woman sitting on the ground. "She's been in Belgrade most of the summer taking care of her mother. Which is good. It's safe there."

"I'm happy to hear that."

"Is your daughter okay? She really doesn't look well." Boris was looking at Adila's face.

"It's fine. It's just a rash."

"I didn't think you had two daughters."

Marija chewed on the side of her mouth. *Do I tell him?*

"She's not my daughter. I just thought it was better if she carried my daughter, to keep the soldiers away."

"Oh," Boris said, his mouth hanging on the word for a moment. "Oh. Okay. I'm sorry. I've only been here a few hours. I didn't think."

"It's okay," Adila said. "How far can you walk with us?"

"Far enough."

He pulled out another chocolate bar and offered it to Adila. She took it and turned around, giving half to Lejla. The soldier looked back, twice.

"Twins," he said, nodding his head.

Boris handed his canteen to Tihana. Chocolate coated the sides of her mouth, her fingers, and both toy soldiers.

The crowd thinned. People took refuge under the shade of trees, waiting out the heat of the afternoon.

"The tree," Boris said, pointing. The large trunk blocked the road. "It's easier to walk around it than over it."

"It's not dangerous?"

"They made sure it was okay. You'll be fine."

They stopped and Boris rested on one knee so that Tihana could jump down. She turned around and smiled, her eyes on the pouch that had held the chocolate bars. "Okay," he said. "One more. But don't eat it right away. You don't want to get a tummy ache, do you?"

She shook her head and took the bar, squeezing it between the toy soldiers.

"I hope you find your husband," Boris said, standing up. "I'll tell my father we spoke."

"Please," Marija said, reaching out for his hand. She shook it, holding on for a moment. "Thank you."

Boris opened his mouth to reply then shut it, his eyes gazing down.

"What is it?"

"When we picked up the table, I remember a boy a little younger than me. Is he in the woods?"

Marija's stomach tightened. She nodded, swallowing hard.

"What's his name?"

"Atif."

"Listen," Boris said, glancing back. Maria followed his gaze. Two soldiers were leaning against the guardrail, smoking. "I'm going back to watch the road after the last bus. I'll keep an eye out."

"Thank you," Marija said. She wiped her eyes with her sleeve.

"I can't promise anything. I'm nobody in this army, but who knows?"

Marija took Boris's face into her hands and kissed it. He blushed and turned away. She watched him join the other soldiers.

Ina took her daughters' hands.

"I think we're safe now."

Marija picked up Tihana, using her shirt to clean the chocolate from her face.

"Yes. We're safe."

# THURSDAY: ATIF STAVIC

ATIF'S LEG SANK in the swamp up to his thigh. He grabbed at bushes on the river bank, trying to pull himself free, but the leg didn't budge. Hands slipped under his arms; Tarak and Salko dragged him forwards. The swamp gave up its grip on his leg and he was deposited on firm ground. He crawled next to a tree and lay back, breathing hard and shivering. The soldiers returned to the Jadar River to help the other men cross the swollen and fast moving current. Atif knew he wouldn't have made it without Tarak's firm grip on his back pack.

Atif shut his eyes then someone shook his shoulder. Opening them, he saw Tarak motioning to the woods where the others stood waiting. Atif climbed to his feet, his clothes sticking to his body. He twisted the ends of his sleeves as he followed Tarak into the forest. Water dribbled down his arm.

"That's it?" Salko said.

Two hours later, Atif crouched beside the soldiers and scanned the forest. Trees and thick brush obscured the steep embankment leading to the road above.

"I don't see the bridge," he whispered.

Tarak handed Atif the binoculars and pointed. Atif adjusted the focus and stared at the patch of green.

"It's hard to see," Tarak said. "Look for straight lines, like the side of a building."

Atif focused on one spot. Unnatural straight lines emerged among the trees, forming an opening not much larger than two men. The ground sloped upwards towards the opposite side of the road. Only a thin sliver of sunlight indicated an exit.

"What's on the other side?"

"That's the sticky part," Salko replied. The other three men leaned in. "There's some brush in the ditch, but beyond that is a farmer's field and I haven't been this way since March, so I don't know what he's growing. If it's corn, we're okay. If it's carrots, we're going to have to cross it in the open. The forest is only about a hundred and fifty metres away. Once we're in there, we can keep to the trees for some distance."

"Can we cross it after dark?" Kemal asked.

"Maybe. Let's wait and see what Ratib has found." The younger soldier had volunteered to scout the area to find out how many Serbs lined the road. "I would prefer to wait until dark, but we run the risk they'll patrol the area and discover the bridge."

"Or us," Tarak said.

Atif gazed at the bridge through the binoculars, chewing on his bottom lip. Once they had crossed, Tarak expected they would make up a lot of time and catch up to the main group before they reached the front lines. There, he told Atif, they should be able to cross safely, with the help of the Bosnian army.

*All we have to do is get across this road.*

As Atif handed the binoculars back to Tarak, he spotted movement in the trees.

"Ratib is back."

The soldier rejoined the group, out of breath. He took a swig of water and then nodded.

"Chetniks are on the road. There's one leaning on the guardrail directly above the opening. I could see him clearly through a break in the trees."

"Which means he would see us," Salko said.

"Right at the entrance." Ratib took another swig of water. "But we can get close without being seen. I could only see about a half dozen others in that immediate area, but a truck stopped down the road and let off at least a dozen more. I heard another vehicle coming from the direction of Nova Kasaba, but I didn't stick around to find out what it was because some of the new troops were already setting up to patrol."

"Damn it," Salko said.

"They looked like they were going in the other direction, towards the Jadar. They probably expect some of us would try to cross where the river goes under the road."

"Only a matter of time before they turn west," Tarak said.

Salko looked at the men.

"Decision time, my friends."

Kemal opened his mouth to speak, but Ratib raised his hand. A truck rumbled by and then squealed to a halt.

"More and more are arriving," the young soldier said, gazing at Salko. "These woods will be infested with Chetniks long before it gets dark."

"Can we go farther west and cross after dark?" Kemal asked.

"The longer we wait, the more soldiers there will be," Izet said. "I would be willing to take my chances crossing here."

"How about we vote on it," Tarak said. "I'm willing to go now."

The three men turned to each other and then looked back at Tarak.

"We will go now," Kemal said. "Before there are more soldiers."

"We go," Ratib said.

"Then that settles it...." Tarak held up his hand before Salko could finish.

"Just a moment. We haven't heard from everyone."

Salko raised an eyebrow and turned to Atif.

"Yes," Atif said, clearing his throat. "No sense in waiting for dark. There could be a hundred soldiers by then. I'd rather keep moving than sit here waiting for the snakes to bite."

Tarak smiled. "Then we go."

"So, what do we do about the Chetnik on the road?" Izet asked. "The one who can see the entrance."

Salko looked at Tarak and they both smiled like a pair of schoolboys.

"Distraction," Salko said.

"My thoughts exactly," Tarak replied. "What do you have there?"

Salko dug into his pack, took out three grenades, and laid them on the ground.

"Perfect." Tarak dropped a handful of elastic bands next to the grenades.

"Got any cigarettes? Matches?" Salko asked the men.

Two men gave up eight cigarettes and three packs of matches.

"I have some," Atif said. He remembered that the Dutch rations included matches. He dropped six packs next to the pile. Ratib added his three grenades.

"What are you going to do with them?" Atif asked.

"I'll explain later," Tarak said, gathering up the supplies. "We need to hurry."

Salko pointed to Ratib.

"You stay with them and in five minutes bring them as close to the opening as you can."

Ratib nodded and Salko looked at the others.

"We should get back before the grenades start blowing. The moment the first one goes, we go together. When you get through, run straight for the woods. Don't stop for any reason. If you can't find us in the woods on the other side, head for Mount Urdc. We will see you there or on the way. Okay?"

The men nodded. Tarak and Salko finished packing up the grenades.

"Wait for us," Tarak told Atif. Then he turned away and disappeared into the woods.

Atif took a bottle from his pack and drank from it, gulping the water between rapid breaths. Prayer beads clicked behind him. He looked back.

"Remember," Kemal whispered. "Everything is as Allah wills it."

Atif stared into the woods.

*This is the right thing. It has to be. If we stay, they'll find us. If we go, they might see us. What choice do we have?*

"We should go down there now," Ratib said.

*Already?*

Atif swallowed a breath and tightened the straps on his pack. He got up and followed the rest.

They took their time moving towards the bridge. When they got there, they stopped a few metres short of the opening. The ground sloped up towards a smaller opening on the other side and, to Atif's relief, bushes hid part of the sky on the other side.

Ratib motioned to the guardrail. Atif shifted his gaze and glimpsed two helmets through the trees. The soldiers wearing them shared a cigarette and spoke. Atif looked back into the forest.

*Where are they?*

He rubbed his palms against his damp jeans. His heart was pounding.

The Serbs above them stopped talking.

One walked away. The other turned to face the woods.

Nobody moved.

# THURSDAY: TARAK SMAJLOVIC

TARAK LAY UNDER a thick tree bough with his face pressed against Salko's boot. A spider crawled across his hand. Mosquitoes buzzed next to his ear; some of them crawled inside and bit. Tarak cringed but remained still.

He opened an eye. A pair of boots stood an arm's length away. Another pair paced, crunching leaves and twigs. A cigarette dropped and a boot smothered it. The Serb coughed. One of the others offered him a canteen.

"Nobody is out here," one of the Serbs said. "Those bastards are having all the fun while we babysit the trees."

Tarak pulled a slow breath in through his nose.

More cigarettes dropped to the ground.

"We've done enough patrolling." The Serb flicked his cigarette into the tree. It lodged in the branch above Tarak's head. "Let's go back. I'm hungry."

The others murmured in agreement. Rifles clinked as they shouldered their weapons. The boots next to Tarak took a step back, crushing part of the bough. He held his breath as the soldier bent down and tightened a lace.

*Five soldiers, maybe six. Thirty rounds.* Tarak's mind settled on the rifle jammed beneath him. He had cocked the weapon as they dove for cover under the tree, but the safety was still on. He imagined the motion necessary to pull the weapon up, disengage the safety, and shoot the soldiers before they had a chance to respond.

Tricky, he thought, but it could be done if Salko reacted as quickly.

The bough shook as the soldier straightened up and the smouldering cigarette butt fell. The Serb shouldered his rifle and followed the others. The cigarette burned against the back of Tarak's arm. His teeth clamped down on his tongue.

One minute.

Two.

When Salko's boot pulled away from Tarak's face, he reached back and swatted the cigarette away. Then he sat up and looked in the direction the soldiers had gone. When he turned around, Salko was making a circular motion with his finger. Tarak crawled out into the open, pulling his pack behind him. He and Salko put the grenades and other supplies on the ground and sorted them into six groups, each containing a grenade, cigarette, elastic band, and matchbook. Salko picked up a cigarette and examined it.

"Low tar," he whispered. "We won't have long."

"But they won't go out."

Elastic bands snapped as Tarak wrapped each grenade. Salko checked to make sure the levers were secure and then he pulled the pins, tossing them into the bushes.

Voices drifted between the trees. Tarak and Salko froze and then looked behind them.

Nothing.

"Just plant them and run," Salko said.

Tarak pulled on his pack and slung his rifle across his chest. He rubbed his hands on his pants and then picked up three grenades along with three matchbooks and three cigarettes. Salko took the rest and they each picked a tree.

Tarak stuck a cigarette in his mouth, lit it, and inhaled. The smoke tickled his throat and he swallowed, suppressing a cough. He drew on the cigarette a second time and then wedged it inside the matchbook. He placed the grenade between the trunk of the tree and a branch and slipped the matchbook under the elastic around the grenade with the lit end of the cigarette pointed down.

Four minutes at least, he guessed. Eight if they were lucky. The cigarette would smoulder until it ignited the matchbook and then it would burn through the elastic, releasing the grenade lever. Five seconds later, the grenade would explode.

Tarak moved to another tree and then another, repeating the process twice more. The voices returned. When Tarak turned around, Salko was motioning him forward.

"Go, go, go," Salko whispered as he passed Tarak.

The pair lunged through the forest, hurtling deadfall. The bridge came into view; Tarak glanced at his watch.

*Three minutes? Already?*

They slowed as they approached the bridge. The others were crowded together near the entrance. Tarak counted five heads, all staring in his direction.

He looked at his watch.

*Four minutes.*

The forest rumbled.

He dropped down next to Atif and the boy pointed up. A Serb soldier was standing next to the guardrail, his rifle butt jammed against his shoulder. He was scanning the forest in the direction of the explosion. Other men shouted. Some ran.

*Come on, come on.*

Thunder rolled again. The soldier looked back and forth. A truck started up. Then the soldier ran.

"Go," Salko whispered behind him.

Another explosion echoed through the trees. The men went through the opening and picked their way over the smooth rocks to the other side. Salko slipped ahead. He reached the top and parted the bushes.

"Damn it."

Tarak climbed up behind him.

"What is it?"

"The field looks fallow."

"Could it be mined?"

"I doubt it."

"The woods will be swarming with Chetniks," Tarak said, glancing at the others waiting behind him. "We can't go back."

"I agree. We run."

The ground shook. Automatic rifle fire erupted to the east. Tarak looked at Atif. The boy raised his hand, four fingers spread out. Tarak nodded and turned, his eyes fixed on the blue sky ahead. Freedom could be seconds away.

So could death.

"Okay," Salko said. "I'll go first."

They shook hands.

"Good luck, my friend."

Salko disappeared through the bushes and then returned, waving to the others to follow. Ratib scaled the embankment and vanished.

"Don't stop for anything, Atif," Tarak said. "Nothing. Do you understand?"

Atif looked up, his face drained of blood.

"Yeah. Nothing."

"Good. Go. Stay ahead of me."

The boy hesitated when the ground shook for the fifth time.

"Go," Tarak said, pushing Atif up over the embankment. He followed, pausing on the far side of the bushes to look left and right. The thick greenery ended on the edge of a wide furrowed field. Tarak swore under his breath and looked behind him. The road sat three metres above them. He saw no one but knew the Serbs would be able to see them as they crossed the field.

The last grenade popped.

Tarak tore after Atif through the heavy, damp soil. His feet sank deep into every furrow.

*Not fast enough.*

When he caught up to Atif, he looked back. A dozen men and three trucks crowded the far side of the road. The Serbs were still facing south. They were shouting and firing their weapons at random into the forest.

*Don't turn around.* Tarak stared at the trees in front of him. *Just a few more seconds.*

Salko and Ratib vanished into the forest. On his left, the other three men were spread out, struggling in the deep, sticky soil.

*Sixty metres to go.*

Tarak focused on a large beech tree at the edge of the field. It was directly in front of him and he was desperate to touch it. The voices behind him changed. Rifle rounds pierced the air above them.

*Forty metres.*

"Keep going, Atif," he shouted to the boy. "I'll be right behind you."

Tarak flipped the safety off on his rifle and turned. Soldiers were pouring over the embankment like water breaching a levee. Trucks revved their engines. The Serbs raised their rifles. Without bothering to aim, Tarak fired his rifle, spitting out the entire magazine in seconds. The Serbs dropped to the ground. Tarak turned around and sprinted the last few metres, slapping the beech tree as he passed it. Atif had stopped inside the treeline, gulping air.

"Keep going. They're coming."

The boy's eyes widened and he ran.

Tarak took one last look. The three men were nowhere to be seen. At least a dozen helmeted heads bobbed around the edge of the field.

*Will they follow us into the woods?*

He ran ahead of Atif, zigzagging his way between half-dead trees that didn't provide a lot of cover but didn't slow them down.

"This way," he said to Atif, shifting to the right. He searched for more cover, but the woods had thinned. He shifted their path again, hoping the troops following them would run in a straight line.

"I hear a truck," Atif said, slowing.

Tarak grabbed a tree and swung around, listening. The truck rumbled unseen in front of them, growing louder. Behind them, voices drifted through the trees. Tarak remained still, until the sound of the truck faded, then shifted direction. They broke out onto a narrow dirt road.

Deserted.

Tarak patted Atif on the back and pointed straight ahead.

"Keep going."

The boy hesitated long enough to pull in a mouthful of air and then he crossed the road. The shouting on the left grew closer. Gunshots rang out in the distance. The terrain now sloped downwards and they picked up speed. They ran and slid through thickening brush and trees. Atif slammed against a tree and stopped.

"I'm stuck," the boy said, yanking at the backpack.

Tarak reached under Atif's left arm. A branch had found its way through the strap on his pack. He pushed Atif back, but the pack didn't move.

"Leave it," Tarak said.

Atif flipped his arms back, and left the pack hanging from the tree. They slid down the nearly vertical slope. Tarak broke through the bushes first, coming to rest on a wide gravel road. A river bordered the far side. Beyond that lay another uncultivated field.

"Shit!"

Suddenly, the ground around Tarak's feet spit dirt. He turned, raising his empty rifle. The Serb truck had stopped up the road. Three soldiers were running towards them. He heard grunts behind him and turned around. Two soldiers dropped from the woods farther down the road. They raised their rifles and ran towards Tarak and Atif. Another soldier came out of the woods closer to them. Atif crouched at Tarak's feet and wrapped his arms around Tarak's leg. Tarak swung his rifle right, left, and then right again, trying not to lose his balance. The boy clutched tightly, his head down.

"Drop the weapon," one of the soldiers shouted.

Tarak held it high, shifting aim between the three Serbs approaching from the truck. The pain in his stomach told him he and Atif had run out of options.

"Hey, Turk."

The voice was nearly at his shoulder. As he was turning, the butt of a rifle came down on his face.

The blue sky blackened.

A voice shrieked.

# THURSDAY: NIKO BASARIC

NIKO STOOD ON the road, staring at the house where Ivan had dragged the girl. The screaming had stopped an hour ago. Niko had no idea if the girl was dead or alive. Anton and Pavle remained next to the guardrail. Vladen sat on the front steps. Twice Drach had come out and stood on the porch, waving to them to join him and Ivan; twice they had declined.

"You see, Petar," Niko whispered, leaning close to the recruit's ear. "They're all just talk."

Petar jerked his head towards the house. "Yeah? What about Drach and Ivan?"

Niko straightened up and rubbed his nose.

*What about them?* He watched for movement inside the house. *Are they asleep?*

Sweat dribbled past his eyes. He took off his helmet and rubbed his head with a towel. Then he looked at the photo of his family.

*The girl in that house is someone's daughter, someone's sister. What do I do?*

Vehicles rumbled in from the east. Niko took a step forward; a train of buses crested the hill in the distance. He stepped back and tapped Petar on the shoulder.

"Get up." Petar got to his feet and Niko led him across the street. "Do me a favour. Keep the last bus here."

Petar stared at Niko, his eyelids heavy.

"What? Why?"

"Just do it," Niko said.

He hopped over the short concrete fence and walked across the lawn. Vladen stood and held out his arm when Niko tried to climb the steps.

"Where do you think you're going?"

"Inside."

"Sergeant said to leave them alone."

"He can go to hell," Niko muttered, slapping Vladen's arm away.

The young soldier tried to block Niko's path.

"He said to leave them alone."

Niko's nostrils flared. He shifted his rifle on his shoulder and then reached up and grabbed Vladen's collar, pulling him close enough to smell the rancid smoke and plum brandy on his breath.

"Listen to me, you loudmouth coward," Niko whispered. "I'm not going to The Hague for something those two bastards did. I'm guessing you're thinking the same thing."

"Fuck you."

"News for you, little boy. They can get you for doing nothing to stop them, too."

Niko released Vladen and pushed him away.

"Help or don't help, but don't stop me."

Vladen sat back down on the steps. Niko licked his lips and then stepped inside. Silent and still. The floor creaked under his feet.

*They must be asleep, but where?*

Placing his feet heel to toe, he moved forward and peered inside the room on his right. It was empty; the pieces of a smashed table littered the floor. He sidestepped to the left, took two steps forward, and looked into a larger room. Drach was asleep on a couch on the far side. Niko leaned in. Ivan lay sprawled over a shorter couch, snoring.

*But where's the girl?*

Niko backed up into the hallway. He looked at the stairs.

*Damn it.*

He tiptoed towards the steps, grasped the banister, and shook it. Rock solid.

Staying close to the banister, he crept up the stairs, stopping to listen on each step. No one stirred. He reached the landing and moved towards the first room. The girl was curled up on a ragged mattress in the corner, covered with a filthy sheet. Niko shifted his rifle to his back and stepped inside. She didn't move.

*Is she alive?*

He crossed the room and touched her shoulder. She flinched and Niko jumped. He watched her pull the sheet up to her neck, whimpering.

*My God. She's just a child. Sixteen? Seventeen?*

Niko raised a finger to his mouth. The girl stared at him and then her eyes moved to the door.

"Asleep," he whispered. "The buses are coming. I can put you on one, but we have to go now."

She sat up, holding the sheet around her with one hand. He reached out, took the other hand, and helped her to her feet. When they were outside the room, Niko raised a finger to his lips and pointed to the stairs. The girl nodded and came closer; she leaned against him and he half-walked, half-carried her down the steps. When they reached the bottom, he looked inside the large room. Drach and Ivan were still asleep. He could feel the girl tense under his arms.

Niko pointed to the front door. Hand in hand, they walked quickly through it and down the front steps. She tripped, skinning her knee. Niko scooped her up and carried her over the concrete fence. Petar stood next to a bus. The door was open and the driver was waiting next to him.

Footsteps pounded the steps of the house behind them. Niko held his breath and crossed the shoulder.

"What are you doing, Turk?"

Niko dropped the girl into the driver's arms.

"Take care of her," Niko said. The driver scaled the steps and passed the girl off to a woman who helped the girl inside. Niko waved at the driver as he sat in his seat. "Go. Now!"

The driver's eyes shifted to Ivan as he shut the door and hit the accelerator.

Ivan grabbed Niko and yanked him back.

"You stupid Turk."

Drach swung his fist into Niko's jaw. He staggered back and collapsed where the bus had been sitting moments earlier. Drach and Ivan followed. They stood over him and Drach spit, just missing his face.

"Just what were you thinking, you goddamn fool?"

Niko climbed to his feet, rubbing his chin.

"There can't be that many buses left. I just thought it was better if she left now." He gazed at Drach. "Or were you planning something else?"

Drach pulled his pistol and grabbed Niko by the collar, jamming the barrel into his temple.

"Do something like that again and dead Turk whores will be the least of your problems."

Drach shoved Niko to the ground and stuffed the pistol back in its holster.

"Go sit with your pet and don't move."

Niko got up, glared at the sergeant, and turned away. He walked across the street and lowered himself next to Petar. The sound of the accelerating bus in the distance made him smile as he rubbed his aching jaw.

# THURSDAY: MICHAEL SAKIC

MIKE LOOKED AT the three photos drying on his bed. He raised the bottle of vodka to his lips and drank until his stomach protested. Then he walked to the end of the bed and stared into a fractured mirror on the wall.

"He said it wasn't your fault," he shouted at the mirror.

He swallowed more vodka.

"But he died when he did because of me. I robbed him of the last minutes of his life."

He slammed his hand against the wall. A piece of glass tumbled from the mirror.

Mike turned away and stared at the photos again. Jure had wanted to stay with the peacekeepers when Mike returned to Kladanj, so he dropped Robert off and drove straight to a man who had developed photos for him in the past. This time Mike paid extra to use the dark room himself. He didn't want anyone to see the pictures.

*Not yet. Maybe never.*

The Serb sergeant shooting the wounded man filled all three photos. Blurred but recognizable. As were the bits of brain and skull flying away from the man's head.

He drank again.

"I'm sorry. Goddamnit all. I'm so sorry."

He backed up against the wall and slid to the floor, crying.

The door opened.

Mike's head flipped back and struck the wall, tears still wet on his cheeks.

"Christ, Mike, where have you been?"

Brendan dropped his bag on the floor. Mike kept his eyes low.

"You're drinking again?" He tore the half-empty vodka bottle from Mike's hands. "This isn't what I'm paying you for."

Without a word, Mike crawled to his feet and stumbled, bent over, to the bathroom. He emptied his stomach into the toilet. A wet towel appeared next to him. Mike rubbed his face raw and then he threw up the rest of the vodka. When he went back into the bedroom, Brendan was sitting on the edge of the bed, holding up the damp photos.

"What the hell happened?"

Mike wanted to march across the room, rip the photos from Brendan's hands, and tear them into a million pieces, but his feet refused to cooperate. With the help of the wall, he managed to collapse into the closest chair.

"Where'd you get these shots, Mike?"

He told Brendan everything. The trip to Kladanj, the soldiers, the refugees, and the execution.

"The soldier is right," Brendan said after a long pause. "It's not your fault."

"It is my fault," Mike shouted back. "I have no way of knowing if those shots were for the other two men. They were wounded. Maybe the Serbs got someone to carry them to Kladanj. Or back to the Dutch in Srebrenica. I don't know."

"What about the men in the ditch? Christ, Mike, you've heard enough to know they were going to shoot them anyway."

"He would have lived another ten minutes. Twenty minutes. He could have prayed. I robbed him of that. I robbed him of a chance to think about his family. Because of me...."

Mike trailed off, wiping a tear from his cheek. Brendan pointed to the photos, shaking his head.

"No. You didn't rob him of anything." He held up one photo. "Do you know the last thing to go through his mind?"

*Besides the bullet?*

Brendan held the photo closer to Mike.

"Look at the picture. Look at his eyes. He's looking at you. He knew you were going to take the picture. He knew it was going to be evidence. A record of what the Serbs are doing to them. Don't you think he gladly gave up those twenty minutes, knowing it meant the world would see this?"

"I can't publish that."

"Yes, you damn well can publish this. You have to. The French and Americans are sitting with their thumbs up their asses because they don't know who to believe. The Serbs are saying they are only fighting the soldiers. They're saying the men are going to be treated in accordance with the Geneva Convention. The French and the Americans are drinking that Kool Aid and they're going to keep drinking it while the Serbs march into Zepa and Gorazde. Hell, there are rumours now the Ukrainians are being pulled from Zepa."

Mike looked up.

"What?"

"Yeah. They're giving up the safe areas. Just like that general wanted them to when he spoke to the UN in May."

"You think this was all planned?"

"Look, I don't know. But when something stinks, there's usually a lot of shit around."

"Publishing that photo won't make any difference. The Serbs will just say they executed a war criminal. Or they'll call it staged. Heck, they still think Capa staged his photo." Mike drew in a long breath. His stomach settled. "No. All this will do is call my objectivity into question. None of them would trust me anymore. I'd be thrown out of the country."

Mike leaned forward, rubbing his face in the towel. His thoughts made sense again. He wouldn't publish the photo, but he wasn't going to give up. He couldn't help the men out there now. That much was clear, but he could ensure the Serbs didn't get away with it. Somewhere, somehow, he was going to prove to the world the Serbs were murdering thousands while Western leaders sat back and did nothing.

He dropped the towel and walked over to the bed. He took the photos from Brendan's hand and tore them up. Brendan leapt forward, trying to stop him.

"What are you doing?"

"I still have the negatives, but this is going nowhere for now. I'll get something else. Something better."

*Something that will honour that man's death.*

# THURSDAY: ATIF STAVIC

THE TRUCK BUCKED and Atif felt his tailbone crack against the metal floor. He clenched his teeth, pulling in a sharp breath against the pain. His arms pulled his legs tighter against his chest and he kept his eyes away from the two Serb soldiers standing next to the tailgate. He looked over at Ratib, bruised and bleeding from a gash on his jaw. Atif had said nothing to him since the soldiers loaded him into the truck. Tarak lay between him and Ratib, still unconscious. Blood trickled from his nose.

Tarak stirred. A Serb kicked him in the leg.

"Wake up, filthy pig."

Tarak's hand crossed his face, wiping away the blood. He opened his eyes, blinking.

"I think they broke your nose," Atif whispered.

Tarak pulled himself up next to Atif. "No, it's fine. Where are we?"

"No idea."

"Ratib?"

"I don't know."

"What about Salko?" Tarak asked.

"Got away, I guess. We separated. I haven't seen him."

One of the Serbs stepped back, kicking Tarak.

"Shut up, *balije*."

"Alija abandoned you." The second soldier laughed. "He's in

Sarajevo sipping American beer."

The soldier kicked Tarak again and then returned to the tailgate.

The truck turned onto a dirt road. Dust enveloped the vehicle behind them. They passed two wooden buildings and then swung around. The truck went into reverse. Atif looked up. The dust settled as they backed towards a brown barn. One soldier released the tailgate and jumped to the ground.

"Out," the other soldier screamed, pushing them over the edge.

Atif hit the ground hard and rolled. Tarak and Ratib landed behind him. Soldiers who had been loitering next to the barn entrance descended on them. They stripped off Tarak's shirt and boots, leaving him only his khaki pants and T-shirt. One of the soldiers dug through the pockets of his shirt but found nothing. They had better luck with Ratib's shirt which contained Deutsch marks. A sergeant smacked Ratib across the back of his head and then turned his attention to Atif.

"Let the boy go," Tarak said. "He's only fourteen."

The sergeant raised his hand to keep one of the soldiers from striking Tarak with his rifle.

"Fourteen? No. He looks older. Sixteen. Seventeen," he said, gesturing at Atif's clothes and boots. "He certainly looks like a soldier."

"I gave that to him. He had nothing on his feet."

"If he is what you say he is then he will be okay. We have to check your names. War criminals will be tried and punished. The rest of you we will exchange for prisoners."

A soldier pulled off Atif's green shirt, leaving his neon yellow T-shirt alone. Another soldier took his boots, checking to see if they were his size.

"Inside," the sergeant said.

The soldiers pushed them through the barn door. Two dozen heads turned in their direction. Atif looked around. The men sat in small groups in the empty stalls. There were no boys and only three of the men were wearing military green. Ratib dropped to the ground near the door. Tarak led Atif to the back of the barn, to a stall with a window too high for Atif to reach. He sat down. Tarak peered over the window sill for a moment then lowered himself down beside Atif.

"They're watching out there."

"Do you know anyone?"

Tarak shook his head. "Don't think so."

"Do you know where we are?"

"Yeah," Tarak replied. "I grew up not far from here. We're just south of Zvornik. They've brought us a lot closer to the front lines."

"What's going to happen to us?"

"I don't know."

"Do you think he told us the truth? That they'll exchange us?"

"Could be," Tarak said then met Atif's gaze. "I'm sorry I didn't get you to Tuzla."

"You got me farther than I would have on my own. I'm not sure I would have made it through that minefield without you. I would have stepped on a mine or turned back when I saw the flags were gone. Or I would have gotten lost after Kamenica and walked into an ambush."

"Or the *blautsauger.*"

Atif smiled.

Or I would have given up, he added to himself, his smile fading.

A Serb soldier stepped inside. "Who's from Cerska?" he shouted. "I'm looking for anyone from Cerska."

Four men put up their hands. The soldier told them to follow him outside.

Another soldier entered. "I'm looking for anyone from Lolici or Kravica?" He motioned to a man near the front. "Are you from Kravica? Lolici?"

Atif looked at Tarak.

Tarak shook his head. "Don't raise your hand."

"But why do they want to know? Where are they taking them?"

A man shrieked outside the barn.

Pop. Pop.

Atif flinched and looked up at the window. Tarak stood up and peered through it. The screams continued. He dropped down.

"What is it?"

"Nothing," he replied, staring straight ahead. "They're just celebrating. Shooting into the air."

"I'm not a child, Tarak. What did you see?"

Another man screamed. Tarak's next breath was long and hard.

"They have some sort of gauntlet out there. The soldiers are beating the men. One man has a pitchfork in his head."

Atif shrank against the wall as the soldier called again for anyone from Kravica.

*What if they find out I'm from Kravica?*

"They're going to kill us, aren't they?"

Tarak said nothing.

"Aren't they?"

"I honestly don't know, Atif. I really don't. The exchange may be real. They've done it before, many times."

"Then why are they killing those men?"

"Revenge, I guess."

In the opposite stall, a group of men were praying.

"My mother won't know," Atif said.

Tarak stared at him for a few moments and then reached inside his sock and pulled out the laminated ID he had shown Atif earlier.

"Put this in your back pocket."

"Why?"

"Like I said yesterday, if anything happens to me, you can give it to the army in Tuzla."

"What good will that do? If anything happens to you, it'll happen to me, too."

Tarak shook his head with purpose.

"No. You'll be okay. I made a promise. I intend to keep it."

"But...."

A man's voice begged for death on the other side of the wall.

"Take it, Atif. Please."

Atif took the card, poking it into his back pocket.

"You will see your mother again."

# THURSDAY: MARIJA STAVIC

*SIX KILOMETRES?*

Marija looked down at Tihana, asleep in her arms, and tickled her cheek. Tihana opened her eyes.

"Can you walk for a little while?"

Tihana nodded; Marija knelt down and stood the little girl on the hot pavement. Then she checked the bottles in her bag.

Empty.

"I haven't any left either," Ina said.

"Are you sure they said six kilometres?" Adila asked. "It feels like twenty."

"Yeah. Six."

Marija took Tihana's hand and started walking. Tihana pulled the toy soldiers from her waistband with her other hand.

"The tunnel," Ina said, pointing ahead. "It can't be much farther."

Marija swallowed, her throat sticking. They walked into the tunnel and paused in the shade. A cool breeze brushed their sweat-soaked hair and clothes.

"I can see tents," Ina said. "And some buses."

"Oh thank God," Marija said, hugging Tihana. "We're almost there."

Peacekeepers and doctors were crowded along a line of tables. Marija picked up bread and juice before they boarded the bus. She shivered as a blast of cold air met her at the door of the vehicle.

"Air conditioning!" Adila said. She stopped and took a long deep breath.

Marija followed them to the back of the bus, where Adila collapsed into a window seat. Tihana sat on her lap and went to sleep. Ina cuddled up with Lejla next to them. Marija laid her head back.

She woke to the swaying of the bus as it turned into the Tuzla air base. They stopped next to an ocean of white modular tents. Tihana held the soldiers up to the window.

"Are we really safe?" Adila asked.

Marija rubbed her eyes.

"Yes. We'll be okay here." Marija whispered.

When they stepped off the bus, the heat rose from the pavement to meet them.

"Where do we go?" Lejla asked.

Marija pointed to a blue beret moving among the crowd.

"That way, I guess."

They followed the others into a makeshift receiving area. More peacekeepers sat behind a line of tables, taking information.

"My son's name is Atif," she told the Pakistani peacekeeper.

"Where is he?" he asked without looking up.

"He's in the woods. With the men."

"Oh."

"He needs to know that I am here."

"Yes, ma'am." The peacekeeper turned a page, looked up, and pointed to the opposite side of the tent. "You can proceed. There are doctors there if you need medical attention."

"But what about my son?"

The peacekeeper scratched his forehead and stifled a yawn. "I don't know what to tell you about that, ma'am. You know about as much as I do. You might want to check with the Bosnian army."

Marija turned away. She found Ina in the medical tent; a medic was examining Lejla's arm.

"They want to take them to the hospital to treat the rashes," Ina said. "They want us to go now."

Marija caught her breath.

*Is this good-bye?*

"If you need a place," she said, "you know where we are going."

Ina nodded and wiped a tear. "I'm pretty sure I still have a cousin nearby. When we are settled, we will try to come by to see you."

They put their arms around each other and held on for a long time.

"Thank you," Ina said. "For everything. And let us know when Atif shows up."

"I will," she replied, letting the tears fall. "I promise."

The twins hugged Marija and Tihana. Behind them, a medic was motioning to a truck waiting outside the tent. The women embraced again, quickly this time, and walked outside together.

"Take care," Marija said. "All of you."

They climbed into the truck. Ina rolled down her window and took Marija's hand. Tihana waved with her fingers opening and closing like spider legs. Then Ina rolled the window up and the truck drove away.

Marija stood on the tarmac and looked around.

*What do we do now?*

Refugees were flocking towards a large tent. Marija picked up Tihana and followed. They joined the line; soon tables full of food came into view. Trays of sandwiches, fruits, and vegetables covered the tables and cases of water and soft drinks towered above them. Three years of near-starvation, of watching her children cry themselves to sleep from hunger, and here, only a short drive away, was more food than she had seen in all that time.

"Marija!"

She turned around. Yassir's older brother, Vlatko, was standing alone, grinning from ear to ear. He wore clean jeans and a T-shirt and his face was shaved. His smile reminded her of Yassir.

"Oh my God, how did you find me?" she asked, giving him a quick hug.

Vlatko kissed Tihana. "I saw you get off the bus and then I lost you in the crowd. Where's Atif?"

Marija grit her teeth for a moment and then told him everything.

"I didn't realize they were taking boys so young," he said, picking up Tihana. "I will talk to the army, but I should get you home first."

Marija looked at the food.

"Don't worry. We have plenty." Vlatko looked at Tihana. "Your aunt Kata is at her mother's place until Monday, but I'm sure I can bake cookies as well as she can."

Tihana smiled.

"Okay." Marija picked up her bag and followed Vlatko towards the gate. They passed a wall full of notes written on paper and cardboard tacked and taped to it. Marija stopped to read them.

"They're notes for the men," she told Vlatko. "I should leave something. For Atif."

"We can make something at home. I will come back after dinner and put it up."

"Thank you."

"Come," he said, tousling Tihana's hair. "We have so much to talk about."

# THURSDAY: ATIF STAVIC

ATIF WAS TREMBLING. He had his hands against his ears to dull the screams. The lengthening slats of sunlight moved up the side of the stall as the Serbs kept piling men into the barn then coming back to prey on them. When the men stopped responding to requests for residents of certain villages, the Serbs picked anyone.

They selected Ratib.

Atif imagined the young soldier's walk around the barn to the gauntlet of soldiers armed with rifles, bats, shovels, and axes. A high-pitched squeal penetrated Atif's hands. He squeezed them harder against his ears.

He'd heard that sound before and his mind slipped back to Kravica.

*The pigs.*

A Serb neighbour had kept a few pigs; they squealed the same way when he slaughtered them.

Atif's stomach churned. He began to gag and spit.

"Are you okay?" Tarak asked, squeezing Atif's shoulder.

"Why aren't we doing something?"

"What do you mean?"

"There must be three hundred men here. Why don't we just rush them when they open the door?"

"You didn't see them out there, did you?"

"See who?"

"There are two trucks parked on the edge of the cornfield. Chetniks have a fifty-calibre machine gun set up inside each one. If we rushed the door, they'd cut everyone down."

Atif spit, trying to clear the burning sensation in his throat.

Silence.

No screams. No gunshots. No soldiers dragging men from the barn.

"What's going on?"

Tarak shook his head. An engine revved up. People shouted. Three hundred heads turned towards the barn door. Atif's heart slammed against his chest. Then the door opened. Soldiers poured in. A truck backed up against the door.

"Get up," a soldier shouted, pulling a man to his feet and pushing him towards the truck. "Fifty. We need fifty for this exchange."

Two soldiers grabbed the man, yanked his arms behind his back, and tied his wrists with wire. They helped him onto a wooden box and then into the truck. Other soldiers seized more men, striking them with rifle butts and bats as they pushed them towards the truck.

*Why would they beat them if they were going to an exchange?*

Atif glanced at Tarak. He was facing the door, but his eyes were unfocused and shifting.

"What was your little brother's name?" Atif asked.

Tarak looked at him. "Fadil."

"What happened to him?"

"Doesn't matter."

"It does to me."

Tarak looked away, nodding.

"I told you I was in Srebrenica when the war started. I spent three days trying to get back home. Salko and some others came along to help me find my family. When we got to Zvornik, the Chetniks were already there. We sneaked into an empty building to watch while they rounded up all the Muslims and brought them down to the river." He hesitated for a moment, clearing his throat. "They tied the families together. Husbands and wives and children. Then they shot the parents and pushed them over the bridge. The children drowned."

Atif realized his jaw had dropped; he clamped it shut.

"You couldn't stop them?"

"There were only five of us. When I saw my family up there, I went crazy. Salko and the others had to hold me down so that I didn't give away our position." Tarak paused. "He was only eleven years old."

"You used to call him *Braco*."

A smile crept up one side of Tarak's face.

"Yeah. I was so much older. He liked it when I called him that because it used to remind everyone that we were brothers."

"I'm sorry."

"They died together," Tarak said with a shrug. "That's all that matters."

"If...." Atif said after a few moments. "When we get out of this, will you come with us?"

"What do you mean?"

"To another country. You could come with us. You said you have no one left here. You don't have anything left to fight for. Come with us. You could be my big brother."

Tarak's smile went up the other side of his face and he draped an arm around Atif.

"Is that what you want, *Braco*?"

Atif's head bobbed.

"Then I'll go with you." Tarak held him tight. "We'll be okay."

Another truck arrived and left with a load of men, then another. Eventually, only a few dozen of them remained. Atif wiped his face hard; his hands were shaking. He wished he could change the past. When their Serb neighbour offered to smuggle them out, he had given his father the choice between Tuzla and Srebrenica. Atif's father had chosen Tuzla, but the Serb said it would be safer to go to Srebrenica and his father had agreed.

One decision and it changed the course of his life.

He could have spent the last three years in Tuzla. He could have eaten more than one meal a day. Maybe even gone to school and played soccer in the streets.

Another truck arrived and the Serbs herded the remaining men towards the entrance. The soldiers had run out of wire, so they piled the men aboard unbound.

"Stay close to me," Tarak said, grasping Atif's hand. He pulled him into the centre of the group at the back of the truck.

"Where is Alija now?" one of the Serbs said, pushing them forward with his rifle.

"He's having dinner with Oric in Tuzla," another replied. "He doesn't care about you. They've left you to rot."

Tarak kept Atif in front of him and they managed to scramble into the truck before a rifle butt made contact. Tarak pushed Atif as deep inside as possible. Shouts and gunshots echoed behind them. Tarak pushed his way to the side of the truck and peered through a slit in the tarp.

"What's happening," Atif asked.

Tarak told him what he had seen. Four men had sprinted away from the truck into a cornfield. The first man was shot dead then the Serbs ran into the field after the other three, firing bursts from their weapons. After a few minutes, they came out pulling a body between them.

"We'll get them later," Tarak heard one of the soldiers say.

He looked at Atif.

"They got away."

*Escape is possible!*

"It'll be dark soon," Tarak said. "That will help."

Atif allowed a hint of optimism to creep into his mind. As long as he was alive, he had a chance. The only question was how to exploit it.

The Serbs grabbed a man from the back of the truck and threw him to the ground. They beat him until his screams faded.

"Stupid Turks," a soldier shouted. "You're going to be exchanged. Now we don't have enough for all the prisoners they want to give us. Try it again and we'll find fifty others to take your place."

The soldiers pulled the tarp down and secured it, leaving the men in darkness.

"They're still talking about an exchange," Atif said, trying not to sound too excited.

The truck remained still for more than an hour. The man next to Atif fainted.

"Switch places with me," Tarak said, pushing hard against the man behind them. "Put your head against the tarp."

Tarak pulled Atif as close to the hole as possible; he drank his fill of the cool dusk air. Then something splashed inside the truck. Someone made a slurping noise. Atif looked back into the darkness.

"Does someone have water?" he whispered to Tarak.

"He's not drinking water."

"Oh."

Atif peeked through the slit in the tarp. A red car pulled up next to the soldiers and a silver-haired man in a camouflage uniform stepped out. The soldiers greeted him with kisses, handshakes, and salutes. The officer spoke to them for about ten minutes then returned to the red car and left.

The truck started up. As they drove, Tarak relayed information. The Drina River was on the right; they were travelling north but were still south of Zvornik.

"We're getting even closer to our territory," Tarak said.

Makes sense if they are taking us to a prisoner exchange, Atif thought.

The truck slowed and pulled onto the side of the road, in front of a small building.

"I know this place," Tarak told Atif. "It used to be a butcher's shop. But it's been closed since the war started."

Atif looked out of the hole. Soldiers were coming out of the building.

"Must be a command post or a barracks now," he whispered to Atif.

The soldiers opened the tarp and stared up at the men.

"Anyone here from Zvornik?" one asked.

"Or Grbavci?" said another.

The man standing next to Atif moved towards the tailgate. Tarak caught his arm, but he pulled away.

"I know," the man said. "I just need it to be over, one way or another."

Two men dropped from the truck and were taken inside the building. Moments later, their screams filled the air. Atif shivered.

"Anyone from Lehovici?"

Another man jumped to the ground. Atif fought the urge to follow.

*Perhaps they would realize their mistake if I jumped off now. Would they beat a boy?* His mind sifted through the possibilities. They had already refused to consider his age when Tarak pleaded with them. The Serb in Potocari hadn't cared about his age, only what he looked like. And he doubted they'd let him go after everything he had seen.

Atif squeezed his eyes shut and leaned against the tarp.

He waited.

# THURSDAY: NIKO BASARIC

A GREY-HAIRED MAN scrambled out of a ditch and raised his hands high above his head. He wore pants and the shredded remains of an undershirt; his ribs were visible underneath it.

"Don't shoot," he said. "There are five more. One is hurt."

"Tell them to come out," Niko said, motioning with his rifle. "We're not going to shoot."

The man waved at the forest and the men emerged. They looked like the hundreds of men that had already surrendered: gaunt, exhausted, frightened. One man leaned on two others, his leg covered in dried blood. Another was barefoot; his feet were cut, blistered, and swollen. Petar led the group across the road, lining them up next to an empty truck.

"Take off your shirts and shoes," Anton ordered, pointing to piles of clothes, shoes, and documents.

The men added their shoes and shirts to the two piles. A few dropped documents. Niko stood beside Petar, his helmet low over his eyes. Anton and Vladen searched for valuables, pocketing money and jewelry. Ivan pulled an empty pistol from one man and smacked the trembling man on the head with it.

"What were you going to do with this?"

The man said nothing, staring at the ground. Ivan stood behind him and cocked the pistol.

Click.

Click.

He poked the barrel into the man's neck.

"How many Serb women did you kill with this pistol?"

"None," the man replied. "The firing pin is broken."

Ivan struck him on the head, driving him to the ground.

"Liar. Get on that truck."

The rest of the men shuffled towards the truck. Petar offered his hand.

"I'm sorry," Petar said, helping the men aboard. "I'm sorry."

Niko grabbed him by the collar, yanking him back.

"Will you stop that?"

"Leave me alone," Petar said, pulling away. He offered his hand to the next man. "I'm sorry."

Niko turned away, tugging his helmet lower.

"Turk."

*What does he want now?*

Drach pointed to a truck. Ivan and the others were already climbing aboard.

"Get on, Turk. Your pet, too. I've volunteered us for something even you can't screw up."

Niko climbed into the back of Drach's truck. Petar sat next to him. There were four other soldiers Niko didn't recognize. He studied their uniforms, taking note of the patches on their sleeves.

*They're paramilitary. Scorpions.*

"I don't like this, Niko. Why are Scorpions here?"

"I don't know, Petar. Maybe we're just giving them a ride. Don't worry about it. In a couple days, we'll be home. Just think about that."

"I don't want to think about it. I can't think about it."

Niko eyed Petar. Two days ago, the recruit had been as excited as a schoolboy at the thought of combat. Now, he would do anything to get out of it. Niko knew from the beginning Petar wasn't a soldier. He was worried that these few days had changed him, and not for the better. His mother might not recognize her son.

Niko leaned back and looked outside. Darkness enveloped the east; the Drina sparkled in the fading light.

"Why are we going so far north?" Petar asked.

"I don't know," Niko replied. "Maybe they found the men who crossed last night."

He sighed at the thought. The majority of the men who had

crossed the night before were soldiers. If they were going to the front to stop them from crossing the lines, Petar might see the real combat he craved. And he wouldn't be able to cope.

They turned left.

"Where are we now?" Petar asked.

"This is the road to Tuzla. The front line cuts it in half, near a village called Memici."

Soon after they turned onto the Memici road, they pulled up next to an abandoned farm. Niko dropped from the back of the truck and looked around. A field of tall grass extended as far as he could see in the dying light. Several trucks idled near the treeline, their lights illuminating the area.

"Why so much light?" Petar asked.

"I don't know."

The lights would attract the enemy. *Or was that the point?*

Drach led the group towards the trucks. Several other Scorpions sat in the grass next to them. The sergeant dug into an ammo box, tossing magazines to everyone.

"What are we supposed to be doing?" Petar asked.

"Doing your job, Recruit. You're going to shoot the Turks." Drach walked towards a red car and a group of officers.

Petar stared at Niko.

"What does he mean? Are we doing patrols again?"

Niko glanced around. They were too far north for the men to have made it from the road in one day. He sucked in his cheeks and stowed the extra magazines in his webbing. Drach was still with the officers when a line of buses turned into the driveway and pulled up behind their truck.

"They're the buses they used for the women and children," Petar said. "I thought they were all gone. What are they doing here?"

"No idea," Niko answered, stepping forward.

The first bus switched off its engine; an inside light came on. Men.

"Form up, single rank," Drach shouted from behind.

The sergeant walked up to Niko and motioned with his arm. The section lined up to Niko's right. The Scorpions stood near the buses.

"What are we doing?" Petar whispered.

Niko waved him silent.

Drach faced the buses. The Scorpions got on the first one, hauled a dozen men off, and forced them to form a line in front of the trucks.

Headlights illuminated the men. They had been stripped of their shirts and shoes and their hands were bound behind their backs with wire. They wore blindfolds.

"Prepare to fire," Drach said as the Scorpions joined the line.

"Fire?" Niko blurted out.

"Yes, I told you. We're here to shoot the Turks."

"Shoot them?" Niko said. "You mean murder them. No fucking way. I won't do it."

Niko turned and began walking away. Behind him, he heard the tall grass whipping against leather boots. Metal on leather and then cold steel against the back of his neck.

He halted.

"Coward," Drach said next to his ear. "I have the authority to kill you if you threaten the integrity of this unit."

Niko turned around. Drach jammed the pistol against his chest.

"Spout regulations all you want, Sergeant, but this is wrong and you know it."

Drach pressed the muzzle into his flesh. "What did you say?"

Niko glared at Drach. "This. Is. Wrong."

Drach grabbed Niko by the collar and yanked him forward then pushed him towards the line of bound men.

"If you don't want to shoot them then go stand with them and let the real soldiers do their work."

Niko eyed the men.

Civilians. Neighbours. Friends.

"Make your decision, Turk."

Images of Mira and Natalija filled his mind.

Drach pushed him. "Now, Turk."

Niko squeezed his eyes shut, apologizing to them.

*I have no choice. I have a family to consider. Dying with them will serve no purpose.*

He glanced at Petar. The recruit's jaw trembled.

"Damn it," Niko muttered. He nodded.

Drach shoved him back into line; Niko took his place next to Petar. He cocked his rifle and then faced the line of men. Drach's voice suddenly entered his ear.

"And don't let me catch you firing into the air, Turk."

Niko struggled to quell the nausea. He stared at bare backs, the sweat glistening in the headlights.

"Prepare to fire."

Barrels swung up. Butts smacked against shoulders. Metal slid on metal. Niko aimed at the heart of the man in front of him.

"God forgive me."

"Fire!"

# THURSDAY: JAC LARUE

JAC SAT NEXT to the tailgate of the truck driving their group into Nova Kasaba. The Serbs had decided it was too dangerous to send the Dutch back to Potocari and offered to put them up for the night.

There were hundreds of soldiers in the town. Trucks passed them carrying anti-aircraft guns and mortars. A tank was idling near the main road. Soldiers were loading ammunition into a jeep.

The truck turned into a parking lot and stopped. Jac stood up and looked around the tarp.

*A school?*

The Dutch dropped from the truck and followed their escort inside, past soldiers sitting on the steps smoking and others moving in and out of the building. The Serb led them down a corridor filled with desks and lockers and then into a classroom converted into a barracks. Desks lined the back of the room, piled three and four high. Sheets of paper hung from the walls. Jac turned one over. Several crayoned stick-children were holding hands. A dove flew above them.

Serb soldiers were sitting or sleeping on three cots near the door; the Dutch claimed the rest. Jac dropped his gear on the cot next to Maarten. A soldier appeared at the door.

"You can get something to eat and drink across the hall."

"Smells like chicken," Maarten said.

Jac faced the door. All he could smell was school.

They crossed the hall and went into another room where they

were handed plates. Jac stared at the food, his mouth watering. A full chicken breast, a large scoop of near-liquid mashed potatoes and peas smothered in steaming gravy. He devoured the dinner, his first hot meal in weeks. Afterwards, he went outside and sat down on a step, grateful for the cool dusk air. Soldiers were eating and smoking in the playground across the street. The sky glowed red behind them.

"I think you could use this."

Jac glanced up. Maarten stood above him holding two glasses.

"Vodka?"

"What else?"

"No thanks."

Maarten sat next to Jac. "Well, more for me."

"I think it's best if we keep our heads clear."

"That, my friend, is exactly what I don't want anymore. I'm sick of this crap. I'm sick of being played like a violin." Maarten took a mouthful from one of the glasses. "If it isn't these bastards holding up our convoys, it's the locals stealing our stuff. I mean the soldiers, not the civilians. No, they're great. Great pawns. Sitting around and starving while the politicians and generals play chess with their lives."

Maarten paused to swallow the rest of the vodka. He laid the empty glass on the step and took a sip from the second glass.

"Who are the bad guys today, Jac? We're supposed to be impartial. You remember them telling us that? No good guys, no bad guys. This is royally screwed up, Jac. I know I've said it before, but it just keeps getting even more screwed up."

"How many of those did you have before you came out here?"

"Well," Maarten said, lifting the glass up. "Let me put it this way. I'm actually going to sleep tonight."

A group of Serbs was walking towards them; one of them had a growling Alsatian dog on a leash. He loosened his grip on the leash and the dog lunged forward. Jac jumped up and back. The dog halted with a jerk less than a metre away, snarling. The Serb laughed, pulled the dog in, and marched away.

Maarten had not budged.

"Bad guys," he shouted at them. He took a sip and looked at Jac. "Now, the chef who cooked that steaming hot chicken dinner, he's a good guy. The medic who sewed my head back together? Good guy. The sergeant who gave me this fine vodka? Good guy."

Jac considered taking the cup for himself.

"Well," Maarten said, standing up. He looked down the road. "What's going on over there?"

Jac turned around. Maarten used the glass to point. Under the streetlight, two Serb soldiers were pulling a man from a truck. He was shirtless, barefoot, and his torso was covered in blood. The soldiers pushed him into a shed next to the school. Maarten looked back at Jac.

"Bad guys?"

"Sit down before you fall down," Jac said. He stood up and took several steps towards the shed. Then a soldier stepped in front of him.

"Where are you going?"

"For a walk."

The Serb shook his head. More soldiers joined him.

"Stay inside," he said. "Too dangerous out here."

Maarten stood and held up the glass, toasting the soldiers following Jac.

Jac turned him around and gave him a gentle shove towards the door. They spent the evening in the classroom under the eyes of the Serbs who shared it with them. The soldiers followed the Dutch to the washrooms and the cafeteria. As the evening progressed, they brought out vodka, plum brandy, and a deck of cards. Some of the peacekeepers played and drank. Others slept. Karel entertained the Serbs with his jokes. Maarten passed out before midnight.

When the lights went out, Jac settled into his cot and tried to sleep. He rolled, pulled the blanket up around his shoulders, and rolled again. He punched the pillow and checked the time.

Three o'clock.

Light and voices drifted in from the corridor. He rubbed his eyes and glanced around. A bright moon lit up a figure standing next to an open window.

*Janssen?*

Jac threw the blanket aside, sat up, and pulled on his shirt. Maarten was asleep in the cot next to him, pulling in deep nasal snores. Jac got up and walked around the end of the cot. He joined Janssen at the window.

"Can't sleep?"

"Maybe an hour." Jac looked at the moon hanging high in the southern sky. *Is my mother looking at the same moon?*

Janssen motioned outside. "Do you hear it?"

The moon lit up the terrain like a dull day. It was easy for Jac to make out buildings, hilltops, and tracts of forest. An engine revved. Drunken soldiers sang around a distant corner.

And gunshots punctuated the cool night air.

He leaned closer to the open window.

Pop.

Silence.

Pop.

Silence.

Pop.

*The soccer field?*

Pop.

No return fire.

Pop.

"That's not....? Is it?"

Pop.

"They're putting them down," Janssen whispered.

Pop.

"This is insane."

Pop.

Silence.

"There's going to be hell to pay when we get back," the sergeant said. "You know that, right?"

"For what?"

"Shit rolls downhill, Jac. We're at the bottom."

"That's crazy. What could we have done differently? The Serbs blocked all our convoys and kept half our guys out. No fuel. No ammunition. No heavy weapons. No air strikes. You said they told New York and Sarajevo what was happening. If they cared, they wouldn't have waited four days to send two planes."

"I'm not saying it's right, Jac. It's going to be easy for the men on top to put blame on the men on the ground. I think we need to be prepared for what is going to come out of this."

"That's ridiculous."

"Not really. It's happened before. I told you I had a cousin in Canada, serving with the air force."

"Yeah."

"Well, a couple years back they had a unit in Somalia. One night, a group of soldiers went too far with a kid who tried to steal stuff from their compound. They took him into one of their bunkers and beat him to death. The guy who did most of it, I think he was a sergeant or something like that, he tried to kill himself. Didn't finish the job and was left with brain damage, so he never went to trial. They convicted some private and the leadership pretty well walked. Big inquiry going on now, apparently. Last I heard they're considering disbanding the unit altogether."

"That's crazy."

"Remember everything you see, Jac," Janssen said, leaning closer to him. "If you get your hands on a piece of paper and a pen, write it down. In fact, when this is over, write down everything you remember and I mean every last detail. Your memory will never be as good as it will be over the next few days and weeks. Write the truth as best as you can remember it. When people lie, it's easy to catch them trying to remember the lie. Tell the truth and your story will never change."

A thought swirled in Jac's head and he drew in a sharp breath. "You think they might charge us with something?"

"Anything is possible, but I don't see how they can charge any of us as individuals. Heck, half our guys don't even realize what's going on around them. They don't know or don't believe it or they just don't want to see it."

"What about what happened on the road coming back from the outpost?"

"I don't know, Jac." Janssen sighed. "I spoke to some of the refugees that came down the road the next day. None of them reported any bodies on the road."

"That's good to know. I mean, when I walked back, all I saw was a crushed wheelbarrow. We might have just run over their stuff."

"I hope you're right, Jac. I really do. Believe me, I want to know the truth more than anyone."

"There was nothing else you could have done, Sergeant. We were the target. If we had stayed still, the fifty-calibre would have torn those people to pieces."

"You know that. I know that. Do you think the average person sitting at home watching it reported on TV will think that?" He shook his head. "All the best sailors are on dry land, Jac. People who've never heard a shot fired in anger will decide we were cowards or brutes. Tell Maarten and Arie to do the same. I want the same story from as many perspectives as possible."

"Erik?"

The sergeant remained silent for a moment and then shook his head.

"No. He's having a hard time. No sense in making him relive it all."

"If what you say is true, he is going to relive it all, over and over, when we get back."

"I know," Janssen whispered.

Pop.

Jac looked outside, his eyes scanning the shadows for muzzle fire.

"Why didn't we try to stop them? We could have blockaded the road and blew up the first tank the moment we realized they were really going for the town."

Pop.

"Hindsight is a wonderful thing, Jac. If I told you on Monday that they were going to take the whole enclave and start murdering the men, would you have believed me?"

Pop.

"No. I never would have thought they'd try something this bold." He waved his hand towards the window. "And I'm still having a problem believing they're this stupid. They can't possibly think they'll get away with it."

Pop.

"Just remember everything, Jac. Write it down."

Pop.

"Write it all down."

# FRIDAY: TARAK SMAJLOVIC

TARAK WATCHED THE shop through the hole in the tarp. The truck hadn't moved in five hours, but the Serbs refused to let them sit down or go outside to relieve themselves. A soldier had handed up a cup of water and the thirsty men had fought over it, spilling it on the floor. The Serbs didn't refill the cup. They'd stopped asking for men after eight had given up.

"We're trying to arrange an exchange," one of the soldiers had told them. "But your army is not cooperating."

*Do we believe them?* An exchange made sense given how long they'd made them wait, but taking the men inside in order to kill them made no sense at all.

Tarak glanced at Atif. The boy was leaning against the tarp. He'd stopped shivering hours ago.

"You okay?"

"Yeah."

"Thirsty?"

"No. Not really. Just tired."

Tarak looked at the far side of the truck.

*East?*

He mumbled words he had not spoken in years.

Soldiers streamed from the shop. One vomited against the truck. Others shouted insults at the men then crammed into their own trucks and left. Two soldiers counted the men.

"Thirty-six," one of them said.

"That'll do. We're going to the exchange now."

The soldiers pulled the tarp down over the back. The moment the interior went dark, the men collapsed to the floor. There was little room to sit; Tarak pushed hard against the man next to him and Atif sat in the space he'd made. Tarak stayed on his feet, looking through the hole in the tarp.

The vehicle started up, spitting gravel as it lumbered onto the road. The gas station should be close, he thought, but when they reached it, he saw only a bulldozed lot under a weak street light.

The store would be next. Then the bakery. Tarak caught sight of them, outlined in moonlight.

*We're still going north.*

They entered Zvornik.

*It looks normal.* Except for the empty lots where the mosques used to stand.

"Turn left," he whispered as they approached the road to Memici. "Turn left. Please. Turn left."

The vehicle geared down and made the turn.

"We're on the road to Memici," he told the men. "It's not much farther to our territory."

Atif said nothing.

"Keep going straight," he said quietly, over and over. Every moment they were on the road brought them that much closer to freedom. But minutes later, the vehicle slowed.

"Damn it. No."

The full moon lit the area; he recognized the farms.

*Only halfway to Memici.*

The truck heaved from left to right as it turned off the road and followed a dirt track. In the distance, a bright light illuminated soldiers.

*Could this be the exchange?*

Tarak's pulse raced as they moved through the field. The headlights revealed the silhouette of a bus, but little else. He strained to see anything as the truck pulled up next to the bus and then stopped. He squinted, trying to focus. The ground looked as though it were covered with mounds of discarded carpet and bedding.

*What are they growing?*

The bus turned on its headlights and lit up the harvest. Tarak sucked in his breath. Bodies covered the field as far as he could see.

A bulldozer sat farther up the field. A dozen soldiers waited below.

*Blautsaugers.*

Tarak took a moment to find his breath. His stomach contracted until it hurt. His lungs resisted the next breath.

*Think. Think.*

He dropped down next to Atif.

"What is it?" the boy asked. "Where are we?"

"We're at a farm. We're only a couple kilometres or so from our territory. It's to the northwest."

"Why are you telling me this?"

*Think. Think.*

"Listen to me, Atif. I need you to do as I say. If we're going to get out of this, you have to listen."

"I don't understand. What do you mean?"

"When we get down off the truck, stay to my right."

"Why?"

"Do you trust me?"

"Yes."

"Then promise me you'll do it."

Tarak focused on Atif's face, trying to make out his features in the shadows. Shouting erupted outside. Tarak stood up and looked through the tarp. The soldiers forced the driver off the bus and were pushing him towards the truck. The tailgate tarp swung up and a man dropped out. The soldiers shoved the man towards the closest mound of bodies. They pressed a rifle into the bus driver's arms.

"No," the driver said, trying to return the rifle. "I'm just a driver."

A soldier shoved him forward. "Shoot him."

The driver held the rifle as though it were crawling with insects. The barrel wavered, pointing in the man's general direction.

"Open your eyes!" the soldier shouted at the driver.

The driver pulled the trigger and the rifle spit out half a dozen rounds. The man toppled, three holes in his bare back. The soldier retrieved the rifle and patted the driver on the back.

"Good job. You can go."

"What's happening?" Atif asked.

Tarak helped the boy to his feet. "Stay to my right. Do you understand? Just stay to my right and when they start to shoot, fall down."

The boy was breathing rapidly. "What do you mean, fall down?"

Tarak held Atif by the shoulders. He couldn't find the boy's eyes in the darkness. "They're shooting everyone."

The boy's knees buckled. Tarak held him up.

"I can get you out of this, *Braco*. The light out there isn't good. Stay to my right and fall as soon as you hear the gunfire. Fall and stay still. Then when they move on, you can crawl out and escape. Go northwest, Atif. Our territory is not that far away."

"I can't. I can't."

"Get out," a Serb voice shouted.

"Take them all," another voice said. "Then we're done."

"Promise me, *Braco*."

"But what about you?"

"We'll see. Now promise me."

"Okay. Okay. I promise. But you're coming too. Right?"

"Get out. All of you."

Tarak grasped the boy's left hand and followed the men out of the truck. Something struck his head before he could straighten up and he fell, dragging Atif with him.

"Get moving," a soldier shouted. "Over there."

Tarak's vision blurred. White light became red. Warm liquid trickled down his neck.

"Lead me," he said to Atif. "To the right."

Tarak felt the boy tug him to his feet. Another man crumpled next to them. A gunshot rang out and the man remained on the ground. Tarak fought to stay conscious.

*Only a few more minutes. Don't lose it now. Not now.*

He struggled to stay with Atif as they walked over bodies. Atif kept pulling him to the right. They stepped out of the light on the far side of the line. Tarak could only make out shapes and shadows. Bile rose in his throat. He held onto Atif's hand, pulling the boy close.

"You'll be okay, *Braco*. I promise."

Then he took a step back.

# ATIF STAVIC

*YOU STAND STILL, sucking air in through your mouth and nose in short, sharp breaths. Your teeth chatter, but you're not afraid. He pulls you closer.*

*You glance back at the soldiers.*

*We were friends and neighbours. We celebrated birthdays and holidays together regardless of religion. We went to school together. Worked together. Married each other.*

*Now we murder each other.*

*You turn away and squeeze his hand tighter. He says everything will be okay.*

*You believe him.*

*Metal slides on metal.*

*You look down and wonder if you'll see the rounds slice through your chest.*

*Someone screams out orders.*

*Muscles tense.*

*Images of your mother flood your mind. You tell her you tried. You tell her you're sorry.*

*The world explodes behind you.*

# FRIDAY: NIKO BASARIC

NIKO WATCHED THE last man collapse on the heap of bodies.

*So many.*

Eight buses. At least a hundred men in each one. They had killed at least eight hundred men. He had killed four or five dozen.

No, he corrected himself. Murdered. How do I go home and face them after this?

He wanted to throw the rifle away, tear off his uniform and run. They could shoot him in the back for all he cared. Petar sat on the ground next to him, staring straight ahead. He had vomited earlier and sat out half the executions before Drach hauled him back into the line.

All but two of the Scorpions had left. Niko looked to his right. Ivan and the two Scorpions were walking along the edge of the killing ground, calling out to the men they had just shot.

"Is anyone alive?"

"Raise your hand," a Scorpion said. "We will take you to a hospital."

An arm rose up from the mound. Ivan sidestepped until he was standing over the wounded man.

"You want to go to a hospital?"

Niko didn't hear a response. Ivan pulled out his pistol.

Pop.

"Anyone else want to go to a hospital?" Ivan climbed on top of the bulldozer and switched on the lights then stood, staring across the field. "I said does anyone else want to go to a hospital?"

No response.

Drach was standing next to a red car, talking to an officer. They saluted each other and the officer left. Then the sergeant called out to them and Niko and the rest of the section joined him.

"New orders," Drach said, "but first we must check them over, make sure no one has been left alive." Drach pointed at Niko and Petar. "That means both of you, too. If I catch either of you leaving even one Turk alive, you will join them. Now go."

Niko turned away. He didn't care anymore. They were done for the night. Nothing else mattered. He pulled the empty magazine from his rifle, threw it away, and then inserted a full one. He followed the others as they spread out, shooting anyone who moved.

No one taunted the wounded.

Every shot made Niko flinch. He nudged at a macabre jumble of limp arms and legs. He shot into several bodies just to keep Drach away. He glanced back. Petar was behind him, bent over and retching. Niko struggled to keep his last meal down.

"You okay?"

Petar responded with a wave of his hand and he straightened up. Niko turned back and looked down. A pair of eyes was looking up at him. He swallowed a breath.

*A teenager?*

The boy didn't move. Blood was dripping from the point of his nose, but Niko couldn't see a wound. He looked up. The sergeant was leaning against a truck, having a conversation with one of the Scorpions; the rest wandered among the dead. Niko heard Petar take a sharp breath.

"Walk the other way, Petar," he whispered.

"But...."

"Walk away."

Niko didn't have to look to know the recruit was no longer behind him. He stepped closer to the boy.

"Close your eyes," he whispered. "And stay still."

The boy squeezed his eyes shut. Niko raised his rifle and fired a shot into the ground then stumbled away. Drach called them back. Petar came to Niko's side and they walked together in silence.

"We have to go to another site," Drach said. "There are a few hundred more waiting and we need to get it done before dawn."

"No," Niko said, shaking his head. "I've had enough. I'm not going."

"What was that, Turk?"

"I said I'm not going. I've done enough. If you want to shoot me then go ahead. Otherwise, send me back to Bratunac."

Drach marched up to Niko, raising his pistol. He jammed it against Niko's temple. "I'm not sure I heard you right, Turk?"

Niko returned the sergeant's glare.

"I. Am. Done."

The pistol wavered. Niko stood his ground.

"I'm done, too," Petar whispered from behind. "I want to go back to Bratunac."

Drach ignored Petar and pushed the pistol tighter against Niko's head.

Then Anton stepped forward.

"I'm done, too. You're not going to shoot us all, so to hell with this; send us back to Bratunac."

Vladen and Pavle stepped up beside Anton and Niko permitted himself the luxury of a deep breath.

"Cowards," the sergeant said, lowering the pistol. "You're all cowards."

"Last time I checked, Sergeant," Anton said, "it doesn't take courage to shoot an unarmed man in the back."

"Fine," Drach said, his eyes shifting between them. "You can all stay here and watch over the dead. It seems that's all you're good for. If I feel like it, I might send a vehicle back for you."

The sergeant kicked an ammo case at Niko, striking him in the shin. A Scorpion spat at Niko's feet and walked away. Drach, Ivan, and the Scorpions drove away.

They were alone with only the lights from the bulldozer. Niko struggled to keep his mind clear. Petar climbed up in the bulldozer, turned off the headlights, and sat silently in the seat. The others wandered near the bodies, smoking. Niko turned away, dropped his rifle, and walked into the darkness until he was sure no one could see him.

Then he collapsed into the tall grass and pulled off his helmet.

The picture of Natalija and Mira shone in the moonlight. Niko pulled them out and kissed them.

He struggled to breathe.

His chest hurt.

Then his shoulders convulsed and his teeth clamped together.

Tears poured from his eyes.

# FRIDAY: ATIF STAVIC

*"BRACO."*

Atif opened his eyes.

Darkness.

His eyes adjusted to it. The moon. Treeline. A faint glow in the east. A man called out to his wife.

*"Braco."*

Atif stiffened and then relaxed.

"Tarak?" he whispered, trying to move. "You're alive!"

Tarak grunted behind him.

"Are they all gone?"

"I think so," Tarak said. He coughed then spit. "Some of them stayed for a while, but then a truck came and took them." He paused and took in a laboured breath. "I don't think they left a sentry."

Atif looked: all he could see was the treeline.

"Can you move?"

"No."

"What's wrong?"

"I can't feel my legs. My arms are numb. You're going to have to pull yourself out."

Atif tried, but his own legs were not responding. "I can't feel my legs," he whispered. "Am I shot?"

"Your legs are probably asleep." Tarak drew in a long breath. "Use your arms. Quickly."

When Atif tried to move, he knocked his head into someone's knee. He pushed it aside. An arm dropped on him. He flipped the lifeless arm across a body and planted his hands on a chest. He raised himself up, but then one of his arms slipped between the bodies. He pulled the arm free, planting his hands firmly on the unmoving chest. He pulled his protesting legs along; they snagged on a limb. Atif shifted course, his hands finding muddy earth between the bodies. He pulled hard and slipped free. Tarak grunted. Atif looked back: he could see his bare feet. His legs ached from his thighs to the tips of his toes.

He looked around. Nothing moved. He turned to Tarak.

The soldier lay on his stomach, his face upturned towards Atif. Atif pulled up Tarak's shirt and inspected his back. There were two holes, one dead centre and the other to the right.

"I think one of the bullets is in your spine. The other one might be in your liver." Atif bit his lip. If they were near a hospital, Tarak could survive either wound.

"It's going to be light soon," Tarak said. "You have to go."

"What? No. I can't leave you like this."

"I can't walk."

"I can carry you," Atif whispered. "Into the woods. I can leave you there and get someone to come back for you. I can...."

"Stop it, *Braco*. You can't do any of that and you know it."

"I can't leave you."

"If you stay here, the Chetniks will find you. Is that what you want?"

"I want you to live. I want you to come to Tuzla. I want you to meet my mother and my sister. I want you to come with us."

"I know. I know. But I can't." Tarak coughed and spit out a mouthful of blood. "I don't have much longer. I need to know you're safe in the woods. I need you to tell the army where I am. Where we all are."

Atif wiped Tarak's face with his shirt.

"It's not far," Tarak said. "Go. Keep walking until you find someone."

"I don't know if I can do it without you."

"I'll be with you, *Braco*. Promise."

An engine revved. Atif froze.

"They might," Tarak said. "They might be coming back. Go. Please, little brother. Go now."

The rumbling grew louder. Headlights bounced off the buildings next to the road. Atif ducked between the bodies.

"I think they're coming here."

There was no response. Atif looked down. Tarak's eyes were wide open, staring straight ahead.

"Tarak?" Atif pushed his shoulders. "Wake up. They're coming. Please, Tarak. I can't do this alone. Wake up!"

The headlights turned towards the farm.

"Tarak?"

Atif swatted a tear.

"Okay. I'll go." He drew his hand over Tarak's eyes, closing them, then leaned down and kissed his forehead. "I won't forget you."

When Atif tried to stand, his legs collapsed in a bed of pins and needles. The vehicle lights struck the trees above him. Atif crawled over arms, over legs, over heads, feet, and torsos. Then he touched wet grass. His legs came to life, pushing him towards the woods, his bare feet digging into the soft ground, his fingers clawing into the grass.

The headlights floated above him.

He heard voices.

A branch struck him in the head.

*Bushes!*

The trucks stopped. Doors slammed.

Atif crawled away.

# FRIDAY: JAC LARUE

JAC STAYED AT the window until the sun broke the horizon and the echo of gunshots were replaced with those of engines, dogs, and human voices. He'd counted over three hundred gunshots. At six o'clock, the Serbs offered the peacekeepers breakfast. Jac didn't eat. Maarten threw up.

"We have an escort for you," the Serb captain told them after breakfast. "You can return to Potocari immediately."

"About time," Maarten whispered next to Jac's ear.

They walked out of the school. As they waited, Jac loitered towards the shed where he'd seen the man the night before. After a few steps, he realized its doors were wide open and no one was standing guard.

"Is that the shed?" Janssen asked Jac as they jumped into the back of the truck.

"Yeah. Looks empty now."

"Write it down, Jac."

Jac sat next to the tailgate, watching the scenery pass by in a blur. Hundreds of Serb soldiers patrolled the road. Trucks and armoured vehicles moved north. Bodies littered the shoulder and ditches. Jac committed every sight to memory.

The truck ran unmolested through roadblocks and dropped the peacekeepers at the entrance to their camp. Jac stood in the middle of the road and stared at the deserted street and the factories. Where there had been thousands of women and children the day before, only garbage and clothes remained.

"I didn't think they'd all be gone by now," Maarten said.

"Yeah." Jac shook his head. The compound was quiet.

Too quiet.

He and Maarten trotted across the yard and stood in front of the building in which five thousand people had been sitting the day before. The building was empty.

"Where are they?"

Maarten took a few steps inside.

"They're gone," said a voice.

The two peacekeepers turned around. Amir, the translator, was sitting on the bottom step of the interior staircase. His eyes were vacant. Jac walked up to him.

"What do you mean they're gone?"

Amir raised his eyes. "Like I said. Gone. All of them." The translator stood up and walked into the sea of garbage. He picked up a doll and held it up. "You gave them to the Chetniks. You walked them out the front gate and gave them to those murdering bastards. The women, the children, the men. My little brothers."

"I'm sorry, Amir. I didn't know."

"I tried to stop them." He threw the doll deeper into the building. "I tried to get them identification, tried to pass them off as employees, but no one would give them identification. They're dead now because of you."

Jac stared at the translator.

"That's all that mattered to you," Amir said. "Just get them out of here so that you don't have to be responsible."

"That's not true."

"It is true. You came here and took our weapons and told us that you would protect us." Amir stepped forward, throwing out his arms. "Where was that protection?"

Jac looked away, his eye catching a glimpse of a rope hanging from a rafter.

"Where are they, Jac?" Amir said, picking up a boy's jacket and throwing it at his feet. "Where are they?"

"The buses got through to Tisca."

"My brothers didn't get on a bus, Jac. The Chetniks put them on a truck. How many trucks do you think went to Tisca?"

"I don't know."

"That's because you don't see what's going on around you. The buses took hours to return. The trucks were gone for less than half of that. Do you really think they went all the way to Tisca?"

"The officers must know about it."

"They don't give a damn. They're too busy having drinks with Mladic."

"I don't know what you're talking about."

"Of course you don't, Jac," Amir shouted, tears streaking his cheeks. "You're walking around with blinders on just like everyone else. Fuck the UN. You're the fucking Mafia."

The translator turned and strode away. Jac looked at Maarten.

"You're quiet all of a sudden."

"What am I supposed to say? I don't know about you, Jac, but I'm beginning to feel like the bad guy."

Jac went into the building. It reeked of urine, feces, and vomit. He scanned what remained of the people of Srebrenica. Garbage, plastic bags, diapers, clothes, luggage littered the floor. He looked up at the rope and took a step towards it. His foot slipped. He looked down: his boot was immersed in shit. He stepped back and wiped it against a canvas bag. Maarten handed him a rag. He examined the piece of white fabric: cotton, long sleeves, collared neck.

*A man's shirt?* Jac dropped it and backed out of the building. He turned away and rubbed his boot clean in the grass.

"Hey, guys."

Jac looked up. Arie was jogging up to them.

"Nice to see you back in one piece," he said. "Erik is cleaning out the carrier. He has mail for you."

"Mail?" Maarten asked.

Arie motioned to the empty building with his head.

"After they left, the Serbs let our convoy in. We got fresh food, mail. Even coffee and chocolate."

"Bastards."

"You better get back there before Erik throws your kit out," Arie said as he walked away.

"Oh shit," Maarten said. "My porn."

Maarten sprinted around the building. Jac glanced back inside. He thought of Atif. *Did I make the right choice? Was there even a choice to begin with?*

He wiped his face with his sleeve and then followed Maarten. Erik was sitting on the ramp of the carrier sorting through his kit.

Karel was already there, digging into his own bags. Jac crouched next to Erik.

"I'm fine, Jac," the gunner said before Jac could open his mouth.

"I heard what happened."

Erik looked up. "We had to stand there and listen to the women beg us to take their sons. We did nothing when those bastards piled all the men into trucks. No, no," he said, raising a finger. "We did do something. We wrote down their names, as if that is going to magically keep them all alive."

"Who cares," Karel said, dropping his kit on the ramp. "Let them kill each other. Just as long as we can get out of here."

Jac's mind flashed. Atif cowering under the bus. The old man beating himself in the head with a rock. Bodies on the roadside. The girl screaming in the factory. The empty building.

A fist formed.

Jac stood up and spun around. The momentum carried his fist into Karel's jaw.

"Jac!"

He ignored Maarten and followed Karel down, landing hard. He grabbed Karel by the collar and swung his fist.

He connected.

Once.

Twice.

Maarten grabbed Jac's arm and pulled him off Karel.

"Jesus, Jac. He's not worth it."

Karel wiped blood from his lip. "The sergeant will have your head for this."

"For what?" Maarten replied. "I saw you fall off the carrier, you clumsy idiot."

"Erik saw it."

Everyone looked at the gunner.

Erik picked up a pebble and tossed it away. "I didn't see anything."

Jac pushed Maarten aside and glared at Karel. "Get out of my sight."

"I did my job, Jac. Nothing said I have to care about these people. What would that get me? Hey? Tell me that?" Karel leaned down and snatched his kit bag. "That kid you sent in the woods. He's dead, like the rest of them. So, what did you get for caring about him? Nothing. He was dead one way or the other and now you have to live with that."

Maarten tackled Jac before he could reach Karel.

"Get out of here, Karel," Maarten shouted. "Or I'll let him go."

Karel smirked and ambled away.

"Don't listen to him, Jac," Erik said. "We went up there this morning."

"Where?"

"The road. They needed to bring fuel up to the guys stuck at Tango so that they could drive back. I went with them. I saw a lot of garbage and junk on the road but nothing else. We didn't stop, but I didn't see any blood or anything. I think we just ran over all the stuff they dropped."

Jac crouched next to Erik and nodded. "That's what I think, too."

Erik picked up a stack of mail and handed it to Maarten and then he handed a single envelope to Jac. Maarten glanced over his shoulder.

"It's from your mother, right?"

Jac stood up and stared at the envelope; his mother's writing was unmistakable. He flipped it over and started to open it. Then he stopped. His hand dropped to his thigh pocket and felt the book. *Still there.*

He folded the letter in half and stuffed it into his back pocket. He opened his kit and pulled everything out.

"Anyone got a pen?"

Jac felt a tap on his shoulder. He turned around. Maarten was holding a pen and a blue sheet of letter paper.

"Promise me you won't start this one with 'Dear Mother,' okay?"

"Yeah, sure." Jac replied, folding the sheet. He walked a few paces. "I'll be back."

"I'll be here," Maarten said, shuffling through his stack of letters.

Jac went back to the building. Civilian employees were shuffling among the former belongings of their friends and neighbours, clearing away the garbage.

Jac looked up. The rope was gone.

He sat on the staircase where they'd found the translator and pulled the book from his pocket. Inside was the letter to his mother, its edges crinkled and soaked with sweat. He opened it.

*Dear mother.*

Jac smiled, tore up the letter, and threw it into the sea of garbage. He laid the clean blue sheet on the book and wrote:

*Hi mom....*

# FRIDAY: ATIF STAVIC

ATIF LAY ON his back, staring at the sky. He raised his finger and traced the constellations the way his father had taught him. Cassiopeia, the Little Dipper, the Big Dipper, Draco. Lyra drifted directly above him. He turned his head to look south. Jupiter hung above the horizon; to the left, the full moon was rising.

*Must be close to midnight. Have I been here that long?*

Hours earlier, he had crawled away from the field and through the woods to the edge of a meadow bathed in the early morning sun. But the pasture had been too exposed to cross in daylight; he'd spent the day hiding in the bushes. He'd listened to a bulldozer chew at the earth a few hundred metres to the south. The grinding, cracking, and pounding continued until dusk.

When nightfall came, Atif found he didn't have the strength to keep going. His feet were cut, blistered, and swollen; every step like walking on a bed of razors. He had soaked them in a nearby creek, but the pain had gotten worse.

He remained on the edge of the meadow, forcing his eyelids to stay open. Every sound was a Serb soldier searching for him; every rumble a truck driving in his direction; every branch swaying in the wind a *blautsauger*. Gunfire and explosions echoed from the south.

"I can't walk two kilometres, Tarak," he whispered to the night sky. "I barely made it a few hundred metres. What if the front lines have moved? They could be five or ten kilometres farther north by now. Maybe I'll just stay here. Someone will find me. Eventually."

*But no one found Tata.*

"I can't take you this time, Atif," his father had said that day in April.

"But you're not going that far."

"It's not how far I'm going," he said, pulling on his blue shirt. "It's where I'm going. There have been attacks in the area."

Atif didn't reply. Nothing he said would change his father's mind. They went downstairs and Atif stood back as his father said goodbye to Tihana and his mother. Then he followed his father into the early morning fog.

"I was thinking," Atif said as they walked, "that I might get a job."

His father adjusted the pack on his back and glanced at Atif. "What kind of job?"

"I don't know. Maybe I'll see if the blue helmets need a translator."

"You have to be sixteen."

"Then maybe Ina can get me something at the hospital. Or I can get something at the post office."

His father stopped and raised a finger. "No. Not with the army. Listen, Atif, when you're old enough I'll see what Ina can do for you at the hospital. For now, your mother needs your help."

Atif looked away. He felt the weight of his father's hand on his shoulder.

"If it weren't for this war, you'd be more worried about which girls like you than about getting a job. Go play soccer with your friends. Go to the movie room with them. Find a girlfriend. Just be a boy for a little while longer."

"But I want to help."

"You have been helping. You don't see it, but you have been a great help. More than you know."

Two soldiers materialized out of the fog.

"Coming, Yassir?" one soldier muttered without stopping.

"I've got to go," his father said, touching Atif on the chin. "I left my razor if you want to shave off that scruff."

"What? No. I like it."

"Because you think it makes you look older?"

Atif smiled. His father kissed him on the forehead. "I think it looks scruffy."

He patted Atif on the shoulder and turned to follow the soldiers. Just before the fog swallowed him whole, his father turned and waved.

*So long ago.*

Insects chirped. Stars shot across the sky. Branches swayed in a light breeze. Atif's eyes closed.

*Stay awake!*

He shivered and rubbed his arms. After the oppressive heat of the day, the night air felt as though the temperature was just a degree or two above freezing. Atif stuffed his chilled hands inside his pockets.

Curious.

He fingered something in his pocket.

*Did the Chetniks miss something?*

He pulled out the bag of salt his mother had given him. Atif sat up and stared at the plastic bag. He'd forgotten about it.

*I need water.*

He listened for vehicles, voices, and footfalls.

Nothing.

He used his elbows to crawl to the edge of the creek. Opening the bag, he dipped his fingers in the salt, licking them clean in between gulps of water.

*Is this what Kemal meant? Was it a sign from God? Or was it there because a mother had been looking out for her child and a lazy soldier hadn't bothered to check every pocket?*

Atif lay back and let the water soothe his swollen feet while the salt rejuvenated his spent body.

"Thanks, Mama. I'll try. I promise."

*For you. For Tarak. For my friends. For Tata.*

He knotted the bag closed and stowed it safely in his pocket. Then he considered his feet. He had a choice between being cold and not being able to walk.

Not a difficult decision.

He pulled off the blood-soaked neon yellow T-shirt and used his teeth to tear it in half. Then he used it to wrap his feet. He stood up.

Razors. Knives. Needles.

He sat back down and massaged his painful feet. A machine gun popped to the south. A dog barked.

Atif got up again and gasped. Blades sliced to the bone. He turned his back to the moon and walked to the edge of the meadow.

*Is it mined?*

He knelt and felt the ground for a stick, then crawled into the field, probing the loose, moist soil as Tarak had taught him. The stick sank deep with every attempt.

*Maybe it's just hay.*

Vehicles rumbled on a road to his left. Gunfire erupted some distance away to his right. He heard nothing ahead. The moon was high by the time he crept into the trees on the far side of the pasture. Gunfire reverberated from the south.

*Kalashnikovs.*

He recognized the rifle's distinctive sound. Automatic gunfire followed by single shots. No one returned fire.

*They're still doing it.*

Atif grabbed a branch and climbed to his feet. He took a step onto a bed of nails. Another step and the nails caught fire. Atif leaned against a tree and chewed on his lips until he tasted blood and salt.

*I can't stay here. I have to walk.*

He spit and took a step, then another and another. He stopped to give his feet a break and to listen then repeated the process, three steps at a time.

*"Keep walking until you find someone."*

"But what if that someone is a Chetnik?" he whispered.

He took three steps. Then another three.

The woods opened onto a road. Atif dropped to his knees and felt the ground.

*Gravel.*

*Damn it.*

He looked to his left. Darkness.

To his right, lights. He glimpsed part of a house, its light hidden behind heavy curtains. Something moved next to the house.

*Laundry on a line?*

He looked at his feet and then at the gravel between the edge of the road and the clothesline. A shirt waved.

*Too far.*

He drew in a long breath and started to crawl across the road, the gravel clawing at his knees.

*Voices.*

He froze and then looked right.

An orange glow floated above the road near the house. A match flared like a sparkler on a birthday cake. Now two orange glows walked in his direction.

*How stupid can they be?*

Atif slid back into the woods and crawled under the bough of a fir tree.

*Are they soldiers? Are they walking this way?*

Voices drifted through the trees. Gravel crunched.

"It's not football," one voice said. An orange glow swung up, glowed brightly then swung back down. "They don't even use a real ball."

"But it's exciting," another said. Atif counted four helmets, the features under them shaded from the moon. They stopped a few metres away. "The American game is full of strategy. They plan every move. They don't just kick it around and hope someone on the other team doesn't get it. All you do is sit for three hours and you're lucky to see one or two goals."

"It's easy to get excited about that when you're drunk."

One of the orange glows dropped. The other one brightened for a moment. Air seeped between Atif's teeth.

"You don't understand. I mean, in the last Super Bowl I saw, they were apart by a single point. All the other team needed was a field goal. That's three points. So, they march down the field and are well within field goal range. Only seconds left. The kicker comes out to make a sure thing. He kicks the ball and it sails to the right and misses by a metre. They had the win within their grasp and they lost it. You don't get that kind of excitement with our football."

"I don't need excitement. I just need a reason to get drunk."

"I'm out."

"Here."

A match flickered. Something splashed against a tree on the other side of the road.

"After the war, I'll take you to England to watch a good rugby match. No padding. No helmets. Just brute force. Those bastards know how to play."

Boots crushed gravel. The orange glows floated away.

Atif's muscles relaxed. He released the rest of the air in his lungs and filled them without a sound. He counted the seconds until he hit one thousand and then he rolled out from under the bough and crawled to the edge of the road. He looked left, right, and then left again.

Dark. Quiet. Deserted.

*Or had the soldiers doused their cigarettes? Were they sitting on the side of the road waiting for me to move out into the open?*

He swiped the gravel aside and crawled out. Rocks stabbed at his knees. He brushed more gravel away, watching the road and the house and crawling until his hand touched grass that smelled of urine. He stood, checked the moon, and stepped into the forest. Every step found more red-hot razors. The land sloped up and he hiked until he came to a steep embankment. He sat on a rock to rest and stared up at the hill. Then he looked behind for the moon.

*Zenith?*

He turned his back directly to the moon and looked at the hill. If he wanted to go north, he had no choice. He had to climb.

*This is going to hurt.*

He stood and waited for the hot blades to recede into the ground and then grabbed a tree. Sap coated his fingers. He placed a foot at the base of the tree and grabbed a branch. Then he pushed himself forward with the same foot, cringing from the pain now radiating up through his legs. He moved from tree to tree like a monkey in slow motion until the slope levelled near the top. Then he dropped to his knees and crawled the last few metres. He lay back on the grass, panting quietly.

A sound.

He held his breath and listened.

Soft, rhythmic, nasal.

*Snoring?*

Atif crawled towards the sound, planting his sticky hands and knees carefully so he wouldn't crack twigs or crush brittle leaves. The moon lit the small clearing above him.

*Does the blautsauger snore?*

Then he saw the outline of a boot beside a tree.

*Another survivor?* No, he told himself. They had been stripped of their footwear. *Would a Chetnik patrol the area alone?*

He rose to his feet, his teeth clenched against the pain, and stepped up to the tree. He peered around it, catching himself before he reacted to what he saw.

A Serb soldier was sleeping against the tree. His rifle was lying next to him. Atif stared at the weapon and then at the soldier.

*What do I do? Leave?*

That risked waking the soldier.

*Steal the rifle and shoot him?*

But that would bring other soldiers.

Atif crouched next to the rifle. The soldier's hand lay motionless next to it. Then the soldier stirred, taking in a nasal breath. His head jerked back against the tree.

No choice.

Atif grabbed the rifle and skipped backwards, fumbling for the safety. He switched it off as his feet landed on the thorns of a wild rose. He grunted from the pain. The Serb woke up.

The soldier's arm swiped the ground and found it empty.

"Stand up," Atif said.

The soldier hesitated and then climbed to his feet. He stepped forward, his wide eyes reflecting moonlight.

*He looks my age.*

"Don't shoot, please," the soldier said.

"Why shouldn't I?"

"I'm not going to hurt you."

"Liar. You're killing us by the thousands."

"What? Where?"

Atif motioned with the barrel of the rifle. "Down there."

The soldier looked south for a moment. "What are you talking about?"

"Don't be stupid."

"I don't know what you're talking about."

"How can you not know?"

"I've been up here for weeks on the checkpoints near Memici."

Automatic fire erupted in the distance.

"Don't you hear that?"

"The fighting?"

"That's not fighting."

"Of course it is."

"No. That's your people murdering people like me."

"They wouldn't do that."

"They're killing thousands."

"That can't be true."

"They tried to kill me."

"I don't believe you."

Atif stepped forward and aimed the rifle at the soldier's head. "They killed my friend."

The soldier stepped back into the shadows. "I'm sorry. I'm sorry."

"No, you're not."

"I didn't kill anyone."

"I don't believe you."

"They drafted me."

"You're still a soldier."

"I don't want to hurt you."

Atif glared at the soldier through the rifle sight. Images of his friends, his father, Ratib, and Tarak raced through his head. The look on the faces of the men who had given up. Their screams as they were beaten with bats and iron bars. The arm hanging from the car. Tarak's lifeless eyes.

And the Serb who had stood above him and spared his life.

"Why are you by yourself?"

"They said soldiers were coming this way. Tonight was my first patrol."

"By yourself?"

"I got separated. I don't know this area very well. I thought I'd wait till morning to go back."

"Take off your boots."

"Okay."

"I want your shirt and any food or water you have."

"Okay." The soldier removed his shirt and tossed it to Atif and then he sat on the ground and removed his boots. "That's my webbing. There's water and ammunition. There are extra socks too. They're new. You can have it all."

He stood up.

"What's your name?"

"Stefan. Stefan Maric."

"Are there any mines along the front lines here?"

"There's a map in my pack. All the mines are marked."

"Okay. You can leave, then."

Maric looked around. "But I'm lost."

"Just walk towards the moon."

"What?"

"The moon. Walk towards it and keep walking until the sun comes up. It will bring you back to your people."

Maric glanced at the moon and then back at Atif. "Okay. I'll go. I won't come back. I promise."

He turned and began to pick his way down over the embankment. Atif waited until the sound of cracking twigs and pained grunts faded and then lowered the rifle. He peeled his fingers from the stock, rubbing his hands on his jeans to remove the sap. Then he shouldered the rifle and webbing and slipped his swollen feet into the boots. Walking north, he found two trees with overlapping boughs; he hid underneath them, listening.

Nothing.

He leaned back and gently took off the boots. Then he emptied out all the pouches attached to the webbing. He felt the contents.

Cloth. Wool. Leather. Canvas. Foil. Long hard plastic cylinder.

Atif felt for a button on the cylinder and found one. A red light flickered on and off. He tightened the battery cap and pointed the light down.

Towel. Socks. Wallet. First-aid kit. Half eaten chocolate bar.

Atif devoured the bar.

Inside the medical kit were bandages, a bottle of pills, and alcohol rubs. He cleaned his feet with some water from the canteen and the towel and then used the alcohol rubs, biting on the towel from the pain. As it subsided, he wrapped his feet in the gauze bandage and pulled on the socks.

*That feels so good.*

He lay back and listened. Once he was sure no one had heard his grunts, he sat up and pulled on the boots.

A perfect fit.

Two days ago, the boots would have been two sizes too large.

Atif hauled on the shirt and picked up the bottle of pills, hoping they were for pain. The label was torn. He opened it and inspected the round white tablets.

*Aspirin?* Atif's shoulders slumped. *Why would a soldier carry Aspirin?*

Ina had told him that Aspirin keeps the blood from clotting. If he took them, they might make his feet bleed more.

He stuffed the bottle back into the medical kit and repacked the supplies. He picked up the wallet and opened it, pulling out money, identification, and a picture of the soldier standing next to a man.

*His father?*

The thin man was tall; he had his hand on the boy's shoulder.

*The man looks like Tata.*

Atif stared at the photo, stifling his tears.

*No, it's not him. Tata's gone.*

Atif stuffed the wallet back inside the pack. He would send it back to the soldier. He slung the webbing over his shoulders and picked up the rifle, the stock, and the grip coated with sap. He looked south. The moon had begun its decline into the southwest. Atif kept it to his left and took a step. The razor blades were dull now. He took another step and reconsidered the Aspirin.

*Keep walking. Just keep walking.*

The terrain sloped down and he lost sight of the moon. A glow emerged from the east.

*Already?*

He looked around. He would have to find somewhere safe to spend the day. Somewhere with more cover.

He resumed walking north, willing his second wind to kick in. Willing his feet to stop aching.

*A little farther. Just a little farther.*

Every step brought him closer to freedom and safety.

And peace.

The eastern sky brightened. Atif walked through a dense forest, which ended in a large meadow. A dark house sat on the edge of the field.

*Abandoned?*

Atif sat down. Dew soaked through his jeans. He picked at the soft foliage carpeting the field.

*Carrots!*

He pulled one out and chewed on it. Dirt crunched between his teeth. He swallowed and then pulled as many carrots as he could carry and stepped back into the trees. He sat down, brushed the earth from the carrots, and ate. The moon set below the trees and the sun rose over the farmer's house. There was no movement.

*Stay or go?*

Stay.

Rest.

He curled up and fell asleep.

# SATURDAY: MICHAEL SAKIC

MIKE SAT ON the hood of the truck, nursing his vodka hangover for the second day. Never again, he had promised himself as he emptied his stomach for the fourth time that morning. He popped another Aspirin and drank the last mouthful of Coke.

"Well, that's a good sign."

Mike looked up. Brendan and Robert strolled towards the truck.

"Yeah, he's moving," Robert said, opening the back door. He laid his camera on the seat.

"Anything new?" Mike asked, dumping his notebook into his bag.

"Not much more than Jure has told you. I've gotten some confirmation that the Bosnian army is finally going to move south to help the men break through the front lines."

"Oric's not too happy with the slow response."

"Yeah, I heard that, too. Anything new with you?"

"I'm waiting for Jure now."

"Can he get you to the front lines?"

"Not now. And I tried the UN, the Red Cross, and Doctors Without Borders. They're either not going or aren't interested in taking a passenger. Not yet, anyway."

"They expect the men to cross tomorrow or Monday. We'll have a better idea of what's going on then." Brendan checked his watch. "Are you coming to the briefing?"

"No. I'll wait for Jure."

"I'll stay here," Robert said.

"I'll take notes." Brendan walked away.

Robert turned to Mike.

"Now, if we could read his writing that might mean something."

Mike laughed and then put his hand on his head to quell the hammering.

"So much easier to do this job when you can just stand back with a camera on your shoulder, isn't it?"

"In some ways," Robert replied, his eyes darting away.

"Had enough?"

Robert leaned against the truck and motioned to the tent city.

"The stories they tell are like something out of a Stephen King novel."

"Your parents let you read King?"

Robert smiled for a moment. "I mean, if even half of what they say is true."

Mike grunted an affirmative. Robert faced him.

"So, what did you see?"

Mike raised an eyebrow.

"You don't seem to have a problem believing it all. What did you see?"

*Charred furniture. Roasted flesh.*

"To tell you the truth," Mike said after a moment. "I was a lot like you when I first came to cover the war."

"Naïve as hell?"

"Something like that," Mike replied. "I thought I'd come here and expose Serb atrocities against my grandparents' people." He shook his head. "A couple weeks after I got here, I was in a village that had been attacked. I looked into the ruins of this one house thinking it was full of smouldering furniture." He swallowed. "But it wasn't furniture. The soldiers had forced sixteen people into the basement and burned them alive. So, I took pictures thinking 'I've got it, I finally got proof the Serbs are committing atrocities.' Then I see an Orthodox cross on the wall."

"A cross?"

"The Serbs are Orthodox Christians. Their cross is different from the Croat Catholic cross."

"The Serbs didn't do it?"

Mike shook his head. "The Croats did it. My own people were just as bad as the ones I was trying to blame it all on."

"No good guys," Robert said. "So, why do you keep coming

back?"

"I don't know. I just do, even if I file my pictures and stories and watch them get sliced up until they're meaningless."

"I don't know how you put up with it."

"What you see is not true and what is true is not seen."

"Huh?"

"Just something an old friend told me once."

Robert's brow furrowed.

"Never mind," Mike said, turning towards the main gate. A pick-up was stopped at the barrier and peacekeepers were arguing with the driver.

"What's going on over there?"

"C'mon," Mike said, gathering up his camera bag. Robert followed him to the barrier and they slipped under it.

"I can translate," he said to one of the peacekeepers.

"Please," the Pakistani peacekeeper said, motioning to the driver, a short man in his fifties wearing jeans and a white shirt. "He keeps pointing to the boy and saying Srebrenica, but I think he's just trying to offload an orphan. The boy can't possibly be from Srebrenica. The men haven't crossed over yet."

"Srebrenica?" Mike glanced behind the driver to see a boy curled up like a kitten, his head buried in his arms and knees.

"Who is he?" Mike asked the driver in Bosnian.

"My dog found him in my field this morning," the driver replied. "He had eaten some of my carrots. He was wearing military clothes, but I don't think he is a soldier. He had blood all over him and his feet are a mess. All he said was that the Chetniks tried to kill him. I don't think he has slept much. He can't stay awake for more than a few minutes."

Mike told the peacekeeper what the driver had said.

"Ask him to bring the boy out," the peacekeeper said.

Mike started to translate, but the driver seemed to understand. He roused the boy, who sat up, rubbing his eyes.

"Yes! He's from Srebrenica." Mike pulled the camera from his bag.

"How do you know?"

Mike raised his camera and stared at the boy, his finger hovering over the shutter release. Movement drew his attention to the left. A crow landed on the grass and hopped towards the pavement where a rat had been run over. The crow picked at the rodent and then flew away.

Mike lowered the camera.

"I know him." He poked the camera back into his bag and pulled out the laminated photo of Atif, waving it at the peacekeeper. "His name is Atif Stavic. I took this picture in Srebrenica almost three years ago."

The peacekeeper looked at the picture and shrugged.

"Okay."

Mike turned to Robert and dropped the keys into his hands.

"Bring the truck over here."

"What? But I don't know how to drive."

"You're shitting me."

Robert shook his head. Mike spun the cameraman around and gave him a polite shove.

"It's time to learn. Just put it on D and bring it over here. The brake is the one on the left."

Robert ducked under the barrier and jogged towards the truck. Mike returned his attention to the driver.

"I'll take him. He'll be okay." He walked around the pick-up and opened the passenger door, the rusted hinges creaking. "Atif?"

The boy stared at Mike.

"Do I know you?"

"Remember?" Mike asked, showing Atif the picture.

Atif struggled to keep his eyes open.

"You're exhausted." Mike looked at the driver. "Where did you find him? What town?"

"I'm not far from Memici."

"Really?" Mike replied. "That far north?"

He did the calculations. Four days since the enclave fell. Srebrenica to Memici was too far to walk in that time. And the boy was alone. It didn't make sense.

"He had some money on him. I took enough for my gas. He has the rest."

"Thank you."

The driver shrugged and climbed inside the truck. Mike picked up Atif; the boy fell asleep in his arms.

Skin. Bones. Weightless.

"I'll take him to the doctors," Mike told the peacekeepers and then he walked through the open gate, Atif's elbow digging into his chest. He shifted Atif's arm, slowed, and then stopped.

Robert was inching the truck in their direction.

# SATURDAY: ATIF STAVIC

ATIF WOKE TO a white sky.

*Cloudy?*

He reached for another carrot, but his fingers found smooth cotton instead. He felt the soft fabric, his hand moving from side to side until it found an edge.

Straight. Soft. Unnatural.

Adrenaline drove him upright. A blond blue-eyed man wearing hospital whites was staring back at him.

"I hear you speak good English," he said in a thick accent.

"Where am I?"

"The UN base in Tuzla."

*I'm dreaming!*

He looked around. Cots lined both sides of the tent. Men and women in whites were attending to the needs of the people who occupied the other cots. One man was draping a stethoscope around his neck. He glanced at Atif and smiled.

Atif lay back on the pillow.

"I made it?"

The medic wiped Atif's face with a cool cloth.

"I guess so. Are you really a Muslim from Srebrenica?"

Atif ran his tongue over his cracked lips.

"I'm from Srebrenica."

The medic dipped the cloth into a bowl of water.

"Well, how you managed to make it that far on those feet, I can't imagine."

*Feet?*

"A farmer found you stealing his carrots," the medic said. "He cleaned you up and brought you here. Your journalist friend brought you to see us."

"Journalist friend?"

"Yeah." The medic showed him a newspaper clipping. "He'll be back in a few minutes. He left you this to read when you woke up."

Atif took the laminated clipping and read the caption.

"That's me."

"Your friend said that picture was printed all over the world."

*The world!*

"Where is he?"

"He's gone to see if your mother is here. He's assuming she came in on the buses."

"Yes, yes. She said she would meet me at my uncle's house." Atif sat up and tried to throw his feet over the edge, but the medic stopped him. "I need to get to her."

"As soon as we find you some crutches, young man. Your friend has a vehicle. He can take you. Do you know the address?"

Atif nodded and laid back.

"Hungry?"

He nodded again. The thought of food made his mouth water and his stomach churn. The medic left the tent and Atif propped himself up on his elbows. A group of medics stood at the end of the tent whispering. One of them, a woman, pointed towards Atif and every face in the group looked at him and then turned away. The group broke up; each member eyed Atif as she or he walked by him.

The medic arrived with a tray and set it on a table next to the bed. Steam rose from slices of chicken and two ice cream scoops of potato. Gravy smothered everything except a pile of sliced carrots. A large square of chocolate cake sat on a saucer, covered in a thick layer of icing. The medic pulled two small cartons of milk from his pocket and laid them on the tray.

"Is this okay?"

Atif stared at the food and swallowed.

"Are you kidding?"

"Don't eat it all," the doctor said, catching Atif before he could dig into the food. "You probably haven't eaten a lot in a while. Just take a taste of everything and stop before you're full."

"I understand. Thank you."

He savoured every mouthful. Moist chicken. Chunky potatoes. Mushy carrots. Salty gravy. Creamy icing. Ice cold milk.

"You're awake," a familiar voice said from behind.

Atif looked up: the face was older than he remembered.

"How are you doing?"

"I'm okay," Atif replied, handing back the photo.

"You can keep that if you like."

"Thanks." Atif placed the photo in the chest pocket of the clean shirt he was wearing. He had no idea where it had come from. "The medic said you could take me to my uncle's house. My mother might be there."

"Yeah. I can. She's in the town, right?"

"Yes," Atif said through a mouthful of cake. "How did you know?"

Mike held up a piece of paper with his mother's writing on it. Atif read it. His vision blurred.

"She made it."

Mike pulled up a chair.

"You must have quite the story to tell. I can't imagine how you got so far north so soon."

Atif stopped chewing as the memories returned. Dani. Tata. Tarak. He willed the thoughts to stop.

"I want to tell it to you," he said. "I want everyone to know. Everyone."

"I think I can arrange that."

"Will you take my picture again?"

"If you like."

"I don't want to hold in my stomach this time."

Mike laughed.

"You won't have to." He reached into his back pocket and pulled out a card. "They found this in your back pocket."

Atif stared at Tarak's identification card.

"Who is he?" Mike asked.

"He saved my life," Atif whispered. "He wanted me to give this to the army and tell them where he was."

"I can do that if you like."

Atif stared at the faded, outdated picture.

Tarak Smajlovic.

Tarak hadn't told Atif his last name. He handed the card back to Mike.

"I want them to know what he did for me."

"I can do that, too."

Mike helped the medic adjust a set of crutches to Atif's height while he nibbled on cake and chicken. The medic fitted a pair of slippers over the bandages on Atif's feet and helped him stand.

No razors. No blades. No fire.

"Don't lean on them with your armpits," the medic said. "Put your weight on your hands."

Atif hobbled the length of the cot and back.

"I can go? Now?"

"The doctor wants to see you back here in two days. Do you think you can do that?"

"Yes."

"Okay." The medic handed a clipboard containing a release form to Mike. He signed it. "Two days, young man."

"I'll be back."

Atif fumbled around the corner of the cot and then hopped towards the exit. Outside, he squinted against the late afternoon sun. A cool breeze drove dust across the tarmac, spinning it like a tornado. A field of white tents bustled with activity.

In front of him, a white truck with "TV" stenciled in black on the hood was parked next to the curb. Mike opened the passenger door and helped Atif inside. The breeze flowed through the truck, leaving a layer of dust on the dashboard and seats. Mike climbed in the driver's side.

"Do you know the way? I have a map if you can't remember."

"I know where to go," Atif said.

They drove to the main gate. Mike showed papers to the sentry; he opened the barrier without a word. They turned right.

*Tuzla. I'm really in Tuzla.*

Two women pushed strollers along the sidewalk, chatting. A bus stopped to pick up passengers. Men stood on a corner, smoking and arguing. No one watched the hills.

Someone squealed. Atif shrank behind the door and then straightened up and looked out the window. Children in uniforms were playing soccer in a field. The members of one of the teams were hugging one another and the spectators on one side of the field were cheering. Atif turned away.

"Is this it?"

"Yes. Yes. Turn left. It's at the end of the street."

Atif felt his pulse race as they approached his uncle's home.

*Mama. Tihana. Have you given up on me yet?*

"That's it," he told Mike, indicating the second last house on the right.

Atif opened the door before the truck came to a stop. He left the crutches behind and slid out. His feet exploded in pain the moment he hit the ground and he collapsed. He grit his teeth, waiting for the ache in his feet to subside. When he looked up, Mike was holding the crutches out to him.

"You go ahead. I'll wait here."

Atif fumbled with the crutches and then stood up and stared at the quiet house. A wrought iron fence bordered the small yard. A vegetable garden in full bloom had replaced the grass and a short pile of firewood leaned against the wall. Curtains waved through open windows.

Mike held the gate open and Atif crossed the yard and stopped in front of the door. He raised his hand and hesitated, looking at the window to his left.

On the windowsill sat his mother's walking shoes and the toy soldiers he had given Tihana.

Atif knocked.

# EPILOGUE
## MICHAEL SAKIC | OCTOBER 12, 1995

MIKE APPROACHED THE checkpoint, his fingers drumming on the steering wheel. It had taken him an hour to bluff his way through the first checkpoint and he wasn't sure how much longer he could maintain the charade.

The Serb soldiers loitering around the barrier gave his credentials a cursory glance. They assumed he'd made it through the checkpoint near Memici and let him pass.

Mike knew they had other things on their minds.

Zepa had fallen shortly after Srebrenica, but NATO air strikes convinced the Serbs to keep their hands off the largest safe area—Gorazde. Rumours of large scale massacres around Srebrenica circulated throughout the Western media, but the reports, including Atif's, were not deemed credible. No one wanted to believe another European genocide was possible only fifty years after the Second World War.

Despite denials from the Serb leadership, the West quietly lifted the arms embargo that had hobbled the Bosnian army from the start of the war. With arms flowing freely into the country and with support from their Croat allies, the Bosnian army reclaimed more than half the country in a matter of weeks. The United States brokered a cease-fire in early October and the three sides promised to hammer out a peace deal. The Serbs, who were on the verge of losing everything they had held from the earliest days of the war, were eager to comply.

Mike glanced at Atif's hand-drawn map as he drove. He could have walked the same route Atif had taken through the brush, but he decided to try the bluff first. The site wasn't far from Memici. He could be in and out in a matter of hours.

He drove until he spotted the reddish brown buildings and then pulled off to the side of the road. He tilted the map. The configuration of the buildings matched Atif's drawing. He glanced up and down the road.

Movement.

He sat still, waiting for a vehicle, but nothing appeared. Switching lenses on his camera, he focused on the movement in the distance.

It was a cow walking beside a fence.

Mike laid the camera aside and drove in behind the abandoned buildings. He parked out of sight. Shouldering his camera bag, he walked into a meadow covered with high grass.

*Overgrown? Already?*

Mike watched his feet, brushing aside the grass as he walked. He studied the ground, flipping stones and rotted lumber until he found a brass casing.

*Would they have left the brass?*

He took a picture, pocketed the casing, and kept walking. Then his foot struck something metallic.

He froze.

*Mines?*

He leaned down and held the grass aside. An empty ammunition crate sat on its side. He wiped the sweat from his brow with his sleeve.

"I'm getting too old for this," he said.

He took a picture and kept walking. The tall grass ended in clay, rock, and weeds. Empty magazines and dozens of brass casings littered the edge of the disturbed earth. The imprint of a bulldozer's track covered the entire area. He took out his notebook.

*About thirty metres wide.* He looked up from his notes. *More than a hundred long. Did the satellites miss this one?*

He walked along the edge, taking pictures and inspecting shredded pieces of fabric, papers, and more casings. Then he stopped and lowered his camera.

A piece of shredded cloth fluttered like a flag from a short white pole in the middle of the disturbed ground. Mike stepped forward, his foot sinking in the loose earth. He drew back, wiping the clay from the bottom of his boot.

He changed lenses and focused on the flagpole. The cloth flipped around revealing that the white pole was really two.

*An arm?*

Mike shifted a few steps to his right and refocused on the pair of arm bones. The hand, still attached, hung parallel to the ground. The fingers were missing, but the skeletal thumb remained.

"Gotcha, you bastards."

The wind brushed through the tall grass.

Birds sang. Grasshoppers chirped. The cow bellowed.

The shutter release clicked.

# ACKNOWLEDGEMENTS

I'd like to express my gratitude to Rebecca Rose and the staff of Breakwater Books including Elisabeth de Mariaffi, my editor James Langer, and Rhonda Molloy for making this publication possible.

I'd like to thank Paul Butler who was there from the beginning and helped bring this novel to life. I'd also like to thank Marjorie Doyle and Michelle Butler Hallett for their mentorship and the Writer's Alliance of Newfoundland and Labrador for sponsoring the Mentorship Program. I also want to thank the Newfoundland and Labrador Credit Union for sponsoring the Fresh Fish Award and thank the three judges: Annamarie Beckel, Sue Goyette, and Craig Francis Power.

I'd like to express my appreciation to Memorial University's Department of English and Donna Walsh for getting me started in the program. Thanks to Lisa Moore, Kathleen Winter, Marie Wadden, Mary Lewis, Nancy Pedri, Robert Finley, Lawrence Mathews, Jean Guthrie, Lynette Adams, Scott Bartlett, Matthew Daniels, Susan MacDonald, Leslie Vryenhoek, John Reiti, Zach Goudie, Mark Bath, Aimee Wall, Wanda Nolan, Heidi Wicks, Mary Pike, Danielle Tucker, Gavin Simms, Danny Bridger, Stephen Gosse, Sara Inkpen, Chris Hibbs, and Penny Moores.

A special thank you to all those who helped with various programs and readings and to those who offered information, translations, and editorial feedback: Susan Rendell, Debbie Hynes, Mary Dalton, Danielle Devereaux, Théa Morash, Marilyn Dumont (Athabasca U), Gill Eaton, Ruth Ryan, Lisa Ryan, Stephan Ryan, Hannah Heale, Kali Heale, Andrew Heale, Chris10a (Netherlands), Gasper Atelsek, Hafiz Cej, Chris Joy, Rik Taafe, Sherry McGarvie, and finally, an extra special thanks to OzT for taking care of the cats.

Thanks to The Netherlands Institute for War, Holocaust, and Genocide Studies for their comprehensive report on Srebrenica and to the following authors whose works have helped ensure a realistic depiction of the events in and around Srebrenica from July 11 to 16, 1995: David Rohde (*End Game*), Emir Suljagić (*Postcards from the Grave*), Sheri Fink, M.D. (*War Hospital*), Chuck Sudetic (*Blood and Vengeance*), Jan Willem Honig and Norbert Both (*Srebrenica: Record of a War Crime*) and Nicholas Kent (*Srebrenica*).

And I'd like to thank Jacques Rioux for bringing Atif into my life.

LESLEYANNE RYAN was born and raised in St. John's, Newfoundland. A Canadian Armed Forces veteran, she served as a peacekeeper in Bosnia from October 1993 to April 1994. For her years in service, she received The Canadian Forces Decoration, United Nations Protection Force Medal, and the Canadian Peacekeeping Service Medal. Her writing has won four Newfoundland and Labrador Arts and Letters Awards, and in 2011, she won The Newfoundland and Labrador Credit Union's Fresh Fish Award for Emerging Writers. *Braco* is her first novel.